INVITATION
TO AN
ANNIVERSARY BALL

The Lyon family and Lyon Broadcasting Corporation
request the honor of your presence
at the celebration of our
50th Anniversary.

Please join us on
Saturday, the third of July,
nineteen hundred and ninety-nine
at eight o'clock in the evening
at
The Fontenot Hotel
New Orleans

RSVP
Mrs. Margaret Hollander Lyon

From the Authors:

A lot can happen in fifty years. Love grows...and dies. Families bond...and rip apart. Lies told for the best of reasons can haunt generations to come. Family secrets can threaten family ties.

To help Harlequin celebrate its fiftieth anniversary, the three of us have been privileged to create a series of stories about a family business celebrating its own golden anniversary. And what better industry with which to launch this dynasty than television, just getting off the ground in 1949?

We hope you'll enjoy getting to know the Lyon family of New Orleans as much as we enjoyed creating them. They're a complex bunch—powerful and strong willed, creative and passionate. They don't always get along, but they know in their hearts that the most significant force in their lives is *family.*

Join us in celebrating their anniversary—and Harlequin's!

Peg Sutherland
Roz Denny Fox
Ruth Jean Dale

From the Editors:

Superromance is celebrating Harlequin's fiftieth anniversary with *The Lyon Legacy*. This very special project is a departure for us—we've brought together three popular authors to tell you the story of a family dynasty. We take pride in presenting this book...and the following three full-length novels about the Lyon family and its legacies.

Family Secrets by Ruth Jean Dale (available August 1999)
Family Fortune by Roz Denny Fox (available September 1999)
Family Reunion by Peg Sutherland (available October 1999)

Peg Sutherland
Roz Denny Fox
Ruth Jean Dale

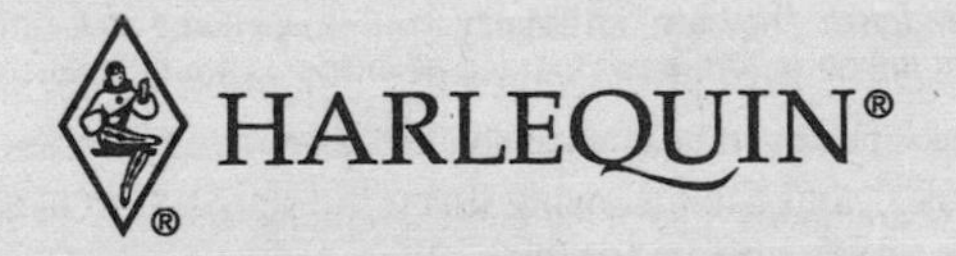

TORONTO • NEW YORK • LONDON
AMSTERDAM • PARIS • SYDNEY • HAMBURG
STOCKHOLM • ATHENS • TOKYO • MILAN • MADRID
PRAGUE • WARSAW • BUDAPEST • AUCKLAND

ISBN 0-373-70847-5

THE LYON LEGACY

This edition published by arrangement with Harlequin Books S.A.

Visit us at www.romance.net

Printed in U.S.A.

ABOUT THE AUTHORS

Award-winning author **Peg Sutherland** has been writing Harlequin Superromance novels for the past nine years. Her books have been both critically acclaimed and popular with readers. Of particular note is her occasional mini-series, HOPE SPRINGS. Peg is also the author of the third novel in THE LYON LEGACY trilogy. *Family Reunion* will be published in October 1999. Peg lives with her husband, Mike, in Charlotte, North Carolina.

Since **Roz Denny Fox** was first published in 1990, she has written six Harlequin Romance novels and eight Superromance books. Her second Harlequin Romance title was nominated for a RITA Award. Roz enjoys doing in-depth research for her stories and isn't shy about asking her husband, Denny, to help her. Roz and Denny have lived in many places throughout the U.S. and are currently residents of Tucson. They have two grown daughters and are very happy grandparents. Roz's next book, *Family Fortune*, the middle book in THE LYON LEGACY trilogy, will be published in September.

Ruth Jean Dale lives in a Colorado pine forest within shouting distance of Pikes Peak. She is surrounded by two dogs, two cats, a husband (her one and only) and a passel of grown children and grandchildren. A former newspaper reporter and editor, she is living her dream: writing romance novels for Harlequin. As she says with typical understatement, "It doesn't get any better than this!" Watch for her book *Family Secrets* in August. It's the next novel in THE LYON LEGACY.

THE LYON FAMILY

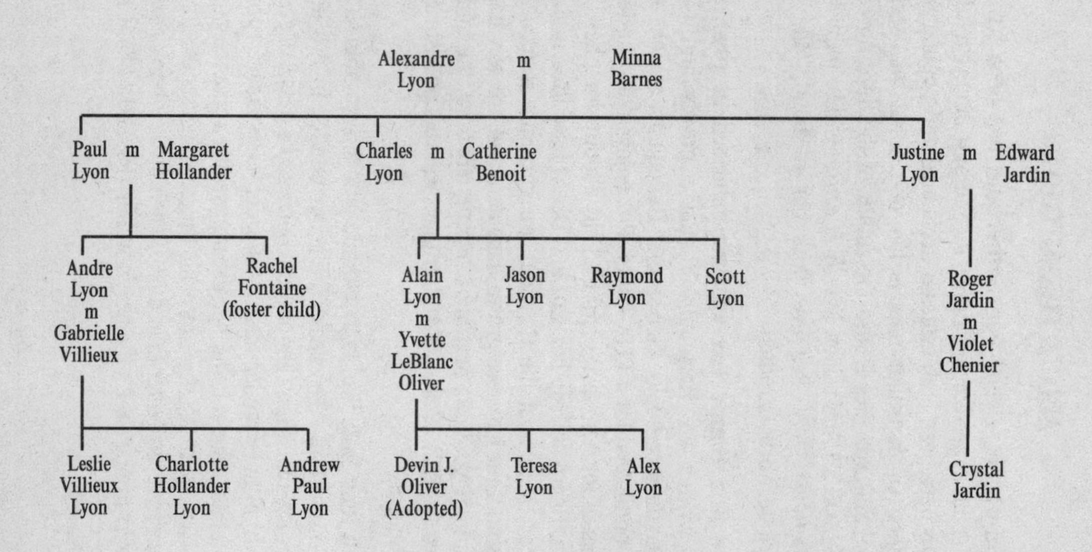

CONTENTS

BEGINNING
Peg Sutherland

PROLOGUE

New Orleans, 1998

THE CONVERSATION about fireworks and parades and gala balls swirled around Margaret Hollander Lyon. But it didn't capture her attention. It couldn't break through the web of thoughts about a lifetime of lies and dissension and the enduring myths that were her legacy.

''What do you think, Mother?''

André's impatient voice drew Margaret away from her regrets, back into the austere boardroom that reflected the iron will of her reign at Lyon Broadcasting. She smiled at André and, having no idea what had been said, replied, ''Whatever you decide is fine with me.''

She saw the glances exchanged by the members of Lyon's board of directors and its management team, both made up of a granddaughter and nephews and others she had mentored through the ranks over the years. Her apparent lack of interest made them nervous. Margaret Lyon never lacked interest in the machinations of Lyon Broadcasting, especially when it came to WDIX-TV.

WDIX-TV.

Her fifty-year-old baby. Her other legacy, along with the fraud and the feud. Its growing pains caused, always, by the fraud and the feud.

''We'd really like your thoughts on this, Mother.'' André's voice still carried the edge of impatience, although he'd made an attempt to temper it.

It grew harder each day, now that André was almost sixty, to see the little boy he had been. He had the hint of Lyon aristocracy in the line of his jaw, the sharp slope of his nose. He also had the streak of Lyon stubbornness.

Smiling slightly, she looked around the burnished burled table and calculated how many others whose gaze was now focused on her also bore that stubborn streak.

Mary Boland, director of engineering for the past decade and privy to everything—almost everything—that Margaret was privy to, snapped everyone to attention when she spoke. "Margaret, nobody here's going to make a single decision without your opinion. You may say it's up to us today, but we all know you. Tomorrow you'll be on a rampage, wanting to know why we didn't do whatever it is you wanted all along."

A few of the younger people, who didn't yet know that Margaret's bark was worse than her bite, seemed to stop breathing as the room waited for her reaction. At seventy-seven, Margaret knew she seemed formidable to many in the room. A legend, even, with her snow-white chignon, her age-spotted hands that never shook when it mattered, and her trademark navy suits and dresses that never sported a trace of lace or frippery.

She laughed, a deep, short laugh that sometimes meant she was amused and sometimes merely meant she knew she'd won. "All right, Mary, let's go over it again. How are you suggesting we spend the Lyon money just to remind the citizens of New Orleans that Paul and I have been around longer than God?"

This time she did listen as the committee that had been appointed to plan a celebration of WDIX-TV's fiftieth anniversary reviewed its plans: weekly documentaries between now and July the Fourth, tracking the city's many changes since 1949; stepped-up public appearances by the station's best-known personalities; T-shirts and ball caps; fireworks and a parade; and, the pièce de résistance, the launching of a literacy initiative, with initial funding to come from a gala ball on Independence Day.

And, of course, a biography of Margaret and Paul Lyon.

Margaret made a mental note to quietly nip in the bud the biography at some later date.

"We're going to keep things moving in this city all the way through until summer," said Mary. "With a grand finale on July the Fourth!"

Margaret heard the murmur of excitement around the table. She liked enthusiasm in people, even liked to think she could still conjure it up herself from time to time. Certainly she had in 1949.

She'd managed to ignite Paul, hadn't she?

She frowned at those around the table, decided to see how easy it would be to extinguish that spark of excitement. She knew from experience that success depended on a high level of enthusiasm; she needed to test their level of committment before she agreed to anything. "This is New Orleans, after all," she said. "Mardi Gras. Super Bowls. A party town like this won't be easy to impress."

"That's just it, Margaret." Mary jumped to defend the plan. "New Orleans loves an excuse to party. Let's give them one."

And so it was agreed. WDIX-TV would set New Orleans on fire—just as it had in 1949.

Margaret remained in the boardroom after the others left. She looked around the room, at the matted-and-framed black-and-white photographs of the New Orleans skyline over the years. Canal Street clogged with dreary black sedans. The art deco New Iberia Bank building, chosen to bear the signal tower for the city's first television station. Audubon Park. The St. Charles streetcar line winding through the elegant Garden District. Jackson Square. The riverfront, with all its many faces over the years.

And her favorite, the photograph of a horde of people clustered around Maison Blanche department store on July 4, 1949, to watch the tiny black-and-white television screen in the display window as WDIX-TV signed on, setting the town on fire.

Margaret looked at the aged hand in front of her on the table. That hand had controlled the switch that sent the first TV signal to those few lucky people in the city at that time who'd had a set to watch. She remembered the way that hand had trembled with fear and excitement. She remembered the way the fire of a new day roared through this town. Through her life. Through her heart.

Margaret Hollander Lyon had done that.

Had it all been a mistake?

CHAPTER ONE

New Orleans January 1949

MARGARET HOLLANDER LYON stared at the man passed out on the rickety dock.

At least, she hoped he was only passed out and not dead. From the looks of him, it could go either way. Thin to the point of gauntness, pale to the point of sallowness. Hardly the man to salvage her career.

Hardly the man she'd married almost eight years ago.

She fought unexpected tears. She hadn't cried over Paul Lyon in a long time. She didn't plan to start tonight. She had no time for sentimentality.

"Take him to the car," she said to Patrick. "If he's still alive, that is."

Patrick McKenna, the burly driver from the city's Irish Channel who had been with the Lyon family longer than Margaret had, sent her a chiding glance. She responded with a look few twenty-seven-year-old women could have pulled off. Patrick respected Margaret, but he wasn't afraid of her. He bent over, grunting as he hoisted the limp body over his shoulder. "Sir's not apt to like this, missy."

"Stop calling me that, Paddy," she said, more out of habit than out of any expectation that he would change his ways. He'd known her since she was in braids. "Sir has had it his way long enough."

Margaret looked around her as Patrick negotiated his load. For this she had worn her best navy Dior dress? Not to mention new navy pumps, matching leather handbag and a jaunty hat with a demure if silly-looking veil that touched the tip of her nose. The moss-slicked dock was rotted in places and the fishing shanty was worse. The windows were bare of either glass panes or mosquito netting. The tarpaper roof probably dripped like a bride's mother. And the screen on the door was curled and rusty. The swamp smelled of decay and fish. Beneath her veil, Margaret wrinkled her nose and walked carefully to avoid becoming mired in the damp ground.

What demons, what hatred, would make a man choose to live here when he had a fine home in town? And a family business holding a place for him. A wife.

A son.

Margaret once again ignored the lump in her throat and made her way to the shiny Pierce Arrow. Paul was now slumped against the passenger window in the front seat. Patrick held a back door for Margaret.

More to the point, Margaret thought as Patrick drove across the rutted roads to the main highway, what desperation would drive a woman like her to seek out the man who had abandoned his home and his family?

"Where to, missy?" Patrick asked as the Pierce Arrow lurched onto the highway.

"Lyoncrest."

He turned to look at her. "Missy, you're aiming to stir up a fearsome ruckus."

"Yes, I am, Paddy."

He chuckled. That would not be the universal reaction, Margaret was confident of that.

PAUL LYON KNEW before he opened his eyes that he was back at Lyoncrest.

The fragrance of winter camellias touched him, a world away from the sharp smells of the bayou. A feather bed cradled him, softer than anything he'd bedded down on these past seven years. And he heard the whispering movements of a servant, the muffled ping of a silver serving tray placed on a table by the door.

He groaned. At least that meant there would be coffee, dark and rich with chicory and maybe strong enough to coax him into movement.

Without opening his eyes, he shifted to one side of the feather bed. His head spun for a moment as he sat on the edge, a linen sheet tangled around his legs.

Lyoncrest. What in the blue blazes am I doing at Lyoncrest? His head started pounding. *Somebody's gotten one over on me.*

Thinking that would be nothing new here at Lyoncrest, he forced his eyes open. Through lids that felt puffy and scratchy, he surveyed his surroundings. No doubt about it, he was back home. Back in his old room, in fact. The four carved cherry bedposts, as graceful and shapely as a woman's thigh, smelled of familiar lemon polish. Lace crocheted by Grandmère Lyon draped over the posts and tickled the top of his head—which was enough movement to call attention to the screaming ache in his skull. The massive chiffonier that almost touched the ceiling, the marble-topped bureau with the glass knobs, even the discreet Matisse originals on the far wall were all still here.

He might never have been gone. And the way his head was filled with cobwebs, he might, indeed, have been lying here unconscious all these years. Everything in between might have been nothing more than a bad dream.

The French doors leading to the second-story gallery were open; a morning breeze wafted in, fluttering the sheer curtains that spilled to a graceful puddle on the floor. It occurred to Paul to wonder—for the first time in his life—who saw to it that the lace drifted so perfectly. He'd taken it for granted before. But since leaving Lyoncrest, he'd been in plenty of places where a waterfall of lace was unheard of. Foxholes and air-raid shelters and concentration-camp bunkers where only the maggots found enough sustenance to keep themselves alive.

A very bad dream.

Taking a deep breath, he pushed off from the bed and took one staggering step. He steadied himself on the nightstand, struggling to remember the most recent events. By the time he made his way to the adjoining bathroom, he had recaptured snatches of memory. None of it pretty.

It had started with the cabdriver.

No, actually, it had started long before the cabdriver. It had started yesterday morning—at least, he hoped it had only been yesterday—when he'd awoken with the knowledge of the date. January fourth. A birthday.

Her birthday.

Somewhere between remembering the date and awaking this morning, he'd found himself in the company of a cabdriver who'd never gotten over D-day. The walking wounded, that was how Paul thought of them. He saw them everywhere he went, even four long years after the war had ended. Men who couldn't forget the hell they'd seen in Europe or the Pacific. Men who sometimes carried the physical scars—wounds that still ached or limbs that had been severed—and always carried the emotional scars. And they could mention those scars only to others who had been there. And usually only after enough alcohol had been downed to loosen their lips.

Paul lowered himself to the edge of the claw-foot tub and reached for the faucets. The pipes groaned as the hot water began to run. Shedding the clothes he'd put on the morning before, he lowered himself into a tub full of scalding water.

"Never again," he vowed hoarsely.

Alcohol never worked for Paul the way it did for some men, resulting in blessed oblivion or a few hours of false euphoria. No, a couple of drinks and he passed out. He supposed he ought to be grateful he didn't have what it took to become a rum hound. He'd seen too many men back from the war who had gone that route. Like the cabby yesterday, who had recognized Paul's voice and launched into a conversation neither of them wanted to have, but neither could resist.

And look where drinking had gotten him this time. Lyoncrest.

At least he could soak in a really hot tub long enough to clear his head, then escape before he got caught up in anything going on at Lyoncrest.

As he soaked, his mind drifted.

He wondered how she'd celebrated the day before. What would she be now—twenty-seven? Younger than he'd been then. He remembered when she'd turned nineteen. They'd served a cake at the radio station because she hung out there, making a pest of herself and wrapping everybody around her finger. Paul had planned to go in for a piece of cake when he signed off, thinking he'd say something to make the day memorable for his father's partner's kid. Something swell from the Voice of Dixie, something she could giggle over at the Maison Blanche soda fountain with the other Holy Cross seniors.

By the time his shift was over, most of the cake was gone.

She was sitting on Maizie Donnelson's desk, swinging her legs like a schoolgirl and laughing at something one of the engineers had said. When Paul came into the room, she dipped her head. He noticed how long her legs were, hanging off the edge of the desk, bare from her knees down to the little socks she rolled around her ankles.

Too bad she's such a long drink of water, he thought. *A beanpole.*

She cut the cake herself and handed it to him on a little plate. When he took it, he noticed, too, that she'd lost her braids, no doubt in honor of turning nineteen. Her hair hung loose to her shoulders now and he noticed the way it shimmered golden in places.

He ate the cake, and the banter in the room continued. When he was all ready to say something witty, something worthy of Cary Grant or William Powell, she smiled at him and said, "You're a mess. You've got icing on your face, Mr. Voice of Dixie."

It flustered him, not because he minded the icing. No, it was her voice that sliced through him. Husky and alluring, not at all the voice of a nineteen-year-old kid who ran errands for the station. He swiped at his face, but he apparently missed, because she slid off the desk and came right up to him. With her pinky, she dabbed at the corner of his mouth. Then, eyes glittering, she touched her finger to his lips, inviting him to suck the icing.

He did it because he didn't know how to deny her without making more of it than it was.

He did it because her silver-blue eyes caught him in some kind of dangerous magic.

And when he did it, his body told him that little Margie Hollander had graduated from the category of schoolgirl.

That afternoon he decided to take up with Riva Reynard, the gum-popping receptionist who'd been coming on to him for months. Riva had been around the block. Riva was a safer companion for a twenty-eight-year-old man who had also been around the block. Safer than a nineteen-year-old with a voice and eyes that could grab a man by his privates, and a pair of legs that wouldn't quit.

Paul groaned again. His head was slightly better, although it still hurt like a son of a gun. But the water had grown cool. It was time to drag himself back to the bayou before something happened that he would regret even more than he regretted those last two shots of whiskey the day before.

He stood in the tub and reached for a towel. He wiped his face, burying it in the soft cotton as he momentarily envied the luxuries he'd denied himself. When he withdrew the towel from his face, he realized he was no longer alone.

A woman stood in the door.

Startled, he clutched the towel to cover himself. "What the..."

Then he saw her eyes, those silver-blue eyes that could down a strong man in a matter of seconds. "Margie."

"Get dressed, Paul."

She turned and walked away. He jumped out of the tub and followed her, wet feet slapping on the hardwood floor.

"What the bloody hell am I doing here?" he called after her retreating figure.

She paused at the door and glanced back. "We'll confer in the library when you're dressed."

She looked so cool she might have faced down an unclothed man in a bedroom every morning of her life. For all he knew, that was precisely what she did. He reached her in a heartbeat and grabbed her by the arm.

"I want an answer. Now."

She glared back at him, tensing her arm. She was still thin, he realized. As thin as she'd been at nineteen. He remembered the way her small breasts had stood high and taut, crying out for his touch, his taste. His mouth went dry. His body went hard.

Before either of them could react to his arousal, the bedroom door burst open and a little boy burst into the room. "Mama, where are you? I went down for breakfast and..."

He was dark-haired and fine-boned, a boy with eyes so large and thick-lashed he should have been a girl. He looked startled by the naked man clutching a towel to the front of his body. The little boy's eyes immediately zeroed in on the hand that gripped his mother's arm.

"Mama...?"

Margie freed her arm and moved to position herself between Paul and the boy. "Go down to Grandmère, André. I'll be right there."

"Yes, Mama." He hurried off.

Margie turned back to Paul. When she spoke again, her voice was colder than before. ''In the library, Paul.''

She ordered him as confidently as she'd ordered the boy, then closed the door behind her. Paul stood there with his towel and his withering erection, finding no comfort in the rage growing inside him.

André. Margie's bastard son, the one she had schemed to palm off on the world as his. Apparently she had succeeded.

CHAPTER TWO

MARGARET SAT in a leather chair in the library, facing away from the door, striving for an air of calm.

She should never have brought him here without telling the family.

Her hands, she noticed, were clenched in her lap. She willed them to loosen.

What if someone—Charles or Justine or, heaven help her, Mother Lyon—saw him before she had a chance to talk to him?

Margaret stood and paced in the direction of her father-in-law's decanter of brandy and remembered it was barely nine in the morning. She walked to the window overlooking Lyoncrest's side garden. It was her favorite view, the same one she enjoyed from her bedroom window. This morning, she barely noticed it.

What had she been thinking, walking in on him like that? The image of him stepping out of the tub had taken hold of her mind and refused to let go. He was lean, leaner than he'd been before, although he looked to be firmer now. More of his wiry body was muscle. And it was brown from the waist up. Hard and brown from living in that ridiculous fishing shanty on Bayou Sans Fin. Hard and brown and slick with water.

Her cheeks burned. ''Curse the man,'' she muttered.

She should have taken greater care to keep André away from him, too.

''Who was that man in your room, Mama?'' he'd asked as she'd buttoned his jacket before he left for school.

She'd cast about for a way to avoid lying to her son. ''You don't know him,'' she'd said, the evasion tasting bitter. But what else could she have said? *Your father. Your father, who doesn't want to see you, who wants nothing to do with you.*

The answer hadn't satisfied the boy. He'd pressed for more. "But you do?"

Sighing, she'd kissed him on the forehead. "Yes. I knew him when I was younger. He's been away for a long time."

"Like Papa?"

Thinking back, Margaret despised herself for being unable to tell him the truth. But she wouldn't expose him to Paul's rejection. She'd seen the bitterness in Paul's eyes the moment they'd lit on the seven-year-old boy. She knew what Paul believed. But she would convince him otherwise.

In fact, she might have to do that first if she were ever to persuade him to work for the family again.

She drew a deep, shaky breath. Were things never to be easy? Apparently not for a woman who wanted more than what society dictated. Her hands shook. Maybe she should have that brandy, after all. Maybe she should have worn the soft pink dress with the white lace collar, the one she saved for taking André to Sunday morning mass, instead of this navy dress with its high collar and long sleeves. But she had a staff meeting today and that demanded navy, not pink. Although she knew that some women believed the way to get on in a man's world was to use feminine wiles to good advantage, Margaret had never played that game. Those women were probably right, she thought now. After all, she was the one about to get the boot. She, who'd been a trooper all during the war, when there weren't enough men to do the work necessary to keep WDIX radio running.

And it was Margaret who was no longer needed now that the men were back. And, of course, her father's death meant she was no longer protected by her status as daughter of the co-founder of Lyon Broadcasting.

She seethed for a moment, remembering the weasel-faced little solicitor explaining her father's will. "Mr. Hollander was confident that, as mother of Alexandre Lyon's first grandchild, your future was secure. He believed it simpler to bequeath his share of the company to his partner, Alexandre, where it would pass on to young André at the proper time."

Oh, yes, her future was secure, all right. As long as she was willing to stay home and run charity fund-raisers and host bridge parties for society matrons. As long as she was willing to keep her mouth shut when she saw her shortsighted, stodgy in-laws squander Lyon Broadcasting because they wouldn't see that the future...

She heard footsteps on the stairs. She resisted the impulse to rush into the foyer. She waited for him, counting the blushing blossoms on the Lenten roses spreading along the ground in the shade of the massive magnolia. She denied the urge to smooth her hair or check the seams in her stockings. She—

The front door slammed shut.

With a cry of outrage she dashed to the door. She caught up with him on the walkway. Her legs were long enough to match his stride, though her high heels made it difficult. Why was being a woman always so accursedly inconvenient?

"Paul, we need to talk."

"I think not."

"You have to listen to me."

He flung open the front gate between the sleek bronze lions on their pedestals and stalked through it, not even pausing to close it. His jaw was set and there was a frown line between his eyes that looked permanent.

She remembered, for a moment, the time when she'd had the power to capture his attention. Could it work again?

No, she was a businesswoman now, contrary to what her in-laws believed, and not a coquette.

She set off after him, leaving the iron gate creaking out a slow complaint beneath the predatory gaze of the bronze lions. Her mother-in-law would hear it and be very displeased. Margaret rarely pleased her mother-in-law.

She caught up with Paul at the corner. He turned toward St. Charles. She had one block before he reached the streetcar line.

"Let me call Paddy. He'll drive you."

"Is that what you did? Sent Paddy after me?"

His voice was the menacing growl the networks had broadcast across the country during the war. It was a voice that had brought the war home for Americans, that gave expression to their pride in sending their sons, their husbands, their sweethearts off to fight for hearth and home. It was a voice that had made Paul Lyon trusted and revered—and famous.

It was that voice Margaret now wanted. And not because she remembered with equal clarity how that same gruff voice could caress and seduce.

"Don't snarl at me, Paul," she snapped, irritated with her weak, foolish thoughts. "I'm not afraid of you."

"Don't I know it."

She heard the clang and rattle of the streetcar. They would reach St. Charles about the time the car rolled up. God help her, she had to speak up and she had to do it now. No time to plan her strategy, to think about precisely what to say and how to say it.

"He's your son, Paul. I know you don't believe—"

He stopped dead in his tracks. "If you ever bring that up again, I'll vanish so deep into the bayou that no one will ever find me again. You can take that to the bank, Margaret Hollander."

His eyes bore into her, rock hard and unflinching, and she knew he meant every word he said. Then he took off again. She stood for a moment, watching the long, sure gait she had sometimes never expected to see again. She felt like giving up, but that lasted only a second. She never gave up.

"Margaret Lyon," she corrected him as she caught up with him again. "And you can believe whatever you darn well please about that. But if you let that get in the way of being part of a revolution, you aren't the man America thinks you are."

"You're right about that."

Wryness touched his voice, but she ignored it. "I'm going to bring television to New Orleans, Paul. Not just entertainment, either. News. Television news, Paul."

She caught the split second of hesitation in his gait and knew she'd grabbed him. Her heart gave a glad leap. "But I need you to make that happen. Nobody else can do it. Nobody else has the voice. The authority. You'll make people sit up and notice."

The rumble of the wooden streetcar drowned out the last of her words, but she knew he'd heard enough to at least pique his interest. Her hands began to tremble with excitement. Looking at them, she realized she'd come out of the house without gloves. Her mother-in-law would have a conniption.

They were all going to have a conniption before she was through.

"We can turn them on their ears, Paul."

He leaped onto the streetcar, not even looking back. The car began to move off and she hurried along beside it, calling to him through the open windows. "Four-thirty today, Paul. We're still on the waterfront."

The car was moving faster now. Margaret began to run, wondering which of Minna Lyon's society friends would see her making a spectacle of herself and report back to her mother-in-law.

"Be there, Paul! I'll show you the future."

Then he was gone and she could only pray he would come. What would she do if he didn't? What could she do but sit back and watch someone else live her dream?

Being a woman was so accursedly inconvenient.

PAUL WATCHED the Garden District roll by through the open windows of the streetcar. The scene was familiar. He'd watched it all his life, from the time he was old enough to take the streetcar into town and wander down to the old converted warehouse near the riverfront that had been Lyon Broadcasting since 1921.

It was all part of the fabric of his life—or had been, until he'd walked away from it in 1941. The gracious mansions along St. Charles, the little shops where merchants catered to the wealth and influence of Garden District families. The old warehouse where, as a boy barely old enough to run errands, he had first understood the magic of sending voices through the air to people sitting in their kitchens and living rooms. The maze of windowless rooms where he'd monitored the news teletype as a teenager and memorized the complicated control panels that made the magic possible. And the stuffy little booth where finally he'd been the one whose voice floated over the airwaves. Broadcasting. It had been in his blood for decades. But no more. No more than Margie Hollander was still in his blood.

"What'd she mean, mister?"

He looked into the eyes of a schoolboy on his knees in the seat ahead of him. The boy rested his arms on the back of the wooden seat and stared at him intently. He was about the same age as the other schoolboy Paul had seen that morning, wearing a similar Catholic-school uniform.

The boy pressed when he got no answer. "About showing you the future, I mean."

"Didn't your mother ever tell you, children should be seen and not heard?" Paul said.

"Yes, sir."

"Then do what your mother says."

The boy continued to stare for a moment, then faced forward again. Paul turned back to the passing scenery to distract himself.

He's your son, Paul.

She still thought she could make him dance to her tune as easily as she had all those years ago. Well, Paul Lyon was a changed man. Paul Lyon had seen boys torn apart on battlefields and troops fleeing Paris and walking skeletons in German death camps. Paul Lyon could no longer be taken in by a pair of smoky eyes and a set of endless gams.

Neither of his passions—for broadcasting or for her—ran in his blood any longer. If Margie was counting on either of those things, she was going to be damned disappointed.

The streetcar lurched to a stop and Paul realized he was now on Carondelet, only a block from Canal Street. End of the line. He hadn't intended this. He'd meant to take the car in the other direction, past Audubon Park, to the fringes of town, then make his way back to the bayou. But with Margie snapping after him, he'd taken the first car that pulled up when he reached St. Charles. And here he was.

Old familiar territory.

Canal Street was busier than ever. Cars, many of them new and shiny now that the war was over and production in Detroit was finally up and going again, clogged the wide boulevard. People bustled past on their way to work or shop. Some jostled him in their rush, never knowing they brushed shoulders with a man whose voice they had probably relied upon for news of the war.

Despite himself, Paul thought about what Margie had said. Television. Picture boxes right in people's homes, so people could see where the voices came from. He wondered for a moment what it would be like if all these people bustling past knew his face as well as they knew his voice.

Ridiculous, he thought. Television. A flash in the pan. A fad. Everybody knew that. Why buy a box with a tiny picture for your living room when the movie houses had huge pictures? The almost breathless enthusiasm in Margie's voice came back to him. She believed in it.

He walked the streets, telling himself he would soon turn back along St. Charles and take the streetcar out of town. Or hail a taxi. Soon. But he kept looking. At diners where he'd sat with others in broadcasting, soaking up their cynicism and their romanticism, all a part of the same paradoxical package. At corners where the destitute had sold apples in 1935 and soldiers still in uniform gathered to talk of jobs in 1945. At familiar department-store windows, with their displays of the long, flowing dresses that women had turned to since the war. He stopped and ate lunch at one of the diners, and never saw a soul he recognized.

He told himself it was time to leave and kept walking. He wandered into the French Quarter, a small town within the city, where antique stores peddled respectability next door to places where respectability was not even a desirable commodity. He saw familiar faces, but managed to keep his head down to avoid unwelcome conversation. He found himself on the river, where the dark water churned past warehouses and docks. He kept telling himself to leave, to go back to the bayou, back to the silence and the solitude that had kept him sane at a time when he thought his memories would drive him mad.

But he didn't leave; he kept going till he found himself in front of the riverfront warehouse where he'd spent most of his life from the age of seven until he was almost thirty.

It looked hardly any different, still very much like a weary old warehouse striving for dignity. The brick was painted a warm tan, and the sparse windows were shuttered in green, the way they had always been. The jasmine had flourished. Shiny green leaves covered the walls. In a few months, the block-long building between Canal and Poydras streets would be dotted with tiny, star-shaped flowers, their sweet fragrance so powerful it came to him now, from memory. The iron gate and fence were also a dark green, except where the scrollwork was formed like trumpet-shaped flowers. Those were painted pink and white.

Paul leaned against the lamppost at the corner and let the building, with its memories, fill him.

The first radio broadcast, to which his father had dragged a sleepy little boy against his mother's wishes.

The company of men, rich with cigar smoke and rough language, both aphrodisiacs for a boy.

The heart-pumping, rapid-breathing pace of life when a big

news story had to go on the air or you'd concede to the competition, which was never an option.

And the cramped quarters of the studio, finally invaded by a pig-tailed girl who refused to be barred from the company of men.

"I'm going to be a broadcaster, just like you."

That was how Margie Hollander had announced herself to him the first time he really took notice of her. She was fifteen; he was twenty-three. She wore braids behind either ear and the starched navy-and-white uniform of a schoolgirl. He wore his fedora shoved back on his head, where he'd forgotten it in the heat of a deadline, and starched cuffs now rumpled and rolled almost to his elbows.

He'd grinned at her with the tolerance of wisdom and age. He'd debated, for a moment, telling her the truth—that women couldn't be broadcasters. What the hell, she'd learn it soon enough. Or forget it, when some guy in college turned her head. "You don't say."

She'd plopped into the chair the engineer had vacated when the broadcast was over. "Oh, yes. I certainly do say. I'm Margie Hollander and I listen to you every day. When I'm not in school, that is."

"You listen to me?"

Paul knew grown-ups listened to him of course. He was the number-one newsman in New Orleans already. Tough and hard-hitting, which was an eye-opener here in the Crescent City, where even broadcasters could be as easily corrupted as the cops and the politicians. But kids? Why would a kid listen to his stuff?

In response, she'd held an imaginary microphone to her mouth, adopted a serious expression and said, "Coming to you live from City Hall, this is Paul Lyon with news that the latest charges against Councilman Mike Halloran have been dropped. Ladies and gentlemen, a very bad aroma is emanating this afternoon from the office of District Attorney Pete Fontenot."

She broke into a grin. "That means you think something stinks."

Paul laughed. "Kid, something always stinks at City Hall."

She laughed with him and once again her voice dropped to a deeper octave, as it had when she'd imitated him. It occurred to him that she had a distinctive voice, a voice that people would listen to. But it didn't matter. She was going to be a woman when she grew up, no matter how striking her voice might be.

"You ever think of singing?"

Her grin vanished then. She stood up and looked down at him, her silver-blue eyes narrowed to challenging slits. "I'm going to be a broadcaster."

"You know, kid, this really isn't a world most women feel comfortable in."

"I'm not going to be most women," she'd said.

And from that moment she'd been an ever-present fixture on weekends and afternoons at Lyon Broadcasting. Nobody could get rid of her, of course, because she was the daughter of one of the co-owners. Just as he had been impossible to run off. He wondered, sometimes, if he'd ever been such a pest. But he'd been a boy. A future broadcaster.

And Margie Hollander had been just a girl.

A girl who'd hooked him into marrying her when he was twenty-seven and old enough to know better.

He tossed his cigarette butt onto the sidewalk and realized she'd hooked him in again.

He approached the building, opened the iron gate and walked up the cobblestone sidewalk to the front entrance. He hesitated at the door, then opened it. Standing in the lobby, flirting with the pretty young receptionist, was the one person, after Margaret, that Paul would have paid the entire Lyon family fortune to avoid.

All the color faded from his brother Charles's face when their gazes locked. Then, tight-lipped, Charles said, "I kept hoping the rumors were true. But I see you're alive, after all."

CHAPTER THREE

THINGS HAD CHANGED even less than he'd thought, Paul decided as he looked around the lobby. The ugly yellow walls were still decorated with the station's broadcast licenses; the spindly old furniture still looked uncomfortable and cheap. And his younger brother's attitude was still spiteful and petty.

"I see that sitting out the war didn't change you one iota," Paul said with a casualness calculated to irritate.

Charles's blue eyes shifted in the direction of the girl behind the reception desk. With his sandy hair and blue eyes, Charles should have been the lady-killer in the family. Paul never had understood why Charles didn't have better luck, unless women didn't like petty whiners, either, even if they did have plenty of Papa's money. With women, who knew?

"You're a jerk, you know that, Paul?"

Charles whirled and disappeared down the corridor. Paul turned to the sweet young thing and said, "He's forgotten everything I did for him when we were kids, hasn't he?"

She giggled. "Are you really Paul Lyon?"

Belatedly he removed his hat and made the shadow of a bow, the way he'd learned from the British flyboys. "The pleasure is all mine, Miss..."

"Finnigan. Rosie Finnigan." Her cheeks flamed. "My pop thinks you're the stuff, Mr. Lyon. Sir."

"I hope you'll tell him what a pleasure it is to have his lovely daughter representing Lyon Broadcasting to the public."

"Oh! Oh, I will. That is, I'll tell him you said so, Mr. Lyon."

Paul headed in the direction Charles had disappeared. But before he made it out of the lobby, Rosie Finnigan said, "Does this mean you're coming back to WDIX, Mr. Lyon?"

The moment of pleasure that had come from annoying his

brother and charming a lovely colleen from the city's Irish Channel fizzled out. "Is Hades freezing over, Miss Finnigan?" He smiled to soften the question.

Her eyes grew wide. "Well, no, sir. Not that I'm aware of."

"Then I don't expect I'll be coming back."

The corridor, which ran between the offices on the outside of the building and the glassed-in studios that had been constructed like a doughnut hole in the center of the old warehouse, was gloomy. Both Alexandre Lyon and Wendell Hollander were tighter than Dick's hatband, saving every penny they could. Thus, the same old ugly furniture out front, the same lack of lighting to save on electricity.

The door that had once led to the executive suites stood open, spilling a triangle of light into the dim corridor. Paul hesitated. Did he really want to see Margie? Did he want to risk running into the old man? Alexandre could be a crusty son of a gun, and Paul doubted he was pleased with his older son's disappearing act after the war.

Maybe he'd just wander around, see who was still around from the old crowd, then duck out before anybody else knew he was there.

The engineering booth was manned by strangers, two young guys who were probably mustered out of the army a few years back. But when Paul got to the broadcasting booth, he immediately recognized Red Reilley, the old-timer who had taught him the ropes. Red's raspy voice came to him through the windows that sealed off the booth. Paul listened as Red closed out an afternoon news report. When Red cued up Nat King Cole's new song, "Nature Boy," and settled back, Paul caught his eye.

Red tossed his earphones onto the console and was at the studio door in seconds.

"Well, I'll be a teetotaling sailor if it ain't the world-famous Paul Lyon!" Red slammed him on the back and grinned from ear to ear. "Word on the street had you hanging out down in Sans Fin, but I always said, nah, not Lyon. He's living the good life in Tahiti with a geisha girl he liberated from Tokyo Rose."

Hearing the old man's rough affection gave Paul the first rush of nostalgia he'd had since returning stateside. "How's it going, Red?"

The big man shrugged. ''Same old stuff. We fight a little evil. We expose a little corruption. All in a day's work.''

Paul laughed, noting that among all the things that had stayed the same, Red Reilley had changed. His freckled jowls sagged more, his once carrot-colored hair was mostly white and his broad shoulders were beginning to bow. ''Better you than me.''

Red's smile faded. ''Ah, Paul, you don't mean that. You was born to it, son. It's in your blood. You ain't telling me that's changed.''

Paul reached for his cigarette pack to avoid looking into his old mentor's eyes. ''Times change. People change.'' He tapped the bottom of the pack and offered one to Red.

''Nah. I got to get back before Nat finishes up. Say, I bet you're here for the board meeting. Hear they're gonna skewer Margaret.''

''Margaret?''

''Margie. She's trying to light a fire under 'em, but they ain't having it. Talk is she'll be out of here soon. Maybe in the next hour.''

Red ducked back into the booth just in time to segue smoothly out of ''Nature Boy'' and into an ad for New Iberia Bank. Paul stood for a moment and watched the familiar process, felt a familiar excitement stir in his blood. He sensed the weight of the earphones, the cool metal of the microphone. He remembered how long he had hungered for all this after walking away. A year or more the old longing had stayed with him. Well, it was out of his system now.

He turned away abruptly. The spill of light from the executive offices beckoned again. Might be fun to watch the old heads roast Margie, as long as he was here.

He slipped quietly into the back of the room. A few surprised faces noted his entrance, but mostly the argument going on was so heated that he was able to ease into a chair against the wall without causing a ripple. His father caught sight of him but didn't turn a hair. Paul swallowed back his disappointment. Alexandre Lyon—A.J. as he was known—wasn't one to waste time on sentiment.

''You're going to lose your shirts if you ignore this!'' That was Margie, her voice fierce and insistent. ''In ten years radio is going to play second fiddle to television.''

"Second fiddle," A.J. said scornfully. "Fiddlesticks, I say."

He waited for his flunkies to respond with a chuckle, which they did. The old codger was as manipulative as ever.

"Television is a fad," said the comptroller, a mousy man with a voice to match. "Do you know how much those sets cost? It's exorbitant. People won't pay it."

"This country is booming," Margaret said. "All the GIs have college educations now and good jobs. They spend money. You've talked to our advertisers, Don. Tell him."

Don Ziobro looked uncomfortable being called on as an ally. "People are spending money, A.J."

A.J. dismissed the comment with a gruff snort and a displeased glare. Don Ziobro's job was not as secure as it had been thirty seconds ago; Paul knew his father well. "They're spending money on homes," A.J. said with his usual air of authority. "On automobiles. Not on nonsense."

Margaret caught sight of Paul. She faltered for a moment, then rejoined the fray. "You weren't paying attention last summer when the networks in New York broadcast the presidential conventions, were you, A.J.?"

"And neither was anybody else." He smiled, pleased with his retort.

"You weren't on Canal Street when they stood five deep around the appliance-store windows, hypnotized by the TV sets."

"In five years—"

"In five years, one-fourth of the homes in this city will have a television set."

A.J. and the accountant laughed.

As the battle raged, Paul found himself moved more than once to stand and argue on Margaret's behalf. But she didn't seem to need anyone's help. She matched every one of A.J.'s unreasoned thrusts with a well-reasoned parry of her own. Paul was enthralled by the picture she painted of the future of broadcasting. More than that, he found himself enthralled by the woman she had become.

She stood, leaning across the table. Her color was high. Her hair was swept back from her face, revealing eyes that sparked with enthusiasm and certainty. Her body was taut with excitement and strength. Even his presence hadn't shaken her. He'd seen that same kind of strength in the WACs and WAFs who'd served overseas. They were dedicated, they were fearless, and they were determined to prove they had as much to contribute as a man. He'd admired those qualities in those women, and he was straining right now not to admire this woman.

When, he wondered, had his impish Margie grown up?

But as he listened, as he watched, it came clear to him. This was the woman she had always been.

He'd fallen in love with an impetuous young woman who wanted to shake up the world. With the foolishness of a young man, he'd married her and expected her to turn into a copy of his society-conscious mother. But Margie had always vowed to be different. She wanted to go to college, work in the business. After their marriage, determined to live up to what society expected of a Lyon, he'd ridiculed one idea and forbidden the other.

What he'd found charming in a girl had disturbed him in a wife.

That had been the first rift. But not the worst.

Now Paul had a moment of shame as he realized that Margie had gone on to become strong and sure of herself, more than a match for these men who had once been visionaries but had now settled into conservative old age. The same kind of man he'd been in danger of becoming when he told her, two months after their marriage, that no wife of his needed college and a career. What a fool he'd been.

And what fools these old fogies were being right now. He stirred in his chair, contemplating standing and helping her convince the rest of the board that she was right. When he moved, he glanced around the table and realized that his younger brother's eyes were on him.

Charles stared at him, an insolent half smile on his handsome face.

Paul froze, for he knew what thought hid behind that smug expression. *She's playing you for a fool, big brother. Taking you in.*

As much as it galled Paul to admit it, Charles had probably figured out what had really gone on seven years ago. His brother had hinted that he knew something before Paul had taken off for Europe, although he'd never come right out and admitted it. Margaret had deceived Paul then. Charles was probably right. She would do it again. Paul remained in his seat.

MARGARET WAITED for everyone to finish fawning over Paul and clear the boardroom. Everyone except crusty old Alexandre, who barely barked out a greeting for his son before heading back to his office.

Old goat.

Margaret pretended to be pulling her paperwork together, but the truth was she couldn't walk out of here until her knees quit shaking from the confrontation. Her fear didn't matter, because she was right and she had to convince them, whatever it took.

She capped her pen and shoved away from the table.

"You've turned into a real pistol, Margie."

His voice at her back electrified her. It was still powerful, like silk over horsehair, smooth over rough. It was a voice that made people believe, made them rally behind whatever he called them to.

"You came." She hoped her own voice sounded strong, hoped it didn't quiver the way she did inside.

"I heard there'd be fireworks."

"You weren't disappointed, then." She resisted turning to look at him, although she wanted to desperately. She hadn't had her fill of him that morning. She wanted to see that rough-hewn face again. She wanted to fall into those bottomless eyes that never gave up what he was thinking or feeling. She wanted to reassure herself, once again, that he was still the man she loved. Then, now and always.

"Why, Margie? Why not just let it slide?"

Now she turned in her chair to face him. "The Paul Lyon I knew wouldn't have to ask that question."

"The Paul Lyon you knew is dead and gone, Margie."

His words chilled her. She thought of the shabby little cabin where he'd been living. She noted once again how thin he was, how sunken his cheeks. The war had done it, she supposed. They said a lot of men were still haunted by the war.

My fellow Americans, our enemy's death camps which we have liberated, are a vision of cruelty and horror too evil to be imagined. No words over your radio can convey it. Be thankful it is so.

She remembered his words as vividly as if they'd been spoken only the day before. His voice had broken. The airwaves had been filled with silence, a long silence, before he resumed. Yes, she supposed all of them back home should be grateful they hadn't had to witness what he had witnessed.

"So is the old Margie," she said, trying to lighten their exchange.

He seemed to accept her offer of a momentary truce. "That's right. They call you Margaret now."

"Suits me better, don't you think?"

He studied her. She wasn't what he remembered, that she knew for certain. Growing nervous under his scrutiny, she said, "Let me show you what I'm going to do."

He hesitated, the barest indication of the war within. He didn't want to care; she knew him well enough to understand that. But he hadn't been able to stay away; she'd hoped that would be the case.

"If they let you."

"They can't stop me." It was a boast, an empty one. He would probably realize that. But it would strike a chord with the old Paul Lyon. And that man apparently wasn't as dead and gone as he believed, for he took off his slightly shabby fedora and gestured to the door.

She led him down the corridor, past the broadcasting booth and the control room. She led him to the locked door that sealed the station from the rest of the warehouse, which had been used for storage by a local appliance store for as long as Margaret could remember. She opened the padlock and they entered the back of the building. It was empty now, a long, narrow space. The concrete floor was marked off in chalk.

He studied the chalk marks. He could see it, too, the plans she'd drawn for the new television studio. She knew he could. Suddenly enthused again, she took into the room with a sweeping gesture. "We'll need another control room. More engineering space. A studio of course. And a newsroom."

"A newsroom?"

She paused, amused by his confusion. "Of course. You don't think I want a television station just so we can entertain people, do you?"

"But news? Local news?"

"That's what I know best," she said. "That's what you taught me, you know."

He shook his head. "I don't know. People might stay home

from the movies to watch Milton Berle or Jack Benny. But news?''

He wanted to be convinced. She was sure of it. Her heart raced, as it always did when she talked about her dream. ''City Council fights. Murder trials. Police corruption. You know, things haven't gotten any better in this city.'' She clutched his coat sleeve. ''Paul, one day we'll be reporting live from all over the parish. We'll be able to tell people instantly about the threat of hurricanes. We'll be on the air all night reporting election results. One day, we'll be broadcasting twenty-four hours a day, seven days a week.''

He smiled, the tolerant smile people reserve for the slightly addled. ''They're right. You're losing your marbles.''

''If you think about it, you'll know better. People are hungry for it.'' She felt his excitement rise. His response raised her temperature, as well. ''The war did that. They want to know. And they want to see pictures. They don't have time to read about everything anymore. They got used to the newsreels during the war and they want to see what's going on, hear it.''

He nodded. ''Well, good luck with the plan, Margaret.''

He turned to go. His shoes clicked sharply on the concrete floor. Margaret knew she had him convinced; what was wrong?

''If you let me do it alone, you'll regret it the rest of your life.''

He turned a weary face in her direction. ''You may be hungry for this. The people of America may be hungry for this. But I've had a bellyful.''

MARGARET SOUGHT OUT her brother-in-law that night after André was tucked in. She had already fended off questions from Paul's sister, Justine, who had heard from her husband that Paul had turned up at the station that day. And she'd already been interrogated by her mother-in-law, Minna, and Aunt Ella, who were both aflutter over the news. Minna demanded answers; Margaret didn't have any. Aunt Ella had gone off to argue politics with Alexandre, and Margaret wanted no part of that.

But she did need to know where Charles stood.

Her brother-in-law wasn't hard to find. The door to the library was closed, but she heard the sounds from the grand piano. He was angry tonight, disturbed, and the piano was taking a pounding. He always played Tchaikovsky when he was in a snit. She opened the library door and slipped in quietly, taking a chair and waiting for him to finish.

Charles could sway things in her favor if he wanted to. But Margaret wasn't sure how to convince him. He was usually pleasant to her and especially kind to André. But something about him made her uneasy. She always felt as if he had always resented her marriage to Paul, but could never figure out why.

The music came to an end. Charles dropped his hands into his lap, his head down.

"You're good," she said. Better than good, actually. Concert quality. Why he wasted his time at Lyon Broadcasting she had never understood.

"A steady hand, that's all," he said, straightening and reaching for the brandy on the bench beside him. "Paul's greatest talent, I believe, was billiards." The piano bench scraped the floor as he stood. "Is he going to help you?"

It struck her, not for the first time, that Charles sometimes seemed obsessed with his brother. Even when Paul was gone, Charles seemed to compete with his absent brother. Had anyone heard from Paul? Shouldn't the family pack up his things and store them in the attic? Had Margaret ever noticed that Paul wasn't particularly handsome?

Sometimes his obsession was annoying. Sometimes it evoked Margaret's compassion. Living in Paul's shadow couldn't have been easy. And for reasons that were hard to understand, that was exactly where Charles had spent his life—overshadowed by a brother six years older than he was.

Paul had charisma; Charles often seemed inept socially. Paul had talent; Charles had to work twice as hard as anyone at the station just to keep from making mistakes, while turning his back on the talent he did have. Paul had become a national hero during the war, while Charles had sat the war out because of his asthma. And despite a face that was a little too rough to be good-looking, Paul appealed to women. Whereas Charles—with his sandy hair and blue eyes, with the two inches and ten pounds of broad shoulders and chest that he had over his older brother—couldn't seem to hang on to a woman for more than a few months.

"He says he's not interested," Margaret said.

Charles refilled his brandy and poured one for her. "You don't need him. I told you I'd help."

Irritation gnawed at Margaret as she took the snifter. "You won't even speak up when they're ganging up on me."

"You haven't said you wanted my help."

The truth was, she didn't. He might have a valuable vote on the board, but nobody at Lyon Broadcasting seemed to have much faith in him. She wasn't sure having him on her side was an asset. Besides, what he wanted was the on-air job. And every broadcaster in the city knew he was a stiff on the air; how much worse would it be with pictures?

"Charles..." She floundered for an excuse.

He waved her off, his expression bordering on sullen. "I know, I know. He's a hero. People will tune in for him. But you can't depend on him, Margaret. You know that. Not like you can depend on me." He sat in the chair beside her and leaned closer, his handsome face intense. "With André, for example. He doesn't care who's a hero. He just knows who's there for him."

That was hard to deny. Charles did his best to be a father to the boy. Anytime Margaret grew too uneasy about Charles, she reminded herself of all he'd done for André. He loved André. That was undeniable.

"You know I'm grateful, Charles."

"Are you? Without me he'd be fatherless."

Every time she softened toward Charles, he seemed to make another unwelcome comment about her fatherless boy. She reminded him, sharply sometimes, that André was not fatherless. Each time she did he gave her the strangest smile. She supposed it was possible that Paul had shared his suspicions with Charles, but that seemed unlikely. They'd never been close. Still, the way Charles harped on it bothered her, annoyed her, reminded her that she'd failed her son.

Because Paul refused to believe that André was his own flesh and blood. With good reason, she knew. Because things didn't add up. Because she hadn't been able to tell him the whole truth. She'd been not quite nineteen and frightened, terrified of losing the man she loved with all her heart. And there had been things she couldn't explain about André's birth, not without running the risk of losing everything.

But André *was* Paul's son. Only her immaturity and her fear had made it impossible for Paul to believe that, even to this day. And her need to correct that failure, she knew, was even more important to her than her career or the future of Lyon Broadcasting.

She knew that, even if no one else believed it.

THE CRICKETS and the frogs were loud on the bayou that night. Clouds hid the stars. But Paul lay in the hammock and stared heavenward as if they were visible.

What he saw in their place was Margie.

He thought about her plan. Her dream. She'd always had a dream. He'd tried to deny her that dream, stubborn fool that he was. But it wouldn't be denied. He saw that in her eyes, and her fire had sparked a fire in him.

Television news. What an idea. What a remarkable, improbable, thoroughly intriguing idea.

But he thought about more than her plan. He thought about her eyes. Silver-blue and heavy-lidded, they were sultry and provocative, suggesting things no man could refuse. He thought about her voice, husky and soft, drawing a man's attention to her lips. And he thought about her body, lean where a woman's body should be full and somehow all the more alluring for it. Because once he possessed her, he'd never found another who satisfied him.

He wanted her, boyish curves and husky voice and all. After all this time, after all the care he'd taken to stay the hell away from her, he ached with wanting her.

But he didn't trust her. And he never would.

CHAPTER FOUR

LYONCREST WAS TUCKED amid sheltering live oaks, dense magnolias and sprawling rhododendron.

Paul stood on the opposite side of Prytania Street, taking in the shades of green, the camellias in both pink and white, the iron scrollwork fence that had been the inspiration for the one at Lyon Broadcasting. And there behind it the three-story stucco mansion, columned and elegant, the color of a fat gulf shrimp.

He'd watched his father's car leave by the back gate and felt the old doubt that anything he could ever do would be good enough to satisfy the old man. He'd thought of his mother, whose belief in his perfection was too heavy a burden for anyone to bear. And he thought of Justine, who had been just a girl the last time he saw her. What kind of woman had she become in his absence? Had she missed him?

He hungered for Lyoncrest and his family almost as much as he hungered for the woman who still dwelled there and still carried his name. Impatient with himself, he turned toward St. Charles. He should go back to Sans Fin. But he couldn't ignore the call of Lyoncrest and all that it held. Before he could fathom his foolhardiness, he was at the front door, tapping the polished brass knocker, waiting with his heart fluttering higher and higher in his throat. He couldn't even open his mouth in explanation as an astounded housekeeper gasped and admitted him.

"They're in the sunroom, Mr. Paul," Lena said, her impeccable professionalism overcoming her personal astonishment. "Your mama likes breakfast there."

"I remember, Lena."

"Sure does these old eyes good to see you, Mr. Paul."

"Thank you."

He forced himself to smile despite the guilt her warm greeting stirred. He walked toward the sunroom. Once again he was awash in memories. He remembered sunshine winking through the branches of the oldest live oak on the property. He remembered the ancient Oriental runner in the foyer, always slightly askew no matter how often Lena straightened it. The heavy, gilt-trimmed furniture—mirrors, library table, umbrella stand, bench—remained as familiar as the raised welt on the back of his right hand, where Charles had jabbed him with a fireplace poker when they were six and twelve.

He followed the gentle tinkle of silver and china to the open French doors into the sunroom.

Margaret had the business pages of the *Times-Picayune* spread open in her lap, a triangle of toast and jam in her right hand. She was dressed for work, again in navy, again very unadorned. It vexed him to realize he remembered exactly what she'd worn the day before.

"Good morning," she said without faltering. She lowered the toast to her plate. It was his mother's favorite morning china, white with a ruffled edge, decorated with yellow and blue flowers. "Coffee?"

He turned to the sideboard without replying and poured himself a cup from the silver pot, doctored the coffee with cream and sugar and sat across from her. He stared at her over the rim of his cup, just to make her nervous. She didn't shrink under his gaze. She lifted her own cup. Her hand was long and elegant. He remembered that hand, trailing timidly over his body.

The trembling virgin, he thought bitterly. "You know the FCC isn't granting licenses right now."

"I applied last year. It's already taken care of."

"Always attentive to the details, aren't you, Margaret?" She didn't bother to answer. She went back to her toast. He was miffed by her apparent unconcern.

"Is anybody else moving in that direction?"

"In New Orleans? No."

"You're sure?"

She didn't bother to answer that, either. He found he wasn't as much miffed as he was impressed. She had brass, that was for sure. He liked it.

"When do you want to be up and running?"

"Why should I tell you?"

"Because you need me. And you haven't got me yet."

She patted her lips with her linen napkin, although there wasn't a dab of jam or a crumb of bread anywhere near them. Being contrary. She might need him, but she wouldn't let her desperation show. "This summer."

"Why so soon?"

He saw a glint of excitement come into her eyes, knocking the edge off her tough exterior. He liked that, too. "The president makes a whistlestop on the Fourth of July."

He remembered what apparently didn't even faze her. July fourth was also their wedding anniversary. Well, if it didn't bother her, it certainly didn't bother him. "You don't have time to build a studio."

"Pasco Blaine says he can have it done in two months."

"If you can get my old man to come around."

She wasn't coy; she didn't hesitate to admit the truth. "That's right."

"And if you have me, the old man will come around."

"Yes." This time her admission sounded tight.

"Why should I do this for you?"

"Some people might ask why I should do this for you." She didn't sound haughty, just tough. Businessman tough.

He stood and drained his coffee. "Not the ones who know all the facts."

"Paul, I—"

"Paul! Mercy on my soul, Paul!"

Paul turned toward the voice and in seconds his mother had collapsed into his arms. She didn't weep, for that would have been unseemly, but there was nothing amiss in a near-swoon for a carpetbagger's granddaughter turned pillar of Southern society. Paul held his mother tightly, unsure how a prodigal son behaved.

"Good morning, Mother."

He held her arm while she looked up at him, fanning herself with her fingertips. Minna Barnes Lyon had grown old in seven years. Always petite and fragile-looking, she now appeared frail and weak. Her hair was snow-white, swept up in a soft chignon. Her everyday pearls fell against parchment-like, lined skin. The arm he held was thin.

"Pour me some juice, Paul. I must sit before I fall."

He helped her into one of the cushioned wicker chairs and

turned to the sideboard for a glass of juice. He glanced at Margaret, noticed her frown and felt his own concern rise. Just how much of an invalid was his mother?

When he set the glass of juice in front of her, she was dabbing her eyes with the corner of a handkerchief she'd pulled from the breast pocket of her dress. Her hand shook slightly. "Oh, thank you, darling." She sipped at the juice, sniffed at her handkerchief and studied her son. "You gave me quite a start, Paul. I had heard, of course, that you were at the station yesterday, but seeing you here was so unexpected...."

"I'm sorry, Mother. I wasn't thinking."

"Indeed."

He knew from the tone of her voice that his mother the society matron had regained control. Decorum had been restored. "How are you, Mother? I trust your health is good."

"If you're concerned about my health, you might have inquired before now. Margaret, please pass the jam."

Margaret complied, her expression unchanging. With a tiny silver spoon, Minna placed a dollop of raspberry jam on her bread plate. She barely flinched when the sunroom door was flung open by a lovely dark-haired woman. Justine was quite certainly no longer a girl. And noticeably in the family way.

"Paul! Oh, Paul!" She rushed over to him, wrapped her arms around his neck and gave him a big kiss on both cheeks.

"Justine, please," Minna said. "You mustn't excite yourself."

Justine winked at Paul, then settled into a chair across the table. "Of course not, Mother."

"Your brother was just apologizing. Were you not?"

"My behavior is inexcusable, Mother." All the harder to say because he knew it was true. No matter what he thought of Margaret, he'd had no right to treat his mother so badly.

"I am up in years and I am not entirely well, to reply to your question," Minna announced crisply.

A quick calculation told Paul she was all of sixty-one. "I'm sorry, Mother," he said. "Is there any way I can help?"

"You certainly may. You may return home. I would like my children with me for whatever time I have left."

He opened his mouth to ask what, specifically, was wrong with her. But he knew she would view that as a breach of etiquette. "Mother, I really don't think that's the best idea."

"No?" She raised one eyebrow at him, then smiled. "Let me be the judge of that. How soon can you be home? A homecoming soiree sometime during Carnival would be nice, don't you think?"

Justine covered her grin with her juice glass, but her dark eyes flashed wickedly at him. A soiree to welcome him home? What an abominable thought.

He glanced at Margaret, hoping for an ally. Surely she would agree it was impossible for him to return to Lyoncrest. She stood.

"More coffee, Paul? Some for you, Mother Lyon?" She poured for them both, then placed her hand on Minna's shoulder. "Mother Lyon, Paul and I will be away for a few days. Perhaps he could think about this while we're away...."

Minna stared at her daughter-in-law. "Away? The two of you?"

She seemed unsure whether to be delighted or aghast.

"We're going to Philadelphia, Mother Lyon. There's a station up there we need to see."

"Oh, business. How nice of you to help Margaret, Paul."

Paul looked at Margaret, not daring to glare at her, which is what he felt inclined to do. "Mother, I—"

"There will be plenty of time to finish our discussion when you return from Philadelphia."

Margaret glanced at her watch. "We should run, Paul. The train leaves in an hour."

Minna patted his hand. "Run along, dear. I'll have Lena prepare for your return."

Paul discovered he simply couldn't argue with his mother, and he didn't really want to argue with his wife. An hour later he was at the Southern Railway Station at Canal and Basin with Margaret, wondering what he would wear tomorrow.

And where he would sleep tonight.

THE TRAIN RATTLED and hummed its way north to Philadelphia, the vibration resounding through Margaret's body. The air in the crowded car became cooler, but Margaret grew warmer. She flattened herself against the window, but Paul still seemed to take up an inordinate amount of space. His elbow brushed her arm; his scent invaded her nostrils.

This had been a bad idea. How could she deal with it for two whole days? How could she deal with it if Mother Lyon had her way?

"Will you move back to Lyoncrest?" she asked, shifting once again to take her arm out of contact with his.

"Is that a proposition?"

"I don't have to proposition you. I'm your wife."

Now he shifted away, as well. "You could remedy that."

Is that what he'd hoped for by staying away? That she would end things despite all the teachings of the Catholic church? "Father Flynn tells me that isn't part of the divine plan," she said wryly.

He matched her tone, except he did it better. "It hasn't exactly been divine."

That almost made her chuckle. "Mother Lyon had gallbladder surgery last year."

"Is she all right now?"

"And her bones are brittle, they say. A fall..."

"She should stay off those stairs."

"You tell her. She won't listen to any of us."

He grew silent. "Was this your plan all along? To drag me off to Philadelphia with you?"

"Of course."

"You're so sure you'll convince me."

Didn't he realize he was more than half-convinced already? Aunt Ella was right. Men were hardly a challenge.

"You'll never change their minds."

She smiled. "First I'll change yours. Then you'll change theirs."

After a moment's hesitation he laughed out loud. Margaret thought it was worth putting up with his irritating ways just to hear one of his rare laughs. That sobered her enough to send her back to the window.

She took in the passing scenery—clouds of smoke over the iron mills in Birmingham, rag-tag farms and dense pine forests in Georgia, the rolling hills of Virginia. Time moved slowly in the company of a man she knew intimately, yet not at all.

They were on the outskirts of Baltimore when a woman in the seat behind them tapped Paul on the shoulder and said, "Excuse me, I couldn't help but hear your voice earlier and, well, please forgive me for being so bold, but aren't you Paul Lyon? The man on the radio?''

Margaret stifled a grin. She glanced at him, saw the struggle on his face. Should he be polite or should he brush her off? Margaret decided to help him out. She smiled at the woman.

''Oh, no, ma'am. The man on the radio is really quite a dashing figure. Nothing at all like my husband.''

The woman smiled and nodded. ''I thought so.''

Paul looked inclined to protest, but the woman settled back into her seat.

It wasn't the last such incident during their trip.

Of course, neither of them was surprised when it happened at the television station they toured in Philadelphia. Paul Lyon was a legend in their profession, a candidate for the broadcasting hall of fame, had there been such a thing. His voice was as well-known as FDR's had been, his reporting as revered as General Patton's battle strategies.

Everyone at the station wanted to shake his hand. A few got his autograph—''For the wife. She's crazy about you, Mr. Lyon.'' And because of him, everyone was eager to share the secrets of successful television broadcasting.

Margaret greedily made notes of everything.

By the time they'd wrapped up their afternoon tour, Margaret was so excited she felt as if she could sign on and send a signal without bothering to build a signal tower. Her excitement faded only when she came back from powdering her nose and overheard the words of the station manager, who had taken Paul aside in the lobby.

''We're an established station,'' he said. ''We're affiliated with one of the networks. If you want to do television, you're wasting your time down there. Come to Philadelphia. We can take you places, Paul.''

Margaret held her breath and checked the impulse to dash in and snatch Paul away from the thieving little rat.

''I've been places, Mr. Lovatt.''

There it was, that same hollow tone he'd used when he told her the old Paul Lyon was dead.

''Begging your pardon, Lyon, but not the kind of places television can take you. Television will create the next American royalty. Clark Gable on a small screen. I can see it now. And you could be the first.''

Margaret could see it, too. She wondered a moment if it was fair to ask Paul to limit himself to a little station in New Orleans when he could have the world at his feet. But frankly, she didn't care about fair. She cared about WDIX-TV.

And she cared about giving André back his father. With Paul in Philadelphia, that would never happen.

''I appreciate your interest, Mr. Lovatt. But the family's already promised I can be the Humphrey Bogart of the small screen and, well, I guess that's more my style.''

They spent the evening in a Philadelphia appliance store that had four television sets for sale, watching the programming and tuning out the appliance salesman's pitch on the merits of each set. They soaked up what each station did—how they announced their programs, the background music some of them used, what drew the attention of the people watching and what bored them so that their eyes strayed to the next set, the next network.

By the time they were sitting in a little bar across from the train station, they were full of ideas, their conversation animated. Margaret sipped a rum toddy and he had coffee while waiting for the midnight train headed south.

''Did you notice how their voices faded every time they looked at the people they were talking to?'' she said.

''Because they were turning away from the microphone,'' he said. ''The microphones were set up all wrong—you have to be looking right at the camera for them to pick you up.''

''But don't you want to be looking at the camera?''

''Not if you want it to look like you're having a conversation with the other person on the set.''

She nodded. ''And the camera work outside the station. This station uses a movie-newsreel company. Do you think we can find a company like that close enough to New Orleans to get our film for us?''

''No,'' he said. ''And you don't want to.''

His conviction stirred her. He was involved, whether he knew it yet or not. Seeing the opinionated Paul of old warmed her far more than her toddy. ''What do you mean, you don't want to? That's the way it's done.''

''If you want to do it the way it's done, we may as well keep feeding them a radio signal,'' Paul said. ''Television is a revolution. Isn't that what you keep telling me? Who says we have to do it the way they're doing it everywhere else?''

''Then how would *you* do it?''

''I don't know yet.''

''But you'll let me know when you've figured it out?''

He sat there fiddling with a matchbox and his cigarette pack, rattling the matches, rolling an unlit cigarette back and forth between his fingers, occasionally striking a match but forgetting to light the cigarette while an idea held him captive. Funny how little he'd changed. He had the same mannerisms, the same expressions. And yet...

''Was it bad over there?'' she asked softly, regretting the question as soon as she saw the shift in his expression.

He shrugged, an attempt at nonchalance his rigid expression belied. ''Bad enough.''

She plowed on despite his obvious reticence. ''It changed everybody.''

''Yeah. If you were lucky, you only got killed. The rest of us had to come back and...''

His voice trailed off. He lit another match and this time brought it to the tip of his cigarette. Smoke swirled around him.

Smoke screen, she thought. ''Come back and...?''

''Live with it.''

''Are you? Or are you hiding from it?''

''No, Margie.'' He stubbed out his cigarette, then reached across the small table and twirled a finger in her hair. ''That's not what I'm hiding from.''

Words caught in her throat. His knuckles whispered against her cheek. She forced herself to smile, to play the tough broad to his tough guy. As long as he thought they were playing, maybe he wouldn't run again.

''But I found you.''

He grinned, a wry, brittle grin. ''How far are you willing to go, Margie, to get me?''

Still a game, she reminded herself. Play along. ''You don't expect me to play all my cards right up front, do you?''

''I guess not. You're a pretty good bluffer, as I recall.''

André. He meant André. She resisted the urge to explain, to tell him the whole truth. Now wasn't the time. Not unless she wanted to take the train back to Louisiana alone and leave him in Philadelphia to become Clark Gable of the small screen.

"Let's approach it this way, Paul. What's it going to take to get you?"

He studied her then, the way a man studies a woman when he's trying her on for size. His eyes on her made her warm. She'd managed to forget the feeling over the years. But it came back to her now; she'd begin to bubble and boil inside, until her knees melted out from under her and her eyes could barely focus. She realized too late that she couldn't play these games with Paul, because she wanted to win too badly. And for all the wrong reasons. Not because she wanted him for the station. Not even because she wanted him for André.

But because, deep down in a place she hadn't allowed herself to visit since he'd left, she wanted him for herself. She wanted him to make her a woman again.

Longing froze the breath in her chest.

He slugged back the last of his coffee and stood. "Nobody gets me, sweetheart. And if I want anything you've got, you'll know the minute I come after it."

MARGARET PRETENDED that the train ride home, through moonlit countryside and sleeping cities, wasn't awkward. They spoke little, feigned sleep, studiously avoided physical contact. She pretended that it didn't even matter what he meant, although the image of him coming after what he wanted stayed with her, no matter how many times she banished it.

When they reached New Orleans, he hailed two taxis.

One took her to Lyon Broadcasting, the other presumably took him back to the bayou. She didn't even ask when—or if—she would see him again. She rode off in the taxi without looking back.

But she thought about him the rest of the day. And at home that night she had a pickle of a time making sure the rest of the family understood that it wasn't time to talk to André about his father's return. They acquiesced only when she told them of her fear that Paul would disappear again if too much was forced on him. Minna, in particular, was hard to convince.

By the time Margaret was tucking André into bed that night,

she was exhausted from battling her family and her own wayward thoughts.

"I missed you, Mama," her son said sleepily, his cheek resting against the teddy bear he insisted could not sleep alone.

Her heart contracted. A thousand Pauls weren't worth this. She would remember that next time she saw her husband. If there was a next time. She kissed André's forehead. "I missed you, too, *mon cher.* I miss you every single minute we aren't together."

"I read two stories in class today," he said, then yawned.

Margaret knew she should turn off his light and urge him to sleep, but she hated to end these moments with her sweet boy. Besides the station and her own mother, he was all she had now that her own papa was gone. "Did you?"

He nodded, his eyes drifting shut. "One was about a bear and one was about a brother and sister."

His words were barely audible. He would sleep soon. She smiled at his dear face, a face that would one day be just like his father's. If Paul would only open his eyes, he would surely see that. Even Mother Lyon insisted that André was the very image of her son. For a moment Margaret's heart broke at the realization of all that Paul had missed.

She remembered when she'd seen André for the first time, his eyes squeezed shut, his face tiny and red and round. Dark fuzz stood up all over his head and he shook his fists at everyone. A Lyon, she'd thought at the time, no question about it. She remembered his first clumsy step and her apprehension mixed with pride when he'd toddled off to school in his crisp little uniform. Too small to spend the day away from home, she'd thought, and yet so big, this little baby who could no longer be cuddled in her arms.

"When can I have a brother, Mama?"

Margaret's heart grew heavy, as it always did when André asked questions that were impossible to answer. *Why don't I have a daddy? But if he's not dead, why doesn't he live with us? Doesn't he love us, Mama?*

"Not everyone has a brother, *mon cher.*"

"Then a sister? That would be fine, too, as long as we could climb trees together. Can sisters climb trees, Mama?"

Margaret smiled at his sleepy words. ''Of course they can. But...''

He was asleep. That fast, his eyes closed, his breathing fell into a pattern, and the hand clutching his teddy bear slackened. Margaret didn't move. She didn't want to give up the warmth of him pressed to her side. If there were any way to give André the brother or sister he wanted, she would do it, as she had always done everything she could for him. She had sacrificed college for him. She'd given up years at Lyon Broadcasting to concentrate on caring for him, only going back to the world she loved when he started school.

And, as determined as she had always been to be a career woman, she had never regretted a moment devoted to André. She would do it all over again—except for one thing.

She should never have tried to deceive Paul.

Finally she tiptoed out and down the hall to her room. She was exhausted. It had been a long trip, with only catnaps on the train throughout the day and night. She could already feel the feather pillow, the quilt pulled up under her chin. Sleep. And tomorrow she would be revived and able to figure out what to do without Paul Lyon.

She opened the door to her room.

There stood Paul, an old army duffel bag at his feet.

Heart skittering, she thought immediately of his arrogant boast the night before. *If I want anything you've got, you'll know the minute I come after it.*

CHAPTER FIVE

If Margaret's presence in the bedroom that had been his for almost thirty years was intended as a sign that coming home was a bad idea, Paul was convinced. "What the devil are you doing in my room?"

"Your room?" Outrage shuddered through her voice. "This has been my bedroom since 1941!"

"Since you married the heir apparent and took possession, is that it?"

"Since you walked out!"

She grabbed the drawstring of his duffel bag and started dragging it toward the still-open door. He put a hand on top of hers and stopped her. Her fingers were cold. He felt suddenly warm.

"If I'm coming home, I'm certainly not giving up my own bedroom," he said.

"Don't use that menacing tone with me." She snatched her hand away and backed away a couple of steps. "You gave up your room seven years ago. It's too late now."

He thought for a moment of showing her that it was never too late. He wondered what she wore beneath those prim and proper dresses that covered her from neck to wrist to ankle. He wondered if she was still as passionate at twenty-seven as she'd been at nineteen.

He wondered if she'd learned any new tricks along the way.

That thought revived his anger. He stood by the open door and pointed to the hallway. "Get out."

She stared at him, her chest beginning a rapid rise and fall. She gave his bag a kick. "You get out."

"You haven't learned a damn thing, have you, Margie?" He slammed the door before she could get his belongings into the hallway. "You know, nobody likes a stubborn woman."

"Women have to be stubborn to stand up to pig-headed bullies."

"You're not being reasonable."

She took a deep breath, then marched over to the chiffonnier, flung open the carved door and rattled the clothes hanging there. "See this?"

She snatched a silky robe off the hook on the back of the door and stalked over to wave it under his nose. A sweet scent assaulted his senses. His body responded.

"This is my robe. Those are my dresses." She threw the robe over his shoulder and went to the dresser, where she snatched open drawers and began tugging lingerie out. It spilled over the lip of the drawer, little bits of white, lace-edged and probably as sweet-smelling as the silk she'd left lingering against his neck. "These are all my clothes, Paul." She pointed at the duffel bag. "In that bag—reeking of the swamp—are yours. Now you tell me whose room this is."

Damn her all to hell and back. She wasn't as stubborn as she had been before. She was worse. Because she wasn't a girl any longer, not even a headstrong, intelligent girl. Now she was a woman. And dangerous. With a fierce toss, he threw her silk robe toward the drawers of disheveled lingerie, then heaved his bag directly into the middle of the room again. Without thinking of the consequences, he began to unbutton his shirt.

"What do you think you're doing?" Alarm rose in her voice.

He tossed his shirt onto the top of the bag. Then his undershirt. He slid the belt out of his trousers next.

"Don't you dare!"

He turned to face her as he dropped his trousers. Her cool eyes were growing wild. So was his heartbeat. He felt himself stir again and wondered himself what in God's name he was doing.

"Paul, so help me—"

Her words broke off in a strangled gasp as he unbuttoned his skivvies and let them fall to his ankles. Her eyes grew wide. He grew hard. He suppressed a groan. He'd lost his mind.

Pretending he was in complete control of his faculties, he flopped onto the bed and lay there, hands behind his head, erection boldly beckoning. "Okay. So maybe this is your room. But I think this is my bed."

She seemed to be panting. Her eyes were focused on him, and

not on his charming face, either. Lord, he thought he might explode. Even if this drove her away, it might surely drive him crazy first.

"But you're welcome to join me."

He hoped she would. He would remind her of a thing or two.

MARGARET THOUGHT for a moment she might just take him up on his invitation. He had reminded her of things she'd thought long forgotten. What a man looks like when he's ready and eager. How a woman feels when she knows she's responsible for the way a man throbs and swells. Her body ached and yearned.

Damn him. She would need confession in the morning.

Except...he was her husband. Did it count as lust if he was her husband? Was that a sin worthy of confessing?

She swayed for a moment between giving herself something truly worthy of confession and not giving this arrogant man something to hold over her head. She made a decision.

As calmly as possible she slipped off her shoes. She unbuttoned her dress, a long, slow process, for these longer dresses had interminable buttons. She let it drop as carelessly as he had dropped his clothes. Not even looking at him, telling herself he might not even be there for all she cared, she slid the straps of her chemise off her shoulders. She stood there in her underpants, brassiere, stockings and garter belt.

She heard him groan.

She thought about the sounds he would make if she touched him. She tried to remember what a man felt like. Silky and hard, the way she remembered? Impossible to be sure after so long.

But she could find out. Now.

She thought she might explode.

She unhooked the stockings from the garters and rolled them down. Drawing a deep, steadying breath, she took off her brassiere. The night air caressed her breasts, bringing her nipples to peaks. She shivered.

She forced herself to look at Paul. He seemed mesmerized. She smiled and thought about how damp and hot she felt, how easily he would slip into her right now. Then maybe...

She found her nightgown in the tumble of lingerie and slipped it over her head. Then she closed the drawer, put away her clothes, took an extra quilt from the top shelf of the chiffonnier and walked toward the French doors that led to the gallery.

"What the—"

"Good night, Paul. Sweet dreams."

As she closed the door, she heard his muffled curse. Then she curled up on the chaise longue and waited for her body to stop pleading with her to go back inside. It was a long wait.

SHE AWOKE WITH THE DAWN, her back stiff, her body instantly alert to needs that wouldn't be satisfied. She was also mortified at the memory of undressing in front of Paul the night before. Oh, she was reckless, but not, she discovered this morning, completely shameless.

She thought of staying on the gallery until she heard him dress and leave her room, but she had to get André ready for school. Maybe if she rose early, she could get out without waking Paul. So she opened the French doors quietly and crept stealthily across the room.

Taking a peek at Paul, sprawled across her bed, was more than she could resist. The bedcovers were in havoc, sheets and quilt tangled around his legs. He lay on his belly now, revealing his buttocks and back. The back was strong, firm with compact muscle, the buttocks taut. She thought once more about the feel of his skin beneath her fingers.

"Sleep well, Margie?" he murmured against the pillow, and she realized that, even with his eyes closed, he must have been aware of her staring.

She composed herself the best she could, marshaling the impassive society voice she'd learned from Mother Lyon. "I had the most frightful nightmare. At least, I had assumed it was a nightmare. Until now."

He rolled over. She forced herself not to look away and was startled to realize he was aroused again. Or still. Either way, panic rose in her.

"Still not too late," he said, stretching and yawning.

"You should cover up before Lena comes up with coffee. You'll give her a heart attack."

He laughed. She watched, fascinated, as all the muscles of his body joined in his mirth. How had she forgotten what a miraculous piece of work the male body was?

Without another word, she went into the adjoining bathroom. She considered forgoing her bath to avoid disrobing with him nearby. But she refused to let him disrupt her life any more than he already had. She would proceed as usual. She bathed—although quickly—and pulled on her robe.

Was it too much to hope that he might have behaved as a gentleman would, dressing and leaving while she was in the bathroom?

Apparently the gentlemanly thing had not occurred to him. He stood at the open gallery doors, wearing a striped satin robe and sipping coffee.

"I asked Lena to bring an extra cup for you, my dear," he said. "And how is my loving wife this morning?"

"Your playful mood isn't amusing, Paul." She busied herself dressing, doing her best to keep the essentials protected from his prying gaze.

He chuckled and moved across the room. "My dear, if you aren't in a cheerful mood this morning, I'm afraid my reputation with the servants is going to suffer."

Margaret told herself it didn't matter what the servants thought. She tugged on her dress. Paul moved in to secure the hooks in back.

"Don't do that," she snapped.

He ignored her. "How do you get by without a man around the house? Or maybe you don't."

She jerked away from the whispering touch along her back. "You're despicable."

"I'm only a concerned husband, my dear. And I'm sorry you're in such a snit this morning. Here, we've gotten off on the wrong foot. Let's patch things up."

Without further warning, he framed her face with his hands and dropped a light kiss on her lips. He backed away an inch, a mocking expression on his face. But as he looked into her eyes, his expression changed, grew dark and intense. He lowered his lips to hers again, but this time it was no sham of a kiss, intended to taunt her. This time his lips pressed insistently to hers, and she felt the warmth of it flood her entire body.

When she realized how her body was betraying her, she pulled away.

"The game is over," she said, then marched out of the room and down the hall to her son's room, shaking all the way.

PAUL FINISHED HIS COFFEE on the gallery, sitting on the chaise longue where Margaret had spent the night.

He listened to the birds, to the trees rustling in the breeze. Early morning here at Lyoncrest was as peaceful as it was on the bayou, if you could ignore the undercurrents within the family. The place could seduce him, make him forget all the reasons he had stayed away so long.

But the real danger, of course, was Margaret.

Clearly, if he didn't keep his distance, he would fall under her spell again. He already wanted her so badly he feared she would manage to convince him of her lies, if he listened to that husky voice, looked into those eyes long enough. Hadn't she already ensnared him with her big plans for a television station?

And hadn't his mother helped lay the trap by convincing him to come home?

Margaret had power over him the way no other woman ever had, before or since. Why else had he stayed away so long? Nevertheless, he refused to end up a slave to his baser needs. And the first order of business was to find another bedroom. He wouldn't be able to handle even one more interminable night with her so close. He could sense her arousal.

And she had been aroused. He shifted in the chair, suddenly uncomfortable. The way she'd disrobed right in front of him, as if it meant nothing to her. My God, she was bold as brass. He smiled. Still, he'd seen the way her nipples hardened, the flush that heated her body. He'd seen her eyes go soft and bright. She'd been ready for him, and heaven knew he'd been ready for her.

Cursing softly, he headed for the bathroom. If he was lucky, she'd have used all the hot water and he could get himself under control with a cold bath this morning.

Tonight he would make other sleeping arrangements. The thought brought another smile.

"That's not what I meant," he muttered as the pipes groaned

and rattled and delivered a rush of steam and hot water. He sank into the steam and gave in to one final daydream.

CHARLES ENTERED the sunroom briskly, gave his mother a peck on her powdered and scented cheek and headed for the coffeepot.

"My, what an early bunch this morning," Minna said. She sounded especially cheerful, Charles thought.

"Are we?" He gave her a smile as he loaded a plate with salt-cured ham, fluffy scrambled eggs and a flaky croissant.

Minna nodded. "Your father left before daybreak, Margaret directly after that and Paul couldn't be bothered to have breakfast before he left. I suppose his eating habits aren't what they should be. I imagine he didn't have a cook out there in the swamp, did he?"

"Paul? Paul was here?" Charles's knife and fork paused over the slice of ham.

"Oh, yes." Minna looked and sounded unconcerned, but Charles spotted the delight in her eyes.

"What is he doing here?"

"Why, this is his home, Charles. Whatever do you mean?"

"Mama, this hasn't been Paul's home for a decade."

"You're exaggerating as usual. He's only been gone a few years. The war took many young men away from home."

"The war was over years ago."

"Nevertheless, he has returned at last. We discussed this possibility last night. You haven't forgotten our agreement about André, I trust."

Charles clenched his knife so tightly his hand began to shake. Paul, skulking around the station. Paul, back at Lyoncrest. Charles's morning coffee soured in his belly. Everybody's favorite son was back from the war. Charles knew what that meant. Soon he would fade into the shadows again, eclipsed by the family's shining star.

Sure enough, Minna Lyon's face held a contented glow. "I declare I slept better just knowing he was back in his old room where he belongs."

"What?" Charles shoved back from the table.

"Charles, he does have a wife who's waited faithfully for him all these years."

Back at the station, back at the house, back in his own bed.

With Margaret.

Jealousy flashed white-hot in Charles, planting wild thoughts in his mind. Thoughts of betrayal and revenge. All these years, he'd kept Margaret's secret, waiting patiently for the day when she would realize which of the Lyon brothers was truly worthy of her.

And now this.

He would tell them all. Make it known. Disgrace her and that little bastard.

The thought of André calmed him, took the sting out of his fury. He loved the boy, would do anything for him. It didn't matter to him that André wasn't a real Lyon. Someday, when Margaret wised up, they would find a way to circumvent the Catholic church. Then he would marry her, adopt the boy, make him a true Lyon heir.

At least, that had been the plan until somebody dragged Paul Lyon out of the swamp.

Charles stood abruptly. "That is obscene."

"Now, Charles, don't excite yourself. You know your asthma—"

"My asthma be damned!"

Minna gasped. Charles was instantly contrite, but still could not tame the impotent rage in his heart. Was his entire life to be ruined by his brother? He left by the front door, running out of steam halfway to the garage as he realized he'd forgotten his briefcase. Deflated, he heaved a sigh and dropped to the bench beside the bed of roses that were Aunt Ella's pride and joy. She was there already this morning, on her knees, wearing that enormous straw hat that made his mother shudder whenever Ella wore it off the property.

"Weeding," Ella said. "It's been such a wet winter the weeds are thriving. You can't let them get ahead of you."

"They'll choke out everything, I suppose," Charles said, identifying with the poor rosebushes that wanted nothing more than to bloom where they were planted, but had to battle weeds and bugs and who knew what in order to fulfill their birthright. Yes, Charles himself was like one of Aunt Ella's prize roses. The thought gave him comfort.

His aunt got to her feet, dusted the knees of the breeches she wore to garden in—which also appalled her older sister—and kneaded her lower back. Ella was almost sixty, but not at all like the other women that age that Charles knew. His maiden aunt was what some might call eccentric. She'd always been his favorite, and he hers.

"You're looking morose this morning, Charlie boy."

"Paul is back."

She nodded and joined him on the bench. "I heard that."

"Mother even wants us to lie to the boy about him. He's going to do it all over again, you know. Usurp everything."

Ella patted him on the knee. "Let him take it. All of it. You're better than any of it, Charlie boy."

"Ella, you don't understand—"

"Don't be witless," she said. "Of course I understand. Haven't I lived here ever since your grandparents died? Haven't I practically raised you myself since then? I've watched while that big brother of yours stole away everything you ever thought you wanted, haven't I?"

It comforted him further just to hear her say it, to feel that someone understood.

"Minna always worshipped him, while all she could spare for you was fussing over your asthma. A.J. loves success and Paul had plenty of that. Including Margaret."

Charles felt himself flush. Aunt Ella knew everything. She always saw straight into his heart. He remembered the first time he'd seen Margie Hollander at a family get-together, maybe twenty years ago. He'd been enthralled by the seven-year-old, by her impetuous spirit. She'd taken him exploring in the Hollander attic, a musty, spider-infested place that had given Charles the creeps and had him wheezing and coughing before it was over. Margie had been dauntless. He'd known then that he loved her. Aunt Ella had spotted his feelings right away.

"Play your cards right," she'd whispered to him in the car on the way home, "and she'll be yours. Everyone loves a match like this, uniting the two dynasties."

At ten, Charles hadn't completely grasped what she meant, but he'd understood enough. Margie Hollander would be his bride someday.

Then, while he was away at college, he'd lost her. And not to just anyone. To Paul. That was what had made it so unbearable.

One more thing lost to his charming, talented older brother. Paul, adored by Minna, admired by A.J., loved by Margie and worshipped by the American public, while Charles languished in New Orleans with his asthma, a man not even able-bodied enough to fight in the war.

Through it all, he'd loved Margaret. Been loyal to her. Even her shabby behavior regarding André hadn't disillusioned him. She was young. Young people made mistakes. He could forgive her, something Paul couldn't do. Surely, soon, she would see how noble that made him.

And now Paul was back. In her bed. Charles had to get out of the house without delay. He simply couldn't bear this.

"Now is the time to get out of that place, Charlie boy," his aunt was saying. "A radio station is too callow, too mundane for a man of your talent. You belong on the concert stage. That is your true calling. You know that."

The words weighed him down even further. If there was one thing he wanted more than Margaret, it was just what Ella spoke of. But he had realized long ago that pursuing a career as a classical musician would never get him the things he wanted most—his father's respect, Margaret's love, the satisfaction of besting Paul. No, he had to make it in the broadcasting arena for those things to happen.

"I told her I'd do the announcing for this silly television station of hers," he said woefully. "Why is nothing I do ever enough?"

"Because they are beneath you, Charles. Until you follow your heart and do what you're meant to do, you'll be forever miserable."

"I do follow my heart, Aunt Ella." But Margaret had never noticed. And now, it appeared, she never would.

CHAPTER SIX

SEEING THE LYON BROTHERS together later that day, sharing a booth at The Pearl diner, was the last thing Margaret expected when she arrived to pick up the food ordered for the engineers.

Charles was leaning intently over the table, where their po'boy sandwiches sat barely touched. Paul was leaning back in the booth, the epitome of indifference. Margaret thought she'd never seen two brothers less alike. Charles, fair yet intense, tall and broad-shouldered despite the asthma that had dogged him all his life. And Paul, dark, slight of build and to all appearances easy-going, despite the tension on the inside.

They could've complemented each other with their differing personalities. Instead, for reasons she couldn't fathom, they had become rivals. At least, Charles saw them as rivals. Paul didn't care a fig.

Indeed, she wondered what her estranged husband did care about. Once he had cared passionately about broadcasting. Now, it appeared, he could take it or leave it. As easily as he could take or leave her.

Seeing them like this made her nervous. The brothers could banish her from Lyon Broadcasting. Everyone would be happy then.

She sauntered over to the table, trying for that heedless unconcern Paul had mastered. "Well, if it isn't the brothers Lyon, plotting to take over the empire, I suppose."

Charles slid to one side to make room for her in the booth. Paul didn't budge. Margaret slid in beside her brother-in-law.

"Actually," Charles said, draping his arm across the back of the booth, "we were deciding how to divvy things up."

"Oh, really." She should have realized that being this close to Paul would make her jumpy. The memory of that unexpected kiss just a few hours earlier had her completely rattled. How could Paul remain so cool? "You take the executive offices, Paul gets the break room and I get the studios and engineering booths? Are you sure A.J. will approve?"

Charles laughed, but there was an edge to it.

Paul took a long swallow from his glass of tea. "I don't think you were part of the equation. Was she, Charles?"

"Now, listen, you two. My father helped found—"

Charles put a hand on her shoulder. "He's baiting you, Margaret."

She forced herself to relax.

"Besides, he knows about your father's will."

To her chagrin, Margaret felt her face flush. What her father had left her when he died was a position of no power. With Paul gone, her father had given his share of Lyon Broadcasting to Alexandre. Theoretically it would all be passed on to André when he was of age. But Margaret wasn't quite as trusting as her father had been. A.J. Lyon was manipulative and shrewd. If he saw a way to benefit from doing something else with André's rightful shares of Lyon Broadcasting, then he would do it.

Being merely a daughter, Margaret got nothing, which she also knew would be Justine's fate unless she had a son. Thanks to her own father, Margaret couldn't even count on the job she'd held since the shortage of men on the home front had boosted her into the position of acting news director. During the war, women had built ships and manufactured munitions and even made decisions at radio stations. But when the war ended and the men came back, the women went home.

Margaret had held on to her position only because she held sway with her father. But Wendell Hollander had died last year and Margaret's clout at WDIX was slipping. Fast.

Charles had probably taken great delight in passing along the news to his brother.

"I was telling Charles there was no reason he and I can't do television," Paul said. "We certainly wouldn't have any trouble getting the board behind us."

Paul and Charles working together? And the only reason Paul would even consider it, Margaret knew, was to cut her right out of the project. "Now, listen, this is my idea. I've done all the work so far. You can't—"

"Sure we can."

Charles put a placating hand on her shoulder. But Margaret's wrath was directed entirely at Paul, who smiled. "You wouldn't dare!"

"No?"

"You listen to me, Paul Lyon. I made WDIX radio number one in news in this city while I've been in charge," she said. "Tell him, Charles. There's no reason—"

"You're a woman," Paul interjected. "That's reason enough."

The look in his eyes said he'd been reminded of her womanhood quite recently. She'd been reminded of her own womanhood, for that matter—the way she'd felt looking at his lean body sprawled on her pristine white linen sheets, the evidence of his manhood on prominent display; the way she'd burst into flame the instant he touched his lips to hers. And his lips had been hard and unyielding, which was how she imagined he would have felt the night before, if...

"I'm a broadcaster," she said stiffly. "And I can do as good a job as any man. Better than some. My record speaks for itself. So if the two of you are cooking up any deals, you'd better deal me in."

Paul went on as if he hadn't heard her. "The thing is, Charles isn't crazy about the whole television idea."

"And I hold the swing vote." Charles looked immensely pleased with himself.

"So we've reached a compromise."

And left her completely out of the negotiations. Of all the conniving—

"I vote for your television station," Charles said, "if the family hands me the reins of the radio station."

For a moment Margaret felt elated. It was going to happen. She was going to make it happen. Then she realized what Charles was saying. He wanted complete control of WDIX radio, the station she'd nursed along for years. Her boasts weren't empty boasts, either. She had raised WDIX from the bottom of the heap, where it sank when Paul left, to the top again. Charles would ruin all that. She knew he would. He had no feel for radio, no sense of why people listened or what they needed from their radio broadcasts. He had no business sense, either. He would run WDIX into the ground. Could she let that happen?

She looked at Paul. For an instant something blazed in his eyes—a passion for the future of broadcasting. It might not be much, but it was something they could share. It was a new beginning.

"All right," she said. "We'll do it."

"It's settled then," Charles said. "Now, if you'll excuse me, I need to get back to the family business."

Margaret stood so he could leave.

Charles looked at them for a moment. "Oh, by the way, I'm going to be leaving Lyoncrest, too. I hope you won't mind, but in six months, I'll be running the best station this city has ever seen. And you two will be the laughingstock of New Orleans. I think putting a little distance between us is for the best."

He walked away whistling. Margaret eased back into the booth, both relieved and stunned. Too much was happening too fast.

She felt the heat from Paul's knees under the table, so close to hers. "So we're going to be partners," she said.

"Don't let it go to your head, kid."

What a stinker he was. "We'll need some ground rules."

"Oh?"

"This is purely professional. Nothing personal. Nothing..."

He spoke the word she couldn't utter. "Sexual?"

What a word to use in public. She glanced around to see if he'd been overheard, saw no one choking on their gumbo. "Yes."

"I think I can manage to restrain myself."

His dry proclamation offended her. "Can you really?"

"I like a little flesh and blood, a little heart and soul in my dames," he said.

"I'm not a dame."

"No? You're not much in the heart-and-soul department, either, Mrs. Lyon. Congratulations. You've achieved everything you ever wanted, haven't you?"

"What are you talking about?"

He stood, tossing a bill onto the table to cover the tab. "You always wanted to be a businesswoman. Dollars and cents, right to your core. Congratulations. You made it."

His words were like a slap in the face. She wanted to deny them, but knew there was little she could say to convince him. Of course, from his perspective it appeared as if she'd been perfectly content to leave him alone until she needed him to save her professional hide. He couldn't know how many sleepless nights she'd spent, wondering where he was, wondering if anything would win him back.

When it came to Paul Lyon, she was nothing *but* flesh and blood, heart and soul.

PAUL STROLLED THROUGH the grounds of Lyoncrest with his mother, her slender hand tucked into the crook of his elbow. The January night was cool, pleasingly so. And his mother's presence was a balm to his spirit after the recent conversation with his father.

A.J. had given in to the idea of a television station, although it was clear he would be glad to see it fail. More galling than that, however, had been his comments in private. "You're just another employee here," he'd said in his usual gruff way. "Until you prove you can be trusted, you're just a hired hand. Understood?"

Oh, Paul understood all right.

He sighed and tried to put the bitter discussion out of his mind.

"So, you have decided to rejoin your family," Minna Lyon said, her voice as soft as the night air. "Your father informed me of the board's vote. I am quite satisfied. Yet you were not with us for dinner." She gave him the searching look that had always kept him honest.

"I'm not ready to face...all of it. Not yet."

She patted his arm where her fingers rested. "You wronged her, Paul. It is time you faced it."

He tightened his jaw, resisting the impulse to lay out the ugly truth about Margaret and her child. His mother had blinded herself to the truth and she was too old now to be robbed of the boy she considered her only grandchild.

"It was complicated."

"Between men and women, it is always complicated," she countered.

He wanted to tell her about Margaret's blind ambition, about her bankrupt moral code, about the ice water that ran in her veins. He wanted to tell her that even now, when maturity might have changed her, Margaret still wanted success more than she wanted love or happiness. Or him.

"She doesn't want me, Mother."

She stopped beneath a bare dogwood tree. "If you believe that, you are a fool."

He had no choice but to believe it. "That certainly seems to be the case, regardless."

Minna laughed. "Even a foolish son is better than an absent son. I am glad you're home. I will light a candle for you tomorrow that you will no longer be a fool."

He smiled and brought her hand to his lips. "Better light two."

They walked until the chill was too much for her, even in her cashmere shawl. Then he escorted her back to the house, poured her a brandy and delivered her to her bedroom.

He prowled the softly lit house, restless and irritable. The day's events kept spinning through his mind. Learning from Charles just how powerless Margaret's father had left her, hearing from Margaret's own lips that she wanted nothing more from him than his professional skills and his vote, the eerie feeling of moving into an office adjoining Margaret's. So much had happened it almost eclipsed the way the day had begun, with Margaret in his arms. Warm and yielding. A reasonable imitation of a woman who cared.

He heard Charles in the library, the soft melody of something melancholy. He turned away. No companionship there. He paused outside the back parlor and overheard a strident discussion between his father and Aunt Ella. Something about race relations being the next crisis to grip the nation. He wasn't up for it. The door to the family game room stood ajar. Maybe he would turn on the Victrola, rack the balls and have a solitary game of billiards. When he stepped into the room, however, he realized he would have been better off facing any of the others.

Margaret sat curled up in one of two leather chairs in the corner near the Victrola, her feet tucked beneath her full skirt, her shoes on the polished floor. At the billiards table stood the boy, André. He handled his cue stick deftly, like someone used to the game.

Paul's first instinct was to turn away, to leave without even the courtesy of an explanation. Confronting the evidence of Margaret's duplicity was as painful as it had ever been. But as he stood there, with both Margaret's eyes and the boy's trained on him, Paul remembered what his mother said. He had made a commitment to live here and become a part of the family business again. He couldn't avoid the boy. He'd better learn to deal with it.

"Hello, Paul."

He heard the anxiety in her voice. He wanted to ease it. He wanted to make it harder on her. He loathed her and he loved her. He dreaded learning which urges would win out. "This is cozy." He strove for as little emotion as possible.

"André loves billiards."

"I suppose you encouraged that. Or Papa, perhaps."

She shifted in the chair, slipping back into her shoes. Back straight, chin high, she sat with her hands clasped calmly in her lap. "He disappeared one day. We couldn't find him anywhere. He was four at the time. We were frantic. Mother Lyon finally found him in here. He was barely tall enough to reach the table, but he was trying."

Her story left a sour taste in his mouth. Margaret had no doubt heard the story of Paul's early affinity for billiards. Charles had been a musical prodigy; Paul had slipped into something a little less praiseworthy. Always thinking, always scheming, Margaret had used that to her advantage. Before he could figure out what scathing remark to direct at her, the boy marched up to him, cue stick upright in his left hand.

"I'm André," he said in a clear, strong voice. "You're Mama's old friend."

For decades Paul had made his living using his voice, but at this moment it failed him.

"*Mon cher,* this is Mr. Paul. He's here to help Mama at the new television station." She came and knelt beside the boy. "Remember I told you about the television station?"

"With pictures in front of my eyes, instead of pictures in my 'magination?"

"That's right."

She stroked the little boy's dark hair back off his forehead. The obvious tenderness of her touch drew forth a sharp longing in Paul. There was some heart and soul in her, after all, even if she did hoard it all for her son. They looked nothing alike, this mother and child. Instead, the boy was apparently the image of some nameless man.

André again turned his dark eyes on Paul. "Do you live here, too, now?"

"That's right." Paul was struck by the little boy's straightforwardness, a trait he did share with his mother. At least, a trait Paul remembered the young Margie—the girl he'd fallen for—had possessed.

"Did you live here before?"

"Yes, I did. In fact, I used to play on this billiards table myself."

"I can beat you," André boasted. "I'm the best."

Paul surprised himself by laughing. "You're on, young man. Your break or mine?"

He told himself there was no reason to despise the little boy for his mother's dishonesty. He actually enjoyed the game and André, especially the boy's delight when Paul's game disintegrated at the very end, delivering him to a shameful defeat at the hands of the seven-year-old.

He watched Margaret lead the boy off to bed and felt something unyielding begin to shift within him. Margaret knew he loved kids. She had it all planned, he supposed. He would have to be wary.

MARGARET CHANGED FOR BED, wrapping herself in her silk robe. She was restless, too excited for sleep, as André had been. He had talked incessantly about his new friend, Mr. Paul, who had shown him billiards tricks that no one else at Lyoncrest knew. He hadn't wanted to sleep.

Neither did Margaret. She kept thinking of this room just twenty-four hours earlier, when Paul had been here, charging the air like a summer thunderstorm roaring in off the gulf. Now the room was empty. Terribly empty.

And she kept thinking of the amazing spectacle of Paul Lyon coaching his son. Inwardly, she had wept with joy at each touch, each smile. Outwardly she'd mustered every bit of willpower she had to remain in control. She ached to tell André the truth about his new friend. But for his own good, she couldn't. Not yet. Soon, she prayed. Soon.

She opened the French doors to the gallery and drifted out. It was cool tonight and the air was fragrant. She saw irony in the fact that neither the temperature nor the scents in the air had registered with her the night before. Then, she had been conscious only of Paul in the room behind her. Paul, sprawled on her bed in the altogether. She could have had him if she'd wanted him. She was sure of it.

But she hadn't.

Supposing she had, though. How might things have been different now? she wondered.

"You're not planning to sleep out here again, are you?"

His voice, close by and unexpected, startled her. Hand at her throat, she turned. Her heart fluttered wildly beneath her fingertips. "You're here."

He leaned against the wrought-iron railing that encircled the wide gallery. He still wore his dress pants, white shirt and vest, although he'd shed both his necktie and his suit coat. The vest was unbuttoned, his cuff links gone, as well, leaving the cuffs of his shirt loose, rolled once to reveal his wrists. A cigarette hung loosely from his fingertips; smoke curled up, drifting off over his head and into the night.

"Don't panic. I'm here," he said, "not there."

He smiled. The gallery outside her room was shared with the room on the opposite side of the hall. The French doors leading to that room were open, as were hers.

"I like the view," he said. "Hope you don't mind that I settled in nearby."

She tried not to read anything into his words. He liked the view of the gardens, nothing more.

"Not at all," she said. She realized she was moving in his direction. She stopped. It wasn't easy.

"Well, I'll leave the gardens to you," he said. "I expect morning will come early."

"Yes. I... Thank you. For being kind to André."

He shrugged and snuffed out his cigarette in the pot of trailing verbena in the corner. "Thank you for not saddling the boy with the erroneous impression that I'm his father."

Margaret felt some of the hope begin to wither in her heart. "Paul—"

"I realized tonight it's going to be easier than I thought," he said quickly. "I've simply made up my mind to let go of the past. And that won't be difficult because I can see now I don't have any bad feelings for you or the boy. He means nothing to me, you see. No more than you do these days."

Margaret made fists in the pockets of her silk robe, pressing her nails into her palms until they hurt. "I'm glad you can view it that way, Paul," she said when she could control her voice. "I believe I'll go in, as well. I think I'll sleep like a baby tonight."

"One more thing, Margaret. If you try to shove that boy down my throat, to put pressure on me...if you tell me one more of your appealing little lies, I'll have you and the boy thrown out of here. I'll do whatever is necessary to make that happen. Am I making myself clear?"

"Perfectly."

Crushed, she retreated to her room. She carefully locked both the French doors to the gallery and the door to the upstairs hall. Then she buried her face in her pillow, fighting tears, unwilling to give in to the anguish in her heart. Would her foolish, youthful mistakes never be forgiven?

CHAPTER SEVEN

August 1941

MARGIE STARED at the angry face of the man she'd eloped with just seven weeks earlier and wondered how to get around the fact that she'd made a mistake. She should never have married this impossible man.

"How many times do I have to say this?" His voice tight, Paul went on about the business of dressing in his dark gray suit. But his lean face had grown hard, rigid with his anger. "No wife of mine needs to run off like some schoolgirl for a college education."

Margie sat on the edge of the high four-poster bed. Her marriage bed. She felt like a child. And not just because her feet didn't quite reach the floor. *He's too old for you.* How many times had Wendell Hollander warned his headstrong daughter? *Too worldly for a girl like you.*

Margie never had been one to listen when others disagreed with her plans. It had worked with her overindulgent parents, sometimes even with the nuns, who thought her bright and talented and therefore gave her more leeway than they gave other students.

It wasn't working with Paul.

"But, Paul, you knew I wanted to go to college." She tried to sound rational and mature, not like a whining child. "I've been accepted at Ladycliff. Classes begin in two weeks. It's all planned."

"Then you can unplan it," he said, bending over to shoehorn his feet into shiny leather shoes.

"But I want a career. I want—"

"I thought you wanted to be my wife."

She thought of his kisses, his caresses, the feelings he stirred in her that she had never, in all the whispers with her friends, imagined. She thought of the way he'd always seemed to understand her as no one else did. Until now. "I do. But—"

"Then stay home. Start a family. Margie, I want a son."

The words chilled her. "What?"

"We're married now, Margie. That's what marriage is for."

"But you never said anything..." Of course, their whirlwind courtship hadn't left much time for sharing secrets.

"Well, now I am. I want a son more than anything."

Margie's cheeks prickled with anxiety. How could this be happening? She should tell him now. Had to tell him now. But how? How to explain that an appendectomy when she was eight had scarred her fallopian tubes, leaving her barren? How to explain that she hadn't known herself until she returned home from their elopement, when her mother had taken her aside and given her a halting, pained explanation? None of them would have known had it not been for the unusual pain that had accompanied the onset of her monthly cycle. At twelve she had accepted her mother's explanation of the surgery to make the pain go away.

What she hadn't known until a few months ago was that the surgery had been successful in removing the scar tissue that had caused the pain. But nothing could restore her ability to bear children.

No, she dared not tell him that. Not yet. Not until he realized how happy they were going to be without children, just the two of them. Partners. Forcing down her misgivings, she said, "Paul, we have plenty of time for that later. First let me go to college. Let me learn the business—"

"No wife of mine is going to work in radio. It isn't done."

His words sounded suspiciously like orders. Her own anger taking over, she got to her feet and looked him squarely in the eye. "Nobody bosses me around, Paul Lyon."

Some of the tension went out of her when he smiled. "You're cute when you get tough. Did you know that?" Then he kissed her on the nose. "I'll see you tonight, kiddo. Don't you have the garden society with Mother today?"

"No!" She barely stopped herself from stamping her foot. "I most certainly do not!"

He walked out of the room whistling. She followed him, shouting as he descended the stairs, "I'm going to college, Paul Lyon. Then I'm going into broadcasting. You knew that all along. I'm going to be the most famous woman in New Orleans. You'll see."

He never stopped whistling. A cheerful Glenn Miller tune carried him out the front door. Now furious beyond measure, Margie whirled to return to her room and slammed into Ella Barnes, Paul's maiden aunt.

"Oh, Aunt Ella, I'm sorry." Her voice suddenly trembled. Ella put her tiny hands on Margie's shoulders and looked up at her. "Stick to your guns, Margie. If you let him rule the roost now, he'll still be crowing over you in forty years."

Margie's convictions wavered with Ella's support. After all, how much could Ella know? She'd never been married. Margie might be only nineteen, but already she had more experience than Ella. Still, she thanked the little woman, submitted to a hug and went back to her room. Paul's room, actually. She couldn't face the family, knowing others had heard her shouting. And she certainly couldn't face a car ride with Mother Lyon, followed by an interminable afternoon with the powdered and corseted members of the Beautiful Crescent Garden Society.

But she also couldn't face the solitude that was filled only with the unrelenting voice in her head. Paul wanted a child. More than anything. A son. The one thing she could never give him. Never.

On the verge of tears, she thought of running home to her mother. But her mother would tell her father, and Margie wasn't yet willing to admit he'd been right and she'd been wrong. After pacing for an hour, Margie realized she had to get out of this room.

Grabbing her pocketbook, hat and the little white gloves she was always forgetting, she sneaked down the servants' stairs and out the back door. She would take the streetcar into town. She would have a malted at the Maison Blanche lunch counter. She would show Paul Lyon that he couldn't run her life.

Of course, the truth was, he did run her life, just as he ruled her heart.

Margie had been head over heels in love with Paul Lyon since she was sixteen. She'd followed him around at the station like an adoring puppy, doing his bidding and learning everything she could about broadcasting in the faint hope of impressing him.

She'd had her first glimmer of hope on her nineteenth birthday in January, when she'd seen a look in his eyes that she'd been sure was...well, adoration.

That hope had been dashed when he started going around with Riva Reynard, the receptionist at WDIX. Riva was cheap-looking, not nearly good enough for Paul Lyon, in Margie's opinion. Margie had suffered agonies of jealousy that entire spring, until Riva had vanished from her post in April.

In May, Margie had launched a bold campaign to capture Paul's attention.

By June, he was courting her.

In July, they eloped, the most romantic thing Margie could ever have imagined.

Here it was August, and Margie was already proving the old adage she'd heard her mother repeat to her bridge club many times: marry in haste, repent at leisure.

Walking briskly to the streetcar line, Margie tipped her head politely to the woman standing on the corner of Prytania and Third streets. The woman was dressed with dime-store flash and looked vaguely familiar. She must be a servant at one of the neighboring houses, and Margie had been brought up never to slight a servant.

When she reached the streetcar line and stood waiting for the next car into town, the woman came up behind her. That, of course, was not remarkable. How else was one to get into town? The St. Charles streetcar rumbled up and Margie boarded, taking a seat near the back. The showy woman sat in one of the seats facing the back. Margie avoided her gaze. She was caught up in her own gloomy thoughts when the woman slid into the seat beside her.

"You don't remember me, do you?"

The woman's forwardness startled Margie. "Well, certainly, I— Oh! You're Riva Reynard, aren't you?"

"Sure, that's me all right." The woman smiled. "And you'd be Mrs. Paul Lyon."

Despite her earlier misgivings, Margie felt a thrill at being addressed so. She twitched her ring finger and felt her wedding band tug on her glove. "That's correct."

"Best wishes, Mrs. Lyon. Your husband, he's a fine man."

Margie felt uneasy, sitting beside this woman who had quite

possibly been intimate with Paul just a few short months earlier. What, she wondered, would Mother Lyon consider proper social etiquette in this situation? The nuns certainly never covered it in catechism class. She smiled and hoped that would suffice.

"I'm bringing you a business deal, Mrs. Lyon." Riva's voice had dropped. Her tone made Margie anxious.

"I believe this is my stop, Miss Reynard," she said as the streetcar slowed near a caterer that her mother always used for significant events. "If you have business to discuss, perhaps it would be better if—"

As Margie rose from her seat, Riva put her hand on Margie's arm to detain her. "I'm in the family way, Mrs. Lyon."

Her piercing gaze left no doubt in Margie's mind who the father was. Margie dropped back onto the wooden seat to catch her breath. Her head was spinning. She'd never fainted in her life and tried to imagine Mother Lyon's consternation if she made her fainting debut on the St. Charles streetcar line.

"Breathe slow, Mrs. Lyon," Riva said. "Slow and deep. You'll be all right."

Margie did as the other woman suggested, until her head began to stop spinning. What now? she thought. What happened now in this happily-ever-after world she'd believed she was entering? That world was already fraying. But this. What did this woman want? Would there be a scandal? Margie tried to imagine disgrace, but it was beyond her ability to imagine.

"Sorry to be springin' it like that," Riva said. "I couldn't think of an easier way to say it."

"Wh-what do you want? Why are you telling me?"

"Because I want to give you my baby."

Margie's heart lurched. "You can't be serious!"

"Dead serious. I want you to raise it as a Lyon."

"I can't listen to this," Margie said, standing and pushing her way past Riva. She made her way to the exit and when the streetcar made its next stop, she got off. She was still six blocks or so from town. Riva was right behind her.

"Please, Mrs. Lyon. Hear me out."

"You are quite insane. You must be."

Riva grabbed her arm again and yanked Margie around to face her. Her expression was fierce. "I am going to be a mother. All

I want is what all mothers want—the best for my baby. I'm not crazy."

Margie softened at the honesty in the woman's words. "It's insane to think it would work. Paul would never agree to it."

"You're goin' away. To school. While you're away, who would know that a child was not born to you?"

"But we've only been married a few weeks." She felt her face grow warm. "The timing..."

"First babies, they're lots of times early. You've seen this even in fine families."

Margie felt herself blush furiously now. She could never explain that she and Paul had not been intimate until their wedding night. Speaking of such things wasn't done.

"I'll buy you a coffee. We'll talk." Riva looked at her with such despair and such hope that Margie found herself sympathizing with the woman. "Please."

Margie nodded. They entered a diner that Margie had never noticed before, a place where she would have been inclined to wipe the rim of her coffee cup if she hadn't been reared always to exhibit politeness. And as the waitress poured a cup of coffee for each of them, it came to Margie that Riva Reynard had perhaps just presented the solution to Margie's own dilemma. Riva would soon have a baby for whom she wanted to provide the best. Margie herself could never have the baby her husband so desperately wanted.

No, that truly was insane thinking.

"Let me tell you what we can do," Riva said. Margie held her breath.

THE PLAN WAS SIMPLE, but carrying it out was the hardest thing Margie had ever done. First she had to leave for college as planned despite Paul's vehement protests. Because the first thing Riva had insisted on was secrecy. No one must know, not even Paul. She didn't want to risk his rejecting the baby and ruining their plans. Knowing Paul as she did, Margie had to agree.

She'd cried on the train all the way to Ladycliff College in New York, wondering if Paul would ever forgive her. The set of his jaw as she'd packed her bags said he wouldn't.

Within weeks of leaving home, she had to write the letter

telling the family her news and then wait fearfully for their reaction. Her own mother, on hearing about the "miracle," sobbed into the phone. Paul showed up at the dormitory two days later, looking jubilant.

"Have you packed?" he asked.

"Don't be silly," she said. "Why would I do that?"

"You're coming home, of course."

"Paul, be reasonable. I can finish out this first semester. The tuition has already been paid and—"

His face had clouded over. "To blazes with the tuition. You need to be home. Off your feet."

She reminded herself that she had to be even more adamant than he was. Going home would ruin everything, spoil the entire plan. "I'll finish the semester. I'll be home by the holidays. I can put my feet up then."

What she didn't say was that, by the holidays, they would be the proud parents of a premature son or daughter. And the only people who need ever know the whole story were herself, Riva and the Cajun lawyer Riva knew from the bayou where she'd grown up. He would make it legal and cover everyone's tracks besides. Riva had promised. Of course Margie knew she would be able to tell Paul the truth once he saw his baby. Then he would have to accept the baby. His heart would dictate it. And so would his strong sense of right and wrong. Once he saw the baby in her arms, he would see it was the right thing to do, no matter what the circumstances.

By the time Paul left Ladycliff, he was furious all over again. He swore that he wouldn't come traipsing after her again, that the next move was hers. She counted on his stubborn pride to keep his word about that.

What she hadn't counted on was the wounded pride that would drive Paul to leave New Orleans in a huff. Her mother wired her the news the day after Riva's baby was born. Paul had been trying for months to get a job with one of the radio networks. He'd finally been successful, and had left for New York City. There was even some talk that, if the war in Europe escalated, he might go overseas.

Frantic, Margie called long distance to the network in the city. Everyone kept saying Paul wasn't available. She made plans to take the train to New York as soon as she had the baby.

The infant was four days old in early December when Riva Reynard handed him to Margie outside a rundown country hospital near the bayou. His hair was a tuft of dark fuzz and his tiny red face looked perpetually frustrated. Margie's heart expanded when she saw him, taking him in.

"I named him André, after my papa. I hope that suits. It...it helps me. Knowing he'll have something of me with him."

Margie looked from André to Riva. Riva still held him clutched tightly to her breast, and she hadn't looked away from his face for an instant. In Riva's eyes, Margie saw a mother's love so powerful she would give up her child in order for him to have the best of everything. And in the tiny baby's face, she saw something of the man she loved. In that instant, this baby took the place of every other dream her heart had ever held.

"I'll love him with all my heart," she said, her throat thick with tears. "He'll never want for anything."

"This I know. He'll never be a rich man's bastard," Riva murmured. She quickly thrust the baby into Margie's arms as if she might change her mind, given the chance. "He's a Lyon now."

Riva smiled, but her eyes glistened with tears.

Margie felt the wonder of the tiny person in her arms and an awed respect for the woman who had given birth to this miracle. She couldn't imagine the sacrifice. She looked up to express her gratitude, but Riva was gone.

"Come with me, André. It's time to meet your daddy."

THE TRAIN FOR NEW YORK left early on Saturday, arriving Sunday morning. All the way up, Margie gave vent to her imagination. She imagined the fatherly love in Paul's eyes when he saw his baby—their baby—for the first time. She imagined how readily he would forgive the mother of his son for her headstrong ways. André would smooth over everything between them. They would make a new start.

By the time she reached New York City, the terrible news had broken. The Japanese had attacked Pearl Harbor. The United States would enter the war.

Anxious to find Paul, Margie rushed by taxi from Pennsylvania Station to the tall building where the network was located. There she learned that Paul was preparing to leave that very afternoon. If she hurried, she might catch him before he sailed for England.

Truly terrified that he might get away before she could see him—before he could see André—Margie hired another taxi. Holding the baby close to protect him from the jostling crowd at the docks, she looked for Paul, growing more distressed with each passing minute. André began to cry and Margie was close to tears herself when she finally spotted him in a knot of men and piled-up trunks.

"Paul! Paul, thank God I found you!"

His eyes held a hint of welcome relief. "Margie!"

"I...I came to..." She glanced at the other men, who viewed them with interest and amusement. She had to talk to Paul, had to tell him the whole story. But how, with all these men he seemed to know watching and listening? "To ask you to come home. We need you. Paul, you have a son."

The welcome in his eyes vanished. "So soon, *ma chérie?* Why, it's only December seventh, a mere five months since we married." His skepticism came out in biting sarcasm.

"Always knew you were a fast worker, Lyon," one of the men in the group said. A round of crude gaffaws followed.

Margie flinched. "He...he was early. Premature."

Narrowing his eyes, Paul pulled the corner of the little blue blanket away from the baby's face. "He's a strapping young fellow for one born so early. Could it be you've miscalculated?"

"Paul, can't we..." She felt the heat on her face and the fear in her heart. She had to get him away from these men. Then, when they were alone, she could explain. She put a hand on his coat and tugged. "Please, I—"

Paul leaned close and spoke between clenched teeth. "If you expect me to do the gentlemanly thing and let you call your little bastard mine, you have definitely miscalculated." Then he turned and walked away, calling over his shoulder, "See you around, kid."

CHAPTER EIGHT

June, 1949

WINTER ROLLS into spring with little fanfare in New Orleans. Cool days and cool nights become warm days and cool nights; the scent of blooming camellias is replaced by the fragrance of jasmine and wisteria. Heat, humidity and honeysuckle aren't far behind.

This year, as it often did, the transition took Paul by surprise. One day, it seemed, it had been January in his fishing cabin on Bayou Sans Fin and the next it was summer and he'd been back at Lyoncrest for half a year. It was only in recounting all that had happened in those six months that Paul could believe so much time had passed.

The months were filled with frantic activity as they attempted to meet Margaret's goal of signing on WDIX-TV on July the Fourth, with President Truman's holiday whistlestop in the Crescent City.

Paul spent weeks with engineers, learning more than he wanted to know about building control boards that would enable them to beam television signals from the station to the control tower atop the New Iberia Bank building to the thousand or so homes in the region that had television sets.

He spent days with construction crews, overseeing the building of a studio and sets for news, for interviews, for musical entertainment, for cooking demonstrations and clown acts.

He spent entirely too much time pitching this new idea to potential advertisers and to local newsmakers and to prospective viewers, even to appliance stores that were reluctant to stock very many of the cumbersome, one-eyed boxes.

He spent meeting after meeting justifying expenses to the stodgy old men who ran Lyon Broadcasting.

He spent hour after frustrating hour relearning his own profession, now that listeners would not only be able to hear him but see him. He had to learn how to communicate with the camera, dress for the camera, hold his head for the camera.

And virtually every hour, every day, every week, Margaret was at his side.

"You have to woo the camera," she said now over the shoulder of the camera man. "I know you can do that."

"That might be easier if yours wasn't the only face I saw when I looked at the camera," he retorted.

She laughed. His displays of ill temper didn't seem to faze her. She wasn't intimidated by him. At first Paul hadn't been sure how he felt about that. Now he knew. He liked it. Respected her. What did that say about him? Weren't men supposed to run the show, be in control?

Not with Margaret around.

With Margaret around, the best you could hope for was an equal partnership. A very disturbing idea. Certainly no man he knew of had ever had an equal partnership with a woman.

He snatched at the knot of his necktie.

She marched out from behind the cameraman and glared at him. "Now that's certainly attractive. Crooked tie. Frown wrinkles."

"Wrinkles are good," he said. "Viewers respect age."

"Viewers respect dignity." She walked over and straightened his tie.

"It's too blasted hot to be dignified." Especially when she leaned over him like that, her eyes cool and assessing. Her knuckles brushed his neck.

"Wait'll we get the lights. I hear they're murder. You're not going to perspire on camera, are you?"

"Maybe you ought to do this."

She tapped him on the cheek with the tips of her nails. "No. You're the beauty, I'm the brains. Don't forget it."

"I'm more than just a pretty face," he said.

"I know. You have a compelling voice, too," she said, heading back to the camera.

And you're more than just the brains behind this operation, he thought, watching her retreat. *You've got a sweet little backside, too.* Maybe he would announce that when the cameras were rolling, see what she had to say about that. He grinned thinking about it.

"That's too much," she said. "Friendly, not wicked, Paul. You must be thinking about murdering your director."

"As a matter of fact..."

Iron Margaret. That was what all the engineers and construction crews called her behind her back. They'd never seen a woman like her. But strangely, they all seemed to like her. They did everything she asked, fell over backwards to please her. And not just because she was a looker. They did it because they respected her as much as they respected any man. They did it because she worked harder than any of them, because she knew her business, because she was always fair even when she was tough. They couldn't put any of those feelings into words, but Paul felt the same way. So he knew what they meant when she walked away and one of the guys said, "That's one helluva dame."

Paul had to agree.

And to his chagrin, she'd managed to become all that by disregarding everything he'd demanded of her. She'd become the woman she was by defying him. Thank goodness she had.

Now if only he could admire her unorthodox virtues without being distracted by her sultry eyes, her full lips, the honey-colored hair brushing her shoulders and her slender body.

"Paul, you are not following orders."

"You're not the only one who never follows orders," he said, getting up from the news set. "Especially when it's this blasted hot. It's half-past six and I'm done for the day."

"Half past!" Margaret glanced at her watch. "Gotta run."

"What's your hurry, kid?"

"There's an end-of-school program at seven," she said, not slowing down as she grabbed her pocketbook, gloves and hat from atop the packing crate where she'd thrown them after lunch. "André has a speaking part. I forgot to call Patrick for the car, but if I can get a streetcar, I might make it."

"I'll drive you."

She hesitated. "You're sure?"

As his roadster rolled toward the school in the dusk, Paul realized he was constantly around Margaret these days, but they were always surrounded by others. Being alone in the dusk felt different. The cozy atmosphere made him want to say some of the things he'd been thinking earlier.

"We're almost there," she said.

He knew what she meant. "We'll be ready for sign-on."

"You bet we will." She muffled a yawn.

"You're knocking yourself out."

"It's worth it," she said.

"This is the most important thing in the world to you, isn't it?" Six months ago he could not have said that without bitterness. Now he understood that men weren't the only ones driven by ambition.

"Second-most important," she said.

Their arrival at the school saved him from comment. Of course, the boy. She'd always been clear that the boy came first. Although her son wasn't the sore point he had been six months ago, Paul still had some ambivalent feelings about him. Margaret had somehow managed to convince the family not to try to make Paul accept the boy, probably by telling them he'd threatened to leave for good if they pressed the matter. Whatever the reason, he hadn't had to confront the issue and for that he was grateful.

Margaret got out, then peered through the open car window at him. "When you get back to Lyoncrest, perhaps you could ask Patrick to bring the car for us in about an hour and a half."

"Sure."

But he didn't. He sat there in the car, listening to the faint sounds of inexpert music from inside the school. Finally he did what was on his mind. He walked into the school and stood near the back of the auditorium.

The children were cute. Kids always were. But this moment wasn't about how sweet all kids were. It was about one kid, the only one he could see on the entire stage.

"And now, ladies and gentlemen, a recitation on faith, hope and charity from one of our most talented first graders, André Lyon," announced a portly nun.

Paul felt a hitch in his heart as the boy came forward. He'd been around André a lot these past few months, had learned not just to tolerate his presence, but to enjoy it. André was a funny imp, a mischief maker who accepted the consequences with a sincere promise never to commit the transgression again. Except that, in the way of seven-year-old boys, he quickly forgot the promise and had to be taught again. Paul liked him. Sometimes he almost liked him enough to surrender his pride and claim the boy as his own, despite what he knew. Sometimes, looking at the child, he thought—or imagined—he could see a slight resemblance to himself. At those times—before he could convince himself that he was wrong—he felt a prick of conscience that said he needed to pay more attention to the boy.

He was a sucker for kids, that was all.

He tried to concentrate on the boy's recitation. Faith, hope and charity. Paul had little of the first, none of the second and was apparently listing too far in the direction of the third, if he was even considering playing father to André.

But then, it wasn't the boy's fault.

Maybe it wasn't even Margaret's fault, either. He saw her, straining forward, her hair glistening beneath the prim navy hat perched on her head. She'd been little more than a child herself when it happened, a child in trouble. Pregnant when they married, pregnant when she started pursuing him, if his calculations were right. That, of course, was the hardest to swallow. Her sudden interest in him that summer had been nothing but a convenient cover-up. She'd gotten herself in the family way, probably by some pimply-faced fraternity boy from Tulane. Happened all the time.

He ought to admire her for coming up with a better plan than a shotgun marriage to some undergrad Romeo. Maybe if he hadn't been so crazy about her, he might have been able to see it that way. Maybe if he hadn't wanted so much to believe she was just as crazy about him.

André was finishing up. He hadn't stumbled over a single word; his voice had rung out strong and clear to the far reaches of the auditorium. The audience clapped. The nun returned to the microphone, beaming. "A chip off the old block, I believe is the way it's said," the nun declared to the dying applause.

To anyone who didn't know better, Paul supposed that would certainly appear to be the case. He startled himself for a moment in wishing it was so. In thinking that it could be, if only he would relent.

CHARLES DECIDED to skip the board meeting. He had no desire to hear how well things were going for the sign-on of WDIX-TV only six short days away.

He decided to skip lunch with Catherine Benoît, whom he'd been dating sporadically for the last few months also. He had no desire to hear Cat's broad hints that it might be time to consider formalizing their relationship. He called Aunt Ella, instead, and picked her up for a late lunch at the little fish house near Lake Pontchartrain. It wasn't fancy and the clientele wasn't desirable, but the food was outstanding and Aunt Ella wasn't such a nose-in-the-air that she would let shabby surroundings spoil her enjoyment.

"What a fine idea, Charlie boy," she said. "You know, things have not been the same at Lyoncrest since you left."

They were sitting at a picnic table, one of a half-dozen under the live oaks dripping Spanish moss. Raucous Cajun music wafted out of the wooden cabin that housed the restaurant. The day was humid. Charles had left his suit coat in the automobile. Despite the shade of a huge yellow hat with a frightful red band, Ella's upper lip was damp with perspiration. Cat Benoît, who hadn't half the class of Aunt Ella, would have died rather than be seen perspiring in a place like this.

Margaret wouldn't have minded.

"It was time to move on," he said, tearing a chunk of crusty French bread off the loaf in a straw basket. "Time to make my own life."

"You're right about that," Ella said. "And it goes well? You're in charge of the entire radio station now, R.J. says."

Charles wanted to tell her the truth, but hadn't the stomach for it. He wanted to tell her that after six months at the helm, the station was losing money and listeners for the first time since Margaret had taken over. "Papa's breathing down my neck."

"He should retire. Leave it to the young people."

Charles savored a plump fried oyster. The best in three parishes. If Cat's father offered food like this at that third-rate restaurant of his in the French Quarter, people would be lined up at the door. That was what Charles would do if he was in charge. Hire the chef from here, change the menu, change the decor. He'd... Who was he kidding? He'd probably run a restaurant into the ground as quickly as he was ruining WDIX radio.

"You're courting someone, too."

Charles winced. "Catherine Benoît."

"She's not good enough for you." Ella smiled. "I suppose I'd say that about anyone, wouldn't I, Charlie boy?" Charles smiled at his aunt. She was good for him. She believed in him the way no one else did. "I'm thirty, Aunt Ella," he said. "It's time I marry. I've been waiting and... It's never going to happen, is it?"

She patted his hand. "No, Charlie, it's never going to happen. Margaret's going to wait forever, too, if that's how long it takes. And that brother of yours, he's such a hopeless case, I think forever is exactly how long it's going to take. You get on with your life, Charlie. Make yourself happy. Forget Margaret and Paul and those fools at Lyon Broadcasting who can't see what a prize they have."

Charles looked into Ella's eyes and saw reflected there all that he'd ever believed he had it in him to be. Maybe she was right. He simply had to forget Margaret and move on.

He had heartburn all afternoon. He blamed it on the oysters.

THE NIGHT WAS SULTRY, the kind of night Margaret longed to throw open the doors to the gallery outside her bedroom. But she dared not. Had dared not since Paul moved home. He might be out there. And she might not be able to encounter him without giving in to urges that didn't suit a lady.

"He is your husband," she said under her breath. She sat at her dressing table, finishing one hundred strokes to her hair. The atmosphere in her room was oppressive. If only she could open the door...

She finished with her hair and turned back the bedcovers. Her skin was damp. She glanced at the door, longing for a hint of night breeze. She surely wouldn't sleep yet. Tomorrow WDIX-TV signed on. Although she was physically exhausted, her mind raced, her heart felt the exhilaration of seeing its dreams fulfilled. *One* of its dreams.

Perspiration trickled between her breasts. She would surely die if she didn't let some air into this stifling room. She opened the doors, studiously avoiding a glance to the right. She remained inside the room, shielded by diaphanous curtains from anyone who might be standing on the gallery.

As if anything could protect her from Paul, she thought as a hint of a breeze kissed her bare arms. For it wasn't Paul she needed protecting from. It was herself. It was the haunting memories of their lovemaking, the long-dead ghosts of their dreams and plans. It was the part of her that refused to accept the truth, that continued to love him and want him no matter how clear he made it that he had no more feelings for her.

Because sometimes, in moments when he didn't think she noticed, she would vow she saw something in the way he looked at her. Sometimes she even convinced herself he felt something when he looked at the son he still insisted on denying.

And those were the times when her hopes clung to life most stubbornly, those times when she saw him with André and saw the flash of their matching smiles, the same dark, thick-lashed eyes. Surely, she would think, he'll see the truth.

He hadn't yet. And no matter how many times she told herself to give up the hope, she hadn't yet, either.

Sighing, she stepped onto the gallery. Never mind about Paul. She would concentrate on that moment when she, personally, would activate the lever that sent the WDIX-TV signal out over the airwaves. She closed her eyes and shivered with the fantasy soon to be reality.

"I can't believe you're cold," he said.

The whisper of his voice didn't startle her. She admitted in that instant that she'd known all along that he would be here, that he would speak to her. And more. She opened her eyes and turned to face him. He was close enough she could reach out and touch him.

She would do exactly that before the night was over.

"No," she said, aware that her voice was huskier than usual. "Excited."

"About tomorrow?"

She didn't bother to reply. About tomorrow, yes. But also about tonight, and what it might mean for all her tomorrows.

"I don't think I can sleep myself," he said.

He held a glass, a tall glass filled with ice and water. He'd stripped down to his trousers and sleeveless undershirt. She noticed that he'd gained some of his weight back since returning to Lyoncrest. He looked better, healthier. Virile.

"It's going to go fine, you know," he said, taking a long swallow of water. His Adam's apple worked, perspiration sliding down his throat.

Margaret felt her body soften, felt her skin prickle with response. "Life is full of surprises."

He looked at her, and she thought from the look in his eyes that he might realize she wasn't talking about their sign-on the next day.

"No surprises tomorrow," he said. "Clockwork. It's all going to go like clockwork."

"No," she said, moving toward him. Her hand touched his when she took the glass. "Unexpected things will happen. We'll have to make adjustments we hadn't anticipated. We won't be sure what to do, how to react. That's the way of it."

She drank from his glass and imagined she felt the warmth of his lips on the rim of the crystal.

"But we can handle it," he said.

"Yes." She set the glass on the wrought-iron table. "We can handle it."

"We're good...together."

She smiled at him; there was no longer any denying the look in his eyes. "Very good."

Despite the breeze, the air felt heavy. She lifted her hair off her neck, watched him as he watched the curve of her bare arm in the moonlight. He would be aroused already. She knew that much.

She reached over with her free hand to test her theory. She was right.

"Oh, God," he groaned.

"Unexpected things will happen," she murmured.

He slipped an arm around her waist and inched her toward him. "You think this is unexpected?"

Only a breath of humid air stood between them. She felt the heat of him burning through her silk robe from breast to thigh.

"Isn't it?"

"No. This is inevitable."

Then he kissed her, a kiss that didn't ask permission to sweep her up in his heat. His mouth was demanding, his body insistent, his passion feeding hers. She clutched his bare shoulders, dug her nails into his flesh, felt the hard grind of his body against hers. When her knees went weak, he swept her into his arms and carried her into her room, to her bed.

Their bed.

He set her on the bed, her legs adrift off the side of the high four-poster. He lifted her gown to her waist and groaned again. Heat flowed through her with the sound. She felt him undo the tiny pearl button fastening her underpants, felt the silk slip to her knees, her ankles. She heard the metallic rustle of his zipper. His arms hooked beneath her knees and she was lifted to him.

With a barely stifled cry, she took him into her.

He moved against her fiercely. She thrust back, wanting him deep, wanting him fast, wanting him forever and ever and caring not that it might be just for this moment. She felt herself rising and rocking to sensations that her memory had not done justice. She felt him spill into her just as she felt herself gasping and grasping and soaring.

THEY CURLED INTO THE MIDDLE of the feather bed, hot flesh on hot flesh, breaths mingling, arms and legs tangled.

"If it was inevitable," she whispered, "why did we wait so long?"

"Test of wills," he said. "You lose."

She smiled against his chest. "I lose?"

"Mm-hmm. You're the weaker sex."

She jabbed him lightly. "I seduced you. Who does that make the weaker sex?"

"You also talk too much," he said, raising himself on one elbow.

His expression as he gazed down at her almost brought tears to her eyes. It was an unguarded look, a trusting look, a look she'd waited years to see. She was wise enough to let it pass for now and keep the mood light.

"You forget who's directing the show," she said.

He chuckled. "Want to stage direct?"

"Yes. Move your hand here."

He followed directions.

"And do this with your mouth."

He did.

"Oh. My. You're...oh...you're not waiting for directions."

"I'm a professional. I know what to do."

Indeed, he did.

THEY MADE LOVE late into the night. They never spoke of love, but Margaret knew what she felt in his touch. It was only a matter of time.

But before she could fall asleep, she knew there was one thing that needed to be done before another hour passed between them. She had to tell him the truth. The whole truth.

"Paul, I have to tell you something."

She felt him tense against her.

"Not now, Margie. Not now."

"I have to, Paul. Please."

There was a long silence. "Then tell me."

"It's André. I know you've never believed that he's your son. But he is." She faltered. After all this time, how to say this? What if the truth enraged him more than the falsehoods he'd always believed? The words stuck in her throat. "He's your son, Paul. You have to believe that. I can explain—"

He yanked upright in the bed. "This? This is all you're going to say? After...tonight? You're going to keep on lying?"

"No, Paul, please. It's not a lie! If you'll just listen—"

He was out of the bed now, heading for the open French doors, heedless of his nudity.

"Not one more lie," he said. "I'll not listen to another single lie from that sweet, poison mouth of yours."

He stalked away. The way he had before. Margaret sat on the disheveled bed, trembling with anger and despair.

CHAPTER NINE

THE ENORMITY OF HER MISTAKE sank in by lunchtime. WDIX-TV was scheduled to sign on at six that afternoon. And Paul Lyon was gone.

"You mean, you don't know where he is?" The cameraman's expression pleaded for her reassurance that he'd misunderstood.

"That's right, Ray. Right this minute, he's gone."

"He must've said something to somebody this morning." That was Rosie. "To his mother at breakfast, maybe?"

Margaret sat in Paul's chair on the news set. The entire crew—engineers, cameramen and other technicians—stood around like people who hadn't yet been told where the funeral was being held. "He... No. Nobody saw him."

One of the engineers said hopefully, "Call the police. That roadster of his won't be hard to spot."

"The roadster is still in the garage," Margaret replied.

Crew members glanced at one another, but their gazes always returned to Margaret. She was their boss, the one they looked to for answers. She had none to give. She knew what was slowly dawning on all of them. Paul had vanished before; apparently he had vanished again. Her plans for WDIX-TV were in ruins. But worse, far worse, she had in all likelihood destroyed the delicate connections being built between André and his father.

Yes, Margaret would create a solution from thin air if need be. But not for the sake of WDIX-TV. For André.

"I'll find him." She stood, adopting a confident stance. "You guys keep working. We're going on the air."

"But without Paul?"

"With or without Paul. We'll sign on if I have to read the news myself."

That drew a nervous laugh from all of them. Margaret gathered her handbag, hat and gloves and headed purposefully out of the studio. She sensed as she left that her determination was giving her crew the drive needed to move forward.

They depended on her not to let them down. They didn't know she already had.

Patrick was waiting at the curb.

"Find him," she said. "I don't care where we have to look. Find him."

Then she would force him to listen, with Patrick to hold him down, if necessary. Even if he despised her for her actions, she would make him listen. Then she would turn over to him both his son and the station. Because once he knew the truth, she knew he would never walk away from WDIX-TV or André. This day, the eighth anniversary of their nonexistent marriage, would become the official end of everything between Paul and her.

But if it assured the future of André, Paul and WDIX-TV, what happened to her mattered not in the least.

WITH THE PRESIDENT'S ENTOURAGE rolling into the city's business district on a patriotic holiday, the streets were crowded. It should have been a good place for an unhappy man to lose himself.

But Paul couldn't seem to manage that. The things that made him miserable stuck close wherever he went. He walked mile upon mile through cemeteries and along the waterfront. He finally ventured into the French Quarter, where the streets were still quiet.

Margaret haunted him wherever he went. Without her, his life seemed empty again, as it had these past seven years. But he couldn't take her lies. He loved her too much to listen to them, and he loved her too much to stay away.

In the morning light, without its music and the mingling aromas of Creole food, the French Quarter was as dreary as Paul's thoughts. He walked without looking around, hoping his feet would take him someplace where he could find peace. The few people who were out, sweeping up or unlocking their little shops, called greetings to him. It was like one of the small Italian villages he'd been in during the war, where everyone knew everyone else. There were no secrets, no strangers.

"You never were an early riser before," came a voice from above. "People change, aye?"

He looked up. A woman stood on a balcony, wearing a bright red robe, a fat white cat cradled in her arms. She was familiar.

"Riva? Is that you, Riva?"

"Yes, darlin'."

"I thought you'd gone back to Bayou Sans Fin."

She shrugged. "Sometimes I stay there. Sometimes I stay here. I'm here all summer. See you twice, no, three times on the street."

He didn't have to ask why she hadn't spoken to him before. She probably figured it wasn't proper. But she'd spoken to him this morning. He wondered why.

"But today I'm thinking I better speak up. You're looking like hell this morning. You can't be looking like hell today. Is your big day, yes?"

"Yeah. My big day."

The cat jumped out of her arms and walked the tightrope of the balcony railing. Riva leaned on the railing and smiled. "Then why do you look like you been out havin' a big night?"

"You might say I've been contemplating the many mistakes in my life."

"You? You got mistakes? Come up here, Paul Lyon. I'll give you coffee and brandy and I'll tell you about mistakes."

He might have been tempted, but for Margaret. His heart was full of her this morning. There was room for no one else, not even an old paramour.

"Just coffee, darlin'. And a little story. About André."

"André?"

"Sure, that's right. I always believed you ought not know the truth. Mayhap I was wrong."

Heart thumping, Paul climbed the dark stairs to Riva Reynard's apartment, beginning to wonder if he really wanted the truth, after all.

The apartment was small and crowded and already steamy on a day that promised to hit a hundred degrees. Riva brushed a kiss on the corner of his mouth; she smelled of dusting powder and all he could think of was Margaret's scent the night before. They sat on the balcony and he gulped down the coffee despite the heat, because he needed the fortification.

Riva studied him. "You want this truth? For sure?"

Paul wasn't sure at all. But he nodded.

"That boy, André, why did you go off and leave him and that wife of yours?"

"How do you know so much?"

She made a dismissive sound. "Everybody in this city knows that much. Why did you do that?"

"Then I suppose everybody in this city knows he isn't my son."

Her eyes grew wide. "You must be crazy. Delirious. Brain fever. That boy is your boy. Anybody with one squinty eye knows that."

"When did you see him?"

She closed her eyes and shrugged. She was enjoying the drama. "I see him. One time or two. I see him the day he is born."

"What?"

Her voice changed. The look in her eyes changed. "I hold him. I ask a blessing on his head. Then I give him to his new mama."

Paul felt as if the balcony below him had suddenly gone into free fall. He barely croaked out, "What?"

"I give him to your Margaret. So he won't be a rich man's bastard. Then you run off. Paul Lyon, what kind of fool man are you?"

Paul dropped his cup. He heard it shatter, as if from a great distance, felt the hot coffee splatter against his pants leg. But none of that really sank in. The only thing he could take in was the harsh truth Margaret had tried repeatedly to share with him.

André was his son. His flesh and blood. A son he had rejected for seven long years.

"I GIVE UP." Margaret slumped against the leather upholstery. "Take me home, Patrick."

She sensed his hesitation. What about the broadcast? That was what he wanted to say. That was what anyone would ask who knew what her passion had been for well over a year. Right now Margaret didn't have an answer. She only knew that she had to see her son. Had to hold him in her arms and pray for some way to make her awful, unforgivable mistakes up to him. Then she would be able to carry on. WDIX-TV would go on the air.

They had looked everywhere for Paul. At his haunts on the bayou, pounding on the doors at the homes of old buddies. Then they'd returned to the French Quarter, where she'd had high hopes of finding him. After all, it would be hard to lose a man in such a small neighborhood. But they'd had no luck there, either. Finally she'd abandoned all sense of decorum to visit a couple of the classier houses of ill repute frequented by the city's power brokers. Margaret didn't care how she humiliated herself this day. All that mattered was finding her son's father.

Aching and anguished, she dragged herself upstairs to André's room. When she opened the door, a cry escaped her lips.

André sat on the window seat overlooking the garden, tucked against Paul's side. Margaret had imagined such a scene so often she felt certain she must be imagining it now.

"Mama!" André sprang up and flung himself at her. "Guess what, Mama! You'll never guess!"

But she did guess—from the look in Paul's eyes as he gazed at the little boy who clutched her waist. Paul knew. He believed.

Tears sprang to her eyes, because she could also see that he was as filled with awe and joy as she had always hoped he would be, if only he could be made to believe.

"Mama, Mr. Paul is my real papa. Did you know, Mama? He said he didn't know it until today. Will we be a real family now? Will we?"

Tears trembled on her eyelashes. She couldn't speak, knew she couldn't trust her voice without dissolving into the sobs she had refused to release for so many years.

"We will." Paul stood and walked to them. "Won't we?"

Margaret swallowed hard. "But...I'm not...not his real—"

Paul pressed a finger to her lips. "Yes, you are. A real mother would want him to have his father's name. No matter what. A real mother would never give up hope."

Tears spilled onto her cheeks. "I thought it was the best thing. I never dreamed..."

"That I'd be such a stubborn fool. Margie, I'm sorry. I'll be sorry for the rest of my life for doubting you. But he is yours. And he is mine. That's all anybody ever needs to know."

She fell against his chest, their son laughing between them as she began to cry. "Oh, Paul, I love you so."

"And I love you. More than ever. I'll show you, every day, for the rest of our lives."

TWO HOURS LATER, Margaret looked across the brightly lit, stultifyingly hot studio at the man who was now truly her husband and gave the signal.

Paul smiled, looked at her, instead of the camera. "Good afternoon, New Orleans. This is Paul Lyon with WDIX-TV. Welcome to the future."

Margaret hadn't expected to cry again for a very long time. But as she looked around her at the crew who had helped give birth to this new baby of hers, she realized hers weren't the only eyes in the room that were wet with tears.

SILVER ANNIVERSARY

Roz Denny Fox

CHAPTER ONE

New Orleans January 1974

ANDRÉ LYON STRETCHED out the full length of the noiseless glider, crossing his ankles on the top rail of the hand-hewn fence that wrapped his rented raised bungalow. A fancy name, he thought, for a swamp shack. Still sleepy, he absorbed the sights and scents of a breaking day in Bayou Sans Fin. Graying, pungent moss draped tinsellike from a huge cypress, shaded his porch and edged out the smell of stagnant water. Beyond, in the wooded thicket, an owl hooted suddenly, startling a great heron, which flapped its wings and rose, dodging branches to hold on to a prize breakfast fish.

André yawned into a curl of steam drifting from his mug of chicory-laced coffee. Not a morning person, he couldn't recall the last time he'd seen a sunrise. Well, yes, there was one he did remember. A day three years ago when the freighter he'd called home for far too long had steamed into New Orleans, ending forever his global wanderings with the merchant marine.

Daybreak in the bayou. Early morning was a time of movement, of activity, of foraging for food; most swamp inhabitants went to ground during the muggy part of the day. André, however, was used to rising at noon. If his young neighbor hadn't banged on his door, fleeing from one of her mother's endless lovers, he'd still be snoring in his hammock.

But it was just as well, because right after that his mother had phoned. Her call had been abrupt. She'd simply said she was on her way over. That rattled André. No member of the influential Lyon family had ever set foot in his humble abode.

Thank goodness for the kid's visit. He often paid Rachel Fontaine to straighten up his place and vacuum. Her mama, it seemed, spent all their money on booze. This latest incident alarmed him. If her mother's overnight visitors were now turning their attentions to this child, something had to be done. Rach had been a skinny ten when André had returned to the city of his birth. Today, after the frightened girl came to him for protection, he realized how much she'd grown.

He wasn't normally so unobservant. But most of his waking hours had been spent developing a swamp-tour trade with J.D. Hawk.

Focusing on Rachel's plight, André knew the best advice he could give her was to go to the authorities. Was her mother blind, for pity's sake? Possibly. Though his privileged childhood had been the antithesis of Rachel's, *his* parents had been blind to everything except the family business. Lyon Broadcasting had consumed their lives—and still did. In a way, André saw a lot of the lonely kid he'd been in Rachel.

At thirty-three, he shouldn't care about a past he couldn't change. But maybe that part of him was closer to the surface than he'd realized. The child who'd been loved yet too often neglected while his parents were preoccupied with work... Maybe it was those memories that had moved him to become concerned about Rachel's plight. To keep an eye on her, help her with homework, give her a few bucks now and then.

Dropping one foot, André lazily pushed the glider. He knew his childhood didn't compare to Rachel's. His mother was a good woman. One truly baffled by what she no doubt perceived as her son's ingratitude. Not that she'd ever *called* him ungrateful. Papa, now—he'd never understood his son's lack of interest in the business. Paul Lyon, the much acclaimed Voice of Dixie, could not fathom André's feelings on the subject. But André had watched the business swallow his parents, and he didn't want that to happen to him. So he'd left home rather than embroil himself in arguments.

Running away only worked for so long. And since his return, he'd mended a few fences. He often met his mother for lunch. Just last Friday, in fact. Which was why her sudden decision to visit struck him as odd.

Whatever her reason, André decided to hit her with a request of his own. A request that involved Rachel. He'd had a positive upbringing, at Lyoncrest, the rambling family mansion in an affluent area of the Garden District. Rachel would be safe there. And certainly there was room for her. Besides, Mama had a history of taking in strays. The first when André was seven, he thought wryly. She'd dragged home a sunken-eyed, unkempt stranger. It turned out to be Paul Lyon, André's father.

Later there were other foundlings. One came immediately to mind—a homeless, pregnant waif named Gabrielle something-or-other. She'd arrived at Lyoncrest about the time he and Papa had their final row over his not joining the family business. Half a lifetime ago, or so it seemed. André sipped from his cup, idly rubbing at the sweat already glistening on his chest. Not even spring, yet the humidity after the last rain was stifling.

Life was stifling. At least that was how it felt now that their swamp tours had caught on. There wasn't much challenge left. The business earned enough for two men to get by, but a single owner-operator could make a comfortable living. J.D. had approached him again yesterday, asking to buy him out.

Maybe he should say yes. Maybe it was time he moved on.

Moved on to what? André drained his cup and climbed to his feet. Better see if Rachel was finished tidying. He didn't want her to be late for school on his account. It'd also be better if she wasn't around to eavesdrop when he discussed her with his mama.

Uh-oh. Too late. His peripheral vision picked up the limousine crawling along the dirt road that passed his shack. André chuckled. Man, did it look out of place. The neighbors would think he was being paid a visit by the Mafia. He watched as a driver disembarked and opened the passenger door.

André slipped behind a thick cascade of wisteria, where he could see and not be seen. In spite of the early hour, his mother looked coolly attractive. Her severe navy blue suit would be drab on some women. It took more than dark colors to dim Margaret Lyon's natural effervescence.

Her controlled expression slipped only minutely as she gave André's seedy bungalow the once-over. Even frowning, she looked queenly as she stripped off her gloves and placed a determined hand on the sagging wooden gate.

André heard the screech of the rusty hinge. She'd soon be at his door—if the steep climb up the rickety steps didn't daunt her. Clearly she didn't belong in the bayou. So why in hell had she made the trek?

Heart slamming against his breastbone, André felt a frisson of fear without knowing why. He dug through his pockets for money. No matter what had prompted the visit, matters involving family deserved privacy. Racing into the house, he snatched the dustcloth from Rachel's hand and replaced it with folded bills. "Treat yourself to a plate of beignets at Bertie's Café before you head off to school," he said, hustling her out the door. "I've got company, shortcake. Time for you to am-scray."

"Ton amour?" she whispered.

"My lover?" André skidded to a halt. That shouldn't be the first question out of a thirteen-year-old's mouth. *"Non,"* he growled. *"Ma mère."*

Rachel's eyes widened. But when she met the regal Margaret face-to-face, the girl ducked her head shyly. In a soft voice she said goodbye and disappeared like a wisp of smoke into the foggy swamp.

Margaret Lyon's gaze flicked from the retreating form to the man whose shoulder-length black hair was tied at his nape with a leather thong.

He stared back, his expression impassive. A growth of beard shadowed his jaw, suggesting he'd just climbed out of bed.

Recovering from her obvious confusion, Margaret grasped André's work-worn hands. "If you've been hiding a daughter from your family, André, I'll never forgive you."

Caught totally off guard, André laughed. He didn't know what made him lead her on. But he stood aside and swept a hand toward the rickety steps. "Care to enter my den of iniquity, Mama? Something important must be afoot for you to go slumming."

Sidestepping her son's unrefined display of sunbrowned muscles, she clasped the railing and marched past him. "Your uncle Charles and aunt Catherine might refuse to accept your cousin Alain's wife, but that doesn't mean Papa and I would ostracize anyone you chose, regardless of her background. Where is the child's mother?"

"She lives a mile up the road," he said with a perfectly straight face. "I'm pretty sure this isn't a social call, Mama. Usually we meet in more civilized surroundings, and it's only been a few days since we had lunch uptown."

At the door to his shack, which still stood ajar after Rachel's hasty departure, Margaret turned. "You're right, André. First things first. I've asked you a million times to join the family business. Today, I've come to beg."

Shaken by the quaver in her voice, André closed the door behind him. Once inside, he took a moment to grab a shirt and slip it on. "The coffee's fresh. Will you have a cup?"

She nodded and followed him into the Spartan kitchen. He looked so...so piratical, she thought, this man who called her Mama. Margaret had always assumed that when he matured, her son would be like Paul. Polished and suave. ''Your papa's had a heart attack.'' Never one to mince words, Margaret had decided to get right to the point. Perhaps all wasn't doomed, she mused when the coffeepot jerked in André's hand and coffee sloshed onto the counter.

''A minor one,'' she said into the strained silence. ''Dr. Young says Paul must cut back on the hours he works—or risk suffering a massive coronary.''

André led her to an overstuffed couch. He was glad Rachel had straightened the throw, which now hid the tattered cushions. ''You and Papa gave WDIX-TV the best twenty-five years of your lives. Maybe it's time to sell like other family-owned stations have done.''

''Sell? Never!'' Margaret clutched the heavy mug in both hands. ''So,'' she said brusquely, ''you've been in touch with your uncle Charles.''

''Not lately. He contacted me when I came back to town. He said a lot of stations had sold to conglomerates.''

''To Charles, the bottom line is always money.'' She paused. ''Do you have any idea how many times your papa has subsidized his brother's ventures?''

''No. And I don't want to,'' André said coldly.

She leaned toward him. ''I'm not here to ask you to take sides, André.''

''That's good. I've tried to make it plain that I refuse to be put in the middle of a family feud.''

''You won't be. But the only prayer I have of convincing Paul to slow down is if I do the same. Like it or not, André, the controlling interest in Lyon Broadcasting will one day be yours. You're going to inherit sixty percent of the shares. It's how Alexandre divided his shares, a portion of what my father left in trust for you. You can't keep avoiding the inevitable.''

That was exactly what had kept André on the high seas for so long. But, as he realized now, he'd returned to family obligations that still existed. Family obligations that needed to be met. Oddly enough, the timing was right. J.D. wanted to buy his half of the swamp tours—an investment that entailed little more than a few pontoon crafts.

''Is Papa in immediate danger of a second attack?'' André

asked carefully. "Could I have a few days to consider your request?"

Margaret almost scalded her tongue in her shock. "I came prepared to arm-wrestle," she said, trying to cloak her raw emotion with a joke. "I hate to push, but I need to make plans. I'll bend over backward to accommodate you, André."

"I'll need at least a week to settle my business affairs," he said, more jolted than he wanted to admit by the urgency in his mother's tone.

"Anything." Turning away, she fumbled for a hankie and blew her nose.

André stroked his stubbled jaw. "I suppose Lyon Broadcasting has a stringent dress code?" It was a feeble attempt to avoid acknowledging her tears and his concern.

Clearing her throat, Margaret searched her purse. She pulled out a business card and handed it across the table. "Paul's tailor. He can make two suits in a week. If you'll jot down your shirt and underwear sizes, I'll stock your armoire. You will take a suite at Lyoncrest, won't you? Commuting from here every day would be impossible."

André tapped the card on his palm. "Would you toss in a room for Rachel?"

"Rachel?" Margaret blanked momentarily.

"The girl you passed on the way in."

Refocusing, Margaret felt her excitement rise. "Oh, André, she *is* your daughter. Of course she can come! I won't even ask why you live apart from her mother."

"I shouldn't have led you on, Mama. A bit of the devil in me, I guess." André told her he was strictly a friend of the girl's. "Moments before you showed up, I'd decided to ask if you'd help her. Rachel's mother is an alcoholic. When she's drunk she brings home men. The kid showed up here today to avoid being raped."

"How horrible! If you think her mother will let the poor child go, I'll gladly offer her sanctuary." Margaret smiled at him, proud of her son's compassion and his honesty. "I'm sorry I jumped to the wrong conclusion, André. Of course you'd never hide any child of yours from us. I should have given you more credit."

"Why? Does sharing your blood automatically make me honorable, Mama?"

Margaret blanched. *If he only knew*. But the truth of André's parentage was a secret only three people besides her shared. His biological mother, a now-dead lawyer and Paul. The secret weighed her down at times. Suddenly feeling faint, Margaret twisted the single strand of pearls she always wore. A strand Paul had given her, not the ones her mother-in-law, Minna, used to flaunt. Finding her voice, she said, ''I'm sorry if my life's choices somehow hurt you, André. I can't alter the past. Reporting the atrocities of war almost destroyed your papa. He needed me. And if Lyon Broadcasting was going to make a successful leap from radio into television, I needed him.'' She bit her lip and glanced away. ''I love you both, André.''

''What about Uncle Charles? I thought you two...''

Her head snapped back. ''What do you mean? I'm his sister-in-law. That's all.''

''Well, he was practically a father to me when I was little. Then Papa appeared and all anyone did was argue and bury themselves in the business.''

''I make no apologies, André. The war changed our lives. Your papa went overseas. Charles couldn't. His health... Nevertheless, he gave up a promising career as a concert pianist to work at WDIX. But your grandfather left Paul the controlling interest in the company. My father put his shares in trust for you. Paul and I let Charles run the radio station and he nearly bankrupted it. He left it in shambles and took over his father-in-law's restaurant. Now Chez Charles is shaky. Walk a mile in our shoes before you condemn anyone.''

''I said I'd give this request serious consideration, but I'd like to know more about what I'd be getting into. Could I stop by the accounting office for a profit-and-loss statement?''

''I'll put together a full prospectus. Oh, and, André, I'll include a list of everything you'll need to do if we're to offer legal shelter to your young friend. Our lawyer can move things along pretty quickly. I'll let him know you'll be in touch.'' She looked at him closely. ''You'll call me, then?''

André inclined his head. ''You'll have my answer next week. If I do accept, I'll bring Rachel to Lyoncrest on Sunday and report to you for work the following Monday.''

Margaret pulled on her gloves, then rose. After an awkward hesitation, she stretched up to kiss his cheek. ''It's the right thing to do, André. For years I've envisioned WDIX-TV passing into your hands. The boundaries of television are limitless.'' Her silver-blue eyes lit up when she spoke of her pride and joy.

"You can quit trying to sell me, Mama. If anything tilts in your favor, it's that I'd look forward to spending time with you while you teach me the business."

"I'm cutting back, remember. But I'll provide a competent teacher."

André tried not to let his disappointment show. "I'll visit Papa when I come to town." Taking her arm, he walked her to the limo. He stepped back and watched Paddy turn the heavy car around. André couldn't help wondering if he'd just made a terrible mistake. He hated family politics.

"YOU LOOK PLEASED, Miss Margie." The white-haired chauffeur, who'd been with the family longer than Margaret had, smiled at her in the rearview mirror.

"Not a hundred-percent pleased, Paddy. André agreed to think about joining WDIX. He's far from committed."

"Are you afraid he'll be dissuaded by Mr. Charles—or those conniving kids of his?"

"André may have strayed from the family tree, but his roots are sound." Margaret gazed at the passing scenery. "Did Gabrielle go off to work before dawn again this morning?"

"She did. That'un would work twenty-four hours a day if she didn't have a child."

"I see Gaby making the same mistakes with Leslie that Paul and I made with André. I can't allow her to become a workaholic. Take me to the station, please, Paddy?"

The chauffeur adjusted his course. He maneuvered expertly through snarled traffic along the river and soon stopped at the curb next to the red-brick building that housed the television station.

Margaret let herself in through the cast-iron gate. She greeted the receptionist and others who bustled through the lobby of the station she'd nurtured from infancy into a local and national media power. Today she didn't waste time on small talk with staff. Instead, she strode purposefully toward Gabrielle Villieux's office. Margaret had gone through school with Gaby's mother. They'd been good friends until Gaby's mother ran off to marry a seaman. Through bad luck and a terrible marriage of her own, Gabrielle had landed broke and pregnant on the doorstep at Lyoncrest. Now she and her small daughter, Leslie, couldn't have been more loved by Margaret and Paul if they'd been bound by blood. The blood ties so important to Charles Lyon and his wife meant nothing to Margaret. It was the love people carried in their hearts that counted.

THE RAVEN-HAIRED, twenty-nine-year-old Gabrielle glanced up from a pile of papers she was sorting as the door to her office swung open.

"Margaret!" Gaby circled the desk to hug her friend and mentor.

"I hate to interrupt, but I've just come from visiting André."

Gaby leaned against her desk. "For breakfast? Didn't you just see him last week for lunch?"

Smiling, Margaret slipped off her gloves. "I bearded the wolf in his den."

"You didn't venture into Bayou Sans Fin alone? Oh, Margaret."

"Relax. Patrick drove me. I decided I had to tell André about Paul and prevail on him again to take his rightful place in the business."

Gaby's hazel eyes flicked to life. Her fine eyebrows arched into her wispy bangs. "I don't know why you continue to let him break your heart. He always refuses."

"Maybe not this time." Margaret paused for effect. "I really think he's going to work here."

Gaby released the heavy swath of hair that had been knotted at the nape of her neck. It fell to her waist in a swirling cascade. Her full lips parted. "Work here? Doing what? We don't have much call for loading freighters or poling tourists through alligators."

Margaret inspected the fit of her wedding band. "Gabrielle, if...no, *when* André joins us, I want you to take him under your wing. One day he'll be in charge. I want him to learn from the best."

"But...I..." Gaby expelled a breath. It was hard to argue in the face of a compliment. The bald truth was, she didn't *want* to train André Lyon. Gabrielle knew she had no right to expect to be handed the job of general manager. But it was exactly what she'd hoped for ever since the doctor had diagnosed Paul's condition. There wasn't another employee here who had the knowledge and expertise she had.

Yet she owed Margaret so much. Everything, really. And if Margaret asked this of her...

Perhaps, Gabrielle thought, locking gazes with the older woman, André Lyon wouldn't stick it out. From the tales she'd heard, and she'd heard plenty, the heir apparent liked his wine, women and song. Maybe he'd crawl back into the hole he'd crawled out of when he discovered how hard he'd have to work at Lyon Broadcasting.

Gaby slapped her hands hard against her thighs. "Your wish is my command, Margaret." She turned to check her calendar. "You expect him when?"

"I'll let you know. List him tentatively for next Monday at eight." The older woman exhaled in relief as she stood and made her way out.

Gabrielle took a seat behind the desk again, but it was a long time before she returned to her task. She'd seen André Lyon once. The day he'd announced to his parents that he'd signed up for a second term with the merchant marine. Gaby had only been at Lyoncrest two or three days, and she'd been frightened of her own shadow. The argument that erupted after André's declaration had left her shaking in her shoes. So did the sight of André Lyon's devil eyes when he burst out of Paul's study. Fortunately Gaby had gained bushels of self-confidence since then. The prodigal son wouldn't find her so easy to unseat.

ANDRÉ STOPPED AT WDIX to collect the information he'd asked his mother to prepare. Over lunch he studied the prospectus. The figures shocked him. His parents had been shoring up the radio station with interest from his mother's trust fund. He wondered why. The country certainly didn't lack for cataclysmic events. Despite the cease-fire the year before, Vietnam wasn't over yet—plenty of news there. All the world was clamoring for information about Watergate. And it seemed that presidential impeachment hearings were more than likely. Hot news brought in influential advertisers—wasn't that how broadcasting worked?

André recalled little of the business chatter that went on at Lyoncrest during his early childhood. One thing he did remember was his mother saying over and over that his father's voice was all WDIX needed to catapult them into fame and fortune.

Obviously not. And André intended to find out what had gone wrong. Well, he had a bit of extra time. Transferring the business to J.D. had gone faster than he'd expected. His parents' lawyer was looking into the situation with Rachel. And André had already visited his father's tailor. Nothing else he had to do for the moment. He paid his check and drove straight back to the station.

He nosed around the production department, spent an hour with the program manager and twenty minutes chatting with the news director. By the time he left the ad sales coordinator and traffic supervisor, he had a better idea as to why WDIX-TV was in trouble. He could sum it up in two words—Gabrielle Villieux, the stray his mother had taken in. Taken in and all but handed the family jewels. At least, some here hinted that the Villieux woman considered herself a Lyon. Oh, André could believe that, all right. He'd poked his head in her office and asked for a minute of her time. She'd curtly told him she was busy and that he was on her calendar for next Monday at eight.

Obviously his mother didn't realize the woman had exceeded her authority. She acted as if she had a natural right to be in charge and owed him no deference whatsoever. As if her last name was Lyon and not Villieux. Hmm, maybe Gabrielle had heard and believed an old rumor that said *he* wasn't really a Lyon. André didn't know how such a rumor had started, but Papa himself had confirmed it was a lie. In any event, the Villieux woman had hoodwinked his parents.

"Tough," André muttered as he strode from the building. *Beginning bright and early next week, things will start to change, Mrs. Villieux. The resident pauper is about to storm the castle and dethrone the phony princess.*

CHAPTER TWO

ANDRÉ'S SUITE AT LYONCREST was shaded by a stately old magnolia. His private balcony overhung a lush green lawn that gave way to a well-tended rose garden. Monday, the morning he was slated to start work, he got up in time to greet a blood-red sun. As he gazed over the remembered landscape, he found himself ill-prepared for a wave of nostalgia. He fumbled with the buttons on his new white shirt, then let it hang undone as he came to grips with the knowledge that he'd missed this place. Why had he manufactured reasons to stay away so long? Time had wrought its changes on the occupants of the house, if not on the house itself. Papa's parents were gone. Aunt Ella, too. He'd missed their funerals.

As he dealt with good memories and the not so good, he tackled the shirt again, finally stuffing snowy shirttails into banker's gray pinstripe pants. Tying a silk tie was a novelty. He could probably count on the fingers of one hand the number of times he'd worn one since leaving college. At first the tie tangled with the leather thong he used to fasten his hair. What with the move, and some unforseen difficulties in making the guardianship arrangements for Rachel—difficulties finally resolved when a large check was handed over to the girl's mother—well, with all that, he'd run out of time for a haircut. Maybe today. Or maybe not. In a way, he needed to show that he had limits to how civilized he cared to be.

Heading the list of those André wanted to show was Gabrielle Villieux. Late on Saturday evening, when he'd hauled the last load of his belongings into Lyoncrest, she'd been seated on the front stoop blowing soap bubbles with her daughter, Leslie. A cute, plump girl of five or six. André had caught a big bubble and laughingly set it on the kid's pug nose. Gaby stuck her snoot in the air, grabbed Leslie by the hand and marched away, leaving him feeling like a leper.

André frowned, remembering. The woman might be a complete bitch, but she had damned fine legs. She was tall. Five-seven or -eight, he'd guess. Close enough to his own six-two. She'd worn white shorts and— André slid the knot on his tie so tight he gasped for air. That'd teach him to daydream. Still, as he slipped into his jacket and smoothed the wide, notched lapels, there was a zing to his blood he hadn't felt in some time. It was the anticipation he felt at the idea of sparring with Gabrielle at breakfast.

She'd disappeared on Sunday. He'd spent nearly the whole day helping Rachel move in and get used to the house. He'd wanted her to feel comfortable with Mama and Papa before he had to report for work.

A swing past the dining room revealed it to be empty. At a table in the kitchen sat Leslie and an elderly woman he didn't know. He coaxed a shy smile from the girl who'd just dripped syrup down the white blouse of her school uniform. ''Is your mother still in bed, squirt?''

She shook her head, making her curls dance, but didn't say a word.

The cook handed André a plate heaped with thick slices of *pain perdu,* a Creole version of French toast. ''I'll sit in here,'' André said when LuAnn, the current cook, motioned him toward the empty dining room. Lena had retired, he assumed, fondly recalling the cook who'd always had a kind word for a lonely boy. ''I'll join you here until someone else comes downstairs.''

LuAnn plunked a silver coffee carafe on the table. ''Miss Gaby's gone to the office as usual. Mr. Paul has an early appointment with his doctor. Your mother went, too, and took Rachel to get her registered at Holy Cross school.''

''Oh. And this is?'' André turned his gaze on the other woman at the table.

''Leslie's nanny, Miss Claire Harris. This is Mr. André, the wandering son returned to the fold.''

André took the woman's limp hand. ''Pleased to meet you.'' Pushing his untouched plate aside, he poured himself a cup of coffee. ''I hope you didn't go to all this trouble for me, LuAnn. Coffee will do me until lunch.''

The cook snorted her disapproval. She picked up his plate and plunked it down in front of the child. "We'll give it to Miss Leslie. She's the only one in this house who appreciates food the way a body ought to."

André glanced over the rim of his cup. Now he understood why the child was so chunky when her mother looked like a Dior model. Another strike against Gabrielle Villieux, allowing others to turn her daughter into a human waste-disposal.

And yet André guessed she had no earthly idea that these women, who should have better sense, sat around stuffing her daughter.

"You've had enough, haven't you, honey?" He gently removed the plate and, with a sour look at the two women, walked to the sink and scraped it clean.

Leslie had ducked her head as André took the plate. She peered at him from beneath thick lashes, but only after she thought he was no longer paying her any notice.

He was, though. He'd flipped pages back to his boyhood in this big rambling house and wondered if Leslie was as lonely as he'd been. It always astounded him when he met people who envied him for being an only child. If and when he married, he'd like a houseful of kids. He intended to take an active part in raising them, too.

But that wasn't going to happen anytime soon. "I'd better quit stalling," he muttered. "Time to get to work. Have a nice day, ladies."

"Don't 'spect you'll be home for dinner," announced LuAnn as André refilled his coffee cup and headed for the door. "Nobody ever is."

"A late dinner, surely."

LuAnn and Claire exchanged a swift glance. "Miss Gaby said she'd give you two days and you'd head back to the swamp," LuAnn murmured.

"She did?" André scowled. "Tell Miss Gaby... Never mind. I'll tell her myself." He stomped out.

STUCK IN TRAFFIC, André considered a lot of things he could say to mouthy Gabrielle Villieux. Unfortunately he was thirty minutes late for work.

"Oh!" a harried receptionist exclaimed as she let him into the building. "Gabrielle's gone to an outside appointment. She said for you to wait here until she gets back."

"When will that be?" André flipped a cuff back to check his watch.

"Eleven. At least, she's scheduled to meet with the sales staff at eleven-fifteen."

"That's two and a half hours from now!"

The receptionist, who was answering a call coming into the switchboard, gave a shrug. Her wisteria-blue eyes conveyed a deeper interest, which André ignored. His mother had been remiss in thinking she could put that Villieux woman in charge of teaching him the business. Did Mrs. Villieux believe her time so much more valuable than his that she could leave him cooling his heels half the morning?

He waited patiently until the receptionist finished her call. "I'm to share Mrs. Villieux's office. Did she leave me a key?"

"No. Sorry. Anyway, she'll probably want you to call her Gabrielle or Gaby. We're pretty informal at WDIX. By the way, I'm Raylene Miller."

"I'm André Lyon—but you obviously already know that. Tell me, Raylene, who would have a key to Mrs. Villieux's office?" He stubbornly clung to the formality of last names.

"Margaret. Oh, or Steffan, the head of maintenance. He can't issue building and office keys, but he'd probably let you in. I'll page him if you like."

"Thanks. I *would* like."

GABRIELLE KEYED into the building at five to eleven. The lobby was empty. Did that mean her pain-in-the-neck charge hadn't shown up? Raylene was talking on the phone and the board was lit up like a Christmas tree. Gaby switched her briefcase to the other hand, fluttered her fingers as she passed and climbed the stairs to her office. Funny, her door was wide open. Maybe Margaret had come in. Smiling in anticipation, Gaby burst into the room. Then she skidded to a stop and blinked. Instead of being in the center of the room where it belonged, her desk was angled across the right corner. A matching desk sat on the left. Her three file cabinets were crowded together to make room for two that were taller.

Gaby's fingers went slack. Her briefcase hit the floor with a thump.

André chose that moment to appear behind her, arms laden with a card file, pencil holder, stapler and other office paraphernalia.

"What is the meaning of this?" Gabrielle waved and several narrow bracelets tinkled musically as they ran up and down her arm.

"I didn't think it would come as a shock. We *are* going to be working together, Mrs. Villieux." He deposited his armload on the desk and bent to retrieve her fallen briefcase.

"Put that down," she ordered, her voice barely below a screech. "And I prefer to be called *Ms.* Villieux."

André straightened and opened his fingers.

Gaby had to jump back to keep the steel-reinforced case from landing on her toes. A hiss escaped her lips. Eyes smoldering, she hefted the case and marched to her desk. Then she set her things down on the polished cherry surface and dropped into her chair. "You were late for work this morning. Our meeting was at eight. Tardiness is an intolerable habit, Mr. Lyon. It's an indication of laziness. I am always early."

He eyed her thoughtfully. After a few moments he sauntered to the door and kicked it closed. "I guess it's not true that the early bird gets the worm, Mrs. Villieux, or you'd have some meat on your bones."

Gaby sputtered. "Ms.," she reminded him.

"Furthermore," André said, planting his hands on her desk, "if you stayed home for breakfast, you'd stop LuAnn and that Claire woman from stuffing your daughter like a Christmas goose."

Gaby's eyes narrowed to slits. "Attacking me is bad enough. Calling a defenseless child fat is low, even for you. LuAnn and Claire love Leslie."

"I never said Leslie was fat. And I'm not saying they don't love her. But some people equate food with love. And you attacked first. You accused me of being lazy."

She leaned back in her chair and studied him as if...as if he was the trail left by a slug. "Your reputation precedes you. I'm well acquainted with your type."

"Well," he said in a soft voice, "it's plain enough what you think of me—regardless of the fact that you know nothing about me. But I have to warn you that, at home, you'd better make sure those feelings don't spill over to include Rachel. If ever a kid needs a woman to look up to, it's her." In a straightforward, matter-of-fact way, he filled Gabrielle in on the young girl's distressing history.

Gaby listened, twisting a lock of hair around her finger. When he finished, she looked shaken. "I-I'm glad you told me. I once knew men who'd consider a night with the mother license to take pleasure with the daughter."

André's stomach knotted. "Are you saying that...that you were raped? I'm sorry, my memory of the circumstances that brought you to Lyoncrest is murky."

"I didn't mean me. The men in my husband's crowd... I was married to Leslie's father, unfortunately. And I've said too much. Whatever Margaret told you about my circumstances, I want it understood that Leslie must never learn the truth about her father."

What exactly was the truth? he wondered. "Mama didn't say anything. I just recalled hearing that you were involved in some kind of trouble."

"Yes. I found out too late that womanizing was the least of Marc Villieux's unsavory activities."

Shaken by her story but still curious, André asked, "How did Mama happen upon you?"

"She and my mother were girlhood friends. My parents both died when I was about Rachel's age. I lived with a great-aunt." Gaby began to straighten things on her desk. "To make a long story short, Marc turned up dead in an alley—murdered—leaving me pregnant and up to my ears in debt. Margaret saved me. Even if I lived forever, I couldn't repay her. I'll do anything she asks—and that includes letting you follow me around to see how the station operates."

Her clipped speech told André two things. One, she had a soft core beneath a brittle shell. And two, she resented his being here. The first he'd tuck away for future reference. The second he'd also leave alone—for now.

He extended a hand across the expanse of her desk. ''Your secret is safe with me. Shall we say hello, shake hands and start this relationship over?''

She clasped his hand so briefly one could hardly call it a handshake. ''We don't have a relationship. With Paul and Margaret cutting back their hours, I'm assuming a bigger load. I don't have time to baby-sit you. So keep up or miss out.''

''Fair enough. But once I get a handle on how everything works, I can handle more responsibility—and you'll have more time to spend with your daughter.''

''Oh,'' she said, polite but remote. ''And how long do you think that'll take?''

''I don't know. A month? Two? Mama's hoping to formally pass the baton to me at the twenty-fifth anniversary wingding. That's what she and Papa spelled out last night, anyway. Didn't they inform you?''

''No...I...not specifically. The anniversary celebration is July fourth.''

''Well, then, there's plenty of time.'' André sliced her a killer smile. ''It's only January now.''

Gaby's brows knit more tightly. She wondered if that was just big-shot talk or if Paul and Margaret really did think he could waltz in and learn in a few months what it had taken her six years and a lot of overtime to perfect. She'd worked days and studied nights in preparation for moving up the ladder at WDIX-TV. It hadn't been easy, but she'd earned her degree in marketing in three years. By August she'd have her masters in communication. Unless she'd been misinformed, André Lyon had graduated with a liberal arts degree that prepared him for nothing. He'd *done* nothing, for pity's sake, except flit around the world loading boxes into ships—no doubt leaving a legion of women panting in every port. At least, according to the tales she'd heard about him.

Gaby brooded and tapped her long fingers on the desk.

''Excuse me.'' André drew her attention to the wall clock. ''Far be it from me to tell you your job, *Ms.* Villieux, but Raylene said you had a meeting with the sales staff at eleven-fifteen. It's after that now.''

''Good grief!'' Jumping up, she grabbed a yellow tablet and a stack of contracts. ''I doubt you'll understand a word of what's being discussed, but you may as well come and get your feet wet. And if you're going to call me Ms. Villieux in that tone, just use my first name, please.''

''Sure.'' He plucked his suit jacket from the back of the chair and shrugged into it. As he crossed the room, hot on Gaby's heels, a dapper, gray-haired man muscled past her and grabbed André's arm.

''André!'' Charles Lyon bellowed. ''You sly fox. I didn't believe...had to come see for myself what the staff's buzzing about. So you finally let Margie twist your arm. Son of a gun! All I can say is it'll be damned good to have another vote on my side.''

''Uncle Charles.'' André pulled out of the hearty bear hug. Glancing over his uncle's shoulder, he saw Gabrielle's eyes turn wintry. ''I, ah, was headed out with Gabrielle for a meeting. For the record,'' he said lightly, ''I'm not on anyone's side. I make up my own mind.''

Charles flashed an equally chilly look at Gabrielle. ''Gaby can carry on without you while you catch your favorite uncle up on this latest development. Or maybe you haven't been here long enough to know that Gabrielle's really Wonder Woman in disguise.''

Gaby's lips tightened. ''I am quite capable of conducting this or any other meeting by myself, Charles. I wouldn't presume to break up your reunion.''

''But I...'' André frowned as Gaby sprinted off. Plainly there was no love lost between her and his uncle.

Charles clapped him on the back. ''Forget the gal. She's nobody. Come along, son, I'll treat you to a drink.''

''It's not even lunchtime,'' André protested.

Charles, refusing to take no for an answer, hustled his nephew determinedly toward the elevator.

CHAPTER THREE

ANDRÉ ENTERED THE OFFICE whistling, hands buried in his pants pockets. He saw Gabrielle seated at her desk, almost hidden behind a stack of ledgers.

She barely glanced up. "Managers don't take three-hour lunches. Employees resent it, as do clients. And right now we need every client we can get."

The tune died on André's lips. "Believe it or not, I wouldn't have gone if you hadn't disappeared so abruptly. And I wasn't away for three hours. More like two. We detoured past my cousin Alain's office. Last time I saw him, Alain was a teenager. Now he's an attorney. Hard to believe he and Jason have grown up and both work here. Makes me feel old."

Gabrielle leaned back in her chair. "I wouldn't have hired either of them, no matter how Charles whined, if it'd been up to me. He wore Margaret down. But then, I assume you know what a soft heart she has."

"Aren't you lucky she does? Otherwise, where would *you* be?" André wasn't normally one to trade insults. But he didn't intend to let this woman walk all over him. "Jason suggested you might be the reason for the station's declining revenue. Alain didn't disagree."

Gaby stiffened. For a second anger flared in her eyes. "Will I be wasting my breath if I rebut that lie?"

André pulled up a chair and faced her across the desk. "Where this family is concerned, I don't wear rose-colored glasses. Just so we understand one another, I've spoken to various of the department heads *and* I've studied the station's budgetary figures for the past five years. So don't try to snow me. Something—or someone—is responsible for the drop in revenue."

This time she made no effort to check her anger. "Now *you* understand *me*. Margaret instructed me to familiarize you with what it takes to run WDIX-TV. So I will, as long as it doesn't interfere with operations. I expect you to adjust to my schedule. I'll answer questions when and if I have time."

"Fair enough," he said, after turning the edict over in his mind. "I still have a question on the table—if you have time." He leaned both elbows on her desk. "The drop in revenue."

Gaby selected a ledger from the stack, opened it and spun it toward him. "Cash flow is our greatest problem. Unless you've had your head buried in the sand, you know the entire nation is staggering under a recession."

"I know. Don't forget I started a business recently. The energy crunch hurt tourist-based operations, too. But I'm not talking about items like increased power bills." He tapped one column with a neatly clipped fingernail. "What caused the revenue loss? Uncle Charles thinks my parents ought to dump this albatross. He said they've turned down several solid offers."

"Margaret and Paul believe the way advertisers have tightened purse strings is only temporary. It's worth mentioning that Charles is one of the major drains on our revenues," she said. "He could buy advertising for his restaurant, instead of expecting us to run prime-time ads for free. And his son might work a little harder to bring in new accounts. Jason's been on the marketing payroll six months and has yet to sign a new client." She grabbed another book, flipped through pages and smacked it on top of the other. "In January we invested a large chunk of capital in memory TV. Portable microwave. It's an innovative process capable of storing one or more frames of a signal and it'll make it possible to broadcast from coast to coast simultaneously. Paul bought the patent. Eventually all stations will need this technology to compete. Charles balked so long we almost lost the deal to a competitor. He resents the fact that Paul had so much authority."

André's dark, brooding gaze followed the animated movements of Gabrielle's hands. "My parents have the controlling stock. If Charles lacks vision and wants out of the business, why don't they buy out his forty percent and get him off their backs?"

"Ah. It seems you aren't up on the terms of your grandfather's will. Both brothers and/or their male descendants have to agree to a sale. Frankly, Margaret believes that family should always remain involved in the business, regardless of commitment or skills. I don't. Which is why I'm so unpopular,'' she added wryly.

''Yet Charles said you take his youngest son, Scott, to the movies and such.''

''Scott's different. He's a sweet little kid. Nothing at all like those other two—or that creep, Raymond. Scottie's a lot younger than the other three. He's smart and sensitive.'' She sounded almost defensive.

André held up his hands. ''Hey, you don't have to apologize for finding one good Lyon in a barrelful of rotten ones.''

''Very funny.'' She threw a pink eraser at him. It bounced off his broad shoulder. ''You asked. I'm telling the story the way I see it affects WDIX.''

''Mm.'' He scooped the eraser off the floor and placed it in the center of her desk. ''Enlightening. But it's only your perspective. I can see I have a lot to learn. Could you provide me with a list of all departments and how they mesh?''

Gaby shouldn't have been disappointed by his cavalier dismissal of her perspective, as he called it. But she was. For a minute there she thought he might actually be open-minded regarding the negative effect Charles and his brood had on the company. She should have known better, tight as André was with his uncle. Gaby had lived with the Lyon family long enough to have gained some insight into problems that existed long before she came to live at Lyoncrest. She didn't know everything of course. But none of that really mattered, because Gaby's allegiance would always lie with the woman who'd taken her in and given her so much more than a home and a job.

Few people knew that Margaret had gone into a most unsavory part of town to pay off Marc Villieux's accumulated debts for booze, gambling and women. Marc owed men who'd stop at nothing to collect. Men who would have forced Gaby to abort her baby and turn tricks or be killed. She'd seen enough ugliness to make her gladly put in fourteen-hour days to keep this job and see her daughter safe from people like Marc Villieux. Leslie would never experience life as Gaby had.

André snapped his fingers in front of Gabrielle's vacant stare. She'd left him for a minute there. It shocked him, discovering that he wanted to protect her from whatever had caused that bleak look.

Gabrielle closed the ledgers with a snap. Briskly she extracted a ring of keys from her center desk drawer and unlocked a file cabinet. "Here's a flowchart and a packet of job descriptions." She tossed them at André.

"Do we have any openings at present?"

"No. Neither have we laid off anyone. A lot of stations have, so if any experienced people call in, get their résumés." She rose and pulled out two drawers filled with neat folders. "Résumés for potential department executives are here, filed by technical expertise. There's also a copy of each one in personnel." She nearly jumped out of her skin when André whistled through his teeth right next to her ear.

The woodsy scent of his aftershave made her stomach knot unexpectedly. Gaby clenched her fists to ward off the silliest urge to smooth a hand over his stubborn jaw. A jaw already fetchingly in need of a second shave. Paired with his ponytail, it gave André Lyon a roguish look she found far too attractive.

She didn't want to find anything attractive about him. He'd turned his back on Paul and Margaret once. In Gabrielle's estimation, the prodigal son had some atoning to do before she'd believe in his right to stand at the helm of Lyon Broadcasting.

She, on the other hand, had spent many long nights at this desk, poring over ideas on how to turn profits around. If she could accomplish her goal of setting the company in the black before the twenty-fifth anniversary celebration, Margaret might put her and not André in charge. To achieve that, she had to stay focused.

André moved closer. He reached around her to riffle through a folder of résumés and whistled again. "You have them in alphabetical order inside each folder. My filing system at the tour office was chaotic. So are my armoire drawers. I'll bet yours are as orderly as rows of tin soldiers."

The soft laughter that accompanied an all-too-personal innuendo pinched the breath from Gabrielle's lungs. "Alphabetical order is pretty standard office procedure," she managed to say.

"Uh-huh." He studied her solemnly, his gaze traveling down her crisp suit. His eyes swept up again, lingering a moment too long on the rise and fall of her full breasts. Her blouse shimmered under the light.

Heather-green, André thought they called that color. The variegated shades matched the mix of colors creating a storm in Gabrielle Villieux's hazel eyes.

Ignited by a sudden wave of heat, Gaby tried to step back. She nearly fell over the file drawer she'd left pulled out.

"Whoa! Careful there." André caught her before she took a tumble. His fingers flexed in the fabric that covered her arms. "I liked your hair better down, the way it was Saturday night," he blurted, removing half his support as he ran two fingers along the ornamental clasp that held her waist-length hair in a twist at the back of her head. "With the weight of that doodad and your hair, don't you have a whopping headache by bedtime?"

Not only did Gaby tilt precariously, his nearness made her head spin. "I, ah, André..." She flattened her hands on his chest and wedged a space between them. "My hair is none of your concern. I don't want to appear rude, but I have a lot of work to do and we keep getting off the subject."

He stepped back immediately, righting her again. He still had a grip on her arm when Raylene charged through the door, carrying a wire basket heaped with mail. Though she plunked the basket down on Gaby's desk without a word and proceeded to collect an outgoing stack of letters, her interested gaze bounced between the two of them.

Gaby wrenched herself from André's hold and hoped the small kick she aimed at his shin wasn't noticeable to Raylene. Gabrielle could practically hear the wheels spinning in the talkative receptionist's head. The flush she felt heating her cheeks didn't help Gaby appear as nonchalant as she would have liked.

Pausing at the door, Raylene turned and wiggled her fingers at André. Then she bestowed Gaby with the barest twitch of a smile and withdrew.

Silence thickened the air left in her wake. Slowly releasing a hiss, Gabrielle slammed the offending file drawer shut. She closed her eyes and massaged the bridge of her nose.

"What was all that about?"

Gaby opened her eyes. "Raylene Miller has dreams of becoming a world-famous television talk-show host. You could say she practices in-house. Which wouldn't be so bad except that she can't resist adding a few interesting details to give her news shock value."

André's eyes lit up. "How sweet of you to worry about my reputation, *Ms.* Villieux."

Gabrielle snorted in a most unladylike fashion before she gave up and allowed an answering snicker. Sharing an office with him might not be so terrible, at that. A person needed comic relief occasionally, and she tended to be far too serious. Her ability to see the humor in situations involving herself had been virtually nonexistent of late. "I can always hope Raylene's scoop will make the staff quit calling me a workaholic."

"But you are, aren't you? That's what I'd call a person who left the house at 6 a.m. and worked till midnight."

Gaby's chin lifted in defiance. "Some nights I leave here at eleven." An engaging smile broke out again. "Come on." She gave him a gentle shove toward the door. "If I introduce you around, it's bound to steal part of Raylene's thunder. I expect you'll be here a few weeks before you meet everyone, though. Reporters are out on field assignments. News, production and sales all work split shifts."

André fell in behind her, his focus locked on the trim feet and ankles that navigated swiftly in spite of T-strapped shoes with the highest heels he'd ever seen.

Gabrielle stopped suddenly and he plowed into her. "Lock the door, will you? By the way, how did you get in today?"

"Surely you don't expect me to reveal my sources." André waggled his brows before he turned back and engaged the lock.

"So Margaret gave you her key?"

André, enjoying her pique immensely, shook his head. He believed she would have continued interrogating him if two women hadn't grabbed Gaby and boxed her in. One a platinum blonde trying to look like Marilyn Monroe, the other a sleek-as-a-peacock brunette.

"Gabrielle," the brunette said, pouting. "Miles promised a week ago that I could interview Donny and Marie Osmond the morning of their concert. Now I find out he's scheduled them with Chatty Cathy at five."

The Marilyn look-alike flew at the brunette. Gaby caught the hand with its curved burgundy nails before she did major damage.

"Tiff always makes snide remarks as if 'Breakfast with Tiffany' has more *class* than 'Chat with Cathy.' She's such a bitch,'' declared the blonde.

The brunette might have responded in kind but she suddenly caught sight of André. ''Well, hel-lo! You look familiar. Someone worth interviewing, I'm sure.'' She fingered his jacket. ''I'm Tiffany Edwards. I'm sure you've seen my morning show.'' Never taking her eyes off André, she murmured, ''I want to book this man, Gaby. Let Cathy interview the entire singing Osmond clan.''

Gaby was amused for all of ten seconds—until Cathy attached herself to André's other arm and, instead of shrugging the ladies off, he boosted his charm. For two cents, she'd leave him to his fate. Or she would have, if something resembling jealousy hadn't niggled.

Deciding to play by their rules, she pried both women away. ''Tiffy and Cathy, I have it on good authority,'' she purred, marching them down the hall, ''that he's a member of *the family*.'' Gaby rolled her eyes toward André. Could she help it if these two nitwits believed he'd blown into town on the coattails of the mob?

They took somber peeks at him before Gabrielle hustled them around a corner.

''What did you say about me?'' André asked when she returned and led him in the opposite direction.

She smiled benignly. ''Nothing.''

''Nothing?'' He sounded skeptical. ''It's not my imagination. They looked at me as if I were some notorious swamp murderer.''

''That's very good. Too bad I didn't think of it. In a way, swamp creature is more appropriate for you than what I dreamed up.''

''So you did warn them off. Come on—give.''

Gaby laughed up at him. ''How you malign me. I said you belonged to the family. I suppose they could have gotten the wrong impression—particularly when I mentioned that we were on our way to see Vic Napier. He's the assistant news director.'' She batted her eyes the way Tiffany had. ''Well, *I'd* never take you for a hit man. But then, Vic's running an exposé on Mafia activity in town.''

André reared back. ''You didn't!''

Gabrielle tried but couldn't contain her glee. "You should thank me, Lyon. Ask any man who works here. Those two are bona fide sharks."

André enjoyed the joke with her. They were still laughing when a harried, balding man burst from an office, practically bowling Gabrielle over.

"Whoa, George. What's your rush?"

He bobbed a blue film canister past her nose. "I borrowed this tape from McKillop at WEZY for our noon news. I promised I'd have it back to him before six. I don't have time to drive across town. I'm going to ask Raylene if she'll deliver it."

Gabrielle glanced at her watch. "I think you missed her. She's got a three-o'clock dental appointment. If you're really tight for time, I'll drop the film off. By the way, this is André Lyon. You'll be seeing a lot of him. André, meet George Collins, our film manager."

André shook the man's hand. "You have a fun job. Provided you get to preview new segments of the 'Planet of the Apes' series."

Gaby made a face. "I won't let Leslie watch that program."

"You'd better warn Rachel," he said as she tucked the canister under her arm and waved at the departing film manager. "Rach got me hooked," he said. "They didn't have television at home. Took me a while to realize she'd pop by asking for help with her homework every night there was a new ape episode."

"You actually helped her with schoolwork?"

"I did graduate from college."

She started to say something sarcastic but had a change of heart. "You just seem so...I don't know. Too much of a jock to spend time helping a kid crack the books."

"A jock?" André mulled that over while Gaby introduced him around another department. An hour later, as they made their way back to their office, he was still trying to figure out if she liked jocks or not. He could speculate till hell froze over. If he wanted to know, he'd obviously have to ask.

"About your jock comment? I didn't go out for sports in college," he said. "I studied hard to keep an academic scholarship. Weekends I worked on the docks to pay what the scholarship didn't cover."

"Now that does surprise me." In the elevator she took a long look at him.

He swiped the key from her hand and unlocked their office. Again she left him wondering what part surprised her. That he'd earned a scholarship or that he'd felt compelled to prove he didn't need the Lyon fortune in order to succeed? But she didn't elaborate or leave an opening for him to delve deeper. He would have tried, but his uncle waltzed in again.

"Don't mean to be a bother, boy. I forgot to give you these two invitations to the Comus *bal masque* on Fat Tuesday. The masked ball kicks off Mardi Gras in style." He nudged André and winked. "This year's crop of debutantes are lush. So put together a dashing costume. Invitations are at a premium, but you don't have to thank me. We're family, after all."

Gabrielle didn't know why she had the feeling Charles had dangled a bribe of some sort under André's nose. She wished he'd refuse, but why would he? Invitations to the prestigious balls were highly prized. Gaby knew people who'd sell their souls to get a single invite, let alone two.

André probably had a mile-long choice of partners, and he'd have his pick of debutantes, too. So what? Gaby didn't have to stick around and listen to their male posturing. She set the film canister down on her desk and gathered a stack of ledgers. "I'm going to return these," she announced at large.

Charles broke off. André turned and smiled. "Sure. See you later. The only other thing I'd like to do today is coordinate our calendars."

She didn't say yes or no. She just sailed out.

André remembered that when five-thirty rolled around and Gaby still wasn't back. She must be dropping off the film. Did she plan to return to the office? Did she expect him to stay late? What? By six o'clock he was plenty steamed at her failure to let him know.

"Tough bananas," he said to no one except maybe the ficus as he snapped off the light, shut and locked the door. She'd probably evaded him on purpose. Except for the lights in the newsroom, all the offices he passed were dark.

Downstairs, only a green exit light glowed in Raylene's area.

"Tomorrow," André promised himself, as he let himself out the main entrance, "I'll stick to Gabrielle Villieux like glue."

CHAPTER FOUR

GABRIELLE RACED BACK to her office at twenty after six. She'd been going over budget figures with their chief accountant and lost track of time. Then it dawned on her that she'd forgotten the promise to return that news tape to McKillop at WEZY. George would kill her. If McKillop didn't beat him to it.

Her entire wing was dark and that irritated her no end, yet it didn't surprise her. André had made clear how he felt about overtime. When she hit the switch, the bright light in her office temporarily blinded her. She shut her eyes and felt for her desk. At last she eased one eye open. "Oh. Where's the canister?"

Getting down on her knees, she checked the floor. No blue canister. "Huh! It can't have just walked away."

She crawled out from under the desk. A pleasant thought began to take shape. André must have decided to deliver it for her. He'd heard George stress the importance of getting McKillop the tape by six.

That thought was followed by another. "Great," she muttered. "What must André think of me making promises I fail to keep?" As a rule she was scrupulous about commitments. Truth be known, André Lyon flustered her. Gaby hadn't felt so much as a twinge of yearning for any man since she'd discovered what a first class louse she'd married. That marriage—six endless, awful years—proved she honored commitments, didn't it?

Married at seventeen, she'd realized her mistake before the ink on the license was dry. If her aunt hadn't made it clear she'd be unwelcome, Gaby probably would have slunk home. Instead, she'd endured. And did her best to be an ideal wife—until she'd accidentally gotten pregnant. There was no way she'd let Marc Villieux or his scummy friends lay their hands on her baby. In fact, she'd been on her way to a shelter when Marc turned up dead in a back alley—knifed by a girlfriend or a creditor. Marc's creditors let it be known that they expected her to pay his debts—or else.

Gaby chose to believe that her guardian angel had left the newspaper with Margaret Lyon's picture in it lying on a bus seat, where she happened to see it. Margie Hollander Lyon, a name Gabrielle's mother had mentioned often and with fondness.

Not a day went by in the six years since she'd made the impulsive decision to seek out her mother's old friend that Gaby didn't count her blessings. Considering everything Margaret had done for her, Gabrielle figured she could ignore the occasional weak knees and tingling spine brought on by proximity to André. Especially if he did nice favors that took the load off her and freed her up to see more clients.

She flipped a page on her appointment calendar. Tomorrow she had a breakfast meeting scheduled with an important advertiser. One she hoped to entice away from WNOG-TV.

"And why not?" Gaby exclaimed aloud as she opened a scrupulously prepared proposal. "If WDIX can sell Rodney Fortner's stupid overpriced face cream to overstuffed old ladies better than they can, why *shouldn't* he switch to us?"

Gabrielle heard, or thought she heard a noise at the door. She glanced over. It wasn't fully closed. *Odd.* She thought she'd shut it tight. She waited for someone to knock. No one did. Her fingers tensed, and she put the folder down. She worked alone in the administrative part of the building almost every evening. Why feel uneasy tonight?

A glance at her watch revealed it was seven-thirty. Where had the time gone?

There, the noise again. Footsteps?

"Hello? Is anyone there? Steffan?" Had he finally gotten around to replacing that burned-out bulb over the stairwell?

No one answered. She felt silly, talking to herself. Gaby smoothed a hand over her French twist. Several strands had wiggled loose but she couldn't be bothered tucking them in. She stood, knees not quite steady, and stiffened her spine, then marched across the room. She jerked the door open. A quick look in both directions revealed nothing. Or was that a man silhouetted in the mirror at the end of the corridor? A smoky flash, and then gone. She must be seeing things.

Gaby stepped back into her office. She closed the door firmly and locked it, surprised to discover her palms were sweating.

"You silly goose," she scolded.

At her desk once more, she picked up the phone and dialed home. Leslie's bedtime was eight-thirty. Whenever Gaby worked late, she phoned to say goodnight and to chat about her daughter's day at the exclusive Catholic girls' school. The same school Margaret had attended. There was comfort in following tradition.

"Hello?" For a second, Gaby didn't recognize the voice on the phone. "Rachel? It's Gabrielle. How was your first day of school?"

The girl seemed eager to talk, so Gaby listened. "Hey, I'm glad your classes went so well. Not math, huh?" Gabrielle laughed. "Paul's a whiz with numbers. If he's feeling fit after his visit to the doctor today, maybe he'll help you with homework."

She was startled by Rachel's response. "Oh, André already did? I...didn't expect him to be home yet. Me? I'm still at the office. Could I speak to Leslie, please?"

While she waited for her daughter to come on the line, Gaby wrestled with an undeniable feeling of jealousy that André should be playing billiards at home with Paul while *she* toiled here trying to save what was left of his inheritance.

"Hi, sweetie." Gaby shed her tight smile for a more relaxed one when Leslie picked up the phone. "Yes, I'm still at work, sugar pie. I know Mommy's gone a lot. You and Rachel are watching 'The Partridge Family' on TV? Bath and bed right after, okay? Mommy'll stop and give you a kiss, I promise. What? No. I'm sure you'll be asleep. I love you too, baby."

Gabrielle blinked away tears. She gripped the receiver with both hands and pressed the cold plastic against her lips as she made kissing sounds—even when the line was disconnected. Several minutes ticked by before she sucked in a deep breath, dropped the phone back in its cradle and opened the advertising proposal again.

She closed the folder only when she was positive she could give tomorrow's presentation backward and forward. The trick to sales, Gaby had learned, was in knowing the material so well clients ended up begging her to advertise their product.

She stifled a yawn. Tired. And no wonder. Five to eleven. Too bad a fairy godmother didn't pop up to drive her home. Gaby sighed as she tucked extra copies of the proposal into her briefcase. Weary steps took her down the stairs, across the echoing reception area, then out through the squeaky gate.

In her rush to get home to bed, Gaby dismissed memories of the earlier noises the same way she dismissed hunger pangs caused by missing both lunch and dinner. She ignored them and searched for a star on which to make a wish.

Before she settled on a star, she caught sight of a disk jockey from WDIX radio trudging up the steps that led to the side entrance. About this time every night, Sam Hardesty brought a picnic to share with his new bride, WDIX-TV's technical engineer, Barbara—Mary Boland's sister. Mary herself was a crackerjack employee who'd been with WDIX for a long time. A woman staunchly loyal to Margaret Lyon.

Gaby returned the bridegroom's wave. What would it be like, she wondered, pausing to dump her briefcase in the back seat, to have a man dote on you that way?

''You'd hate it,'' she said to her reflection in the rearview mirror. ''You're too independent.'' She flicked on the radio, permanently set at WDIX. Rhythm and blues, her favorite sound. When she turned onto Prytania Street, her eyelids were starting to droop. As Gaby expected, the occupants of Lyoncrest had all retired for the night. She let herself in the front door and tiptoed across the marble foyer. A light glowed softly in the kitchen. For all of two seconds she debated raiding the refrigerator, then decided it wasn't worth listening to LuAnn in the morning. That woman was so possessive about her kitchen. Gabrielle grasped the polished newel post and began the long ascent up the winding, spiral stairs.

Moonlight spilled through the glass dome at the top, gleaming on the mahogany banister. She sent a glance down the corridor that led to André Lyon's suite of rooms. If she'd thought he might be up reading or something, she'd stop and thank him for doing her the favor of returning that film to McKillop.

An image of André's dark, slumberous eyes and five-o'clock shadow floated before Gaby's eyes. Today, all those muscles—the ones she'd seen that sweltering Saturday he'd moved in—had been covered by a respectable suit. Gabrielle could hardly breathe imagining him in night clothes. More like *no* clothes.

Ignoring her skittering pulse, Gaby made a hard left and continued on around the circular balustrade.

She slipped out of her high heels and wriggled tired toes in the thick hall carpet before she entered her daughter's bedroom.

Clean, tangled curls and freshly scrubbed cherub cheeks. An undefined longing threatened to crack Gabrielle's heart. She suspected that all this emotion was because she felt so tired tonight. She bent to drop a light kiss on Leslie's dimpled hand. Baby fat. All children had it and shed it in due course—didn't they? LuAnn and Claire *weren't* stuffing her.

But what if André was right? The possibility nagged at Gabrielle even after she'd showered and climbed into bed.

ANDRÉ'S ALARM SOUNDED before daylight. He eyed it, thinking it couldn't possibly be morning. That was what he got for falling asleep in a chair. Since he hadn't caught Gabrielle at the office to find out what she had on her morning docket, he planned to snag her when she arrived home. The last time he'd checked the clock, it was eleven-twenty. Then he must have dozed off. Didn't the blasted woman need any sleep?

Grumbling, he staggered into the shower. He shouldn't have to play hide-and-seek to find out where she was at any given hour of the day. She was supposed to be training him—not hiding from him.

Feeling marginally brighter after shaving and dressing, André went downstairs. Dawn was an ungodly hour to eat. Yet, with the sun only beginning to sprinkle layers of gold along the eastern horizon, he felt pretty cocky about besting Gabrielle at her own game. She'd never expect him to be down there, ready to ride in to work with her.

He whistled cheerfully, as he entered the kitchen.

LuAnn had the *Times-Picayune* spread out all over the table. "I s'pose you're going to work with the chickens, too." Heaving her stout body from the chair, she began to fold the paper with an aggrieved air. "Miss Margaret and Mr. Paul used to leave at a civilized hour. You young'uns wanna set the world on fire. I already told Miss Gaby you two are gonna burn out. Then Mr. Charles and his brood'll be left to call the shots like they want."

She slammed a cast-iron skillet on the stove. “But what do I know about runnin’ a broadcast business? I’m only a cook.”

André listened to her sputter. His whistle slowly died. “Say again—the part about my going to work with the chickens, *too.* Am I not the first to come down?”

“Ha!” LuAnn poured a mixture of grits and sausage into the sizzling oil. “Miss Gaby tore outta here half an hour ago. Didn’t even wait for coffee. Said she had a six-thirty meeting.”

“Where? With whom?” He poured himself a strong coffee, added cream and took a sip, then another. Ah-h! Caffeine. Just what he needed.

“Didn’t say. That poor girl is cracking under the pressure, if you ask me. Not that anybody does.” She waved a spatula at a sheaf of notebook pages that lay scattered across the counter. “Before it was even light, she swept in here and ordered me to put Miss Leslie on a diet. I told her, can’t everybody look like a fashion plate.” The woman dug the spatula into the pan and flipped the concoction. “I ain’t puttin’ that sweet child on no diet.”

André finished his coffee and put the cup back on the table. One thing he’d learned was that good old Southern fare was liable to kill a man before he reached his prime. New Orleans was synonymous with rich food. Always had been. Probably always would be. It pleased André that Gabrielle had taken his comments about Leslie seriously. She needed to learn, however, that a person couldn’t decree change and expect it to come about instantly. Hesitating at the door, he summoned a coaxing smile that had thawed more than one woman. “I’m sure Gabrielle didn’t mean for you to single Leslie out.” He patted a stomach that rippled like a washboard. “The whole family could benefit from paring down. Especially Papa.”

“The doctor did say Mr. Paul ought to eat less fried foods. Less rich sauces.”

“Wouldn’t it help if the family had dinner together? If you get Mama to agree, I’ll convince Gabrielle.”

“I’ll believe that when I see it,” LuAnn muttered.

“Tonight, at six,” he promised. “We’ll all meet in the dining room.” The words were barely out when Paul sauntered in, puffing on a cigarette. He commented on André’s early start. André’s only reply was to suggest they all dine together that evening.

He'd expected his father to decline, but Paul seemed pleased by the idea.

On the drive to the station, André ran through various ideas for enticing Gaby to leave work on time. He had visions of sweet-talking her into it until he went in and discovered her meeting wasn't on site and he was again locked out of the office.

He paced the floor in front of Raylene's desk. "So Steffan is taking a comp day? Someone else in this building must have a set of keys."

"No one. Per Gaby's orders. I wish she was here. George Collins has been calling her every five minutes."

"Well, hell. When's she due back?"

Raylene shrugged. "She's meeting a potential advertiser." The phone rang and she grimaced. "That's probably George again. I don't suppose you could take his call?"

"No," André said gruffly. It galled him that he didn't know enough about the operation to even answer the damned phone. He stalked upstairs to wait outside their shared office. How the hell long could a meeting with an advertising prospect take? An hour?

Three hours later André, slumped mutinously against the wall, watched her stride toward him. From the set of her shoulders, she looked ready to chew nails and spit tacks. That was fine. He was spoiling for a fight.

The fury he saw in her eyes centered on him as she brushed past and unlocked the door. Wait just a damned minute. *He'd* been the one hanging out in the hallway here because *she* hadn't given him a key. André zipped through the door behind her and slammed it so hard the file cabinets rocked.

Gaby smacked her briefcase on the desktop, causing pens and pencils to jump. She whirled to face him. "I don't imagine it entered that microscopic brain of yours that your little prep-school prank actually gave Lyon Broadcasting a black eye."

"What the hell are you yammering about? I've been planted outside this door for three frigging hours."

"Don't play coy with me! I'm talking about the canister of film George trusted me to take to WEZY. You've had your jollies. Now hand it over."

"I don't have your damned canister."

Her eyes clouded. "You...you must."

Glaring at her, André held out his arms airplane-fashion and made a slow circuit. ''You're welcome to frisk me.''

''But...but...'' She gestured feebly toward her desk. ''It was there when I took the ledgers to accounting. It *wasn't* here when I came back at six. I assumed you'd delivered it to McKillop.''

''Why would I?''

''Why, indeed?'' She shook back her bangs. ''To be nice, I thought. To help me out. I was late returning. And...well, you heard George Collins say McKillop needed it by six.''

''I don't know McKillop,'' André said gently, stepping close to capture her nervous hands. ''I'd like to ease your load, Gabrielle. But if I'm going to do that, we have to communicate.''

''André—you really didn't take the film?'' Her eyes begged him to say yes.

He threw up his hands. ''Why don't you trust me?''

''Because you were the last one here, I...think.'' She floundered a minute, recalling the noise in the hall and the silhouette in the mirror.

''You remembered something. What?''

''I... Nothing.'' She expelled a harsh breath and shook off her paranoia. ''Maybe the canister got caught between the ledgers. I'll run down to Accounting and check.''

''I'm coming along. From there we'll go out and have an office key cut for me. After that, you're going to give me lists and times of all your meetings. Oh...and starting tomorrow, we'll ride to and from the office together.''

''No, we will not. The commute is my time to gather my thoughts or to unwind. You can dog my heels at work, but my free time is my own. That's not negotiable.''

He said nothing as they exited the office and he matched his steps to hers. He only offered her a crooked smile—like the one he'd used on LuAnn.

Gaby was not pleased with what his smile did to her equilibrium. She picked up her pace, reminding herself that she wasn't a woman easily impressed by smiles.

CHAPTER FIVE

A THOROUGH SEARCH of the accountant's office didn't turn up the canister. ''I can't imagine where it went,'' Gaby said.

''Why didn't WEZY make a copy before they lent it out?''

''I'm not sure. Timing, perhaps. George said this particular footage of a twenty-car pileup on the Pontchartrain Causeway was one of a kind. A WEZY news car narrowly missed being involved in the accident. They had firsthand shots.''

''I thought WEZY was our competitor.''

''Friendly competitor,'' she said. ''Until now,'' she added, closing her eyes and sighing. ''They'll probably never swap film with us again.''

''They will,'' André said confidently. ''As soon as we break a big story they missed. Am I right? Is that how this system works?''

Gaby nodded as she slid into his car. She wasn't quite sure how he'd maneuvered her into leaving work to go and copy her office key. But here they were, driving up Chartres. ''You catch on fast. You may survive in broadcasting, after all.''

''Thanks. I sort of thought I didn't have a choice in the matter.''

''I wouldn't know about that. Why didn't you join the station after you graduated from college?'' Her tone indicated he must have been out of his mind.

André jockeyed his sports car into a miniscule parking space.

Gabrielle held her breath, sure he was going to hit one of the cars on either side. Miraculously he didn't. She'd given up expecting an answer when he surprised her.

''By the time I graduated, I'd convinced myself that my politics were at complete odds with Papa's. We argued about everything. Whatever stand he took, mine was the direct opposite.''

''Even after I arrived at Lyoncrest,'' Gabby said, ''I heard him grumbling about your into-the-trenches involvement in civil rights. But I think he was just worried you'd be hurt or killed.''

''In high school and college, I hung out with a crowd he didn't understand. He wanted me to be a reporter. I was interested in making news, not reporting it. I had visions of saving the world. In the trenches of the civil-rights war, I saw atrocities you'd never believe.'' Voice fading, André opened the passenger door and helped Gaby from the low-slung car.

''But your parents are both humanitarians,'' she persisted. ''Paul's editorial broadcasts move viewers to tears.''

''They do that. You know...growing up, I felt everyone knew him better than me,'' André said as if trying to work out answers in his mind. Gaby left him to his musing.

Half a block down the street, he handed her key to an old man with scarred ebony skin seated in a rickety booth. ''One copy,'' André said in response to an offer to cut one key for three dollars or two for five. After accepting the finished product, André handed the man a ten-spot. ''Good work. Keep the change.''

''That was generous of you,'' Gaby whispered. ''You're not as at odds with your folks' philosophies as you seem to think. Margaret and Paul give unstintingly to the underprivileged, too. I'm sure they always did.''

''And I'm sure you're right. But I had very few opportunities to observe it personally, although I have vivid memories of Mama's generosity up to when I was seven going on eight.''

''Then what happened?''

''Papa returned from reporting the war. The two of them branched out from the radio station into what was then the risky medium of television.''

''How exciting! What a wonderful opportunity to be in on the beginnings of something that changed the world so drastically.''

André's attention focused inward. ''It certainly changed my world,'' he murmured. ''Hey.'' He flashed another smile. ''That stuff is old hat. I told Uncle Charles yesterday that there's nothing to be gained by digging up the past. You can't change a thing.''

''I doubt he heard you. Your uncle is a bitter man. He's passed his feelings on to his wife and kids. They all circle Paul and Margaret like a flock of vultures.''

André looked at her. If he wanted to add fuel to the fire of her indignation, he could tell her that his uncle and cousins thought *she* was the vulture. He sighed warily. He happened to believe the whole damn family should just let bygones be bygones. When Paul Lyon finally acknowledged André as his son, he'd promised they'd be a family. It was years before André accepted that it wasn't his parents' fault that the new venture demanded virtually all their time.

Lost in his thoughts, he clipped the new key to his ring, took Gaby's elbow and steered her toward the car. In the center of the sidewalk, he stopped and sniffed the air. "Do you smell that?"

"What?" Gabrielle tripped on a raised cobblestone.

Sliding his arm around her waist, André steadied her. Then he deftly turned her up the street. "*Muffulettas.* It's almost lunchtime. Care to share one?"

"And smell like garlic all afternoon? No way. Besides, the bread they hollow out to stuff with that gastric time bomb is so heavy, I'd fall asleep at my desk."

Gaby might as well have saved her breath. He'd already sniffed out the hole-in-the-wall family diner and pulled her in after him. Almost before her eyes had time to adjust to the dim interior, she was holding a glass of red wine in one hand and an enormous half sandwich, dripping gooey cheese, in the other.

A satisfied smile softened André's features. That was enough to make Gaby relax against the vinyl booth cushions. Capitulating gracefully, she tackled the massive sandwich.

André wiped cheese off both their chins after tasting his portion. "Uh, don't mention our lunch to LuAnn. This morning she was complaining about the diet you left for Leslie. I said we could all stand to eat healthier." He set down his bread roll and caught Gabrielle's hand. "LuAnn has a harebrained notion. She thinks the whole family should sit down to an evening meal together." He wasn't about to confess it'd been his grand scheme. "I cross-my-heart-hope-to-die promised to deliver you at six sharp."

"That's impossible. Why, we'd have to leave work early every night."

André traced figure eights over the fine bones in Gaby's hand. As he prepared to launch an assault on her soft heart, he prayed she'd never compare notes with anyone at the house. "It'd help Mama's cause, too. A family meal every night *would* take Papa's mind off not being able to do the evening broadcast."

Gaby stared at the strong, tanned fingers curved around her smaller, pale hand. She felt a steady warmth and the ever-so-slight rasp of André's calloused palm. "You must think I'm terribly insensitive." She leaned forward and curled her other hand over his. "Paul thrived in the fast pace of the newsroom. And now the doctor wants him to give up everything except a weekly editorial." She sighed. "I guess there's no reason I can't go back to the station after dinner to tie up any loose ends."

"Exactly." André counted on the likelihood that she'd find it too hard to go back once they made it home. He watched her pick Italian sausage off her sandwich and tried to imagine a Gabrielle without dark circles under her eyes and with, say, an extra ten pounds. Sleep was essential. The weight, a give or take. Though she did skip too many meals. Someone ought to make sure she didn't. *Him?* The idea hit him like a brick to the head.

"Uh...chow down on that *muffuletta* before it gets cold, Gabrielle."

Moved by a combination of his gravelly voice and killer smile, she tackled it with gusto, fitting coral-tinted lips around the oozing tip of the roll. She wiggled her tongue free to lick a glob of dressing that threatened to run down her wrist.

André felt about a pint of blood rush to an area below his belt and wished he'd let her have it her way this time. He couldn't seem to catch his breath.

"You're a fine one to talk," she mumbled a moment later around a contented sigh. "Why aren't you stuffing your face?"

"I, uh, get a kick out of watching you."

"Into sideshows, huh?" She sucked in her cheeks and crossed her eyes. They both laughed. It relaxed the mood for André. While Gaby sipped her wine, he polished off his sandwich.

"That was sinfully good," he said, scrubbing his hands and face with his napkin. Lifting his wineglass, he clinked it lightly against hers.

"I rarely drink alcohol during a workday. But maybe one glass won't loosen my tongue and make me say something to a client I'll regret."

"Do you always work directly with clients? From the job descriptions, I assumed we served more as administrators to the various departments. You know, establish goals and evaluate staff effectiveness and such.''

''At one time or another I've performed just about every job at the station. Well, except for being in front of the cameras. So has Margaret. And advertisers are funny, you know. They get comfortable with a contact and hate to switch. That's something your cousin Jason doesn't understand. When he came on board, he thought I should turn over all my clients to him. Even after Margaret began sharing management duties with me, I kept the ones I thought needed a personal touch.'' She gave a quick shrug. ''Jason dislikes pounding the pavement.''

''Don't think I'm taking his side, but Alain and Jason claim you're still bringing in new clients.''

''Yes. So? What's wrong with that? You saw the drastic drop in revenue.''

''Instead of getting huffy, help me understand what's going on. My cousins more or less accused you of skimming off the better prospects, while leaving Jason to follow up on the dregs.''

''That's not true!'' Gaby put down her empty wineglass and pushed out of the booth. ''Ask him about the leads I've given him where he's dropped the ball and I've discovered later the accounts were picked up by competitors.''

André stood and peeled off cash for the bill plus tip. ''No need to bite my head off. I barely know my cousins. I told you. I'm only trying to sort things out for myself.''

Outside the restaurant Gaby donned an oversize pair of dark glasses.

André determined from the stiff set of her shoulders and her silence that she didn't believe him.

He should never have brought up the subject. He hadn't fully believed his cousins' complaint. Although, in his conversations with other staff, several had hinted that Gabrielle was both ambitious and demanding. He'd already learned that one of the accusers was the catty type. Hell, for all he knew, everyone working for Lyon Broadcasting might have his or her own ax to grind.

''Gabrielle, what if you pulled back and left all sales to Jason and the others on the sales force? If within, say, two months he hasn't signed a prescribed number of new advertisers, fire him.''

She stopped with her hand on the car door. ''*Fire* him? Your uncle would make life hell for Margaret and Paul. I don't think they need that aggravation right now.''

''Aren't you exaggerating a bit?'' André asked after closing the door and climbing in himself. ''I can't recall Uncle Charles so much as raising his voice.'' Sentimentality crept into his tone. ''He taught me to play the piano and showed me how to ride a bike.''

Gaby lifted her dark glasses and stared at him almost sadly. ''A lot of years have passed since then. A lot of water under the bridge. I've actually heard him scream at Paul.''

André thrust the key into the ignition. ''People do change,'' he lamented as the engine roared to life.

''Yes, they do.'' Gabrielle got sidetracked in memories of a happy-go-lucky Marc Villieux—the man she fell in love with, not the abusive, hateful person he later became.

''WELL, WHERE HAVE YOU TWO BEEN for the last two hours?'' Raylene demanded the instant they entered the foyer of WDIX.

''Out,'' replied André benignly at the same time Gaby stuttered, reddened and finally managed to ask, ''What's happened? I *knew* if we went out without telling anyone there'd be a crisis.''

''You got that right,'' Raylene said testily. ''First, a man by the name of Rodney Fortner has called four times in the past hour. He wouldn't tell me in regard to what. Reading between the lines, I'd say the guy sounds fit to be tied.''

Gabrielle frowned at the pink slips Raylene thrust across the counter. ''Mr. Fortner is a prospective advertiser. We met this morning. I didn't think he intended to call me back until tomorrow.'' She stacked the slips in order of the calling times. ''There's more?''

Raylene tossed back her blond curls. ''You missed a meeting with our host-affiliate officials. Eleven o'clock at the Hilton. Mr. Brock's secretary called to find out how late you were going to be. When paging didn't turn you up, I told her you were obviously on your way. She called back twenty minutes later. Plenty ticked off, I'd say. They'd delayed the meeting, and you didn't show or call.''

''What? I have that meeting on my calendar for tomorrow!''

''Well, it was today,'' Raylene said without compassion.

Gaby turned to André. Her lips trembled. "I wouldn't have put it on the wrong day. I just wouldn't. I'm very careful about checking dates, times, everything!"

"Look." He lowered his voice and urged her down the hall, away from the receptionist. "You're not infallible. No human being can be right all the time."

"Magnanimous of you to make allowances for my foibles. I wasn't trying to say I was perfect. I do make mistakes. I just don't happen to believe I made one in this instance. I am very, very careful with my calendar."

"You also come early and stay late," he said as they ran up the stairs. "You skip meals and get by on very little sleep. To say nothing of the added load you've taken on since Papa's heart attack. How long ago did you set that meeting?" At her impatient frown he said, "I'm trying to keep you from flogging yourself, dammit."

She turned after unlocking the office door. "I appreciate that, André, I really do. And maybe I wouldn't have reacted so strongly if I hadn't just lost that film of McKillop's. Or if—" Breaking off midsentence, she headed for her desk.

"Or if you hadn't played hooky with me today? Isn't that what you started to say?"

"Yes. All right. That's exactly it." Unlocking her center drawer, she dragged out a burgundy engagement calendar. "If I'd been here where I belonged, I'd have been late, but I would have made the meeting. Those network people are all prima donnas. Not a good idea to stand them up," she said, opening the book.

"You didn't stand them up, Gabrielle. We're talking about an honest mistake. Call and explain. They may be prima donnas, but they aren't God."

"You tell them that," she muttered. "Come here." She bent closer to the calendar. "Does it look like something's been erased in the eleven-o'clock slot?"

He crossed the room and put his head next to hers. "Boy, I don't know. It's possible, I suppose."

She flipped back and forth between the two days. "That appears to be my writing where it's listed tomorrow. Darker than I normally write, though. See, compare it with a few other appointments. What do you think?"

He shook his head. "I can't tell. Who else has access to your calendar?"

"No one. I do all my own scheduling to avoid this very problem. Unless... Did you borrow it yesterday?"

"Me? Why would I nose into your stuff?"

"Right before I left with the ledgers, you said you wanted to coordinate our calendars as soon as I got back."

"I don't think I like what you're implying," André said, wary of the suspicion that muddied her eyes. "I waited for you until after six, and then I figured you'd taken off. Give me one good reason why I'd disguise my handwriting and mess up your calendar."

She slung an arm carelessly over the chair back. "Hm. I can't imagine. To make me look like a fool, perhaps?"

"You are flat-ass paranoid, woman. And crazy to boot."

She rose from her chair and would have responded hotly, but the telephone shrilled. Snatching it from the cradle, she snapped, "Hello!" Suddenly her whole demeanor changed. "Certainly, Raylene. Put Mr. Fortner through."

André watched her fool with a lock of hair that had worked its way from beneath the ever-present clasp. The one today was gold filigree. He wanted to strip it off and watch her thick, midnight hair plummet to her hips. The urge was so strong he moved to his desk and put his hands to work unloading the supplies he'd gathered yesterday. Still, he couldn't help hearing Gaby's side of the conversation.

"Mr. Fortner. I didn't expect a call so soon. Do you need additional information?"

André heard her draw a shaky breath. He glanced around and saw she'd gone pale. The finger twisting and untwisting the strand of hair was noticeably trembling.

"Who told you such a thing?" she gasped. "No. I did not bad-mouth your product to the WDIX family. I...well, I'm sorry you feel that way. I see. Goodbye."

"What was that all about?" André crossed to where she sat as if in a trance, still clutching the receiver.

"Someone phoned Mr. Fortner, owner of a cosmetic account I'd hoped to lure away from a competitor. The person said I called his product stupid and overpriced."

"And of course you didn't."

"No. Well, yes, I did, only—" Gaby dropped the phone and covered her face with her hands.

"Did you malign his product or not?" André tucked a finger beneath her chin, forcing her to look up.

She waved a hand helplessly. "I was sitting here, thinking out loud. A bad habit of mine when I'm alone. I *was* alone, or so I thought," she said miserably. "But it doesn't matter now. Fortner was furious. Who can blame him?"

André raked a hand through his own hair, freeing it from the leather thong. "But if you were in here alone...?" He stared at a spot on the ceiling and massaged his neck. "Why would anyone at WDIX-TV try to scotch an account?"

Her eyes met his and hardened. "Maybe you can answer that, André. You've admitted harboring contempt for your parents and for the business. Nothing like this ever happened until you came on board. None of these...*accidents.*"

He leaned on the desk and thrust his face close to hers. "I damn well know I had nothing to do this. Which leaves you, *Ms.* Villieux. Since you weaseled your way into *my* family, how better to run me out and secure the top job for yourself than to pull this crap and pin it on me?"

Silence enveloped the room except for the harsh sound of their breathing.

CHAPTER SIX

"HOW DARE YOU SUGGEST such a thing?" Gaby half rose from her chair. "Yes, I would've preferred if you'd stayed in the swamp, and yes, I happen to think I can handle what this job entails. All by my lonesome. Because I work hard. Not because I weaseled my way into *your* family. While you've jaunted around the world, I've given up any semblance of a personal life and devoted myself to promoting and maintaining this station's image. I'd never do *anything* to jeopardize Lyon Broadcasting. Not even if it means training my replacement."

André refused to give ground, even though he practically had to look cross-eyed to see the angry splashes of color on her cheeks. It might have been a cliché, but Gabrielle Villieux was something when she was mad. Beautiful. Sexy. And sincere. The sincerity reached past Andre's purely male appreciation of her physical attributes. A real coup, considering that her lips were within kissing distance…and he'd resisted an urge to kiss them most of the day.

To maintain that resistance, he planted his palms on her desk. Kissing could wait. They were both feeling angry and insulted. Looking ahead, he decided their entire future relationship, working and otherwise, was at stake.

"Better now?" he asked quietly.

"I'm okay."

"If you're okay and I'm okay," he joked, "why were we shouting at each other?"

She looked startled, then amused. "You practice transactional analysis? How trendy of you."

"Yeah, but don't give me away to the guys I worked with on the ships. It might ruin my tough-guy image."

"I probably shouldn't admit this, but I envy you all your

travel,'' she said suddenly, sinking into her chair. ''I've never been out of Louisiana. Probably never will be.''

''Why? You make a good salary. I know you don't pay room and board at Lyoncrest.''

''Does that bother you?'' she asked sharply. ''Not that it's any of your business.'' She took a deep breath. ''Your mother squared my husband's debts. I'm paying her back by the month. Plus there's the money for my college tuition and Leslie's school. Would you like an itemized account of my personal expenses?''

''You are the touchiest female I've ever met.''

''That's a world record, I'll bet. I understand your little black book would put the New York City telephone directory to shame.''

He laughed and propped a hip against her desk. ''I have sincere concerns about the news we broadcast if you don't check out your sources any better than that. Who passed along *that* piece of false information?''

She glanced away guiltily. ''I don't recall.''

''That's a cop-out. You may as well tell me.''

''All right. It was Alain. Everything hit the fan around here when he married Yvette LeBlanc. Your aunt and uncle consider her socially inferior. Alain said that at least he didn't have a new woman on his arm every week.''

''Alain doesn't even know me. Maybe he was mad because I didn't make it to his wedding. My partner's dad died and I had to run the business alone for a couple of weeks. Yvette's Cajun, isn't she? A descendant of the Acadians who helped settle this area. How socially inferior is that?''

''Ask your uncle. He and Catherine are the ones who carry on like being Cajun is a crime. Catherine is Creole, the real French aristocracy, she claims. To make matters worse, Yvette has an illegitimate son. Devin's four. He's a darling. I can't believe how badly Charles and Catherine treat him and his mother. But haven't we strayed from the subject? We were discussing your array of lady friends.''

''Wrong. We were discussing the disappearance of WEZY's film canister and the loss of an important client. We meandered way off course.''

Gabrielle's brows slanted obliquely. ''Message received. You don't want to talk about your love life.''

André bent over the desk, forcing her to scoot her chair into the corner. "What, exactly, would you like to know?"

"I... Nothing. We should talk about work."

Impossibly long lashes hid André's dark, sparkling eyes. "You already said you have no social life. It's only fair I reveal as much about mine. I'm not currently involved, if that's what you're wondering." He'd never been marriage-bound with any woman. Not that he'd lacked lovers. He was, however, a lot pickier than his cousin had led Gaby to believe. It suddenly seemed important that she understand.

"Who's wondering?" she interjected. "I don't care who you sleep with. Or marry. It makes no difference to me if they're purple, green or polka dot."

"That's a relief. We wouldn't get along if you were prejudiced."

"We only need to see eye to eye on job-related ethics, not on any personal preferences."

André took some time to study her before he said forthrightly, "I've yet to meet a man who can keep the two separate. Show me a guy who's a bastard in his personal life, and I'll show you a guy I wouldn't be quick to jump into a business deal with."

Gaby's lip curled slightly. "Yet it never occurred to you that your uncle might want something in return for those two invitations to the Comus ball next month."

"Oh, it occurred to me. Which is why I said thanks but no thanks."

"You...you refused an opportunity to attend one of the most elite events of Mardi Gras?"

"Did you want to go?"

"No. I...uh..." Gabrielle rolled forward, unlocked a file drawer and pulled out a stack of manila folders. "That's not entirely true." She raised her eyes to meet his. "I've never been to one of the masked balls. A girl can't grow up in Louisiana and not dream of dressing up and going to a Rex or Comus affair. Where, according to the fine print, this same girl meets a wickedly handsome masked pirate."

"And is whisked off on a white charger and lives happily ever after," André finished with a devilish grin.

"You've mixed fairy tales with Mardi Gras, but something like that, yes."

"Why haven't you ever been?"

She fiddled with the folders again. "Lack of money. Lack of connections. In my wilder youth, I didn't exactly hobnob with debutantes," she said frostily.

"But since?" André persisted. "My folks are well connected. If Charles has access to invitations, so should they."

"Maybe I grew up and discovered that wickedly handsome pirates without their masks, are just lecherous men."

"Ouch." André wanted to counter Gabrielle's bitter statement, but they were interrupted by a soft knock at the door. He turned as the door opened and his mother stepped into the room. Today she wore a navy dress with a white collar. She rose on navy pumps and aimed a kiss at André's cheek.

As Gaby rushed around the desk to embrace Margaret, André was enveloped in a cloud of Chanel No. 5, a scent he always associated with his mother. He moved aside, lost for a moment in fond memories as he watched the women express genuine affection for each other. For the first time in years, he wondered why his parents hadn't had other children. In all the whispered tales surrounding the Lyons, and there were many, he'd never heard it said that his father had come home from the war with any injuries that made him impotent. André tried to recall explicit conversations dating back to Paul Lyon's unexpected return to the household. So many years had passed. Memories, resentments, all got jumbled.

One major encounter between his uncle and his mother stood out. Apparently no one had suspected André might creep from his bed to listen. It must've been early in 1949, when Paul had first come home. During their argument Uncle Charles had insisted scornfully that Margaret had been unfaithful to her husband. At the time, André hadn't understood why counting months meant he was or wasn't a Lyon. Later he learned the significance. That was long after his father had held him and, with tears in his eyes, called André *son.*

Uncle Charles might still doubt his paternity, but André didn't. Up to that point, his papa had refused to be in the same room with him. Something important had occurred about then. His parents had begun sharing a bedroom, and of course, they worked together. Aunt Ella ignored him, and his uncle stopped visiting

Lyoncrest. Nothing was the same after that...reconciliation, he supposed, between his parents.

Suddenly André wanted to know the specifics of the feud. His father was the logical one to ask, but Paul's heart wasn't sound. If André had heard Mama say once that people should keep family issues private, he'd heard her say it a million times. And maybe she wouldn't recall that particular night. Significant to a kid wasn't necessarily significant to adults. His grandparents and Aunt Ella were gone. Maybe he should just forget it.

"André?" Margaret waved a hand in front of his eyes. "Gabrielle said the two of you are getting on famously." His mother beamed as she stripped off her gloves. "I'm so pleased. LuAnn said you'll be home for dinner from now on." Tears sprang to her eyes. "If only you knew how long I've wished for this."

Astounded to hear that Gaby would say they were getting along at all, let alone famously, André shifted to get a better look at her. Her expression was fierce. Quick to catch on, André realized Gabrielle intended to keep their differences quiet, rather than add to his mother's woes. If he hadn't already begun to admire Gabrielle Villieux, her selflessness would have led him in that direction. *Whoa! Hold on!* André rubbed a tense jaw. Such thoughts could spell trouble.

"Are you here to work, Margaret?" Gaby asked. "If so, I'll go somewhere else to show André how to interpret the Nielsen ratings and the reports we get from the American Research Bureau. It's important he learn how they translate into setting ad rates."

"Goodness, you two carry on. I brought Paul down to tape his editorial. I was afraid I'd have a hard time prying him away again. Having to get home in time to dress for dinner gives me the perfect excuse. André, I'll be forever in your debt for coming up with the idea of reestablishing the family dinner hour."

André groaned silently. He felt Gabrielle's eyes bore daggers through him. "If there's any credit, it goes to LuAnn," he mumbled, hoping he'd remember to ask LuAnn to take the rap. What a mess it was turning out. He'd begun the whole thing because he thought Gaby spent too many hours at work. For all he knew, the station might collapse without her overtime. She certainly seemed to have her fingers in enough pies. She was infinitely more vital than his cousins wanted him to believe.

"We'll see you at six," Margaret called from the door. "Oh, and Gabrielle, Leslie's ecstatic. She's not often demonstrative, as you know. Today she whooped and danced around so much Claire had trouble getting her to listen to the end of a story they were reading."

André, who'd been watching Gaby, saw a series of emotions ranging from guilt to sorrow cross her face. If he'd thought she didn't know her dedication to Lyon Broadcasting came at a steep price, he'd now discovered his error. Something drove Gabrielle Villieux; he didn't know what, but he did realize she wasn't insensitive to her daughter, as he'd first believed.

After his mother left, André allowed Gaby time to collect herself. He went to his desk and found a calendar that matched the one she kept locked in her center drawer.

"Before you explain the audience ratings, could we match our calendars? That'll avoid future mixups," he said when she gazed at him suspiciously. "And use a pen, all right? That'll make tampering harder."

"Also messier if you need to change a meeting." She sighed. "Read the schedule to me, please. I'll fill in yours. No questions can come up, then."

He grabbed his chair and parked it next to hers. "Okay. Shoot. But give me time to list them on my pocket calendar," he said, plunking down so close that their thighs brushed.

Gaby's stomach tightened. It did again when he reached the date for the twenty-fifth-anniversary gala. A date she'd circled in red, assuming she'd be awarded the job of general manager. She hadn't thought André Lyon would last until July; she now felt far less positive about the outcome.

Her stomach did handsprings when he glanced up once they'd finished and smiled one of his heart-stopping smiles. She felt all thumbs as she leafed through the audience ratings. She couldn't seem to focus on the totals. Gaby hadn't gotten that quivery feeling over a man in so long she was amazed she'd recognized the symptoms. Amazed and disturbed. Up to this minute, she'd have sworn her experience with Marc Villieux had cured her of ever having sexual yearnings again. Obviously she'd been wrong.

She gave up concentrating on the numbers André entered into the adding machine and turned to analyzing why she'd be attracted to him, of all people. She didn't live in a vacuum. Many of the men she worked with were more classically handsome than André Lyon. But there was something...compelling about him. A sense of restrained energy, perhaps.

Gaby decided that if she was going to be honest about this, she'd have to admit he intrigued her on several levels. It went without saying that he was good to look at. He was lean and fit. His muscles moved with fluid grace beneath the crisp cotton of his shirt. But there was more to André than looks. He'd shown a soft spot for the girl, Rachel, whose home life he could have ignored. He cared enough for a stranger who barely eked out a living selling keys to slip him a sizable tip. And he'd paid attention to Leslie, noticed her eating habits. But darn it all, Gaby didn't *want* to feel this way. Why couldn't he be the jerk she'd conjured up in her mind the day Margaret had asked her to train him for a job Gaby herself wanted so badly she could taste it?

His deep voice yanked her out of her thoughts. "This is impressive. Television shows definitely develop patterns. How long do you allow a program to flounder at the low end before you replace it?"

"Depends. If the program manager thinks it has potential, we may juggle the time slot. Cost factors in too."

"Always, I imagine." He tugged on his lips, and Gaby felt an answering tug low in her abdomen that made her squirm. The reaction he drew from her was ridiculous. She was a professional, for goodness' sake. He obviously had no problem keeping *his* mind on work.

"Look, here we have this a.m. kiddie program. For sixteen weeks the ratings have been abominable. Tell me why you struggle along with this local yokel, instead of going with a syndicated show like 'Shari Lewis and Lambchop'?"

"I'd take her in a minute. But in this case, Sydney, of 'Sydney's Tree House' infamy, happens to be related to Catherine Benoît Lyon. At the last board meeting I suggested we cancel his show. Charles gave us a big sob story about how this program is all that's standing between him and bankruptcy."

"And what stands between us and bankruptcy?" André demanded.

Gaby shrugged. "More power to you if you can ax Syd. In my position, all I can do is recommend. Only family has voting authority. It infuriates Charles that his voice carries less weight than Paul's so he badgers the other board members every chance he gets."

"It's beyond me why the family doesn't want whatever will keep Lyon Broadcasting running in the black."

She grinned; she couldn't help it. "Well, André, I have a feeling you'll come out of your first board meeting much wiser."

He grinned back. "We'll see." Then he closed the folder and glanced at his watch. "We'll make it home in time to dress for dinner if we leave now. I'd like to track a few more of these losers we're carrying. If you're coming back to work later, maybe I'll hitch a ride."

"Sure. If you really care about rebuilding profits, I'll give you a folder filled with my last six months' worth of recommendations. Every one of them was tabled, thanks to Charles."

"Oh, I care, all right," he muttered. "But I'll probably just observe at this first meeting. I'd hate to stir up problems, Papa's heart being what it is."

"I understand. That's why Margaret hasn't been making any hard decisions lately, although I can tell it galls her." Gabrielle stood up, slung her purse over her shoulder and turned off the desk lamp before she started for the door. "My goal is to reverse the station's decline within six months—by the anniversary celebration."

André followed her out and locked the office, rattling the door handle to make sure.

"I want to help you, Gabrielle," he said.

He was gazing earnestly at her, and she fought the overwhelming urge to look away. Finally, feeling very brave, she extended her hand. "If you mean that, let's shake on it. But be warned. With or without you, André, I intend to succeed."

A smile kicked up the corners of his mouth. André did more than shake on it. He lifted her hand to his lips and placed a warm kiss in the center of her palm.

Gaby snatched back her hand and, flustered, fled down the hall.

CHAPTER SEVEN

ANDRÉ MET GABRIELLE on the winding staircase at Lyoncrest. Or rather, she'd already begun her descent and was two steps below him.

Leslie, cherubic-looking in a lacy peach dress, gripped her mother's hand and gazed up at her like an adoring puppy. Gaby wore a softly draped cotton dress of bright yellow. André enjoyed the way the dress set off her dark hair. She wore it down this evening; it curved at her shoulders and swirled enticingly around her hips. André grabbed the polished banister as a tremor shot through him. He imagined that fall of glossy black hair, tangled from lovemaking, splashed across his cool white sheets. The slick soles of his dress shoes skidded on the highly waxed step. He lost his balance and fell into Gabrielle. She caught him, which wasn't easy, as Leslie still clung to her arm.

"Oops," Gaby said. "New shoes? You'd better scuff up the soles before you take a real header and break your neck."

André swore under his breath. He righted himself, feeling like a fool. If she knew what he'd been mooning about, she probably wouldn't care if he broke his neck.

Paul and Margaret were already in the dining room. Margaret was arranging a vase of flowers at the sideboard. Paul sat at the head of the antique table—brought from France by the first Lyons to come to New Orleans. André studied his father, trying to assess his health. Paul seemed in good spirits. A charcoal smoking jacket fit snugly around his lean frame. The years had been kind to him; at sixty-one, he had no sagging jowls, no flab of any kind. André found it hard to believe his father had suffered a heart attack as Paul rose and clasped his hand. Perhaps there was less vigor in the handshake, though. "Sit down, Papa. You must be tired after doing your editorial."

"Not on your life. I could do more." He glanced at his wife as he said it.

"Let's assume your doctor knows best, dear," Margaret said, placing the flowers in the middle of the snowy linen tablecloth. "Isn't this nice?" She included everyone in her smile. Her hands found their way to Paul's shoulders as he crushed out his cigarette. She dropped a kiss on his once-dark hair. Though still thick and brushed back from his face, the way he'd worn it for years, the color, a silvery gray, showed his age as little else about him did.

"Where's Rachel?" Margaret murmured when LuAnn appeared asking if they were ready to have dinner served.

"She's not coming down," Leslie piped up. Blushing profusely, the girl buried her head in Gaby's side as all eyes shifted toward her.

"Rach isn't sick, is she?" André paused in the act of pulling out Gabrielle's chair.

Leslie shook her head until her curls bounced. "Rachel said she's not fambly."

She glanced up shyly. "I told her my mommy and me aren't fambly, but—"

Paul made shooing motions toward Leslie with his hands. "Bring her," he ordered, and Leslie ran off.

As André seated his mother, she patted his hand. "If you and Gabrielle want a glass of wine, Paul could open a bottle."

"None for me," Gabrielle hastened. "I'm going back to the office after we eat."

"Oh." Margaret's face fell. "Will you have time to read Leslie a story first?"

Gaby felt the beginning of pressure behind her eyes. "I haven't written the speech I've been asked to give this week at the Chamber of Commerce luncheon. And I barely glanced at today's mail. I think there's a packet of FCC rate recommendations."

"I'm going back, too," André announced.

She sighed impatiently. "Don't bother. Until you know what you're doing, I can get more done by myself."

"The more you do alone," he said coolly, "the less I'll learn."

"André's right." Margaret handed him a crystal pitcher of ice water and held out her glass. "The sooner he takes the reins, the more secure staff will feel. It's important to the employees that there be an owner in charge."

Gaby's headache intensified. She didn't know why she should be shocked by Margaret's pronouncement—and yet she'd persisted in hoping that hard work and unwavering commitment would win *her* that position. She said nothing.

Paul frowned deeply and cleared his throat as if to speak. André opened his mouth to speak, but Leslie's return with Rachel in tow put an end to their conversation about the business. Leslie shoved Rachel, who still wore her school uniform, toward the empty chair beside André. "Hurry up and sit, Rachel," the little girl said. "I'm hungry. Nobody cares if you don't got a nice dress to wear."

"Don't have," Gabrielle corrected automatically. She placed two fingers over Leslie's mouth when the child continued to babble about Rachel's lack of dresses.

The teenager turned red. "It's no big deal."

Paul reached across the table and lifted her chin. "Rachel, child. There's not a thing wrong with the way you're dressed. The first time I laid eyes on Margie, she had on an earlier version of that same uniform. She came by the radio station every night after school and pestered the life out of me." He shared a smile with his wife.

André's heart twisted. He'd spent so much time resenting the loss of his parents to the business, he'd missed important details. Historic details. He hadn't really understood what welded this family together. Both of his grandfathers, Hollander and Lyon, had started together in radio, and he supposed broadcasting must be in his blood. It hadn't been part of his life, though, until now. He'd spent a lot of time on the outside looking in. He remembered the resentment he'd felt, the uncertainty and lack of belonging. Not his parents' fault, but still... André suspected Rachel needed more than words to ease her insecurities.

"Rach," he said, handing her a napkin, "what I wore in Bayou Sans Fin doesn't fit in here, either." Paul agreed, but slipped in an oblique comment implying that André needed a haircut. Letting his father's comment slide, André turned to Gaby. "Maybe we can pry Gabrielle away from work on Saturday long enough to buy you some new clothes. What I know about current fashion can be summed up in one word. Zero."

"Perhaps your mother..." Gaby said quickly.

Margaret shook her head. "Styles have changed so in the last year. Gabrielle's the better shopper. I can't get excited about these fuller skirts. Cathy had a panel of designers on her talk show last week. Seems they're calling it the 'big' look."

Paul motioned for LuAnn to serve. "More the droop look, if you ask me. The coats were like tents. Not that anyone asked me." He leaned slightly toward André. "I saw the same program. Ask your mother about the evening gowns. More like lingerie. And those string bikinis—ooh la la!"

Margaret tried to shush him.

André's laugh sounded rusty. "I might have lived in the bayou, but I worked with tourists. I fell off a pontoon the first time a woman climbed aboard wearing..." He fashioned his fingers into minuscule triangles.

Gaby's look warned him to remember there were little ears at the table.

He laughed, then gestured toward LuAnn, who came in carrying a steaming tureen of gumbo.

"Mmm." André let his nose follow the spicy steam. "*Laissez le bon temps rouler.*" He murmured the popular Cajun saying.

Gabrielle spewed a mouthful of water. "Let the good times roll, indeed," she said primly as she dabbed at the front of her dress.

Her disapproval surprised André. "I take it you object to having fun?"

"When it's to the exclusion of good sense, yes. Joie de vivre. Live to enjoy, whether the rent's paid or not. Wasn't that your philosophy until a few weeks ago?"

Paul and Margaret cast worried glances at the two, as did Rachel and Leslie.

The strained atmosphere disturbed André. "I did run a business, you know," he said mildly. He couldn't figure out why she'd become so short-tempered. "I do believe in enjoying life," he added. "I'm from New Orleans, after all. But I believe in doing my share of the work, too."

With an obvious effort, Gabrielle smiled, shrugged and withdrew from the conversation.

After that, dinner settled into a pleasant, if lengthy, affair. André persuaded the girls to talk about school. Though both were reluctant, Rachel warmed first. She was more naturally exuberant than Gaby's daughter. Leslie answered direct questions in one-syllable words. Mostly she blushed and hid behind her thick bangs.

When at last they pushed back from the table, André groaned. ''If we do this every night—and we should—none of us will fit into our clothes. Mama, I think you need to have a talk with LuAnn. Healthy dining doesn't mean eating for three hours.''

''Tomorrow I'll draw up a menu. The heart specialist recommended a cookbook. He also told Paul to take a walk every day,'' she said with a significant glance at her husband.

Paul rolled his eyes. ''I see it now,'' he grumbled good-naturedly. ''Margie's going to roust me out of bed and make me walk to the Garden District bookstore to get my morning paper. What good is being able to afford a car and driver? Tell me that.''

His wife simply smiled indulgently.

Gaby broke in with a yawn. ''All that food made me sleepy,'' she said, covering her mouth. ''If I'm going to get anything donc tonight, I'd better leave now.''

''Will you read me a story before you go, Mama?'' Leslie asked.

''I'd like to, sweetie,'' Gabrielle said. ''But by the time I change and drive to the station, they'll be ready to sign off for the night. I've stayed there after everyone leaves, but...I...with all that's hap—'' She caught André's frown. He was right; the incidents had been annoying but nothing to worry Margaret and Paul about. To keep them from probing, Gaby quickly began discussing a shopping trip with Rachel as they left the dining room.

''I'll go as I am,'' André called out. ''Let me play chauffeur.'' Turning to Leslie, he tapped her nose. ''How about if *I* read you a story, squirt?''

Leslie's eyes grew dark and round as she studied him. ''I don't like scary ones like Raymond reads Scott. Don't like books with bugs, neither.''

André studied her earnest little face. ''Then you go pick the story.''

"A short one," cautioned her mother from the hall. "It's nice of Mr. Lyon to offer to read to you. What do you say, Leslie?"

"Who's Mr. Lyon? You mean Mr. André?" The child blinked in confusion. "Isn't Scott's daddy Mr. Lyon?"

André patiently started to explain surnames and given names. "It's polite to use a last name when you first meet an adult. But it can get tricky. What if I yelled Ms. Villieux? You and your mom would both answer."

Leslie giggled. "Uh-uh, I'm Leslie. Mama," she shouted, "there are too many Mr. Lyons!"

"You've got *that* right." Gaby poked her head back into the room. "At least one too many."

He laughed, relieved that her mood had apparently lightened.

In the car some twenty minutes later Gabrielle drew up her left knee and turned toward André. "Has anyone ever told you that you have an easy way with kids?"

He let his gaze wander from the road. It was a warm evening. His left elbow rested on the frame of the open window. "Is that your way of saying I'm still in the throes of childhood?" He raised his eyebrows.

"No!" She reached out and lightly clasped his forearm. "I wasn't being critical. Leslie is painfully shy. I know this sounds corny, but it warmed my heart, hearing the way you made her laugh. Not just once. While you were reading, too."

He made a quick study of Gabrielle from beneath his lashes and did his best to ignore the way her touch slammed his pulse into high gear. "Interesting," he murmured.

"What is? All mothers want their children to laugh, don't they?"

"I just find it curious that you're so passionate about Leslie's happiness, yet you have very little time for her—because you're always at WDIX. You're obviously all work and no play."

She dropped her foot to the mat and said stiffly, "We weren't talking about me."

"Let's."

Her head swiveled slowly back. "Let's what?"

"Talk about your aversion to enjoying life, *Ms.* Villieux."

Gabrielle folded her hands. "Wherever did you get the idea that I don't enjoy life? I love previewing new programs and forecasting which ones will please our viewers. Work isn't drudgery. It's satisfying. Like when I've got the right advertiser for a profitable series. Everything I do at Lyon Broadcasting makes me very, very happy."

"Ah." He nodded. "Success is your aphrodisiac, I guess."

"What?"

"You need me to explain aphrodisiac? It means something that turns you on and—"

"I know what it means." Gaby shifted uncomfortably. "Look, my success is for my daughter as much as for myself—believe it or not. As for aphrodisiacs, I'm not interested. Not everyone needs sex to be a complete, contented person. I've seen how being a slave to self-gratification can ruin lives."

Frowning, André rubbed the tip of one forefinger over his lips. Gaby felt a little embarrassed by her stuffy little speech, but she had to draw a line with him. Had to keep him at a distance.

She was uncomfortable being confined with him. She wished he'd drive faster. The way he touched his parted lips drove a corkscrew of need straight through her. She hadn't hungered for the physical touch of a man in quite some time. Gaby hated the urgency André Lyon fired in her. She'd nearly thrown her life away once on a good-for-nothing two-legged rat. Marc had enticed and taunted her with the pleasures of the flesh. Pleasures that, at seventeen, she'd naively believed only got better with marriage.

Well, she'd gotten the gold band and the blessing of the priest. Then she'd found out that passion and pleasure weren't very reliable; not only that, they were no guarantee of happiness. In fact, sometimes there was no happiness involved at all. "Starting tomorrow," she said tartly, "we—you and I—will rely on separate transportation. I like to come and go on my own schedule. Understood?"

Surprised by her sharp tone, André agreed automatically. He didn't know why his teasing had provoked her, but there was no mistaking the rigid set of her shoulders. He doused the car's lights as he coasted to a stop a short distance from the station. His mind whirled with a long list of possible explanations for her odd behavior. One minute, she seemed comfortable with him, joking and even confiding; the next, she was wary and remote. Concentrating on his thoughts, he hadn't noticed how she'd tensed beside him—but then he woke up suddenly to what she was saying.

"It's awfully late. Why do you think Alain and Jason are just leaving work?"

"Is that so strange?" André asked. "We're coming back."

"Those two *never* put in extra hours," she sputtered. "Jason is a master at figuring out ways to leave early." They watched as the two men climbed into a car parked under a streetlight half a block away.

André stifled a laugh. "What the devil are they wearing? I thought Mardi Gras started *next* week."

Gaby poked an elbow into his ribs. "Shh. Where have you been? Those are leisure suits. It's the latest men's fashion."

"Canary yellow?"

"Listen," Gabrielle said. "Those two could've stolen WEZY's film canister. If we go in and find it sitting on my desk, I'll find a way to convince Margaret to fire them."

André sobered. "They'll inherit Uncle Charles's share of the business one day, Gaby. Why would it be in their interests to sabotage the station? You are *so* distrustful."

"I am not! Tell me why they were sneaking around."

"Were they sneaking? They appeared pretty open to me. Like I said, you might not like Uncle Charles, but that doesn't mean his kids are trying to do in the business."

"Why are you sticking up for them? Alain thinks you should be cut out of Paul's will because...because...you were adopted or something." Gaby clapped a hand over her mouth the second she saw storm clouds gather in André's eyes. Oh, Lord, why hadn't she just kept quiet?

"That's not true," he said coldly. "I haven't heard a word of that ancient rumor since I've returned. Or are *you* the one questioning my right to be here?"

"No. Of course not. Margaret's wanted you in the business forever. If you weren't a Lyon, she'd never say you were. *She* never lies."

"But the rest of the family does? First, you accuse me of stealing the damn film. Now you've decided it's Alain and Jason." He gave an exasperated sigh. "Oh, why am I wasting my breath?"

''All right,'' she said. ''If the film isn't on my desk, I'll eat my words. But *something* happened to it.''

André handed her from the car and trailed her through the dark, silent corridors. ''This is a creepy place at night. Aren't you going to turn on some lights?''

''Electricity costs are up, remember? I know the route by heart.''

''I wish you wouldn't work here alone at night,'' he murmured as she unlocked and flung open their office door. The room looked exactly as they'd left it at five-thirty. No canister in sight.

Gaby was confused. And annoyed. Especially when André pressed his body against her back and growled in her ear, ''Will madam have those words medium or well-done?''

CHAPTER EIGHT

GABRIELLE AND ANDRÉ fell into an uneasy truce over the next two weeks. She left for the office before sunup; he took his morning coffee with Rachel and Leslie. At times Paul and Margaret joined him. Unless absence was unavoidable, everyone showed up for dinner. André spent more evenings with his father, too. They'd finally begun to establish the bond he'd always wanted.

André put in long, hard hours absorbing the workings of the television industry. He sat through his first board meeting without a hitch. Or so he thought until one night when he happened to hear his father fretting and saying to his mother, "Margie, I'm afraid the employees took offense at your bringing in my son at the top the way you did."

His son? *As if he wasn't Mama's, too.* The odd exchange stuck in André's craw through dinner and after he'd returned to the office. The more he puzzled over it, the less sense it made—unless Paul was the resentful one. Putting himself in his father's shoes, André supposed he might be bitter about a forced retirement. So how bitter *was* Papa? Enough to cause problems between him and Gabrielle?

No. Now Gaby's paranoia was rubbing off. If he wanted to, Papa could simply ask him to leave. Paul Lyon had as much say in WDIX as his wife. More. The sixty-forty split in Grandpa Alexandre's will left the greater share to his firstborn son.

André was so deep in thought he barely heard Gaby talking about the board meeting. "André, are you listening? I said your uncle Charles surprised me today. He didn't fight every proposal and expenditure. Why do you think that is?"

"Perhaps he was more shaken by Papa's heart attack than you give him credit for. You know the old adage about blood telling. Or is that money?"

Gabrielle didn't respond. Instead, she dragged a fat manila folder out of her in-basket. "Um...speaking of money, have you had an opportunity to read the latest résumés personnel sent up? I starred one. A man from Atlanta who has a great background in marketing, communications and advertising."

André joined her at her desk. "David Crowley does look impressive on paper. Do we have an opening?"

"Jason still isn't producing, and I have little time to devote to sales. Attracting new sponsors is our only hope of showing growth revenue for this year."

"So, invite Crowley in for an interview. Include a rep from personnel, and Frank Reeves from marketing. As sales manager, he'll have to work closely with the guy."

"Would you set it up? While the phone's quiet, I think I'll file this mess. Beth usually files, but she's on vacation. No sense letting the paper pile up."

"Sure, but why not request another clerk? You don't have to do everything yourself, Gaby." He took the résumé and headed for his desk while Gabrielle unlocked the filing cabinet. Her gasp had André turning. "Gaby? What's wrong?"

"The missing film canister." She snatched it from the drawer and brandished it. "As if you didn't know! Now I remember. The first day you were here, I unlocked this cabinet to show you the filing system. I haven't opened the drawer since."

He crossed the room in record time. "Look at me, Gabrielle. For the last time, I'm telling you my hands have not touched that damned canister. Have the police dust it for prints if you don't believe me. Are you so positive you didn't knock it in there accidentally?"

She scrambled to recall more about that day. "I punched in the cabinet locks before I took the budget folders to accounting. The film was on my desk. If you swear it wasn't you, then...okay, I believe you. But maybe it was your uncle. He was with you. Did you leave him alone in the office?"

"I don't think so." But André vaguely remembered Alain dropping by to collect his dad. Had he mentioned the film while they were there? He couldn't be sure. "Does my uncle have keys to your file cabinet?"

"No. But I keep an extra key in my desk drawer."

"Which you also lock. I know it's an unsettling mystery. But we've got no evidence and no way to prove we haven't just been careless. One misplaced film canister and one calendar mixup—they're not exactly capital offenses.''

''On the other hand, if Charles or his sons did either of these things to make mischief, it's...it's sabotage bordering on treason.''

''Well, if you really believe they're responsible,'' he said hesitantly, ''keep quiet about finding the film. After I phone Crowley, let's return the canister to WEZY with an apology but without fanfare.''

''What good will that do?''

''People who are trying to cause a stink generally need a reaction. If they don't get it, they give up—or grow bolder.''

''Let's hope it's the former.''

''Someone wants to see us at each other's throats. The important thing, Gabrielle, is for us to stick together. Agreed?''

''Yes, all right. If anything else happens, it doesn't go beyond these walls.''

He nodded. ''By the way, do you have plans for the first Saturday night in March?''

She leafed through her calendar. ''Mardi Gras will be in full swing. I've got Mass on Ash Wednesday. But Saturday there's nothing scheduled. Why?''

He slipped two gilt-edged invitations from his inside pocket and waved them in front of her. ''Want to go with me to the Bacchus ball?''

Gaby snatched them from his hand. She traced the gold-filigree border with one finger, slowly lifting her lashes to stare at him. ''You said you hadn't accepted the Mardi Gras ball invitations from Charles.''

''I didn't. His were for the Comus ball. I just got these today.''

She handed back the invitations, then wet her bottom lip. ''A real ball. Costume? Of course it is. Oh, André, I'd love to go, but I can't possibly find a decent costume at this late date.''

He tucked the cards in his pocket. ''I figured you'd say that, so I did my homework. Talk to Mama. She knows someone who knows someone...''

''Bacchus,'' she whispered again. ''It's huge. We've been trying for weeks to get interviews with all the Hollywood celebrities they've invited to perform. However did you wangle two invitations?''

''I know Moon Landrieu. He's this year's king of Bacchus.''

''The mayor? You know Maurice Landrieu?''

André shrugged. ''Yeah. I attended high school and college with two of his nine kids. Moon was in the state legislature then. He was practically the only parent who sympathized with our civil-rights activities.''

''Is it true he received death threats?''

''Yeah, but that was after I'd joined the merchant marine. Reaction to the movement got really volatile then. Maurice took a brave but unpopular stand. It's all in the public record. I'm sure you know how discriminatory the original krewes were. Some still are. I'd never support any of those.''

''Hmm. Landrieu must think a lot of you to give you two invitations. They're very hard to come by.''

''He sponsored me to the krewe. I thought if I worked on next year's ball committee, it'd help us put together our twenty-fifth-anniversary bash. New krewe members receive a book that lists every local entertainment resource available. I imagine we'll need balloons, food, decorations and the like.''

''What a great idea, André. I'd have never thought of something like that.''

''So you'll go?''

''You mean I forgot to say yes—and thank you? I thought the way I drooled all over the engraving sort of indicated my acceptance.''

He laughed. ''Then it's settled.'' He whistled on his way to make the phone call to David Crowley.

THE NEXT EVENING, dinner talk among the adults at Lyoncrest revolved around the ball and possible costumes.

''You lucky guys,'' Rachel sighed. ''Someday I'm going to go to one of the balls.''

''Can me and Rachel go to Mardi Gras?'' Leslie piped up.

''No, sweetie.'' Gabrielle tucked a curl behind her daughter's ear. ''People drink too much and some get awfully wild prancing through the streets in masks.''

Leslie pouted. ''Don't want you to wear no mask. Masks are

scary. Raymond said people in masks make voodoo and you die.''

Margaret nearly knocked over her water glass. ''Really, Paul, you must have another talk with Charles. Never mind, I will. Ray seems to delight in scaring the younger children.''

Leslie's pout began to tremble. ''In church on Sunday, Ray said his big brothers are gonna make a voodoo doll of my mommy. He said Alain and Jason are gonna stick pins in the doll and Mama'll get sick and quit work. She might even *die*.''

Forcing herself to sound calm, Gabrielle assured Leslie that she was just fine.

Margaret and Paul both gasped in shock.

André reached across the table and took Leslie's hand. ''Next time Raymond starts saying things like that, just walk away. He's lying to scare you, Les. Voodoo can't hurt your mom. It's fake. Do you understand?''

Eyes teary and wide, the little girl nodded.

''Good. Finish your shrimp étouffée,'' he encouraged her, pushing her plate closer.

''That Raymond is a jerk,'' Rachel declared, setting down her fork and reaching over to straighten Leslie's hair ribbon. ''If he bothers you again, come find me. I learned a thing or two in the bayou that'll frost his ears.''

André didn't doubt it for a minute. He was tempted to let Rachel handle Ray the way troublemakers were handled in Bayou Sans Fin. Then he thought better of it. ''Uh, Rach, I appreciate your willingness to stand up for Leslie. But some things are better left in the bayou.''

Rachel's black eyes narrowed. ''I s'pose. Can I at least tell him if he doesn't lay off Les that *I'll* do some voodoo on him? Turn him into a toad?''

Gabrielle patted her lips with her napkin to hide a smile. Her daughter had a great champion in the spunky Rachel. Gaby's twinkling eyes sought André's as she waited for his reply.

Leslie giggled happily, obviously picturing her nemesis as a fat toad.

''A toad?'' André cleared his throat. He glanced at Gabrielle and his parents, who all shielded grins. ''Oh, yes, I'd say a toad with warts might be in order for Raymond.'' With that, a disturbing conversation ended in levity.

Throughout the rest of dinner, however, André pondered Leslie's innocent announcement. Had Ray Lyon overheard his older brothers plotting treachery? André's experience with kids was limited. Conceivably a boy of Ray's age, fourteen, might just dream up such a tale to make himself sound important. Then again...

André wished Gabrielle wasn't so adamant about preserving her independence. After dinner he'd bring up the idea of their driving to the station together. Maybe they could start again tomorrow. He intended to talk to his uncle, too. About Ray and other problems, too. Various employees had indicated that Alain seemed to think there was a nasty family secret that, if exposed, would drastically alter the stock split in old Alexandre's will. Frankly, André doubted it. Enough of this, after twenty-five years!

LuAnn hadn't even collected the dishes or served dessert when Gaby took off with Margaret to visit a costumer in the Quarter.

"Excuse me, son." Paul pushed out of his chair. "I'll skip dessert. I want to see my competitor's editorial on TV. Bring your coffee and join me in my office."

"I promised Rachel some help with math," André said.

"All right. Then come in later for a chat. I'd like some information on this Dave Crowley you and Gaby have decided to bring on board."

André nodded as he cleared a spot on the dining-room table for Rachel's books. When they finished, Leslie cajoled him into reading two stories. The women still hadn't returned by the time he and his father had finished their discussion about Crowley. Paul agreed with hiring the man and said he'd let Charles know.

Shortly afterward, Paul decided on an early night. André entertained the idea of going back to the office without Gabrielle. But a check of his pocket calendar showed that in the morning they were both scheduled to attend a six-o'clock marketing-strategies meeting. They'd combine it with breakfast at Brennan's on Royal, because Gaby said it was a more relaxed way of introducing the new man to the sales staff.

"I don't know why that woman can't set meetings at a civilized time like noon," he grumbled, electing to call it a night, after all. He'd catch Gaby in the morning and talk to her again about car pooling.

Before retiring, André phoned his uncle. Charles laughed off his suggestion that Ray was attempting to scare the younger kids. "You know how boys are, André."

As for André's other question about Alain's charge, Charles bluntly told him to ask his mother what secret she was hiding. André terminated the call, feeling shaken.

So what *was* the truth? Was he a Lyon or not? Of course he was! He wouldn't cast aspersions on his mother by even bringing up such a question.

THOUGH ANDRÉ HAD SET his morning alarm for five, he still missed Gaby. How could he not have heard her leave her room to go downstairs? "Dammit, the woman comes and goes like smoke," he muttered, tossing his jacket, briefcase and tie into the backseat of his sports car. Then he gunned the engine and peeled off for Brennan's.

Other than introducing Dave Crowley to the marketing staff, André didn't know what exactly was on the morning agenda. That was something he and Gabrielle could have discussed if they'd driven to work together.

In spite of the early-morning humidity, André dutifully knotted his tie before he entered the restaurant. He glanced up and down the tree-lined street, but didn't see Gabrielle's car. Perhaps she'd detoured by the office for some reason.

In the private banquet room, Frank Reeves, the general sales manager, had already taken a seat. Dave Crowley sat beside him. André shook hands with both men and nodded a greeting to the three women who worked in advertising sales. All assessed the newcomer. Pete Terry, the sales coordinator, arrived and looked at the new face with interest. Jason Lyon had yet to appear. And Gabrielle.

André pulled out his pocket calendar to recheck the time. There it was, 6 a.m., in Gabrielle's neat penmanship. "Let's order coffee and give the others a few minutes," he told Frank.

Fifteen minutes ticked by. The waiters and those at the table were growing impatient. "Where's Gabrielle?" Frank demanded.

André shrugged. "I'll call home and make sure she didn't go back for something." The answer was no. He didn't bother to try the office, since the switchboard was still closed. Five more minutes had passed when Jason strolled in. His hair looked uncombed and he'd done a bad job of tying his tie. He pulled out the chair directly across from André and slumped into it. "Let's get this show on the road. The brass hounds us to sell more ads," he complained, "then wastes productive hours on stupid meetings so they can tell us what a piss-poor job we're doing." He glanced at his colleagues as if expecting expressions of support—but received none.

André, who hadn't slept well, wanted to slap him off his chair. Instead, he beckoned a waiter. "We'll order." When that was done and Gaby still hadn't shown up, André worried that she might have had car trouble.

"Shall I go ahead and introduce David?" Frank whispered.

"Sure. Proceed as planned," André said, not knowing what else to advise. But that caused a bigger stir than he could have imagined. Jason vaulted from his chair and knocked it over.

"Does my dad know about this railroad job? It's policy that promotions come from within! I see Gaby bailed out on this fiasco," he sneered. "I guess now you see what a sneaky bitch she is...*cousin.*"

André reacted instantly. "Take that back! Charles does know. Papa called him." He had one hand curled in Jason's shirtfront and the other drawn back, ready to connect with a row of smirking white teeth, when Frank pulled him off.

Jason thrust out a belligerent chin and adjusted his tie. "Crowley will be history after I have a talk with my old man. You and Gaby are just trying to make me look bad."

Frank Reeves focused on André. "Take the little creep outside and I'll help you wipe up the street with him. Hit him here and you'll headline every local channel by lunch. I'm sure he'd love the publicity."

André gnashed his teeth and sat down. He turned to Crowley who, to his credit, seemed unfazed by the melee. "Gabrielle and I have the authority to hire staff," he said, curtly including Jason in the statement. "Dave, welcome to WDIX." André couldn't suppress an ironic smile, one that the other man returned. "Frank, continue, please. I'm sure Gaby will be here soon."

Jason slouched but linked his hands across his chest in a way that displayed his boredom.

The food arrived. They ate in virtual silence, then Frank discussed sales philosophies for half an hour. Gaby still hadn't shown up by the time he closed his notebook. "That's all I have. You want to add anything, André?"

Jason swaggered to his feet. "Yeah, André, step up here and put *your* neck on the line. Gaby wants you to make an ass of yourself. She'll hand you excuses, but the truth is, she's got her eye on the station manager's job."

André didn't like Jason's attitude—or his leisure suit. Did the kid have a whole damned closet full of those things? This one had pearl snaps down a boxy blue jacket. No wonder he couldn't sell ads in the conservative business sector. They probably thought he was a weirdo.

"David is the new assistant sales manager, and that's all there is to it," André said. "We're expecting great things from him."

During the drive to the station, his worry about Gaby increased. As he turned onto Canal Street, he spotted her car parked in its normal space. Curious. *Had* she tossed him to the wolves?

He stalked through the lobby, barely acknowledging Raylene, who as usual was on the phone. Upstairs, he strode into their shared office.

Gabrielle glanced up.

At the same instant they both exclaimed, "Where have you been?"

"I've been at a damned uncomfortable marketing meeting." André put both hands on his hips. "Nice of you and Papa to clue me in about Lyon's policy of promoting from within. How high will I swing for *this* gaffe, Ms. Villieux?"

Looking puzzled, Gabrielle hauled her engagement calendar out of the drawer. After thumbing it open, she blanched. "I had that meeting written in ink." She traced a finger over the space. "I don't believe this. It's been whited out."

André leaned over. Their noses almost touched. "I'll be damned. So it has." Straightening, he paced in front of her desk. "That couldn't have been what Jason and Alain were up to the night we saw them," he muttered. "We hadn't even discussed hiring David yet. So, who?"

"Still, I should've remembered about today." Obviously distressed, Gaby struck her forehead with the heel of her palm. "Blame it on the late night I spent with Margaret, trying on ball costumes. Otherwise, the meeting wouldn't have slipped my mind. André, I'm so sorry.'' She looked truly stricken. ''What happened?''

''Jason tossed out some nasty barbs about your absence. He tried to create doubt in everyone's mind about our right to lead this outfit.'' André paused as she got slowly to her feet and placed both hands on her desk, leaning forward. ''If you recall, I said someone wants us tearing at each other's throats,'' he finished hoarsely.

Gaby couldn't make sense of André's words. He stood so close she felt as if she'd been set adrift on some strange sea. Her senses seemed heightened and she was physically aware of him in a way she'd never been before. She breathed in the scent of his aftershave, his soap, his sweat—a combination that was potent and masculine. It had been a very long time since she'd let herself slip under the power of a man's scent.

In seconds he was beside her. Almost without volition she moved into his arms, sliding her palms up his chest.

André stifled a groan. For weeks he'd lain hot and naked in his bed at night, torturing himself with waking dreams of how Gabrielle Villieux would taste. He bent his head and touched his lips to hers.

Hearing her breath escape a tiny bleat of pleasure—André brought his hands to her shoulder blades and drew her against him. His teeth nipped a trail down her throat to her sweat-damp collarbone. Then his tongue backtracked, soothing her with cool moisture.

Gabrielle went as limp in his arms as one of Leslie's plush bears. She tried to grasp his lapels. Because her fingers refused to close and because she felt as if her knees had turned to water, she looped her wrists around his neck and leaned into him. She took a moment to breathe deeply, recover her strength. Then, never passive in lovemaking, Gaby tunneled her fingers under the leather thong that held his thick hair. She steadied his head until she managed to capture his lips. It was a tempestuous exploration that went on and on.

Had a car not backfired outside the window, a roll on the floor would have been their next stop. Both recognized that the minute they moved apart. André's tie was askew, his shirt half-open, his belt buckle undone. Gaby's gray suit jacket lay in a heap on the carpet. Her blouse hung loose, and her bra had been unclipped.

She spun away, but not before André read the horror that reshaped her well-kissed mouth.

He ran an unsteady hand through his hair and discovered the thong was missing. He found it curled in her in-basket like a snake. Clearly she considered *him* the snake.

"Gabrielle." He tried to touch her and she shrugged off his hand.

Her voice, not quite steady yet firm with conviction, floated back over one shoulder. "I'll accept half the blame, André," she said, busily righting her clothing.

"That's big of you," he murmured, not wanting to hear the *but* that was sure to follow.

"But," she continued, "we can't let this happen again."

"Why not?" He buttoned his shirt and straightened his tie.

She started stacking papers. "Because a relationship that involves sex takes more energy than I have to give. More than I'm willing to give. In my life Leslie comes first. This job second. In a tie for third are eating and sleeping. Don't take it personally, André. Just call it a failed experiment. We were both curious. We satisfied that curiosity and now we can put sex behind us."

André listened. He heard every precisely spoken word. He thought it commendable that her daughter came first in her life. Leslie was special. Granted, in his view, Gabrielle sometimes had trouble keeping those priorities in order. Not necessarily her fault. He knew how this job, this place, could consume you. His own childhood had shown him that.

He liked Leslie. A lot. And she liked him. Needed him. So did Gaby. It stunned André to realize he needed them even more. As far as the rest of her statement was concerned... Nonsense. His curiosity *wasn't* satisfied. This interlude had only whetted his interest. Gaby could pretend if she wished, but he knew that his interest was reciprocated. He wouldn't tell her that sex most definitely wasn't behind them.

But he'd let her figure that out for herself.

CHAPTER NINE

IT SUITED ANDRÉ to let Gabrielle think he agreed that their relationship should be business only. She had a valid reason to be wary of anything else. While he'd never shied away from women, no alliance he'd made had ever been long term. He'd never wanted it—until now. Of all the women he'd dated, only Gabrielle made his head spin. No other woman had him thinking about forever after.

A lifetime with her. To love and be loved. That was what he wanted. He could wait for her to reach the same conclusion, he decided.

Or maybe not. By the end of the day, André ached to hold her, to touch her, ached so badly that even a lifetime together didn't sound long enough.

Several times he caught Gabrielle watching him with hunger in her eyes. If they didn't come up with a way to alleviate the sexual tension clawing at them, André doubted he'd learn anything more about the business. Nor would the plans for the twenty-fifth-anniversary celebration get off the ground.

Yet he muddled through, day by day.

By the end of the next week, André decided that if he left it up to Gaby they'd reside in a permanent state of lust. And not only lust but something he recognized as even more basic. Emotional need.

It was time for a more aggressive approach.

At dinner Friday night, facing a weekend rattling around under the same roof with her, André hit on a solution. "The weather's great. What do you say to playing hooky from work tomorrow, Gabrielle? Let's take Rachel and Leslie to the Audubon Zoo."

Gaby froze. It was on the tip of her tongue to refuse—until she saw the kids' faces. Hope mingled with resignation, as though they'd been disappointed far too often. She shrugged. "If I can work until noon. Perhaps LuAnn will pack us a lunch. I've heard there are picnic tables near a waterfall in the park." She realized she'd just admitted she'd never been there herself—no doubt confirming her workaholic reputation with everyone at the table.

Still, any reservations Gaby had about taking time off died when she saw how unbelievably excited Leslie had become. She and Rachel could talk of nothing else.

André savored his small victory. He entertained the girls throughout the meal with stories of various zoos and wildlife parks he'd visited in his travels.

"Mama, can Scott go with us?" Leslie pleaded.

Gaby deferred to André.

"Sure. If Uncle Charles and Aunt Catherine will let him," André said. "My uncle's been bent out of shape since I told him off for not telling Jason we'd hired Crowley," he said in an aside.

"That shouldn't involve Scottie. I'll phone Charles myself," Paul offered.

NEXT DAY AT TWELVE-FIFTEEN, André circled by Charles's home to collect Scott. He parked in the shade of a giant live oak outside the faded Benoît mansion. The boy ran down the steps and squeezed into the backseat with Leslie and Rachel. They chattered like good friends all the way to the park. Gaby smiled a lot, but said little.

They ate near a beautiful lagoon, then spent hours trekking around the subtropical park. The sun had nearly set by the time they came out of the white-alligator exhibit. Rachel said sleepily, "I'm pooped, but I had a great day."

"Me, too." Leslie sighed.

"We missed one whole section." Scott pointed at the map.

Gaby rumpled his hair. "We'll save that for our next visit." She aimed him toward the car. André fell into step with her and helped himself to her hand. Oddly she didn't shake him loose and even let him take her hand again when they'd dropped Scott off.

"Scott's a good kid," André murmured to Gaby later as he

carried a sleeping Leslie from the car and deposited her on her bed.

Rachel yawned her good-night in passing the room. She blew them a kiss.

André waited until Rachel shut her door before he whispered to Gabrielle, "Rach is losing her haunted look. She really loves Leslie...and you."

Gabrielle smiled as she washed Leslie's face and hands. André stripped off the girl's sweaty sandals. "Like I told you before, you're a natural with kids," she murmured. "Sure you weren't a nanny in your old life, instead of a dockhand?"

"Dockhands are versatile." In hushed tones he told her about once saving a crateful of monkeys in Morocco. The crate had broken open on the docks. "They were a rare breed, headed for the San Diego Zoo. You should have seen me chasing those little buggers through the streets. I had to pay a fruit vendor for the bananas they stole. But I corralled them all."

Her laughing eyes reflected the moonlight streaming through the window. Laughter made her look almost as young as Leslie. André couldn't help himself. He stole a kiss. Gaby ducked away when he would have deepened it.

He didn't think she put a lot of effort into avoiding him, though. And because he didn't want the day to end, he talked her into raiding the refrigerator with him—despite LuAnn's likely objections. Over cold turkey sandwiches and iced blackberry tea, André thought he detected a softening in Gaby's feelings toward him. Yet the night ended before he could work up the courage to point out that Rachel wasn't the only one who loved her....

In the ensuing days André couldn't seem to find a moment alone with her. Work the next week was chaotic. Mardi Gras made for exciting television news. Everyone on staff was in a perpetual party mood. Maybe the biggest shock—Jason brought in his first advertising account. He more or less admitted to André that he liked working for Dave Crowley.

That was all Gaby wanted to talk about as she and André drove to the Bacchus ball. "André, I know the tide has turned. Profits almost doubled last month's. You and I are functioning as a team. Even Jason's come around some. Plus, no one's messed with our calendars lately or pulled any nasty tricks. Life is good.'' She sighed contentedly.

''Better than good. It'd be near perfect,'' he teased, ''if you didn't have that white goo on your face tonight.'' His fingers itched to take the pins out of her hair, too. She'd coiled her hair on either side of her head and pinned it with flowers and beads.

''It was your mother's idea that I go as a geisha.'' Gaby moved slowly amid all her satin trappings. ''You make a dashing D'Artagnan.'' She eyed him over top of her fan. He looked...incredible. Since the moment he'd appeared at the top of the stairs dressed like one of Alexandre Dumas's three musketeers, her stomach had been one mass of flutters. Dammit!

The ballroom was crowded. Dress ranged from ridiculous outfits to costumes that looked as if they were practically museum pieces. The king and queen of the ball, as well as the invited dignitaries, were dressed in formal wear. White tie and tails for men, and one-of-a-kind floor-length gowns for women.

''Elegant. Exciting.'' Gaby kissed her fingertips. ''This is what I have in mind for Lyons' twenty-fifth,'' she whispered. ''But without the costumes. Black invitations, engraved in gold. I want it so exclusive potential advertisers will beg for an invitation. They'll beat a path to our door.''

André studied the tips of his polished boots. ''All you ever talk about is work. There's more to life, you know, Gabrielle.''

''We're finally climbing out of a slump. The staff's happier and Paul's looking better—''

''You think so?'' André interrupted her monologue. ''You know...a while back, I gave some fleeting thought to the idea that he might be behind those stunts.'' André wasn't sure why he'd confessed this. He supposed it was because he had an impulse—constant and irresistible—to share everything with her. *All* his feelings.

''Honestly, André, you wouldn't even consider your uncle and cousins! Why on earth would you suspect your own papa?'' Gaby fanned herself furiously.

''You didn't let me finish.'' He folded her fan and swung her out onto the crowded dance floor. He moved his sword so that he could hold her tightly and shortened his stride to accommodate her abbreviated steps in the long, narrow skirt. ''I overhead him tell Mama after the board meeting that maybe some staff resented

her bringing me in at the top. But I know now that he wasn'
involved. He called me into his study last week and praised ou
performance. Hey, we've talked about work and family lon
enough. This is your first ball. I want it to be special.''

''It *is* special. I feel like Cinderella, even if I'm not dresse
like her.'' Gabrielle sighed into his open-necked shirtfront. Sh
loved feeling the play of his muscles beneath the fabric. His hai
was loose tonight, curled into his collar in the manner of a mus
keteer. Thick and clean and soft. The butterflies in her stomac
spread.

Gaby couldn't dance in her *zoris*. It didn't take long for he
to wear holes in her tabisocks. Near midnight, seeing her toe
peeking out, André suggested they leave. The ball would likel
go on till dawn, but he had other things in mind to make Ga
brielle's first Mardi Gras experience memorable.

She read the promise in his eyes. A little drunk on the passio
of the night and warmed by the fires of need stoked by his hand
as they roamed over her hips and back, Gaby wanted everythin
André's eyes were offering.

At home it took little coaxing to entice her into his room. He
own was between Leslie's and Rachel's. His allowed the privac
they both wanted. Solemnly they removed each other's costumes
André gently scrubbed her face clean of paint. ''I want you s
much, Gabrielle,'' he whispered. ''But it's your choice.''

''I'm here, aren't I?'' Rising on tiptoe, she wrapped her arm
around him and backed him to the bed.

THE STARS WERE WINKING OUT when Gabrielle roused hersel
enough to untangle her limbs from André's. She trailed her fin
gers over his long, muscular back, stopping short of the line tha
separated his tan from the lighter flesh hidden from all but
lover's eyes. ''Are you awake?'' she asked softly.

''I may be dead,'' he groaned, ''but I died a happy man.'' H
flopped onto his back, lifted himself onto one elbow and nibble
at her lips.

She moved into his kiss. Heat rose instantly between them an
would have led to another romp across the wide bed, but Gab
pulled back reluctantly. ''I have to go, André. Leslie often wake

up toward morning. She's always had nightmares. She wanders in to crawl into bed with me. I've never not been there for her."

He wanted to protest. Instead, he kissed her hard one last time, then sat up and turned on a lamp. Unself-consciously, he helped gather her underwear, which lay strewn across the floor. "I had nightmares when I was little. Mama slept soundly. She and Grandmère both locked their doors. I sometimes went downstairs and woke up Uncle Charles. We'd go into the library and he'd play the piano until I fell asleep."

"You truly know a different Charles." Gaby paused, her hand on the doorknob.

André, who'd followed her, gathered her in his arms and kissed her again. Drawing back, he let his chin rest on top of her head. "I do. There've been some family conflicts, though. Life around here and at the station would be a lot nicer if they'd forget the uneven split in Grandpère Alexandre's will. I won't hold my breath, though. Did you see the woman plastered to Alain at the ball tonight?" When Gaby shook her head, he muttered, "It wasn't his wife. They left together, too."

"I didn't see them. Why didn't you say something? Who was she?"

"I don't know and I don't care. Alain has to deal with his own conscience. Obviously he didn't expect to see us tonight." André framed Gabrielle's heart-shaped face with his hands. "All we can do is live our lives differently. Live them right. I'd like to share my life with you and Leslie, Gabrielle. Between us, we'd provide a better example for the next generation. If...you'll marry me." He stroked his thumbs over her cheeks.

"M-marry you?" Gaby stumbled backward. Clutching her costume, she again fumbled with the door. "Do you have any idea how many Mardi Gras marriages there are—and how many fail? I, uh, your head will be clearer in the morning, André." She managed at last to open the door. Slipping through his hands, she fled across the landing to the safe haven of her room without looking back.

For the remainder of the night, until the sun rose, Gabrielle tried to imagine herself married to André Lyon. Her first marriage had been such a disaster she'd sworn never to be so foolish again. Yet André was nothing like Marc Villieux. André's lovemaking, while thorough, made her feel cherished, not dirty or frightened. But Marc hadn't shown his dark side at first, either.

She bunched her pillow and hid her face. If only there was someone she could talk to about these roller-coaster feelings. Margaret was the most obvious. Except she had her hands full caring for Paul. And how could Gaby talk honestly to Margaret about her son, the son she adored.

Nor did Gabrielle trust her own judgment. She'd gone awfully quickly from wishing André Lyon in hell to accepting him into her bed. Well, his bed. It was all too confusing. Too risky. Tomorrow she'd tell him she'd made a mistake.

AND SHE DID. At work, with people milling around so he couldn't argue with her. André didn't like her decision. Outwardly, he accepted it like a gentleman.

For the moment.

By midday, he'd concluded that the best way to court this woman who insisted she didn't want to be courted was to make himself indispensable. Not just to her, but to Leslie. And there was no time like the present.

AFTER MARDI GRAS wound down, throughout March and April and into the hot, steamy days of early May, André planned weekend jaunts with the precision of a military tactician. To the Children's Museum and the Children's Theater. He included Rachel and Scott, and went out of his way to see that everyone had fun, often stretching the excursions into dinners out.

"André, you have to stop spending all your money on us," Gabrielle scolded quietly one night, long after the girls were in bed. It was the first pillow-talk session André had managed to lure her into since the night of the Bacchus ball. "I told myself I wasn't going to have sex with you again, and here I am. You cast powerful spells, André Lyon." She stared at him with troubled eyes. "I'm just weak where you're concerned."

He lightly scraped his thumbs over the tips of her breasts, and indulged in a deep kiss before he pulled her head down on his shoulder. "What more can I do, Gabrielle, to make you understand that I want to be partners with you in every way? At home and at work and everywhere in between. It's about more than sex."

She snuggled her cheek against his chest. His heartbeat was strong and steady beneath her ear. "I can't explain it, André. When we're together I feel as if I've tripped and fallen into a dreamworld. But I sense that something lurks in the shadows nearby, waiting to snatch our happiness away."

"Like what, honey? Tell me. I'll slay all the big bad wolves."

She smiled and kissed his flat, brown nipple. "Isn't that dragons, sir knight? I know I probably sound silly." She sat up and gathered her long hair to one side. "At work, don't you feel as if everyone's watching us? Watching and waiting for us to disagree. Like they're anticipating an irreparable split in the power base?"

"I did believe that. Now I'm less sure." He shrugged. "Well, possibly Alain. Jason's backed off. He's actually been civil lately."

"But they say things. Well, Alain does."

"What kind of things?" André nuzzled kisses from her bare shoulder to her neck. He stopped, letting his mouth curve into the hollow he'd found beneath her hair.

"When…when you kiss me like that, I can't think of a thing. But…in meetings, Alain's forever insinuating that what you wrote in a memo is the opposite of what I'm telling them. Then the staff's totally confused."

André rolled on top of her. He propped his weight on his elbows for a moment before he settled into the warm cleft forged by her hips. "We can solve that problem by putting both our names on every memo that leaves our office. Or better yet," he growled, running a hand between their bodies to test her readiness. "All our problems would be solved if both our names were Lyon."

Her breath hitched, caught and then was rapidly expelled as he lowered his head and drew circles on her breast with his tongue.

"You don't play fair, André," she said unsteadily, rubbing her toes over his ankle.

Suddenly he plunged into her, let her adjust, then slowly withdrew. After several times, Gabrielle felt boneless and she wrapped her legs around his muscled thighs in an attempt to hold him still. Everything he said was true. She wanted to agree.

More so after they lay spent and sated, and he begged her, between kisses, to let him put a ring on her finger. ''I want our families and the staff to know we're committed, Gabrielle. One hundred percent,'' he breathed in her ear.

She gazed into his earnest eyes for the longest time. In the end she rolled over and slid off his bed, quickly slipping into her shorts and tank top. ''Paul and Margaret approved our plans for the twenty-fifth gala, André. I don't think we should let *anything* get in its way. The business is finally beginning to show a steady climb. Why rock the boat?''

''Rock it how? I love you, Gabrielle. I want you in my bed every night. I hate it when you get dressed and sneak out as if we're doing something illicit.''

''You say that so easily.'' Tears gathered in her eyes. ''Well, I want Lyon Broadcasting to be the most successful television station in Louisiana again. I want your mother to be proud of me. I want her to know she didn't put her money on a bad horse when she invested in me—in my future.''

Gabrielle kept her voice low, but to André it seemed as if she was shouting. ''Look at me.'' She gestured with both hands. ''I'm proving the opposite.'' Her hiccuping laugh bordered on hysteria. ''Do you hear yourself, André? Our leaping in and out of bed *is* illicit. We aren't married, and we do sneak around right under your mother's nose.''

''Gabrielle, stop it. No one knows except us.''

She held up her hand as he started to climb off the bed. ''You're wrong,'' she said bitterly. ''Today, Alain suggested to a room filled with staff that I'm spending so much time sniffing at your heels I'm shirking my duties at the station. Please, André. You've got to allow me time to get my priorities straight again.''

He would have objected, dragged out every argument he had at his fingertips, if she hadn't looked so vulnerable—so on the verge of falling apart. Raking his hands through his hair, he reached for his pants. ''You do what you have to do, Gabrielle. I won't stop loving you this month or next. Whether Lyon Broadcasting reaches the heavens or sinks into the pits of hell. But this is the last time you'll hear me say so until you tell me the feeling is mutual.'' He shoved his legs into his pants and stood.

"André, please forgive me." Gabrielle hovered half in, half out of his room. She bit her lip and squared her shoulders as he went to stand at the window. He pressed both palms hard against the wood casing and breathed in the sultry night air. The curve of his back remained a bulwark of tense muscles.

Leaving him, with anger hanging between them like this, wasn't what Gaby wanted. But it was how things had to be.

Covering her mouth to hide a sob, she crept out and softly shut his door. She felt as if she was drowning in her sorrow.

CHAPTER TEN

DURING THE NEXT TWO MONTHS, André felt lucky if he even caught a glimpse of Gabrielle. She'd resumed her habit of going to work before daylight. She'd moved her desk into a small spare office and taped notes on his door apprising him of meetings she'd set up with clients. His evenings were tied up with Bacchus krewe meetings for next year's Mardi Gras ball. He spent his days tallying the sales figures. Gaby brought in phenomenal numbers of new advertisers; WDIX-TV had again become her obsession. She refused to talk about how she was losing weight and looking pale and drawn. Her answer was to work on ideas for the gala late into the night.

Fortunately André had learned enough to take over all the inside office work. "She's tied up with the gala," he relayed over and over to family when Gaby missed family dinners. He felt at least partially to blame for her absence. André was well aware that one reason for her work frenzy was her desire to avoid seeing him.

Because she also spent weekends at the office, and because the kids were out of school for the summer, André continued their outings. Gaby might be avoiding *him,* but that was no reason they should suffer.

"Mommy's busy a lot," Leslie complained one June afternoon when André detoured past a new frozen-yogurt shop in the French Quarter. He would have replied offhandedly but noticed Rachel eyeing him with an anxiousness he hadn't observed in months.

"You kids have heard us talk about the twenty-fifth celebration. Leslie, your mom's in charge. It's coming up soon—the beginning of next month. She's overseeing invitations, decorations, entertainment and...well, everything to do with it. It's an important event."

"My dad says the gala is a big fat waste of money." Scott cast André a worried glance, even though he continued to stuff chocolate yogurt into his mouth.

André searched for a suitable reply. "It's the birthday of Lyon Broadcasting. Gabrielle and I don't think celebrating birthdays is wasteful. Neither do my parents."

Leslie nudged Scott with an elbow. "I like birthdays, too."

Rachel caught a drip of raspberry sorbet with her tongue. "Is that birthday thing *really* why Gaby's always gone? You're not mad at her or somethin'?" Her voice quavered.

André gave a moment's thought to his response. "Look at me, Rachel." When she did, he said, "As Scott told us, not everyone who's in the business is jumping for joy about this celebration. Gaby wants very much to please everybody. Let's try to make things at home go smoothly for her."

"Okay. But I'll be glad when this thing's over," Rachel said. "She never has time for us anymore."

André pushed his sherbet aside. What excuse would he give for Gaby's indifference *after* the anniversary bash?

JUNE SLID INTO JULY. Tuesday, the week of the Saturday gala, André bumped into Gabrielle as he crossed the lobby, headed for a budget meeting with technical staff. She, apparently, had been up in her office and was on her way out again.

"Whoa. Steady as she goes, mate." André grasped her arm for the pleasure of touching her. She wore black and white, a stark complement to her hair and skin tones. Hammered silver disks winked at her ears. A matching bracelet circled the slender arm André gripped. A new perfume flirted past his nostrils, kindling visions of steamy nights and cool sheets.

"We're not mates." She pursed her lips ever so briefly. "However, we do pass like ships sailing in and out of port," she admitted.

He slid his hand to her wrist and rubbed a thumb along the inside. It gave him immense satisfaction, feeling her blood surge. "I'm anchored, Gabrielle. And ready to mate anytime you are." He needed all his willpower to keep from dragging her into the alcove off the reception area and telling her again how much he loved her.

She went limp a moment, then jerked loose. "Stop it, André." Her voice was breathless.

"Yes, ma'am." He knew he appeared anything but contrite.

Refusing to look at him, she dug through her briefcase and produced a pocket calendar. "We really should meet. Did you read the list of objections to the gala that Alain presented—supposedly from Charles? As a principal in the company, he's demanding an itemized account of monies spent to date. I have the figures. No time to compile them, though." She sighed. "Can you see me at two o'clock today?"

"I'm tied up today with technical staff, and tomorrow with the art department. Thursday? I could meet for breakfast." André leafed through his own planner.

She shook her head. "No, but I'll run back to the office between appointments. At three? My office or yours?" Gabrielle shifted to let someone pass. She donned a duty smile until she saw it was Alain. Her smile turned into a grimace.

"Making time for an afternoon quickie?" he murmured, elbowing them aside.

André would have grabbed his cousin around and demanded an apology, but Gaby's frown and a warning shake of her head stopped him. "Three. Thursday. Got it," he murmured. "Your office is fine." He didn't think he could work in his if she left a lingering trace of that perfume.

AS IT TURNED OUT, on Thursday André's afternoon meeting with the other New Orleans station managers ran late. It was twenty past three when he raced across the lobby and down the corridor; he took the stairs two at a time, fearing he'd miss Gaby. He heaved a sigh as her office doorknob turned easily under his hand. At least she hadn't taken off again.

He walked in to what looked like a room that'd been the target of a burglary. "What happened?" he asked Gabrielle, who sat amidst a sea of paper.

She sagged wearily. "I must have forgotten to lock the door when I left last night. Someone came in and broke the lock on one of my file cabinets. I found these three drawers dumped."

''What's missing?''

''I don't know.'' She put a hand to her forehead. ''I'd barely walked in and found this mess when you showed up. Most of these folders contain old production costs, expansion fees, rate increases and the like.''

''Nothing current?''

She pawed through the stack. ''Margaret and Paul both had some personal files stored in the bottom drawer. Mostly to do with opening the station, I believe. I know you weren't here last night, so you couldn't have seen anyone hanging around.'' She paused. ''LuAnn said you sat up with Leslie and let me sleep. I owe you. She seems to be catching the flu, and she's so fretful. I'd been up three nights in a row.'' She closed her eyes and rubbed her temples.

''You were beat. I heard her coughing. And you don't owe me. I care about Leslie—and you.''

''Yes. Thank you, André.'' She didn't react to his declaration. ''Who did this, do you suppose? I thought we were finished with these senseless attacks.'' She cradled her head in both hands, feeling her nerves buckle.

''Does any of this stuff pertain to the gala costs?''

A soft gasp cleared Gaby's lips. ''Oh, you think Alain heard us making plans to meet and tally the figures? That he tried to steal them first?''

''You're putting words in my mouth, Gabrielle. But, yes, it crossed my mind.''

She looked relieved. ''Then I'd say he must be disappointed. I have that folder in my briefcase. I took it home last night to put it in some kind of order, then didn't touch it.''

''What's wrong with your car?'' André asked, changing the subject abruptly. ''I saw you'd left it in the garage this morning.''

''Dead battery.'' She wrinkled her nose. ''I left the lights on all night. Paul lent me his prize Caddy. Thing drives like a tank and doesn't corner worth spit. Which reminds me, I have to dash out to meet a guy who wants to advertise a new wonder cleanser. And afterward, I've got a dinner meeting with the sales group. We'll have to cancel our session, after all.'' She stood, sighing as she studied the mess. ''I'll come in later and clean up.''

''What time? I'll meet you here and help.''

"No need, André. You won't know which papers go in what folder."

"I don't want you here alone, Gabrielle." His tone held finality.

"I promise to arrive by nine and leave before the station signs off at midnight."

"And if you're running late as usual? Don't argue, Gaby. I'll be here. Now give me the key."

"All right. I may be closer to ten." She stifled a yawn. "I won't object if you come early and put the empty folders in alphabetical order."

"Done. In the interim I'll go have a chat with Alain."

He did, but he might as well have saved his breath. His cousin not only denied everything, but Charles walked in during their argument—in time to hear André say, "I'll fire your butt if I ever find one scrap of evidence that you raided those files."

"I'd watch the threats," Alain said coldly. "One of these days *I'll* be finding evidence...and I'll expose Uncle Paul and Aunt Margaret's dirty little secret, *cou—sin.* Then we'll see who's calling the shots around here."

Charles rounded on André. "You owe my son an apology. He's right. There's no need for you to get so cocky. The truth of Margaret's indiscretions will come out."

"Go to hell!" André stormed out of Alain's office and out of the building. His one regret was that half the staff working on the second floor had heard their argument. He rushed past various offices, ignoring the strained silence. Rumors of a split in the family would run rampant by morning. *Damn.* He didn't dare bring this up around his father. Papa had looked unwell for several weeks now.

He knew that his mother was scrupulously truthful, and she'd assured him that Paul was his father. So, what nasty lies were Charles and Alain spreading—and why, exactly? *Was* there any basis in fact? Had Margaret and Paul committed some indiscretion in the past?

After dinner, before André left for the station, he mentioned the bitter exchange to his mother. He was careful to speak out of range of his father.

Margaret walked André to his car. She listened, looking stoic as always—even when André demanded, "*Do* we have something to hide, Mama?"

She shook her head. "Charles continues to refute your grandfather's will. It's pointless. WDIX-TV will be strong many years after your papa and I are gone. Your sons and their sons will carry the Voice of Dixie into the future, André. That's my dream and your destiny."

"My sons, Mama?" André snorted.

"Rachel intimated that you and Gabrielle—"

"The kid's a dreamer. But," he said, diving into his car, "it won't be for my lack of trying. Keep that to yourself, though, okay?"

Glancing over at Margaret in the light of the carriage lamp, he saw her smile. He smiled back as he rumbled off with his windows rolled down. Then he felt foolish for talking out of turn.

As he'd predicted, André beat Gaby to the office. He had all the folders in order and had almost given up on her appearing at all, when at ten-twenty, she walked in.

"Sorry. I was late for my sales meeting, since the cleanser guy was such a windbag. I mean, what is there to say about a cleanser?"

André laughed. "Did you get some dinner at least?"

"Are you kidding? I called Frank and told them to go ahead and eat before I got there."

"Shall I run out and get you a sandwich?"

Gaby stripped off her suit jacket and rolled up the sleeves of her blouse. "Why don't we get this done, then swing by that new bistro that's opened on St. Peter Street? You know the one I mean? I sold them an ad. They're supposed to have great food—and it's good policy to support our clients." She paused. "I checked with Claire. Leslie is loads better tonight."

"I overindulged at dinner." He patted a flat stomach. "Depending on how long this takes, though, I might be talked into coffee and dessert."

"I hear that the chef there makes *choux à la crème* and millefeuilles to die for." Gaby smacked her lips.

"Cream puffs and napoleons? Just once, I'd like to see you gain an ounce."

Gaby blushed. "So, uh...where to begin?" She bent and picked up a pile André had already straightened.

A few minutes before midnight, Gaby glanced at the wall clock. "We're almost finished. No time to eat, I guess." She and André were seated side by side filling the last folders when the telephone shrilled. They both grabbed for it, but Gaby was faster. She covered the mouthpiece. "I hate calls this late. I hope Leslie's all right."

A tinny voice wafted across the wire. "Gab...beee? Here's a news flash for WDIX. There's a bomb in the building set to blow at 2 a.m. If you tip off your reporters before you call the cops, imagine the scoop. BOOM!"

"What? A bomb in the building? Who is this?" Gaby's eyes were huge. Her hand shook. She almost dropped the receiver as a loud click followed a vacuous laugh.

"A bomb?" Sweat beaded André's brow.

Gaby quickly relayed what the voice had said. She stood, grabbed her purse and headed for the door. "Hurry up! Let's get out of here."

André methodically eased out several of her desk drawers. "We have two hours. Grab the most important files and clear out. Drive to a pay phone and call the police. That phone call might have triggered the device. I'll stay and search until a bomb squad arrives."

"Are you crazy? I'm not going without you!"

His eyes bored through her. "Think of Leslie." He finished searching the desk, walked over and started on the file cabinets.

She roused herself. "André, I just saw my entire life flash by in ten seconds. Not all of it is pretty. But I'm no coward. If you stay, I stay."

He whirled. "Whoever's responsible has crossed a line here, Gabrielle. Eliminate both of us, and they virtually destroy Lyon Broadcasting."

"You think a competitor is behind this?"

"Could be." He joined her in the center of the room. "You said he called you by name. You might be the one this sick bastard wants to bring down. We won't let him. So go. Now!"

"No. Because—" she stared at him, eyes misty "—I...I've been lying to myself and to you, André. I love you. I can't—won't go to my grave a liar."

André's body snapped back with a jerk. He let go of her arms and drove his fingers into her hair, loosening strands from the clasp. ''You might have picked a more opportune time to tell me,'' he said with a crooked smile. ''Now, more than ever, we've got to beat this. Go, Gabrielle. Please, sweetheart.''

''There's more to my confession,'' she said fitfully, clutching his shirtfront. ''I'm...I'm...'' Her hands grew damp. ''I've been so tired and draggy these last three months. The doctor...'' She hesitated.

André lost his color and went still. ''Are you sick? Gaby? Something more than the flu that's making the rounds?'' He grasped her wrists.

She stared directly into his eyes. ''I'm pregnant, André.'' She attempted a shrug, but he held her too tightly. ''My fault, because I didn't check the calendar. Typical of my bad luck with relationships,'' she lamented. ''It happened the, um, night of the Bacchus ball, I figure.''

''Bad luck?'' he breathed, running his fingers lightly over her lips, her cheeks, her eyelids. ''I love you, Gabrielle. You love me. We're going to have a baby. A sister or brother for Leslie. This is only a building. It can be rebuilt. We've been given a far greater gift. Come on.'' He tugged at her hands. ''We're leaving together. It's past midnight, so the place will be clear. We'll find a pay phone.''

She tucked her head into the crook of his arm as he herded her out the door. ''I parked in the next block. I still have Paul's car,'' she reminded him. ''It's equipped with his reporter's mobile unit. A dinosaur, but it works. I used it to check on Leslie.''

Not wanting her to run, André scooped her into his arms and hurried for the stairs. ''No elevators,'' he said. ''They may be booby-trapped.'' He didn't speak again until they were well away from the dark, empty building.

Things happened fast once they called the police. A bomb unit arrived on the scene in less than ten minutes. André and Gaby sketched hasty maps of all the floors. Then they huddled together and waited while men in asbestos suits entered the lobby. Any minute they expected the building to blow apart and set the skyline ablaze.

In a surprisingly short time the team returned. ''We found it,'' announced the captain. ''At least, we found a device attached to the receptionist's phone. Can you think of anyone who'd want to make you the butt of a hoax? Your so-called bomb is an elaborate dud.

"A phony. It has no guts," the man explained when Gaby and André both regarded him blankly.

"Lyon Broadcasting is family-owned," André said, pinning Gaby to his side. "We've undergone some...internal discord. Headline-breaking news is only part of what a TV station's about. It also has to do with attracting and keeping advertisers. The station's twenty-fifth-anniversary celebration is Saturday. Ad clients would jump ship in droves if news of a bomb threat leaked out. And once it was proved a hoax, we'd be a laughingstock in the industry. This is asking a lot, Captain, but can we keep it quiet, at least until next week?"

"It's unusual." He turned to his crew. "I'll do my best," he said after they all shrugged. "Of course, there's nothing I can do if one of your staff is behind the hoax."

"Oh," André said with a grin, "I plan to leak some news that'll give them a little more to worry about. The heir to the controlling interest in Lyon Broadcasting is going to elope—if the lady is willing."

Gaby let out her breath as André dropped a kiss on her nose. "Elope? When?" she gasped.

"Right now. Tonight." He tugged on a loose strand of her hair.

"At this hour?"

"I know a priest in Bayou Sans Fin who doesn't run on a regular clock. All you have to do is say yes."

"Yes!"

The police captain and his men slapped André on the back.

"Wait." Gaby stopped the gaiety. "This priest. He's legitimate?"

André gathered her icy hands. "His cathedral is a cypress, but I guarantee the vows we exchange will be binding and sacred. If you don't want to be Mrs. André Lyon from this night until eternity, speak up now."

"I do want, André," she whispered. "It took the fear of losing you to make me see I've never wanted anything more."

His smile, for her alone, promised his love in return. "We'll leave my car here and take Papa's. His mobile phone will come in handy to disperse our news."

''No regrets?'' he asked a few hours later when they left the darkness of Bayou Sans Fin to return to the neon lights of the city.

Gabrielle's smile lit up the interior of the old Cadillac. ''None whatsoever.''

CHAPTER ELEVEN

SURFACING LATER THAN USUAL the next morning, André and Gaby ambled hand in hand down the winding stairs from his suite, where they'd fallen into bed after releasing news of their elopement, first to WDIX, then to competitors. They had yet to tell members of the household.

"What's the shouting coming from Paul's study?" Gabrielle eased away from André, who'd paused on the middle landing after stealing another kiss.

Paul's study door banged open. Alain Lyon backed out, thrusting papers into a brown briefcase. The minute he caught sight of Gabrielle coming down the stairs, he stood still. Glowering, he snagged her arm and spun her around.

"You think your sudden marriage to André solidifies your power at WDIX? Ha! Go ask Uncle Paul if you married a Lyon. He says he knew there's no official parish birth record. Well, I don't accept what's written in the family Bible. My dad swears it's bloody unlikely his brother knew Margaret was pregnant when she went off to college." He waved a paper under Gaby's nose. She didn't look, but tried to loosen his grasp so she could go into the now-silent study.

André plunged down the last two steps and ripped Alain's hands off Gabrielle. "Nobody speaks to my wife that way! And I'm damned sure—"

A loud thud from the study halted their argument. As Gaby was nearer, she ran into the room. Her distressed cry floated into the hall. "Oh, André! Come quick."

Alain jerked out of André's hold. "If Uncle Paul collapsed, you've got no one but your own dear mama to blame. For trying to pass off her bastard as a Lyon for so many years. My dad settled for crumbs from Uncle Paul. Not me. I intend to get what's due me...us."

Margaret, LuAnn and Claire Harris burst out of the kitchen, confused by all the shouting. "André? Alain? Have you two taken leave of your senses?" Margaret pressed a hand to her mouth.

"Get out," André snarled at his cousin. "Before I forget this is Mama's home and not mine. If it *were* mine, I'd spill some of your Lyon blood across the foyer."

Gabrielle, white-faced, a phone to her ear, appeared in the study doorway. She motioned frantically to Margaret and André. "Paul. I think it's his heart. I've called for an ambulance."

As Alain departed in haste, they heard sirens closing in.

In a surprisingly short time the ambulance crew swarmed around the prostrate man. Paul's heart was still beating, though weakly.

"His chance of recovery depends on how quickly we can get him to emergency," advised the attendant strapping Paul to a gurney.

André drove his mother and Gabrielle to the hospital, arriving minutes after the ambulance.

SEVERAL TERRIFYING HOURS later, the family huddled together in a bleak waiting room. Gabrielle clung to Margaret's hand. "I should go make some calls canceling the gala. The guest list is at the office. André can phone me there if there's any change."

Margaret rallied, employing the take-charge voice they all knew so well. "We will not cancel the celebration. When I spoke with Paul, he said you and André must carry on the work we started. This is the dawning of a new era at WDIX."

André knelt beside her chair and said brokenly, "Mother, Alain claims he has proof I'm not a Lyon."

"Nonsense." Margaret's eyes turned flinty, her voice chilly. "Alain's always been jealous of you, André."

"The jealousy created by Grandpère's will has gone beyond petty family squabbling." André hadn't wanted to worry his mother with the bomb hoax. Now he felt compelled. He ended by saying, "I think we should sell the station if you still have a viable buyer. I can't—won't work with Alain another day. Evidently he thinks that if the business can't be split equally between his family and mine, then no Lyon should head WDIX."

"Alain's not solely to blame for Paul's condition. But I will speak with Charles. If he can't control his son, Alain will have to work elsewhere. The position of manager is yours by right of blood. André—" she gazed directly into his eyes "—never doubt that you are a Lyon. Tell everyone that the world-renowned heart surgeon, Michael DeBakey, has been consulted. He recommends an innovative procedure called a coronary bypass and they'll perform it here later today. It's experimental, but Michael is confident it will help Paul. Please, André, do as I ask. The staff at WDIX are like family. I can imagine how unsettled they must feel. You are Paul's son. Hold your head high tomorrow night. As I said, I'll speak to Charles, but whatever happens, don't let him or anyone undermine our family pride."

"All right." Standing, André dropped a kiss on her hair. "We'll leave you, then. Gaby and I haven't told Leslie and Rachel we're married. We'd hate for them to first hear the news on TV. We'll be back for the procedure this afternoon."

Margaret gripped both of their hands. "I'm so happy for you. But I'm saddened that you didn't take time for a proper wedding." Tears glistened in her eyes. "I still have my mother's wedding gown. I'd planned to wear it, then Paul and I eloped. I'd hoped Gabrielle..." She released their hands and dabbed at her eyes. "There's still Leslie of course. And maybe your new baby will be a girl."

Gabrielle's breath caught and she reached for her husband, who slid a supportive arm around her waist. "Margaret...how did you know?"

"Rachel told me she heard you vomiting almost every morning a while back. Please assure that dear child you aren't dying."

"We will, Mama," André said as he kissed her damp cheek. "If I can cut through the red tape, Gaby and I are going to try to adopt Rachel. I don't want her mother to ever take her away from Lyoncrest."

"Raising a family will bring you the greatest happiness of your life." Margaret smiled broadly, in spite of the solemnity of the surroundings.

"Speaking of family," Gaby said, "We also need to assure the girls and everyone at home that everything possible is being done for Paul. And if the surgery goes well, we'll all feel better about proceeding with the gala."

AT THE ANNIVERSARY GALA on Saturday night, Gaby sought out André and pulled him aside. "I heard Charles say we should call this a wake," she whispered. "It feels like it, all right. All Alain does is glare daggers at me, as if it's *my* fault he's been exiled to manage Chez Charles. Shall I tell him that decision is between Margaret and his father?"

"No. That's for Uncle Charles to tell him. But I'd hate to see Alain's moodiness infect everyone else. It's time we kicked some life into this party, Mrs. Lyon. Come with me to the podium." Taking her hand, André led her through a tense crowd of employees, who stood in tight groups as if waiting for bad news.

"May I have your attention, everyone?" André picked up a microphone. The auditorium fell silent.

In a conversational tone, André laid out the information his mother had requested. The news, especially that concerning Paul Lyon's experimental operation, still met with a ripple of unease. André sensed that people were concerned for their jobs under his leadership. And he knew they were worried about Paul, who was well loved by the staff.

"Gabrielle and I have some personal news, too." André held up a staying hand. "Monday, I'm filing papers to adopt her daughter, Leslie. In addition, we'll petition the court to let us keep permanently a thirteen-year-old named Rachel Fontaine. As a family, we'll continue to live at Lyoncrest. Our pledge," he said, smiling into his new wife's eyes, "is to carry on with this business in the tradition set by my parents. Your jobs are secure. Nothing will change." He spoke over the applause to add, "Oh—make that nothing except that Alain Lyon has elected to take over management of Chez Charles, his parents' restaurant."

Clapping swelled to a crescendo.

"That's not all." André cleared his throat and drew Gabrielle into the curve of his body. Throwing Alain a faint smile, he said, "My lovely wife and I want you to be first to know there'll be a new branch on the Lyon family tree later this year. We're expecting a baby," he said, the pride in his voice unmistakable.

Pandemonium erupted. Cheers went up, along with a huge

release of pink, white and blue balloons, exactly as André had prearranged. Champagne corks popped at the tables—a call to relax and party. *Laissez le bontemps rouler.* Let the good times roll.

Alain and his parents shoved through the jovial crowd on their way to the door. André and Gabrielle were too busy being toasted and accepting pledges of support to really notice their absence. For the remainder of the evening, the employees of Lyon Broadcasting sidled up and assured the happy couple that the next twenty-five years would be even better than the last.

André kept his thoughts to himself. In spite of what his mother had said, he sensed she was keeping secrets. He believed he was a Lyon and yet...

SIX MONTHS AFTER THE GALA, Paul was clearly on the mend. All the indications were that André and Gaby's union had strengthened the business—even though Gaby now left work on time every night.

Family dinners had resumed. Life at Lyoncrest was finally as André had once dreamed it could be. His children's excited chatter echoed in every room.

In January, on the eve following six-week-old Charlotte Hollander Lyon's christening, Gabrielle walked the bedroom floor with the baby in her arms, attempting to soothe her into sleep. "I'm glad Charles and Catherine came to Charlotte's service, aren't you, André? It meant a lot to your parents."

"Yes. Although I was prepared for a confrontation."

"Why? Jason's finally getting into the swing of sales. His mother says he's met a nice girl. Maybe marriage will mellow him even more."

"It's possible." André counted the baby's fingers curled over his thumb.

"André, do you believe Alain was guilty of everything that happened at the office last year?"

"Put it this way." André shrugged as he kept pace. "It's stopped. Alain merely laughed when I confronted him about planting the phony bomb. He swore I'd get my comeuppance one day." André grimaced. "He doesn't hide the fact that he thinks the job of general manager should be his because he's Alexandre's eldest—and as he says—*true* grandson."

"He's blowing smoke, André. Today Margaret pasted Charlotte's baby picture in the Lyon family album." Gaby studied their child. "She has the Lyon nose. Like yours and Paul's. I don't understand how anyone could doubt that you're all related." Reaching up, she ran a hand through André's hair. "The resemblance is more noticeable since you got a haircut."

André frowned into her upturned face. "I've been wondering if Uncle Charles was in love with my mother," he murmured. "And that he resented it when Papa came back into our lives. You know," he said speculatively, "maybe it didn't break his heart so much as hurt his pride. Maybe *that* caused the original rift in our family."

Gabrielle kissed the top of Charlotte's silky hair, then raised her lips to André. When he'd kissed her, she sighed. "Quit guessing, André. You and Alain should stop rooting around in the past. Both of you. You said yourself once that no good will come of it."

André looked fierce as he lifted the sleeping baby from Gaby's arms. "Tell that to my cousin. On second thought—stay away from him. I don't trust Alain." Tiptoeing across the room, he placed the baby in the family cradle and tucked a blanket Rachel had knit around the sleeping infant.

Gaby motioned him to back away. "Alain will be consumed by his own marital problems for a while," she whispered. "I hope Yvette has a good lawyer. I hear Alain ended up with custody of Devin and the other kids. That's odd, don't you think?"

"Enough talk, wife. What I hear is a great big bed calling our names."

Gabrielle didn't argue. She welcomed any and every opportunity to make love with her husband. The business, while important, no longer held top billing in her life. She was quite content to split her day between her growing family and WDIX-TV. André didn't know it yet, but her plans for the future included time off for another baby.

But perhaps she was getting ahead of herself....

André's hands slid up under her nightgown. His kiss chased all thoughts right out of her head. Except one that lingered pleasantly. She was more than willing to practice this delightful activity with André—especially if the result was a son to carry on the Lyon name. A son who'd be a descendant of Paul Lyon. Surely then this senseless family feud would stop.

Wouldn't it?

GOLDEN ANNIVERSARY

Ruth Jean Dale

CHAPTER ONE

Early December 1998

LESLIE VILLIEUX LYON would rather be doing almost anything else at this particular moment. Facing a root canal or a firing squad leaped immediately to mind. Those choices were quickly followed by many more as she played mind games with herself in an attempt to deny the obvious: she was about to be trotted out and put on public display for no other reason than her mother had married into a powerful family.

She'd rather eat liver or do without butter-pecan ice cream. She'd rather be an old maid—some believed she already was at thirty—than get up in front of all those people and—

"Leslie, Leslie, think fast!"

Her little brother's shriek broke through her dark thoughts, and she looked up to see a small rubber ball hurtle toward her. She caught it automatically and frowned at seven-year-old Andy-Paul, the happy midlife surprise of Leslie's mother, Gabrielle, and stepfather, André Lyon. The boy's indecorous display also caught the disapproving notice of several adult Lyons clustered around the WDIX-TV conference room.

Leslie mustered a strained smile. The boy was so pampered and adored by the entire Lyon clan that it was a wonder he hadn't grown into a complete brat. Instead, he was a bright, happy child—and young enough to be frequently mistaken for her son, instead of her brother.

Andy-Paul grabbed for his ball, but she held it beyond his reach, touching pursed lips lightly with a forefinger. "You better calm down or Grandmère will come after you," she cautioned, wondering how on earth he'd managed to smuggle in a ball.

With guilty haste, his glance swung to the matriarch of the Lyon family. Margaret Hollander Lyon stood near the boardroom door. As if feeling the weight of his attention, she looked his way.

Even in her late seventies, Margaret remained regal as a queen. Her snowy-white hair was pulled into a chignon, and her still-slim figure was elegant in one of her trademark navy-blue dresses accented by a string of creamy pearls. Although the chances of her being overly severe with him—even if he was unruly—were nil, Andy-Paul still trembled before her gaze.

She hadn't earned the "Iron Margaret" sobriquet for nothing, and in truth, she was almost as intimidating to Leslie as to the boy. Leaning forward, Leslie spoke softly into his ear. "If I get you some pencils and paper, do you think you could sit quietly for five minutes and draw me some pictures while we wait for somebody to get this show on the road?"

"Sure, Les." Andy-Paul lived in the same house with his grandmother and was under no illusions about the consequences of her disapproval. "I like to draw. I'll be good, honest."

"You *are* good, Andy-Paul." She gave him a quick, affectionate hug. "It's just that sometimes you get a little rambunctious. Now sit here at the end of the conference table and I'll be right back."

Rounding up paper, pens, pencils and highlighters, Leslie felt her tension, partially dissipated while she concentrated on her little brother, blossom once more. All available Lyons were gathered in this room awaiting the signal to parade into one of the studios for a press conference to announce final plans for the Golden Anniversary of WDIX, set to culminate July 4, 1999. Watching these sacrificial lambs—or such they seemed to Leslie—would be scads of media in a private viewing booth: radio and television reporters not only from New Orleans but from across the Gulf coast.

The thought that there would be unseen people looking at her on a monitoring screen, as well as in the studio, filled Leslie with a familiar panic, one bordering on terror. Her trepidation went far beyond natural shyness. All her life she'd shunned the limelight, only to have it thrust upon her now in the name of family unity. She knew her parents and grandparents believed she'd long since learned to control her phobia, but in fact she'd merely learned to avoid situations that would cause it.

By the time she'd settled Andy-Paul down with his drawing supplies, her stomach was clenched in a knot and her hands trembled with nerves. Nothing on earth could make her take part in this sideshow except...love, love for her entire family but especially for her grandparents.

Margaret and Paul Lyon, still a handsome couple and still very much in love, stood close together talking quietly while they awaited their cue. Leslie saw her grandfather take the hand of the woman he'd married in 1941. Tears sprang to her eyes at the tender gesture. It seemed as if words were no longer needed between them. They had loved for a lifetime. And that, Leslie believed, was as good as it gets.

Her parents were also present, of course: André, the best stepfather in the world and general manager of WDIX, and Gaby, who wasn't as active at the television station as she'd been before Andy Paul's birth. Her family loyalty remained as strong as ever, though. Gaby and Margaret were as much like mother and daughter as Paul and André were father and son.

Not perfect, but wonderful caring parents to Leslie, her rebellious sister, Charlotte, and their little brother. Leslie would do almost anything to please them. Today, however, was asking too much.

Right from the start she hadn't wanted to share the stage with the rest of the family. She'd tried every way she could think of to worm out of it, but to no avail. Finally she'd resorted to a last desperate argument: she wasn't a true Lyon, being a Villieux until the age of six when her mother married into the Lyon family, so—

"None of that," Margaret had cut her off sharply. "I simply won't have it, Leslie. This family—including you, young lady—will stand together today and always."

Leslie had no choice but to give in.

Now André turned to look around the room, tall and distinguished despite having just passed his fifty-seventh birthday. "May I have your attention, please? It's time for us to go into the studio now. I want to remind you all that this is a happy occasion. I urge you to just relax and enjoy it—and look into the camera if you're called on to speak. The celebration in July will mark a milestone for this station and you all helped make it possible. Take your bows and then we'll buckle down to make our fiftieth-anniversary celebration something that'll be remembered in this town until..."

He paused for effect, his grin so charming that Leslie could well understand the devotion this man inspired. "Folks will remember this as long as there's a New Orleans or until hell freezes over, whichever comes first. Are you ready?"

"Ready!" several voices echoed, but Leslie's was not among them.

"Then let's do it." André opened the door for his parents to lead everyone from the room.

There was nothing Leslie could do but follow, herding her bright-eyed and eager brother before her. At least kid duty gave her something to think about besides making a total fool of herself.

Again.

LESLIE ALWAYS SAW HERSELF as a shrinking violet in a family of roses with more than a few thorns. Sidling into the second row and trying to position herself behind the tallest person, who happened to be André, she pasted a smile on her face and tried not to shake too noticeably beneath the glare of the lights.

Her grandfather took the lead of course. In a deep and sonorous voice familiar to generations of New Orleaneans, Paul Lyon welcomed those unseen hordes of reporters and station employees and launched into a graceful explanation of the purpose of the news conference. He wasn't called the Voice of Dixie for nothing, and she was sure he had them in the palm of his hand in the first twenty seconds.

Licking her lips anxiously, Leslie stole a glance at the sidelines and nearly collapsed. Beyond the set, many WDIX employees lounged around watching the proceedings. Mary Boland, director of engineering, smiled and nodded; blond and predatory Kate Coleman, the ten-o'clock news co-anchor watched with a certain critical detachment on her gorgeous face; and someone else, someone only now moving out of the shadows…

Leslie caught her breath. Michael McKay had come to WDIX as the director of human resources—what used to be called head of personnel—two years ago; Leslie had been secretly enamored of him for at least one year and eleven months. Now she felt herself melting at the sight of him—or were the lights even hotter than she'd thought?

Michael was the most beautiful man she'd ever known, but he was even nicer than he was good-looking. More than six feet tall with thick, dark blond hair and eyes as blue as a Louisiana sky, he had a knack for putting those around him at ease while still maintaining the decorum of a true Southern gentleman.

She adored him from afar while Kate Coleman adored him from just as close as she could get, leaning over to whisper in his ear, putting a hand lightly on his shoulder.

Paul's voice mercifully intruded. "At this point, I'd like to introduce the youngest member of our family so you can all see that the future of Lyon Broadcasting will be in the very best of hands. Andrew Paul Lyon is my grandson, the youngest child of my son, André, and his lovely wife, Gabrielle."

Leslie guided Andy-Paul forward and the boy went, eager for his moment in the spotlight. The plan called for a quick introduction of the child so that he could be excused before youthful enthusiasm got him into trouble.

With her responsibilities successfully executed, Leslie found her attention drawn once again to Michael. He'd managed to extricate himself from the clutches of the blond anchor and now stood alone and a little apart from everyone, his eyes on the magnetic master of ceremonies.

Michael smiled and nodded approvingly, and Leslie had no idea what might have caused him to do so. All she knew was that Michael McKay was the most interesting, most attractive and most appealing man she'd ever met—and she was absolutely certain he'd never look twice at frumpy Leslie Villieux Lyon.

PAUL LYON WAS a wonder. Watching the old man hold his audience enthralled, Michael felt his admiration increase with every word. This was quite a dog-and-pony show the Lyons were staging. Paul was the perfect family member to pull it off, whipping up excitement and anticipation beyond all reasonable expectations.

Of course, Paul was only the front man.

Like everyone else who worked for WDIX, Michael knew of the elderly gentleman's health problems. He'd had a heart attack or two and his activities had been curtailed for many years. Yet when he swung into action as he did now, he gave an impression of such strength and vigor that it was hard to imagine he wouldn't live forever.

Beside him, Margaret steered her grandson off the set. She was the real dynamo, Michael thought. Iron Margaret might not be as well known as her husband outside Lyon Broadcasting, but inside it, *she* was the legend.

The Lyons had always seemed like a family united and Michael liked that about them. His own family was both smaller and less committed to unity. His parents and wife were dead, his cousins and aunts and uncles scattered all over the world and his mother-in-law a source of friction, instead of support. Added to that was his current uncertainty about his seven-year-old daughter, Cory.

His live-in housekeeper, Mrs. Simms, had been with them since they'd returned to New Orleans two years ago. Cory loved her and she returned the compliment, relieving Michael of at least part of the guilt of leaving Cory's care to others. But now Mrs. Simms's own daughter was having health problems, and if she didn't show improvement soon, he was going to lose the best child-care provider he'd ever had to the needs of her own family.

He didn't even want to *think* about that because he had no plan B. What he needed was a wife, not a housekeeper, but everything in him recoiled at the thought. Definitely once burned, twice shy. With an effort, he pulled himself back to the present.

"...stepped up public appearances by the station's best-known personalities," Paul was saying, "plus a series of documentaries tracking the many changes in our city since 1949. We'll also be launching a literacy initiative. And the pièce de résistance is a gala ball July third and formal ceremonies on the fourth."

Michael joined in the applause but found himself unexpectedly jerked from the moment. Looking around, he found Leslie Lyon staring straight at him, a strange look of...yearning on her face.

Yearning to be tucked away safely in the shadows, instead of standing prisoner in the glare of lights, he was sure. He'd never known a woman as accomplished as she was yet also so shy and self-effacing. Pretty in her own quiet way, she'd be a knockout if she ever chose to go to the trouble. Personally, he didn't see why she should. She seemed perfectly happy in her own small world—unless or until someone made her go against her nature, as was obviously happening now.

Making a circle of his thumb and first finger, he lifted his hand just enough for her to notice. *You can do this,* he mouthed, then saw comprehension dawn on her anxious face, saw the quick sweep of color into her cheeks.

If he'd ever seen a terminal case of stage fright, this was it. He felt for her, he really did.

"...INTRODUCE A WOMAN who needs no introduction, the brains behind Lyon Broadcasting and, most especially, WDIX. Margaret, dear, take a bow."

Paul's gallant gesture brought Margaret smiling to the microphone. Nearby, Gaby led enthusiastic applause.

Leslie's sigh was a mixture of admiration and defeat. Margaret and Gaby were so much alike, both self-confident women who'd succeeded on guts and talent and hard work.

At one time Leslie had longed to emulate them—she *had* tried! But she simply didn't have it in her to mix and mingle and talk and lead. She was far happier with her books and her work as a reference librarian in the city system, although lately she'd begun to long for a family of her own. If only she was more like her confident—some said *over*confident—younger sister, Charlotte.

Margaret's words intruded on Leslie's panicky musings. "We hadn't planned to do this, but we're going to call upon each member of the family to introduce him or herself and say a few words about his or her part in the upcoming festivities. We'll begin with my son, André Lyon, station manager of WDIX. André..."

André stepped up to the mike, graciously accepting the applause.

Leslie dug her nails in to her palms, hoping the pain would distract her. She would have to introduce herself and say a few words about her part in the upcoming celebration?

Impossible! She'd die first. She felt like a bug on a pin and fought the anxiety attack that threatened to overwhelm her. She didn't even want to be singled out, let alone asked to say a few words. How could Grandmère *do* this to her?

And then she knew. Because her grandmother thought Leslie at least had a handle on her fear of public speaking. So did Mama, for that matter. Leslie knew she'd brought this on herself by concealing the depth of her aversion, but that didn't make it any easier to bear.

This was too much! They couldn't expect this of her! The very thought of opening her mouth with a roomful of people looking at her while many more judged her on an unseen television monitor was too horrible. She wouldn't do it. She *couldn't* do it, even for family unity.

André was concluding his presentation. "I'd like you all to welcome back a lady who was one of the movers and shakers of WDIX before she chose motherhood over management. My wife, Gabrielle Lyon."

Gaby, completely at ease, stepped forward. Did that mean Leslie would be next? Did that mean they were going to shove her to the microphone, clap politely and let her fall flat on her face?

Gabrielle spoke effortlessly, as if to old and dear friends. "When I first came to WDIX in the late sixties, I never imagined that I would marry the boss's son and still be here twenty-five years later...."

Leslie couldn't concentrate on her mother's words. Instead, she tried to sidle away, looking for a chance to slip off the set without being noticed. If everyone was watching and listening to Gabrielle as they should be—

"Ouch! Watch it, Les."

"Oh!" She glanced around in a panic at the whispered warning, realizing she'd stepped on someone's foot. It was Devin

Oliver, the handsome stepson of Alain Lyon, who was the son of Charles, Paul's brother. Dev worked at WDIX as André's assistant.

Everybody in the Lyon clan was supposed to work at one or the other of the family endeavors, and most of them did. Leslie and Charlotte were just about the only oddballs, turning down offer after offer, enticement after enticement.

"Sorry, Dev," Leslie whispered through clenched teeth. "But I've got to get out of here."

Concern widened his eyes. "Are you sick?"

Yes! she wanted to shout. "I...I don't know. I—"

He caught her hand in his and squeezed. "Look up and smile," he whispered.

"Why? I—"

"Look up and smile!"

This was a nightmare, made worse when Gabrielle's words penetrated. "...happy to present our daughter, Leslie. We're very proud of her for the role she'll play in our little family celebration. But I'll let her tell you about that herself. Leslie?"

Gabrielle scanned the crowd behind her.

Leslie couldn't bear it. She'd turn and walk out of here and never come back. She yanked her hand from Dev's and was about to bolt. But then for some reason her frantic glance again sought that of Michael McKay.

Which was foolish, because she didn't have time to moon over some man when she needed a miracle.

CHAPTER TWO

H*ELP ME!* Leslie pleaded with her eyes. And as if Michael heard her silent shout, he smiled and nodded. *You can do this. It's nothing.*

Dev steered her forward and her mother guided her to the microphone. Leslie felt so numb she wasn't even sure she was moving until suddenly she faced a bank of lights and a massive camera. Her mouth was so dry she doubted words would come out.

"I...I'm..."

She choked and tried to swallow, and when she did she saw Michael again. He'd moved to stand beside the camera, where she couldn't miss him. He smiled again and jabbed at his chest with his forefinger. *Talk to me, Leslie. Talk straight to me.*

"M-my name is L-Leslie Lyon and I'm proud to be a p-part of this..."

A deep, steadying breath and another nod of approval from Michael kept her from collapsing. She spoke directly to him in a low trembling voice. "Part of this f-family occasion. I'm a research librarian, but I've taken...I've taken a leave of absence. My task will be to compile the official history of WDIX and the Lyon f-family. I'll also be working on the literacy initiative."

Oh, let this end! She was dying up here. But Michael was right there with her, mouthing a single word: *Louder.* And smiling. Always smiling. This would be a piece of cake for him. Why couldn't he be doing this, instead of her?

Still, somehow a tiny bit of his apparent faith in her seemed to arc across the space between them, past the lights and the cables littering the floor. Squaring her shoulders, she finished in a rush.

"Thank you for coming here today and I hope you'll all join us as we celebrate a half-century of accomplishment. Thank you!"

The "thank you" was almost shouted. She turned awkwardly from the podium with the sound of applause in her ears.

They were applauding because she was finished with her painful little speech, not because it had been good. Well, she didn't care. It was over and she'd survived.

"LESLIE, DARLING, you were wonderful!" Gabrielle grabbed her daughter in an enthusiastic hug.

"I was awful."

"Nonsense. I know you don't care for things like this, but you rose to the occasion."

Leslie stifled a groan. "I'm just glad I got through it. If it hadn't been for—" She stopped short, not willing to share what Michael had done for her, even with her mother.

"If it hadn't been for your own intestinal fortitude, you could never have done it," Gabrielle said. "Think how far you've come, Leslie!"

"Maybe, but..." Leslie chewed on her lip, knowing she'd deliberately misled her mother. She hated public attention as much as she ever had. The only difference was, she was better at avoiding it now.

"Les, you were wonderful." André appeared and gave her a hug.

The situation was, Leslie realized, hopeless, so she simply said, "Thank you, Papa."

He patted her cheek. "I was enormously proud of you, honey—we all were." He turned to his wife. "Time to mingle, Gaby. Come say hello to Doris Parker from the *Pilot*."

They moved away and disappeared into the crowd. Which was exactly what Leslie intended to do—disappear—only, from the rehearsal hall. The place was packed with family, employees and media representatives, all munching on spectacular goodies catered by Granduncle Charles's restaurant in the French Quarter. She doubted she'd even be missed.

Turning abruptly, she almost plowed into someone. Words of

apology leaped to her lips—and then she saw it was Michael McKay. Gratitude overwhelmed her and she fought the uncharacteristic impulse to throw her arms around him.

"You were great, Leslie."

"I was...barely adequate, but thanks to you I got through it. Oh, Michael..." She chewed on her lip and clenched her hands at her sides.

"Hey," he said softly, touching her arm in a gesture obviously meant to comfort. "It's all over now. Relax."

"I think I'm in shock," she mumbled, wishing she could press her cheek against his navy blazer. She longed to slide her arms around his waist and snuggle against him, but instead, she kept herself stiff and tight. She'd already made a fool of herself once today.

A smile curved his mouth. "You're too hard on yourself," he scolded. "Believe me, you're not the only person I've ever known who has a phobia about public speaking."

She gave a wry little laugh. "Phobia is definitely the word for it."

"Did you know what most people's biggest fear is on a day-to-day basis? It's not dying or being mugged or getting fired. It's speaking in public."

"Really?" Shame on her, giving him an impression of wide-eyed astonishment. Of course she knew it. She was a librarian; it was her business to know things like that. She'd read the same statistic, but nothing could have dragged that bit of information out of her. "You're just trying to be nice," she said.

"Not at all. I'm trying to point out that you're not alone, and also that you were great."

"I couldn't have done it without you," she said with all the honesty in her. "You pulled me through. I'll never be able to thank you enough."

"You already have."

He squeezed her hand and she wanted to squeeze back—and hang on. But she didn't of course. His glance flicked past her and she knew he was about to move on. Desperately she cast about for some way to detain him. "Uh...you'll be at the WDIX Christmas party, I suppose."

"Uh-huh. Have to make an appearance, at least." He cocked his head to one side and a lock of dark blond hair fell across his forehead at a rakish angle. "You?"

"I...might."

"I don't recall seeing you there before. Of course, I've only been to two."

"I go occasionally, depending on my schedule," Leslie said airily. Maybe he'd think she meant her social schedule, that she had so many men clamoring for her attention she— Forget it. The man wasn't an idiot, after all.

"Then maybe we'll meet again soon." He lifted one hand in a friendly salute. "Especially now that you'll be around more, working on the anniversary plans."

She watched his retreating back for just a moment, then whirled around to head in the other direction. Because if she wasn't mistaken, she'd just put her heart on her sleeve for everyone to see.

SHE BOUGHT A NEW DRESS for the WDIX Christmas party.

Her choices had come down to two: a ruby red velvet with a deep V neckline that revealed a decent cleavage, or a forest green crepe that buttoned all the way to a lacy white collar. She wanted to buy the red. She debated with herself for a good five minutes before carrying the green crepe out to the saleswoman.

She just wasn't the flashy type, she consoled herself while pulling a credit card from her wallet. She didn't want to draw attention to herself, after all...well, any attention except Michael's.

Selective attention, that's what she wanted. Yeah, she wanted to have her cake and eat it, too. Unfortunately she'd eaten way too much of it already and it had all gone straight to her hips. How could she possible look sexy?

She carried the dress home to Lyoncrest and hung it in the back of her closet as if ashamed of it. Then, the day before the party, she waited until the subject came up at the dinner table before saying casually, "I thought I might go along to the station Christmas party this year."

A stunned silence greeted this pronouncement as everyone

stared at her: Paul and Margaret, André and Gaby, Crystal Jardin, a second cousin who worked in accounting at WDIX and lived at Lyoncrest, even Leslie's foster sister Rachel Fontaine, a social worker in her late thirties still unmarried and now living in Metairie.

Only Andy-Paul was immune from shock. "Can I have another boudin blanc, Mama?"

"You've already had seconds, Andy-Paul."

Leslie looked down at the Cajun white sausage on her plate. Usually she adored boudin blanc, but her appetite hadn't been the same since her recent brush with public speaking. "He can have mine."

"Thanks!" Andy-Paul stabbed the sausage with his fork and lifted it onto his own plate.

"About the Christmas party..." Gaby ventured.

"I know I don't usually go," Leslie said, trying not to sound defensive, "but this year I thought I might."

"Leslie," André put in, "we're delighted you'll be joining us. We didn't mean to put you on the spot. We're just surprised."

"I go sometimes," she protested.

Margaret smiled. "Of course you do, dear. If I recall you've been twice—in 1987 and again in 1993. Not that I'm counting, of course."

"You're embarrassing her, Margie." Grandpère, who sat at the head of the table with Leslie beside him, patted her hand. "Any occasion is brighter for your presence, ma chère." He glanced around the table. "I assume all the arrangements for the party have been made?"

Gaby reached for a dinner roll in a silver-latticed basket. "Of course. Charles and Alain are catering naturally."

A universal groan arose and Leslie was off the hook while they debated the wisdom of using the same caterer for every WDIX function; the same hors d'oeuvres at every event, no matter how delicious, could get old.

"But Charles and Alain are *family,*" Margaret stated, as if anyone needed to be reminded. "Eating the same food is a small price to pay for family loyalty."

As always, her viewpoint prevailed.

BY THE TIME Leslie arrived at the WDIX Christmas party with her parents and grandparents, the festivities were in full swing. Despite their lack of originality, nibbles from Chez Charles were still popular and going fast. An open bar in one corner of the decorated rehearsal hall served drinks, with the unspoken understanding that no one would overindulge.

To Leslie's knowledge, no one ever had.

Her green crepe looked drab amongst the jewel tones of the other women's dresses. She should have bought the red velvet—but if she had, she probably would have wrapped a shawl around herself and refused to take it off.

It was hell to be fashion-challenged.

"Would you like a glass of champagne, Les?" It was Dev, grinning and holding a glass of the sparkling wine in each hand.

She couldn't resist teasing him. "What are you—a two-fisted drinker?"

"I will be if you don't help me out." He offered one of the glasses and she accepted. "That was supposed to be for Kate, but she found bigger fish to fry before I could get back with it."

Leslie followed his wry glance and saw the anchorwoman standing close to Michael and saying something very earnest, from the determined set of her shoulders. Leslie was more interested in the man, whose expression of alarm was quite unlike any emotion she'd ever seen on his face.

Kate wore red, dazzling, holly berry red. She looked like a million bucks. Leslie felt like a buck-and-a-quarter beside such competition. She caught her breath on a little gasp of surprise. She'd never thought of herself as a competitor for any man's attention. It just wasn't her.

Trying to sound casual, she asked Devin, "Are they an item?"

Dev looked astonished. "Good God, no! Michael's got more sense than that. Good old Kate just likes a challenge."

"She does, does she?" Leslie gave the other couple a calculated glance that confirmed her first impression; Michael was *not* having a good time. She took a deep breath. "What say you and I go over there and rescue the poor man?"

Dev grinned. "Why Ms. Lyon, I do believe you're up to somethin'."

"Could be."

"In that case, I'd be mighty happy to assist you." When he offered his arm with a flourish, she took it.

And asked herself again what she thought she was doing, butting heads with WDIX's star anchor-babe.

"I UNDERSTAND YOUR SITUATION," Kate was saying, holding Michael's forearm with a grip like steel. "I know you have a child to consider, and I'd never try to interfere with that. But there's been something between us ever since you came to work here and I think it's high time we found out what it is."

This human piranha was inviting him to take her to bed. He'd sooner make love to Lorena Bobbit.

"Darlin'," he said, "there's something between us all right, but on my side it's pure admiration. You're a first-class newswoman and—"

"Bullshit." She kept on smiling with those shiny red lips, stepping so close the tips of her breasts brushed his chest. "That's not what I'm talking about and you know it. I'm talking about—"

"Here you are, Kate." Dev Oliver thrust a glass of champagne at the startled anchorwoman. Leslie Lyon stood beside him, her smile a shade uncertain. "Got the champagne, just like you ordered, er, requested."

Kate did not look pleased. "I've changed my mind. I'm not in the mood for champagne."

"In that case, I'll escort you to the bar and you can name your own poison." Dev caught her elbow in a firm grip.

"Yes," Michael said quickly, before she could form a protest. "Don't let me keep you, Kate. I've got something I want to talk to Leslie about anyway."

"But—"

"Later." Dev gave them a twinkling smile, a knowing wink, and dragged the incensed blonde into the crowd.

Leslie stared at Michael, wide-eyed. "Do you really have something you want to talk to me about?"

"I always enjoy talking to you," he prevaricated.

"But specifically *now?* Or were you just glad to get rid of Kate?"

He mulled that over, unwilling to give her a blandly gracious but meaningless answer. "Both," he said finally. "She was making me uncomfortable—but you saw that."

She nodded, unexpectedly long lashes curving against her cheek. "You looked...*very* uncomfortable. Dev and I decided to rescue you."

"For which I offer my heartfelt thanks."

"And the other?"

"Other?"

"About wanting to talk to me."

"I—" he stopped, struck by a sudden thought "—certainly do. Let's get out of here and go somewhere for a quiet drink and quiet conversation. We've put in our appearance so we're free as the breeze."

Was that shock on her face? Maybe she didn't want to leave the party so early.

Maybe she knew something he didn't. "Would it offend your family if we snuck out? I don't want to put you on the spot. If you don't want to leave—"

"I do!" She plunked her champagne glass on a passing waiter's tray, then turned back to slide her hand into the crook of his elbow. "I can't think of anything I'd enjoy more."

She spoke with such artless enthusiasm he felt himself letting down his guard for perhaps the first time since...he couldn't remember when. Leslie Lyon was not like other women.

Leslie Lyon was honest to the bone.

And not half-bad to look at, either, with her eyes shining and her cheeks tinted with roses.

THEY WENT TO A LITTLE PLACE in the French Quarter. Leslie had never been there before, but she liked it right away. With its matchbook-covered walls and old creaky floors, it had a kind of shabby chic she found appealing. Even the tacky holiday decorations pleased her.

Or maybe she'd have felt the same no matter where he took her.

He ordered bourbon and branch and she chose white wine—boring but safe. When they were alone again, she looked at him across the scarred tabletop with a faint frown.

"Kate really got to you," she observed. "I expect most men would have been flattered."

"I can't afford to be flattered." He spoke quietly.

"I don't understand."

"I don't suppose you do." He grimaced. "You see—"

"Michael," she interrupted hastily, "you don't have to say anything you're not comfortable with. It's none of my business, really."

"It's not that I'm uncomfortable. I just don't want to bore you."

She stared at him in disbelief. This was the first crack she'd ever seen in his armor. "Michael, you're one of the most interesting people I know. You could never bore me."

"Nice of you to say, and under the circumstances, I'm rattled enough to take you up on it. Leslie, a single man is fair game and I'm *not* comfortable with being chased just because I'm unattached. It...upsets the balance of nature."

She had to laugh, and her laughter seemed to sweep some of his tension aside. "I've never heard it phrased quite that way before," she admitted, "but you could be right. I'm...aware that wasn't an isolated incident."

"I'm not a skirt chaser," he said sharply. "I'm not a womanizer. I'm just an average guy trying to lead a decent life and take care of my daughter."

"Average"? He seemed way *above* average to her. "How old is your daughter?" she asked, although she knew. Librarians had ways of finding out things.

"Cory's seven."

Leslie imagined a little girl who favored him and was charmed by the image. "You're very lucky."

"Yes." For a minute he was silent; the waitress delivered their drinks and left and still he sat there, looking like a man with a troubled mind. Then he sighed and said, "I think I'd like to tell you about it, if you're willing to listen."

Was she ever.

HIS REAL PROBLEM wasn't anything that would surface in cursory research: a mother-in-law threatening to sue for custody if he didn't move back to New York City where she could be near her only grandchild.

"When Jordan died—"

"Your wife?"

He nodded. "Jordan Edwards. She was a newsanchor at a New York City TV station, where I was doing the same thing I do here. Anyway, when she died her mother, Cornelia, almost went out of her mind. She'd invested her entire life in her daughter and couldn't let go. All that love was transferred to Cory. Cornelia smothered us both." His jaw tightened. "When I got the chance to take this job and come home to New Orleans, I jumped at it."

"That's so sad." Leslie's heart went out to him. "I feel sorry for the grandmother, but I'm sure you did the right thing."

"Yeah, well..." He took a swallow of his drink. "Cornelia's got more money than sense—enough to buy a lot of lawyers if she decides to make a fight of it."

"I have a feeling you're a very good father."

"Thanks for the vote of confidence. I try, but I've got to admit Cornelia's right about one thing. Cory *does* need a mother. Failing that, Cornelia thinks a grandmother is the next best thing."

"Your mother in law would have a hard time winning custody if Cory had a mother. Have you considered marrying again?"

He looked grim. "I've considered it, but not favorably. Marriage is not my favorite institution, in case you hadn't read between the lines. My marriage was not exactly made in heaven. We loved each other—at first, anyway—but ambition and...other things got in the way."

"*Her* ambition?" Leslie guessed. Her second glass of wine was making her braver.

"That's right." His level gaze didn't falter.

"So you'll never marry again, despite the obvious benefits to a man in your situation."

"Never say never." His mouth tilted up in an adorably crooked grin. "Cory needs a mother, with or without her grandmother causing trouble, but I definitely *don't* need another wife.

I got carried away once by love—or lust, moonshine, whatever you want to call it—and I don't intend to let that happen again. I can't imagine any woman would settle for less."

"You...might be surprised."

"Anything's possible. If I could find a woman who'd love my daughter without driving me crazy in the bargain..." He shrugged. "I'm loosin' my grip here, talking to you like this, but the holidays always seem to make me a little desperate."

How well she knew that feeling. "M-maybe there's a way," she whispered.

CHAPTER THREE

MICHAEL GAZED AT HER quizzically. Leslie Lyon was an intelligent woman, but the solution to this particular problem didn't exist.

She licked her lips and drew a shallow, nervous breath. Although they'd been conversing easily up to this point, she didn't seem able to meet his gaze now.

Still looking down, she mumbled something unintelligible.

"Beg pardon?"

"I said—" she looked up and met his eyes "—what about me?"

"What *about* you?"

"I like children. I *love* children."

Shocked, he said, "Are you talking marriage?"

She flinched as if the m-word startled her. "I guess m-maybe I am. It would make your position stronger with Cory's grandmother and the law, in the event of a c-custody battle."

He stared at her, mouth open in astonishment, while she rushed on nervously.

"And it would also shield you from p-predatory females like Kate." She looked positively indignant when she added that.

She was trying to help him, in a sense offering herself as a solution. He simply couldn't believe she'd settle for so little. But then, he'd never imagined this self-effacing woman could look so fiercely determined, either. Perhaps he'd misjudged her.

He gave a low chuckle meant to diffuse an increasingly tense situation. "That might solve *my* problem, but I can't see that there's anything in it for you."

"Do you consider survival 'anything'? Because that's what's in it for me."

She'd caught him by surprise and he said, "I'm afraid you lost me there."

She sighed. "I don't think I'll s-survive my family's extravagant plans for the anniversary celebration without someone I can count on to help me through," she said in a trembling voice. "You saw me at the press conference. If you hadn't been there—"

"I didn't really do anything," he interrupted. "You're the one who mastered the fear."

She shook her head. "Michael, I was ready to turn and run until I saw you. You seemed to know exactly what I was going through and somehow you g-gave me strength to muddle through."

"You didn't muddle, Leslie. You gave a beautiful speech."

"Not beautiful...but with you pulling me along, I at least got through it without breaking into tears or running from the room. My s-stammer..."

"I'd never noticed it before," he admitted. "Does it only hit when you have to speak in public?"

"It h-hits me when I'm n-nervous." She shrugged and raised an eyebrow. "Like now. This is the first t-time I've ever proposed marriage to anybody."

Her sense of humor was reasserting itself, thank God. "You didn't exactly do that," he said. "As I recall, I'm the one who actually mentioned the word, but I—"

"Please don't go on," she interrupted quickly. "I see I've embarrassed us both. It's too ridiculous to consider." She gave him a strained smile. "It must be the wine."

"I hope not. I'd like to think it was a sincere gesture of friendship."

"That, too."

"Don't give it another thought, then. I know it was just an impulsive gesture on your part. After all, you have a life of your own."

"Not really." She looked at him, then turned anguished brown eyes away. "There hasn't been anyone special in my life for a very long time. You wouldn't be depriving me of anything."

"I can't believe that. You're young and well-educated and pretty—"

"I'm thirty years old, thirty pounds overweight and plain as an old sh-shoe. I *will* accept well-educated, however."

"Leslie..." He smiled and reached out without thinking to pick up her hand from the table between them. Her flesh was icy and he chafed her fingers lightly. "Somewhere along the line, your self-confidence got stepped on in a big way. I've never known anyone with so much going for her who had so little grasp of the obvious."

She gave a breathless little laugh and her fingers convulsed around his. "I don't know how you do it, Michael. You can say outrageous things like that and somehow manage to sound sincere."

"I *am* sincere."

"All right, we'll let that go for the moment. I just want you to understand I value our f-friendship and hope I haven't messed it up."

"You haven't. It's just that..." He quirked one eyebrow. "A marriage of convenience to the boss's daughter? Don't you think that might make me look a tad opportunistic?"

"Only if I'm such a dog that absolutely *nobody* can see any other reason you'd choose me," she shot back, color washing over her cheeks. "In which case I—"

"Another round here?" The waitress appeared at their table.

Michael shook his head. "Not for me. Leslie?" He released her hand and sat back again.

"I think I'd like dessert," she said quickly. "Do you mind, Michael?"

"Not at all. I'll join you." Although he didn't want to. He wanted to be alone to try to figure out what had happened here tonight. Because the idea, crazy as it was, had a certain appeal....

"Crème brûlée," Leslie told the waitress, "and a cup of coffee, please."

Michael ordered bread pudding, a popular New Orleans dessert, and coffee. When they were once more alone, he said, "So why *are* you so nervous about public speaking? Seems to me that someone with your bloodline..." Then he stopped, disconcerted, realizing belatedly how daunting it would be to have the Voice of Dixie in the family.

LESLIE HAD NEVER SPOKEN to anyone about these things. Just thinking about doing so now made her squirm. But if she could get up the nerve to all but offer herself to this fantastic man, she could surely manage to answer his questions.

"I'm not really a Lyon," she began. "Did you know that? So it's not a matter of bloodline. I've had the stammer for as long as I can remember. My parents...well, André's my stepfather. I never knew my real father. Anyway, my parents took me to all kinds of specialists and the answer was always the same—leave her alone and she'll grow out of it." She curved her lips in a wry smile. "My mother is constitutionally unable to leave anything alone, unfortunately."

"She is a powerhouse," Michael agreed diplomatically.

"And she means well," Leslie added quietly. "But it was hard for her to see a child she loved floundering the way I did. Plus I was...Grandmère called me pleasingly plump, but it didn't please *me*. I was also shy—a triple threat."

She looked at him helplessly. "In short, I was a mess—but I was a smart mess. I worked hard and made good grades in school and I minded my manners. But every time I had to speak to more than two people at a time, I stammered or, even worse, froze up entirely."

He shook his head. "Poor you."

The waitress arrived with their desserts, giving her time to compose herself to go on. Picking up her spoon, she stared down with distaste at the creamy custard topped with caramel. For the first time within memory, a sweet did not appeal to her.

Instead of eating, she talked. "By the time I got to high school, I had pretty much learned to avoid speaking in class through mastery of the art of the meaningful nod."

"I'm afraid that's a new one to me." Michael paused with his spoon buried in the puffy bread pudding.

"The meaningful nod?" She gave a self-deprecating chuckle. "That's when the teacher would ask a question and look in my direction, at which point I would frown, give a meaningful nod and start writing with such concentration that she'd be loathe to disturb such a significant moment and would call on someone else. When I had to speak in class, I'd start stammering or blank out totally and sometimes it would take me days to recover."

Michael smiled in sympathy. "Then look how far you've come. When you spoke at the news conference, you didn't show any more nervousness than most people would."

"Because of you," she said. "You got me through that, whether you realize it or not. But you haven't heard the worst of it yet." She paused, then added, "Am I boring you?"

"Not at all." He lifted the coffee cup and sipped, his attention never wavering.

Somehow that attention felt like encouragement, which was crazy when she thought about it. Usually the slightest attention from an attractive man was enough to make her stroke out. With Michael, her reactions were entirely different. He seemed to give her confidence she'd never had before.

"There were a lot of little things," she said, "but two stand out. The first was a fourth-grade spelling bee. There were only three of us left—me, Billy Cooper and René Mettier. I'd been fumbling with my words but eventually getting them right. Then the teacher gave me an easy word—garage. I started out okay—g-a-r-a—but I just couldn't say that second *g*, couldn't force it out. I was stammering and starting over and praying that a lightning bolt would strike me dead. Billy got impatient and said, 'Shoot, she doesn't even know what a garage is!' He started laughing, and then everybody was laughing—at me."

All those old feelings were as strong as if the spelling bee had happened yesterday, instead of twenty years ago. "I started crying," she said, her voice low and pained. "The upshot was, Billy got thrown out of school for three days and while he was on suspension he wrecked his bike and broke his leg, and everybody said it was my fault."

"And you believed them," Michael guessed.

"I did then. Of course now that I'm all grown-up..." She gave a cynical little laugh.

"Now that you're all grown-up you know better—with your head but not your heart."

"Yes, but there was worse to come. I won an essay contest in high school. I was so proud—until they said I'd have to read it aloud at the honors assembly at the end of the year. When Grandpère heard, he announced he wanted to come hear me. When the school heard he was coming, they insisted he sit on the stage with the other dignitaries. I was mortified."

"Any kid would be mortified."

"But not any kid has the Voice of Dixie for a grandpa. Somehow I let him and everybody else prop me up to the point where I thought maybe I really could do what they all expected of me. I mean, I was just *reading,* not talking, for goodness' sake."

He groaned. "I think I see where this is going."

"Yes, well—" she stared past him at the twinkling holiday lights scalloped around the bar "—when the time came, I froze. With what seemed like a million faces staring at me..." She gasped for air as if it were happening all over again. "Grandpère came to my rescue. He took my speech from my hand and said I had a sore throat, and he'd read it for me. I swear to God, he made that little essay about good citizenship sound like the Gettysburg Address, he was so magnificent.

"Afterward everyone rushed up to say how wonderful he was and how sorry they were I had a sore throat, but we all knew that wasn't true. I was a washout, plain and simple. Later Grandpère told me he'd frozen once on air, but I didn't believe him. He was just trying to make me feel better."

"But you didn't."

"Of course not. I get stage fright, but I'm not stupid."

"No, Leslie, you're not." He put his spoon beside his empty dessert dish. "But sometimes you talk like you are."

"Michael!" She couldn't believe he'd said such a thing to her.

"I stand by my statement. You have so much going for you, but you consistently focus on this one...problem. None of us is perfect."

"Some of us are closer than others," she said wryly, thinking that he was about as close as it was possible to get.

He looked thoroughly exasperated. "You're a hard woman to reason with," he complained. "Your mind's made up and you won't be confused by the facts.'' He slid from the booth and held out his hand. ''Let's compromise. How about a dance?''

Until that moment, she hadn't even realized that a three-piece combo was playing Christmas carols at dance tempo on the far side of the room. As much as she longed to be in his arms, she demurred.

''I'm not a very good dancer,'' she said. ''Maybe we should just talk.''

''Not a good dancer my...Aunt Alice.'' He grabbed for her hand and pulled her out of the booth. ''We need a break and this is it. Afterward...we'll talk.''

She didn't dare ask what about.

BEING IN HIS ARMS was paradise. Although she felt awkward at first, he was easy to follow. His touch was firm and confident, although more impersonal than she'd have liked. Still, she hoped the music would go on forever.

Her dance skills improved rapidly as he led her around the small floor. He was an excellent dancer but no better than she'd expected. Michael did everything well, including lead her through steps she'd never tried before until she was breathless.

''That was wonderful,'' she said as they walked back to the booth.

''Yes, it was fun.''

''Would you have time...I mean, I wouldn't mind another cup of coffee.''

''I'm sorry.'' He gave her a grave look, his head tilting to one side. ''I promised Mrs. Simms I wouldn't be late.''

''Oh.'' Disappointment made her shoulders droop. ''Is Mrs. Simms your baby-sitter?''

''Yes. At least we can sit down until the check comes.''

Strangely satisfied, she resumed her seat. As busy as the place was, getting the check might take some time. ''About Mrs. Simms...''

''She's housekeeper, child-care provider and substitute grandma. She's wonderful with Cory.''

''Then why don't you sound happy?''

''Because I may lose her to her own family—but let's not talk about that.'' He leaned back against the padded booth. ''Tell me exactly what you're going to be doing for the WDIX anniversary.''

She made a face. ''Charlotte should be the one writing the official history of WDIX and the family, but she wouldn't even talk about it.''

''Your sister?''

''That's right. Charlotte's a newspaper reporter in Colorado. Mama and Grandmère wanted her to come back home to help out, but she's as stubborn as they are. They'll be lucky if she shows up for any of the events.''

''Will you be working at the station, then?''

''Part of the time.''

''Check!'' The waitress slapped it on the table without slowing down.

Michael pulled out his wallet. ''I've enjoyed this, Leslie.''

''Me, too.'' Was that the signal that the evening was over? Wasn't he going to bring up the little matter of marriage? Apparently not.

HE COULD SEE HER fretting. Retrieving their raincoats, he held hers out and she backed into it, her tension almost palpable.

Other patrons brushed past on their way to the door. For a moment at least, they were alone in the entryway.

''Michael...'' She turned, belting her raincoat as she did. A tiny frown marred her smooth forehead. ''Uh, what we talked about earlier...''

He shrugged into his own coat, thinking this might be a good time to lighten the mood. ''You mean about your sister?''

She shook her head. ''No, about—''

''Your spelling troubles?''

She gave a rueful little laugh. Silky brown curls escaped from the decorative combs holding her hair behind her ears and soft strands framed her face. She seemed much more relaxed than when they'd arrived; prettier, too.

''You know what about.'' Her gaze dropped to the floor.

He touched her elbows and she looked up sharply. ''Of course I know what,'' he agreed. ''It was a kind and generous suggestion, Leslie, and only a very special woman would have made it."

"Special or stupid?"

"What's stupid about wanting to help a friend? I *am* your friend, I hope."

"Of course you are."

"Then as a friend, I'm telling you I'm flattered...and honored that you'd even think about making such a sacrifice for me. Believe me, if I was in the market for a wife I wouldn't look any further. But I don't want to take advantage of you or anyone else, and that's what I'd be doing. Because someone always gets hurt, Les. Since it's usually the most deserving, it would certainly be you."

"You wouldn't hurt me, Michael."

"Not on purpose. But things...happen."

Her shoulders slumped. "Not to me," she said glumly. "Nothing ever happens to me."

"It will. Trust me." He was trying to turn her down gently and having a hell of a time doing it.

"Of course."

She looked so forlorn that he cast about for some way to bring another smile to her face. Then his gaze rose and he saw it: wilted mistletoe hanging from a tattered red velvet ribbon almost directly above her head.

"Uh-oh," he said.

"What?" She glanced around.

He pointed toward the ceiling. She looked up and her eyes widened.

"Is that—?"

"It certainly is. Merry Christmas, Leslie." And he leaned down to kiss her, planning a light peck...

CHAPTER FOUR

LESLIE HAD NO IDEA what came over her, nor did she stop to ponder. She wrapped her arms around his neck and met his kiss enthusiastically. His mouth felt warm and firm—and surprised, she realized belatedly. He'd just been going through the motions while she—

She stepped back abruptly, pasting a stiff smile on her face. "Merry Christmas, Michael," she said in an amazingly calm voice. "Thank you for a very pleasant evening."

He blinked, looking at her with a thoroughly confused expression. "We'll have to do it again sometime." He hesitated. "About before—"

"Please don't bother with that. I plead temporary insanity."

His sudden smile was dazzling, and perhaps relieved. "I knew you didn't mean it. You're just a very compassionate woman, Leslie Lyon."

"You think so?" She turned toward the door, pulling up the collar of her raincoat. A very *selfish* woman, she was thinking, but it hadn't worked. Running through drizzle to his car, she tried to put his humiliating rejection out of her mind.

Obviously she had failed to impress Michael McKay.

MICHAEL DROVE AWAY from the magnificence of Lyoncrest to his own comfortable home in one of the older sections of town, his mind far from the wet shine of city streets. Leslie Lyon had astonished him, and he found himself thinking about that kiss with something akin to disbelief.

He'd always thought there was more to the Lyon heiress than most people realized. She had never traded on her family name at WDIX, which he knew everyone appreciated. She'd appear from time to time to assist her parents or grandparents with special projects, or to show the family flag at events such as the Christmas party. But she always remained in the background, stepping forward only when absolutely required to do so.

Now he had a much clearer understanding of how difficult that was for her, and his sympathy increased.

The kiss had been gratitude on both their parts, he concluded, turning into his own driveway. He'd been grateful because she'd helped him escape the clutches of Kate Coleman, while Leslie had obviously been grateful for a sympathetic ear. It was nearly Christmas, they were surrounded by holiday spirit, and...

A feeling of restlessness swept over him, and for a moment he hesitated at a stop sign, tempted to do something he hadn't done since moving back to New Orleans. Bourbon Street would be alive and roaring. He could listen to the music of his choice, have a drink...

He didn't need a drink, and he had too many responsibilities to just take off on a whim. He wondered if Leslie liked music, liked the combination of ebullience and sleaze that was Bourbon Street. Where once he would have instantly discarded such a possibility, tonight he found himself considering her tastes in a new and different light.

Mrs. Simms, his live-in housekeeper, met him at the door wearing a fluffy blue robe and carrying a book under her arm.

"My goodness, give me that wet coat before you drip all over the rug," she commanded. "I thought the drizzle had let up."

"Not yet." He shrugged out of his coat. While she hung it up, he kicked off his damp loafers. "Cory asleep?"

"Sure is. That little thing was worn to a frazzle from roller skatin' all day with the girl next door." Her pleasant coffee-colored face creased into a smile that was quickly gone. "Mr. McKay, I hate to bring this up again..."

"You heard from your daughter today?"

The elderly woman nodded. "She's sick and not gettin' any better. If she has to go into the hospital...well, I'd just have to go back to St. Louis and help her."

"Of course." Michael put his arm lightly around the woman's shoulders and gave her a supportive squeeze. "You know how much we'd hate to lose you, but if you have to go, we'll understand.''

''I'm much obliged to you for that, Mr. McKay. It'd be hard on little Cory, though. I'd feel real bad.''

''Don't, Mrs. Simms. We all have to do what we have to do.''

With a last regretful glance, she nodded and turned away. Uneasily Michael watched her go. And he thought he had trouble now. If Mrs. Simms had to leave...

CORY COULDN'T POSSIBLY remember a Christmas with her mother.

Feeling unaccountably blue, Michael watched his daughter gleefully open her gifts on Christmas morning. Jordan had died almost four years ago, before the child really knew her. Deeply committed to her television career, she'd been a loving but basically absent mother. She hadn't really wanted a child, and when she became pregnant, she'd grudgingly agreed to carry the baby to term only with the understanding that she wouldn't be tied down.

Michael had wanted the child enough to swallow his pride—enough to stay with Jordan even after her affair with a co-worker became public knowledge.

Cory didn't know any of that, though, and he hoped she never would. She didn't know how scornfully her mother would have looked at their holiday preparations: the Christmas tree decorated with construction-paper snowflakes and glue-and-glitter cardboard ornaments, the childish drawings on every wall, the greeting cards taped to the windows.

And unbidden came a question: What was Christmas like at Lyoncrest?

Nothing like this, he concluded, admiring the video games sent by Cory's grandmother. It was just the two of them, since Mrs. Simms had the day off. After the gifts were opened, they'd have the festive if solitary brunch he'd prepared. Then they'd spend the rest of the day quietly with gifts and holiday programs on TV.

That had become their pattern and it had always been enough for him. But today, somehow, it simply seemed inadequate.

And why was he thinking about Leslie Lyon and the evening they'd spent together?

He stood up abruptly, belting the robe he'd received from his former mother-in-law tightly around his waist.

"Gettin' hungry, squirt? I've got the makings for our favorite breakfast."

"Hungry as a gator!" Cory leaped up from the middle of a pile of discarded gift wrap and empty boxes. "Thanks for my bike, Daddy." She gave him a big hug around the waist. "It's just what I wanted."

"Good." He patted her shoulder, thinking she was the best thing that had ever happened to him even if it took a miserable marriage to get her. "Cory...are you happy?"

"Sure!" She giggled. "Kids *love* Christmas."

He smiled back at her. "I guess they do. I just meant...are you happy with Mrs. Simms? Do you ever wish you had a mother like other kids?"

Her freckled face grew solemn. "Not all kids have moms," she said. "I like when it's just you and me, Daddy. That's my favorite."

He felt the same—usually.

CHRISTMAS AT LYONCREST belonged to Andy-Paul, as it should. Gifts were duly handed out from beneath the massive, professionally decorated tree in the formal living room, but everyone's attention was on the boy and his delight as he ripped into the colorful packages.

Once all the presents were open and servants had cleared away the debris and restored order, the boy sidled up to his big sister and gave her a hug.

"Did you like my present?" he asked.

Leslie rummaged through the gifts on the table next to her chair, pushing aside the diamond pendant from her parents, the jeweled and enameled Fabergé egg from her grandparents, the leather wallet from her absent sister and books from both Crystal and Rachel, who knew her tastes well. Finding Andy-Paul's gift, she held it up to admire it—a pair of papier-mâché napkin rings, painted bright red with a design that looked vaguely like lady-bugs.

"Your gift is my favorite," she assured him. "But why did you give me *two* napkin rings?"

"When you get married you might need it," he said artlessly, tracing the design with a stubby forefinger. "Grandmère says you'll probably get married soon because you're not a teenager anymore."

Leslie resisted the impulse to groan. "Sad but true."

"Ladybugs are good luck," he announced.

"I guess we can all use some of that."

She sat there long after he'd scampered back to his new toys, a bright smile pasted on her lips but a hunger in her heart she could barely contain. She wanted a husband and a bright, energetic, lovable child like Andy-Paul.

Be honest, she scolded herself. *You want Michael McKay any way you can get him.*

As if there was a chance...

ON MONDAY, JANUARY 4, Leslie reported for "work" at WDIX with considerable trepidation. She'd tried this once before, shortly after her graduation from Loyola, simply because she'd been unable to withstand the entreaties of her family.

She'd hated it. She'd hated the tension that seemed such an integral part of television, the competition both in-house and with other stations, the public personae of people she loved and valued as her family. Within six months she'd left for a library job she could enjoy.

Her parents and grandparents had been disappointed, but they didn't hold a grudge, especially after her mother became pregnant. All family attention immediately focused upon the upcoming blessed event, to Leslie's immense relief.

Now here she was back again, if only temporarily. She'd insisted on driving herself although her father had offered her a lift. Now she entered through the ornate iron gates and proceeded down the azalea-lined brick walk and into WDIX.

The receptionist grinned and waved her on. Head down, Leslie hurried to the stairs and ran up two at a time to the second floor where the administrative offices were located.

She'd been assigned a small vacant office at the end of the hall, and she hurried toward that refuge. She'd almost reached it when the elevator doors opened and Michael stepped out, accompanied by a young woman Leslie could not immediately place.

At the sight of her, Michael grinned and held up one hand to detain her. She waited while he completed the conversation with the woman in a low, concerned voice.

"Don't worry about it, Cindy. Your job will still be here. You just go give your mother a hand and I'll take care of everything at the station. Once your father's better, give me a call and we'll talk about your coming back."

"Oh, Mr. McKay—" Cindy looked at him with reddened eyes "—you're the best!" She gave him a weepy smile before turning away, sniffling.

"Oh, dear," Leslie said, "I hope everything's going to be all right for her."

Michael sighed. "Me, too. Her father's had a heart attack. We'll just have to wait and see about that, but there's no reason she should worry about her job, too." His expression lightened, became almost impish. "So here you are! Welcome aboard, Les."

She felt herself blushing. "Thank you."

"Do you have plans for lunch?"

"Y yes. My grandmother is coming mid-morning to get me started on this history project, and she said we'd have lunch in the cafeteria. Maybe I could call her and—"

"No, no," he said with a laugh, "don't go standing up the grande dame of WDIX on my account. Although why she'd choose the cafeteria over the executive dining room, I can't imagine."

"I think she likes to see who's around," Leslie said. "She may not come into the office every day the way she used to, but there's very little going on she doesn't know about."

"That's no big surprise. Your grandmother is one sharp lady."

When he started to turn away, she added, "I...I hope you and your daughter had a nice holiday."

"We did. And you?"

She nodded. "I thought about you," she offered shyly. "We had an open house on Christmas Eve—it's kind of a tradition. I wished I'd thought to invite you."

"That's kind of you." He touched a forefinger to his temple in a casual salute. "See you later."

"Yes...see you later."

She watched him walk away and she was thinking about the evening they'd shared, the kiss, wondering if he was thinking about it, too. And wondering if he'd given any more thought to her proposal of marriage. She sighed. He probably figured she'd come to her senses and realized how loony the idea was.

WDIX EMPLOYEES tended to stumble all over themselves when Margaret Lyon was around, while she didn't even appear to notice. Completely businesslike, she treated everyone with the same calm courtesy. Leslie thought they should all be able to see right through the silver-haired matriarch to her kind heart, but that never seemed to happen. Instead, they looked at her with awe.

Seated at a table in the middle of the cafeteria, Margaret seemed entirely unaware of scrutiny. Leslie, on the other hand, felt it intensely.

Leaning forward, she spoke in a low voice. "What may I bring you for lunch, Grandmère?"

Margaret waved the question away with an age-spotted hand. "That's already taken care of, my dear. I called down our order—hope you don't mind."

"Not at all." But the news created considerable anxiety for Leslie. She wasn't very hungry and hoped her grandmother hadn't gone overboard on the order.

A burly man in a white apron stopped beside their table carrying a large round tray, which he lowered with one hand. "Here y'go, Miz Lyon. A bowl of my special chicken noodle soup for you and a *muffuletta* for the young lady."

"Thank you, Tom." Margaret smiled warmly. "I hope your family is well."

The big man grinned broadly. "They are now, thanks to you, Miz Lyon. Mavis said—"

"Never mind that. Please give her my best." She waved off his obvious gratitude.

"Yes, ma'am—and thanks again." He backed away.

"What was that about, Grandmère?" Leslie looked down at her sandwich with dismay. It was huge.

"Nothing, really. I simply referred him to a good doctor for his wife." Margaret shook out a snowy linen napkin. "I hope you don't mind my ordering for you, dear."

"No, of course not. But...this is an enormous sandwich." Her entire life, Leslie had battled calories—and usually lost.

"Nonsense." Margaret picked up her soup spoon. "You need your strength, Leslie."

"Yes, Grandmère."

Leslie mostly played with her food while her grandmother polished off the soup. Margaret never put on an ounce of weight no matter what she ate, while Leslie worried about her weight constantly. Today, though, she had no trouble pushing aside the huge round Italian bread roll with its layers of cheese, ham and salami, all topped with olive salad. It was enough to feed at least two people.

Leslie had polished off any number of them all by herself in the past, but not today.

At last Margaret placed her napkin beside her plate. "This has been lovely, my dear, but Taylor should be here with the car very soon. Have you any questions about the material I gave you this morning?"

"No. I'm looking forward to it, actually—going through all those files and newspaper and magazine articles about the family. I should be an expert by the time I'm finished."

Margaret's smile was wry. "By the time you finish, you'll know everything you need to know. We're quite pleased that you're doing this for us, Leslie. We didn't want to entrust our family history to strangers."

"I'm happy there's something I *can* do," Leslie said earnestly. "The Lyons have been very good to me."

"Because you *are* a Lyon. You're also an extremely congenial young woman."

Not beautiful, which she wasn't, or talented, which she also wasn't. Congenial. Leslie sighed.

"Don't denigrate the value of a winning personality," Margaret said sternly. "Your sister, Charlotte, could take a page from your book."

Charlotte, who really *was* beautiful and talented, wouldn't be caught dead taking anything from Leslie, including a page from her book. Leslie smiled politely. "I just hope I'll do a good job for you."

"You will." This was said with total certainty. Margaret rose to her feet a bit stiffly. "You needn't walk me out, dear. I see Taylor just coming through the door. Will we see you at dinner tonight?"

"Yes, Grandmère." Leslie rose and pressed a kiss on the old lady's cheek, then, along with everyone else, watched her cross the cafeteria to meet the uniformed chauffeur.

How Leslie admired her! How she wished she could be more like her. Deep in thought, Leslie headed for the large double doors leading to the elevators.

She didn't even notice her granduncle Charles until he spoke her name. She turned in surprise. "Uncle Charles, what a surprise to see you."

"I have every right to be here." His expression matched his belligerent tone.

"Of course. I didn't mean..." Leslie retreated a step. He always threw her off guard this way; would she never learn?

Alain Lyon, Charles's oldest son, stepped off the elevator before she could go on. "Good. I found you, Dad. I turn my head for one minute and you're gone."

"I'm hungry," the old man said cantankerously. "I told you that."

"You're not hungry. You just want to find something else about this place to criticize." Alain dipped his head in greeting. "Leslie. I understand you're working here now."

"Just temporarily, Uncle Alain," she said quickly, giving him the courtesy title due to an older relative. She'd never felt that his branch of the Lyon family welcomed her into their midst, and as a result, he always made her nervous. "I'm w-working on a history of the family and Lyon Broadcasting. If you have any information or materials that might be useful—''

''Ha!'' Charles interjected scornfully.

Leslie frowned. ''What is it, Uncle Charles?''

''It's typical family folly to involve an outsider like you in family business,'' he said in a huffy tone. ''You're not a Lyon, no matter what you call yourself—a phony just like that stepfather of yours is what I say.''

Alain cast her a guarded glance but spoke to Charles. ''Leslie's been a part of this family for a long time.''

''No, she hasn't,'' Charles argued. ''She's a Johnny-come-lately, her and that mother of hers both.''

''Not now,'' Alain said sharply. ''Don't waste your breath on Leslie when our quarrel is with André. If you want to eat, come along.''

Charles took a shuffling step forward, but his eyes were on Leslie, his expression sly. ''It's a mistake to put an outsider in charge of any part of the big anniversary celebration,'' he insisted. ''You'll screw it up for sure. I don't know what Margaret and Paul are thinking, but then, I never did.''

Leslie just stood there, crushed by his vengeful words. He was apparently waiting for some kind of response from her, though, and so was Alain. She licked her lips and tried to maintain her equilibrium. ''You m-may be right, Uncle Charles,'' she said. ''I don't know that I have much to contribute, but I'll do my best not to let anyone d-down.''

''And you won't—I guarantee it.'' The voice in her ear and the strong hand grasping her elbow belonged to Michael McKay.

She could have kissed him for that.

CHAPTER FIVE

ALAIN SCOWLED at Michael, standing protectively at Leslie's side. "This is family business, McKay."

Charles's expression clouded over. "Family business—ha! Family folly is more like it. Alain, I'm hungry." The old man's voice changed to a whine.

"You go ahead," Alain said. "I need a word with Leslie first."

"Sorry," Michael said cheerfully, his grip on her elbow tightening. "We've got an appointment, and if we don't leave now we'll be late."

"You and *Leslie?*" Alain didn't even try to hide his disbelief.

"Me and Leslie." Michael turned her toward the elevator.

Leslie's heart bounded with joy. Michael was obviously suffering from a knight-in-shining-armor complex, but that was all right with her. "I'm sorry, Uncle Alain. Perhaps another time—"

Still scowling, Alain shrugged and followed his father into the cafeteria.

When she was safely inside the wood-paneled elevator, Leslie shivered. "Thank you for rescuing me," she said. "I don't know why those two dislike me, but it's always an ordeal to be cornered by them."

Michael shrugged. "It was nothing."

Thrusting his hands into the pockets of his khaki trousers, he leaned against the elevator paneling. When the elevator stopped on the main floor, he started forward, but she didn't. Holding the doors open, he cast her a quizzical look.

"Aren't you coming?"

"Where?"

"I told your uncles we have an appointment."

"But you were only being nice. I was actually going back to my office."

"Well, if you don't *want* to come with me..."

She had to laugh at his woebegone expression. As if there was anywhere in the world she wouldn't follow him! "Of course I do. I thought you were joking."

"No, Leslie." His expression grew serious. "Mrs. Simms—"

"Your housekeeper."

"That's right. Mrs. Simms has some kind of emergency and I've got to pick Cory up at school. That's not a very exciting date but—"

"Date?" She couldn't believe she'd heard him right.

"We could call it that," he said with a mischievous gleam in his eyes. "As much as the idea of us as a couple seemed to disturb Alain, it might be worth a tiny little lie."

She didn't want it to be any kind of a lie, big *or* little. A date with this man—in fact, any date at all—was too good to be true.

"Hey, Michael!" Kate Coleman strode up to the elevator, anchorwoman perfect. "Are you going somewhere, or do you just intend to stand there holding the door open all day?"

Leslie stepped forward quickly. "We're definitely going somewhere," she said almost gleefully. She gestured at the empty elevator. "It's all yours, Kate."

But Michael isn't, she thought with satisfaction as they walked through the lobby. Still, she mustn't read too much into his kindness. He was kind to everyone.

There was nothing wrong with enjoying herself, though.

"YOU MADE THESE COOKIES yourself? I can't believe it!" Leslie stared with exaggerated astonishment at the big round sugar cookie in her hand.

"I did!" Cory almost jumped off the kitchen stool she was so excited. Her face glowed with enthusiasm. "Mrs. Simms helped me, but I cut them out and sprinkled on the sugar."

Michael watched the two chatter on, puzzled at the way his daughter had taken to Leslie. Usually a cautious child, Cory had warmed to her new friend with the speed of light. Now, over cookies and milk, they'd bonded completely.

''Daddy, you're not eating your cookie.'' Cory fixed him with a perplexed gaze.

''Oops.'' He took a bite. ''Great work, kid.''

''Daddy likes brownies more than sugar cookies,'' Cory confided to Leslie, ''but I don't know how to make them yet.''

Leslie shook crumbs from her fingers onto the empty cookie plate. ''I could teach you.''

Michael was amazed. ''You?''

She gave an embarrassed little laugh. ''One of our cooks was quite tolerant of children. She taught me.''

''Let's do it now!'' This time Cory did jump off her stool.

''Oh, not now.'' Leslie glanced at Michael as if she thought she'd overstepped her bounds. ''Mrs. Simms might not like us messing up her neat kitchen.''

''We'll ask her when she gets home,'' Cory declared, then frowned. ''You *will* come back and teach me to make brownies, right?''

Again that anxious glance. ''If it all works out, honey.''

Michael heard the back door open and knew the housekeeper had returned. ''Cory, why don't you take Leslie to your room and show her your Christmas presents?'' he suggested. ''I'll be in as soon as I make sure everything's okay with Mrs. Simms. Do you mind, Les?''

Her glance might be anxious but her voice was understanding. ''Of course not. Let's go, Cory.''

Mrs. Simms entered the kitchen carrying a plastic shopping bag. Michael took it from her and placed it on the counter.

''Is everything all right?'' he asked.

The woman sighed. She looked tired and stressed out. ''I had to go wire my daughter some money, which threw me behind makin' groceries,'' she said. ''I'm sorry I couldn't pick Cory up.''

''No problem. I hope your daughter's all right.''

''So do I.'' Mrs. Simms set about emptying the bag, pulling out a half-gallon of milk and a long loaf of French bread in a paper wrapper.

Still Michael lingered. He'd grown genuinely fond of the

woman in the time she'd lived with them. "If you need an advance on your salary..."

"Not yet," she said quickly. "I'll let you know, Mr. McKay." She glanced toward the door. "Will we have guests for dinner tonight?"

"I'm not sure—maybe. Either way, you don't have to do anything special."

"That's good, 'cause I'm thinkin' spaghetti sauce from a jar. I just haven't found time to do any real cooking today."

"No problem. I'll let you know."

She nodded absently, already concentrating on something else.

Michael walked down the hallway, concerned for his housekeeper and almost equally concerned for his daughter. He paused at the half-open door to her pale blue-and-cream room. She sat on the floor with Leslie, a dozen small dolls spread around them in a semicircle. Cory was talking and Leslie was listening, giving an occasional nod of understanding.

And a thought flashed through Michael's mind: his life would be a great deal less complicated if he married Leslie. It wasn't as if he was interested in anyone else or ever expected to be. His marriage had made him leery of falling in love again, but he *was* fond of Leslie. He knew her to be a woman of high principles. She'd be a wonderful role model for an impressionable child.

It wouldn't be a real marriage, anyway; neither of them wanted that. It would simply be two people helping each other out, providing what the other needed. There was certainly satisfaction to be gained by rescuing a damsel in distress—Leslie certainly had been when Alain and Charles had confronted her—so it wouldn't be *entirely* one-sided.

He was rationalizing. Impatient with himself, he shook free of such self-serving thoughts. Marriage wasn't something to be entered into lightly. But if marriage—even a temporary one—could work with anyone, it would be with Leslie.

"Hey, you two!" Striding into the room, he smiled at the trusting faces turned toward him. "Mrs. Simms is getting ready to cook dinner, and I thought you might like to join us, Leslie. What do you say?"

Cory clapped her hands. "She says yes, right, Leslie? Yes, yes, yes!"

"Yes," Leslie agreed. "I'll just have to call home so they won't wait dinner for me."

"There's a telephone in the family room."

Michael showed her the way, thinking that even when a make-believe marriage ended, this was not the kind of woman who'd turn her back on a child.

As he'd suspected, Leslie Lyon was made of good stuff.

"YOU HAD DINNER at his *house?*"

"Please, Mama, don't get all worked up about it. I told you, he was just being nice because Uncle Alain and Granduncle Charles were on a tear." Leslie felt her cheeks burn with embarrassment. She hadn't had a date in months and everybody in the family knew it.

Paul beamed at her. "Now, now, everybody, leave the girl alone. Michael's a fine young man—doing a terrific job with personnel. I'd be delighted to welcome him into this family."

"Grandpère!"

Margaret cocked her silvery head. "Who are his people?" she inquired. "I believe I heard they're from around here."

"His grandmother was a Broussard." Leslie knew the right things to say to appease *her* grandmother.

"Of course. Didn't they have one of those big old plantation houses on the River Road? Magnolia...Magnolia something or other."

"Magnolia Hill, but the family sold it years ago. I believe Michael's the last of his line." She *knew* he was but didn't want to appear too interested or knowledgeable.

"In that case," Gaby said wisely, "he'll be thinking about an heir."

"He *has* an heir—a daughter. I...I thought I might bring her here sometime to play with Andy-Paul. They're the same age."

Her grandmother and mother exchanged approving glances. "That would be nice, dear," Margaret said.

"Anytime," Gaby agreed. "Andy-Paul will be delighted."

No less delighted than his mama was. Leslie almost wished

she'd made up some plausible lie about missing dinner with the family. But on second thought, why should she? It wasn't her fault if they insisted on getting their hopes up.

However high those hopes went, they wouldn't be half as high as her own.

THROUGHOUT THE REST of January and all of February, Leslie struggled to strike a balance in her relationship with Michael. They'd fallen into a comfortable friendship, which was slowly being accepted at WDIX. But when they were alone, he treated her more like a sister than a potential wife.

So why was he still seeing her? She stewed endlessly over this question without coming up with any real answers. Not once, either by word or gesture, had he referred to what passed between them following the WDIX Christmas party.

What was he thinking? What did he want from her?

There was nothing for Leslie to do but press onward with her duties in conjunction with the Golden Anniversary. But mysterious forces were afoot, forces she didn't recognize herself until one day at breakfast Gaby gave her a critical look and said, "Leslie, that skirt fits like a sack. Where on earth did you get it?"

"I...why, I..." Leslie, standing at the sideboard to pour a glass of orange juice, looked down in confusion at her good blue skirt. She was astonished to see it sagging from a too-big waistband. "I've had it for years."

Gaby's hazel eyes narrowed. "You're losing weight, then. Does the fact you didn't notice mean you're in love?"

"Oh, Mama!" Leslie turned away to hide her embarrassment, but her heart skipped along lightly. Losing weight had always been such an ordeal for her. If Michael's presence in her life had this happy result...

After that she started working out in the gym that had been installed in a vacant room near the kitchen after Paul's second heart attack. Sweating and hoping and praying, she trudged miles on the treadmill and lifted weights until her arms ached.

For the first time in her life, she thought she might actually be able to make a difference.

All because she had Michael in her life.

"ANDY-PAUL'S OKAY," Cory said, "for a *boy.*"

Michael grinned at his daughter. "I'll bet he says you're okay for a *girl.*"

Cory sniffed haughtily. It was Saturday and they sat across the small breakfast table in the sunroom off the kitchen sharing brownies and milk—brownies courtesy of Leslie. She'd come by after work the day before—Mrs. Simms's day off—to take Cory over to Lyoncrest for a visit with Andy-Paul, then back home for the much-anticipated brownie-baking lesson.

"Daddy." The little girl looked suddenly serious. "I like Leslie a lot."

"She likes you, too."

"No, Daddy! I mean I like her a *whole* lot."

He frowned, taken aback by her emphasis. Perhaps he'd been wrong to fall into this friendship with Leslie. Had he given Cory hopes that would not be realized?

Before he could think of a reply, the telephone rang. It was Cornelia Edwards wanting to speak to her granddaughter. He passed the phone to Cory, but sat and listened to the one-sided conversation. Finally Cory announced, "She wants to talk to you, Daddy. Bye, Grandma—I love you!" A multitude of kissing noises followed.

"What can I do for you, Cornelia?"

"You can move back to New York City where that child can have a civilized upbringing." She paused. "Michael, I've contacted a lawyer."

His stomach knotted. Good old Cornelia, blunt as always. "I can only hope you're changing your will or establishing a limited partnership," he said dryly.

"Levity will get you nowhere," she snapped. "I've lost patience with you, Michael. Either you bring that child back East or I'm going to challenge you for custody."

His temper flared. "You have no right to do that."

"I have every right! She's being raised by housekeepers and baby-sitters when she could be raised by a grandmother who adores her. I'm sorry, I really am, but a girl-child needs a woman's care.''

''Dammit, Cornelia, I—''

Cory's alarmed face moved into Michael's field of vision. ''Don't yell at Grandma,'' she said in a stage whisper. ''I love her!''

Michael sucked in a deep breath, covering the mouthpiece with one hand. ''Of course you do, and she loves you, too.'' Into the phone he said, his voice tightly controlled, ''Don't do anything rash, Cornelia. We need to talk about this. My situation may be...changing.''

''I've heard that before. It generally means a new housekeeper.''

''This time it means...'' What the hell was he talking about? It didn't mean jack. ''Uh, it means something more permanent.''

''Why do I have a hard time believing you, Michael? You'll never marry again, so stop hinting that you will. Look, I'll give you a week. If in that time you can't convince me Cory's situation there is better than it would be here with me, I'll instruct my lawyer to go ahead with the suit. I'm sorry, I truly am. You were a fine son-in-law, but now it feels as if you're the enemy.''

He could say the same of her. Hanging up the phone, he forced a smile for Cory.

''What say we go walk around Jackson Square and have lunch in the Quarter? Just you and me?''

''Oh, Daddy, yes! Can we invite Leslie?''

Obviously there was some part of ''just you and me'' she didn't quite grasp. ''Maybe another time, honey. Today I want to be alone with my best girl.''

''Leslie's your second-best girl,'' she argued. ''Call her, Daddy.''

But he didn't. Not this time. He had too much thinking to do.

THEY RETURNED from several hours of daddy-daughter togetherness to find Mrs. Simms hauling a suitcase into the living room. She wore her brown coat with the velvet collar, a scarf tied around her head.

"Oh, dear, I'm so glad you got back," she said breathlessly. "I've gotta go, Mr. McKay. My daughter needs me."

"Just like that?" He felt the vise tightening. "What's happened?"

"She's goin' into the hospital tomorrow morning for surgery, and she's got nobody to watch her kids. I've gotta go, Mr. McKay."

"Of course you do, but...today?"

"I'm sorry," she said yet again. Her head drooped. "I don't like to walk out on you, but I've got no choice. I hope there's no hard feelin's."

"None at all." It would have been easier if there had been. "Can I drive you to the airport? Do you need money?"

She stopped short in her anxious motions. "You know I probably won't be comin' back."

"That has occurred to me."

"And you're still willing to give me money?" Tears sprang to her eyes. "Mr. McKay, you're a true gentleman, but I don't need your money. I just need you to understand."

"I do, Mrs. Simms."

"And you, my little lump of sugar..." Bending down, she opened her arms to Cory.

Who, now that Michael had time to notice, was taking all this remarkably well.

"Goodbye, Mrs. Simms. I love you."

But it was pretty much said by rote. When they were alone, truly alone, Cory turned to Michael with a big grin on her face.

"Now we can ask Leslie to come live with us," she said, her voice trembling with excitement. "Please, Daddy, *can* we?"

SUNDAY AT LYONCREST meant mass at St. Paul's followed by a brunch. Often guests were included, but on this particular weekend, only family members, including Rachel and Crystal, gathered.

When Leslie entered a few minutes late, Rachel was telling a story about how she'd come to Lyoncrest to live some twenty-five years ago as an urchin of thirteen. "I was lucky to be one of Margaret's strays," she concluded fondly. "André brought me here, but the Lyons took me in. If they hadn't, I'd probably have grown up to be the terror of the bayou."

Leslie unfolded her napkin. "Instead, you're the terror of Lyoncrest."

Everyone laughed, Rachel the hardest. Then she did a double take. "Leslie, you look wonderful!" she declared, accepting the silver bread basket from Crystal. "What have you been doing to yourself? Whatever it is, I want some."

Before Leslie could respond, her mother spoke.

"Leslie's in love," Gaby said with a smile. "High time, don't you think?"

Leslie groaned. "I am *not* in love. I...I've been seeing a very nice man, Rachel. We're good friends, that's all."

"Do I know him?" Rachel spooned scrambled eggs onto her plate from an ornate serving dish.

"Maybe. His name is Michael McKay and he's the director of human resources at WDIX."

Rachel's eyes widened. "Of course. I spoke to him for a few moments at the WDIX Christmas party, but then he disappeared."

"With Leslie," Crystal said with an impish grin.

"He's gorgeous." Rachel looked impressed. "I got the feeling he was very highly regarded by the other employees."

"He is," Crystal confirmed. "All the women are after him, but Leslie's got him."

André rolled his eyes. "Can we talk about something else?" he asked. "Can't you people see how embarrassed Les is by all this?"

Gaby looked affronted. "Why should she be embarrassed? We're all delighted for her."

That was Mama; she simply couldn't understand why everyone in her world didn't have the sort of confidence she had, most especially her children.

Two out of three children did.

"It's all right," Leslie said with a long-suffering sigh. "I'm used to being embarrassed. Just don't get your hopes up too high, because you'll be in for a big disappointment."

The doorbell rang. Moments later a maid entered to whisper into Paul's ear. He frowned.

"Leslie, your young man is here. Please invite him to join us for brunch."

Leslie's heart skipped a beat. Why would Michael arrive unannounced on a Sunday? Could something be wrong with Cory?

She leaped to her feet. "Please excuse me." She almost ran from the room.

Those remaining looked at each other with surprise. Then Paul said, "Margie, I'm not sure she even heard me. Would you be so good as to make sure the young man receives our invitation?"

"Of course, dear." Dropping her napkin on her chair, Margaret followed her granddaughter's path at a more sedate pace. Young people today didn't seem capable of concentrating on more than one thing at a time. Why, in her day—

She stopped short, arrested by the sound of Leslie and Michael talking just out of sight in the entryway.

"...to arrive this way without calling first."

"It's all right, Michael." Leslie sounded anxious. "Is it...is it Cory? Has something happened to her?"

"No, no, nothing like that. She's waiting outside on the lawn swing."

"What, then? Why didn't you bring her in? You're scaring me!"

"I don't mean to." Spoken very low.

Margaret knew she should make her presence known, but some sixth sense told her that would be a mistake. So she lingered.

And was rewarded.

"Leslie," Michael McKay said in a voice suddenly filled with determination, "I've looked at this from every angle, and I've come to the conclusion that we should talk seriously about getting married." His deep intake of air was audible. "If you haven't changed your mind...I want you to be my wife."

What a peculiar proposal! Margaret could hardly bear the tension of waiting for the answer. Then Leslie's voice reached her, trembling with intensity.

"Yes, Michael, of course I will. *Yes!*"

Smiling, Margaret turned and walked quietly away.

CHAPTER SIX

THROWING HER ARMS around Michael's neck, Leslie pressed her trembling body against him. Her thoughts were in chaos. Why wasn't he kissing her, telling her that he'd realized he'd fallen in love with her? Why was he just standing here as still as the statue of General Andy guarding Jackson Square?

She pulled back enough to look into his face and her joy faded. She said his name tentatively.

"I've got to be perfectly up front about this, Leslie." His jaw was tight and a certain wariness tinged his expression. "There's a lot I have to explain before I can let you make this commit—"

"Leslie!" Gaby rushed into the foyer, Rachel and Crystal right behind. "Your grandmother told us! We're so thrilled!"

She gave her daughter a fierce hug. Over her mother's shoulder, Leslie's gaze met Michael's, which filled with alarm. "Mama, please—"

Rachel thrust her hand out to Michael. "Congratulations. I've always thought it would be a lucky man who married our Leslie." She added, "I'm Rachel Fontaine. We met at the WDIX Christmas party."

"I remember you, Rachel." Michael took her outstretched hand, but the cautious expression had not left his face.

Crystal hugged Leslie. "You've got yourself a great guy, Les. All best wishes."

"Michael!" Gaby threw her arms around him. "Welcome to our family. We're at the table. Please, come in and join us."

"Cory—my daughter—is outside. Perhaps we should just go and...and come back another time."

"Nonsense! Leslie, bring the child in. I'm sure Andy-Paul will be thrilled to see her. In the meantime I'll take this young man inside and let him ask for your hand in proper fashion.'' Gaby winked, letting them all in on her joke, but she wasn't joking when she dragged Michael away.

''OH, MY GOD,'' Leslie said, so faintly Michael could hardly hear her. ''What have we done?''

Alone in the sunroom at last, Michael sat down heavily on one of the upholstered cane settees and stared out of the glass-enclosed room at the huge oak tree growing close to the house. How had things gone so wrong so fast?

''It'll be all right,'' he said, although he was far from believing it. Having her family burst in on them that way, before he had a chance to say what needed saying, had thrown him. ''Come sit down by me so we can talk.''

''What is there to talk about? They've already got us married and the parents of a dozen children.'' But she did as he requested.

''I was trying to explain,'' he said.

She glanced at him sharply. ''Explain what? I figured your proposal was self-explanatory.''

The pressure on his chest eased. ''Was it? You understood, then, that I was trying to take you up on the offer you made the night of the WDIX party—if you're still willing, of course.''

She grew very still and all expression left her face. ''Perhaps you should spell it out, just to be sure.''

He sighed and nodded. ''Les, I've come to admire and respect you even more over these past couple of months, and Cory adores you.''

''I adore her, too.''

''I thought we'd settled into a fairly agreeable relationship.''

''Agreeable?'' The word left her lips like a curse. ''I suppose you could call it that.''

''But a couple of things have happened.'' He hated to go on but knew he had to. ''Mrs. Simms left for St. Louis yesterday. She won't be coming back.''

''Cory needs a baby-sitter so you thought of me?''

He winced. ''That's not quite how I'd have phrased it, but...yes, she does. Actually, she asked for you.''

For a moment he was afraid he'd made matters worse, but then Leslie gave him a faint, ironic smile. "I see. What else?"

"Cory's grandmother is making threats again." Should he also mention that he'd noticed the way Leslie's family tended to overlook her feelings? How he understood far better now why she'd made the offer in the first place? No, he decided; that would sound too much like he pitied her.

She just looked at him, her hands folded in her lap atop her dark linen skirt. She seemed quite self-possessed—and quite lovely. Was she doing something different with her hair or makeup, something he hadn't noticed before?

"Let me get this straight," she said. "You want to get married to protect your daughter."

"Unless you've changed your mind?" His stomach muscles clenched. In his heart, he'd really expected her to go for this.

"Well—" she looked away, evasive for the first time "—not exactly. I just need to know the ground rules. It would be hard to tell my family we'd made a mistake, but we can if we have to."

"Ground rules. Okay, I've thought about that. You need my help until after the Fourth of July celebration."

She flinched. "That's a start."

He pressed ahead. "And I need you long enough to get Cory into a...a situation her grandmother can't find fault with. So I was thinking...wait a decent period of time, and after the Golden Anniversary, we can quietly separate. Give everyone time to get used to it. Then we can divorce—a friendly divorce of course, and that'll be that."

It all sounded incredibly callous, he knew, but that was what she'd proposed, wasn't it? He didn't need to explain it to her.

"What about Cory?"

"What about her? She loves you."

"I feel the same, but what happens when you and I separate?"

"Would you turn your back on her?"

"Never!" Anger flared in her velvet eyes. "What do you take me for?"

"Exactly what you are. A kind, loving, compassionate woman

who'll continue to be Cory's—" not mother, he couldn't say mother "—friend and mentor. True?"

"True," she whispered.

"That's what I wanted to say to you in the hall, before everybody burst in on us. The way it happened wasn't fair to you."

"Forget fair." She stared down at hands still folded in her lap. "If I say no, what will you do—about Cory, I mean?"

He shrugged, as if the choices he faced didn't put him between a rock and a hard place. "I'll probably move back to New York so Cornelia can see her granddaughter. That's what she really wants, not custody. Actually, I can't blame her. But one thing I know—she'll do what she has to do to get her way." Just like her daughter before her.

Leslie nodded slowly. "In that case...I'll marry you, Michael McKay."

The weight of the world fell from his shoulders. "God, Leslie, I thought for a minute you'd changed your mind." He sagged with relief. "I owe you for this one, hon. You'll never regret it, I swear."

She didn't smile. "I hope *you* never regret it, either."

THEY WERE MARRIED five days later in Las Vegas at a wedding chapel above a casino in one of the big hotels on the Strip. Leslie could hardly believe this was happening; she was married to the man of her dreams.

Unfortunately her dreams had rapidly turned into nightmares. For openers, her mother had pitched a fit when the wedding plans were announced.

"Your wedding could be the social event of the season," Gaby had complained. "You can't do this to us, Leslie. Run off to Las Vegas like a..." Her eyes narrowed. "You're not pregnant, are you?"

Leslie nearly choked on her reply, which should have been, "I wish!" but was, instead, a defensive, "No!"

In the end of course, she and Michael had insisted on doing it their own way. Now the deed was done and the smiling—was he a minister, a justice of the peace, what?—was nodding and saying, "You may kiss the bride. Please pay the cashier on the way out."

It sounded so tacky and tawdry, at least until Michael turned a big grin on her and announced, "Mrs. McKay, may I have this dance?" He swept her into his arms and whirled her around the only space in the room not covered with plastic roses and glittery streamers.

Laughing, she clung to him, her anxiety easing somewhat. Michael always, always made her feel better. He would make this work. She knew he would.

Releasing her, he dropped a light kiss on her nose, another on her cheek. Beside them, Cory laughed and clapped her hands.

"I wanna see the circus now," the little girl declared. "Please? You promised! I wanna go on a roller coaster and a merry-go-round and see a dinosaur." She grabbed for their hands. "Come *on,* Daddy! Come *on,* Mama!"

Leslie melted. She'd never thought to earn the title of Mama. "Yes," she agreed, "let's go!"

And that's how she came to spend a good part of her honeymoon on a roller coaster.

"YOU TAKE THE BED," Michael said. "I'll take the couch and be up before Cory's even awake."

Leslie chewed on her lower lip, and he supposed she'd been dreading this moment. She needn't have. He'd sworn he'd do the right thing—or more importantly, *not* do the wrong thing. It wouldn't be honorable to sleep with her under the circumstances, even though, God help him, he was tempted.

"All right," she agreed, sounding a trifle petulant. "I'll see you in the morning." Pressing her fingers to her lips, she brushed her hand across his mouth.

Michael's entire body reacted to that light touch. Holding himself rigid, he let her walk away, her bathrobe swirling around her. She disappeared into the master bedroom of the suite, closing the door firmly behind her.

Only then did he let his breath out on a low, unhappy groan. This was no way to spend a wedding night. If she was petulant, he didn't blame her. Their situation was unnatural, but they'd get used to it in time.

He still took a long, cold shower that night.

TWO DAYS LATER they flew to New York and rented a car for the drive to Long Island. Leslie was as nervous about this meeting with her predecessor's mother as she was about her fraudulent marriage. Michael didn't seem too relaxed about it, either.

Only Cory bubbled over with excitement as her father drove past one gated mansion after another. "There it is!" she shrieked, pointing. "That's Grandma's house!"

The little girl was the first one out of the car and she practically flew into the arms of the elegant figure waiting at the foot of the front steps. This was no wicked mother-in-law, Leslie realized. This was a woman of iron will who intended to look out for the welfare of her grandchild.

Climbing reluctantly from the car, Leslie couldn't even find it in her heart to fault the woman. But now that Michael was married, surely everything would be different.

She glanced at the tall, handsome man by her side. Slipping her hand beneath his bent elbow, she gave him a tentative smile. He looked down at her with surprise that quickly turned to gratitude.

"That's right," he murmured for her ears only. He patted the hand clutching his jacket sleeve. "She has to believe our marriage is real or we'll never get away with it."

Leslie nodded, just as if it would be hard to pretend she loved this man.

LESLIE SAT on an Italian-leather sofa with her hands clasped politely in her lap while Cornelia Edwards mixed drinks at the bar. Why the woman had asked to speak to her alone, Leslie could only guess, but she'd try to handle whatever came along.

"Here you are—vodka and tonic." Cornelia extended the drink with a hand displaying long, perfect fingernails and dripping with diamonds. She wore a pale gray knit pantsuit that looked like cashmere, and her hair was perfectly frosted and elegantly styled.

"Thank you." Leslie took the drink.

Cornelia sipped her own, a thoughtful expression on her face. "You're not what I expected when Michael called," she said at last.

"Oh? What did you expect?"

"Certainly not a Lyon! I guess I expected some bimbo willing to jump into a phony marriage to get the wicked grandmother off his back." She grimaced. "I know, I know, Michael's not like that. But if a person gets desperate enough..."

"*You* needn't feel desperate," Leslie said earnestly. "Michael just doesn't want to leave New Orleans, although he has the highest regard for you."

"That's good to hear." But Cornelia didn't sound convinced. "He loved my daughter, you know. Even after she...made mistakes."

Leslie's heart contracted. "I do know."

"I'm not sure he loves you."

"Neither am I." The words popped out. Leslie lifted her chin defiantly. "But if I have anything to say about it, he will someday."

Cornelia smiled. "At least you're honest. I like that. I wouldn't want my granddaughter to be under the influence of a woman without moral character."

Leslie relaxed a bit. "If that's a compliment, thank you."

Cornelia laughed. "I suppose it was. At least I don't have to worry about your feelings for Michael."

Leslie caught her breath. "You don't?"

"It's obvious that you love him and Cory, too. He's a fool not to see it."

Cornelia swallowed the last of her drink while Leslie just stared, completely disconcerted. But later, when Cornelia announced that she would reevaluate plans to seek custody of her grandchild, Leslie was *not* disconcerted in the least.

WHEN LESLIE SAW the green and watery New Orleans landscape from the window of the airplane, she wanted to weep with relief. The entire trip had been a terrible strain—who would sleep where, who would believe whom, who would crumble first. Only Cory seemed perfectly delighted with everything and everyone.

They'd no more than walked into Michael's house when a knock on the door announced new trouble. Margaret stood on the step, a limousine at the curb behind her and a bottle of champagne in her hand.

"Welcome home, my dears." She handed the bottle of wine to Michael and hugged Leslie, then Cory. "I hope I haven't come at an inopportune moment." She walked inside and shut the door behind her.

Leslie and Michael exchanged puzzled glances.

"It's not the *best* time actually," Leslie ventured. "We just got back."

"I won't be long," Margaret promised. "I won't even sit down."

"Please," Michael said, "we didn't mean—"

Margaret waved his protests aside. "I just wanted to say that we're prepared to welcome all of you to Lyoncrest as soon as it can be arranged."

Michael frowned. "Anytime you say is fine with us, isn't it, Les?"

Leslie, who was under no illusions, touched his arm in warning. "I don't think Grandmère is talking about dinner."

"Then what?" Michael frowned. "No! You can't mean you expect us to move into Lyoncrest!"

"I do indeed, and so does the rest of the family." Margaret laughed lightly. "Just thank your lucky stars Gaby wasn't the one chosen to come here today to convince you. I think she'd already have the moving van at the door."

Michael shook his head. "It's out of the question, Mrs. Lyon. Leslie and I—"

"Spare me, please." Margaret turned back to the door. "That big old house just cries out for young people within its walls. We've already prepared a suite for you on the third floor away from everyone else, where you can have complete privacy. We've also prepared a lovely room for Cory."

"Grandmère, please, don't do this to us," Leslie begged. "We've just gotten married."

"My dear, you will have a great deal more privacy at Lyoncrest than in this rented house—dear as it is," she added quickly, apparently afraid she might have hurt Michael's feelings. "Cory will be safe and happy and have a child her own age to play with. Leslie won't be required to care for a house and can concentrate on her new family, and you, Michael, you!" She smiled and her silver-blue eyes warmed. "You will quickly come to realize that family means everything to the Lyons—and you're family now."

Michael's jaw hardened. "I thank you for the invitation, but it's out of the question. I didn't marry Leslie to sponge off her family."

Margaret's laughter trilled. "As if anyone thinks you did!" She opened the door and paused there, a striking figure in navy blue and pearls. "You'll have to talk it over of course, but please don't misunderstand. We're doing this for your own good. You can give in gracefully or you can give in kicking and screaming, but you *will* give in."

She walked out and closed the door behind her.

They stood there in stunned silence for a moment and then Michael said, "There goes Hurricane Margaret."

With a burst of nervous laughter, Leslie turned into his arms and hung on until they were laughing together. When the outburst had passed, she wiped tears from her eyes and said, "I'm sorry. I should have known they'd try to do this to us."

"It's not your fault, honey." The "honey" came out naturally and easily. "To tell you the truth, I wouldn't mind so much if it wasn't for our...arrangement."

"Our arrangement." Obnoxious word.

"Living there would make it even harder than it's going to be."

She didn't think it seemed hard for him at all, but didn't say so. "We'll tell them we decline the invitation, then?"

"I think we have to, but it's your family."

"Whatever you say, Michael."

LESLIE AGREED SO READILY that he told himself she must appreciate his restraint. He also told himself it wasn't getting harder and harder to keep his hands off his bride-in-name-only.

But what was a man if he had no honor? Michael would maintain this charade for all their sakes—hell, it was already working. Hadn't Cornelia stopped making threats about a custody battle?

So he told Margaret no as nicely as he could. Then he had to tell Paul no, and then it was André and Gaby, and Michael still said no. On top of that, Andy-Paul must have said something to Cory, because then Michael had to say no to his daughter.

The first time he and Leslie went to dinner at the in-laws and they all jumped on him at the same time, he took a deep breath, prayed he wasn't doing the wrong thing, and finally said *yes.*

It was worth it to get them off his back, he told himself.

Or lied to himself.

LESLIE, MICHAEL AND CORY moved into Lyoncrest one week to the day after they returned from the honeymoon. Cory was so excited she immediately took off with Andy-Paul to explore all the hidden nooks and crannies of the old mansion. She would be transferred to her new school Monday, the same one the boy attended, and she seemed to have no problem with that whatsoever.

Michael looked around their suite with a guarded expression. Their clothing had already been placed in closets and drawers, their toothbrushes hung in the bathroom, their books set on the table in the sitting room.

Leslie, who'd been watching her new husband anxiously, followed his gaze. She gasped.

"What is it?"

She crossed to the cherry four-poster and touched the crocheted lace coverlet with a reverent hand. "My great-grandmère Lyon made this bedspread," she said. "It was nice of them to put it on our bed."

"Your bed," Michael said with a wry smile. "I figure I can sleep on the sofa in the sitting room."

"Oh, Michael." She looked at him, her frustration boiling up inside. How long did he intend to keep this up? Was she so lacking in appeal?

He stopped those rebellious thoughts with a quick kiss on the tip of her nose. "You know it's the only way," he said. "I'm not made of steel, but I *am* an early riser. I'll make up the sofa every morning so no one will be the wiser."

Except me, she thought almost angrily. But all she said was, "Whatever you think best."

She might be dying to make this marriage real, but she was far too fainthearted to let him know how she felt. Ah, for a little self-confidence—the story of her life.

CHAPTER SEVEN

"WHAT IS IT, LESLIE? You're white as a ghost." Michael looked at his bride with concern, taking in her stark expression and trembling lips. He'd left her alone at the breakfast table and gone upstairs. He couldn't imagine what might have happened to upset her as much as she clearly was.

He was getting to know her, this diffident woman he'd married. She didn't have a selfish or vindictive bone in her body, and she would do anything for those she loved—anything she *could* do.

"I need help, Michael."

She reached out blindly and he took her hand, squeezing lightly before leading her to a chair near the French doors. "This time Grandmère isn't taking no for an answer," she added tightly.

"What's the question?" he asked. "Must be a humdinger, judging by your expression."

"She wants me to attend a l-luncheon with her Friday and present a literacy award on behalf of WDIX. She s-says now that I'm m-married—"

"Stop and take a deep breath," he interrupted her panicked recitation. "That's right. Now, just tell me what happened."

She nodded, starting over. "Grandmère says now that I'm married, it's my duty and responsibility to take my rightful place in the family." She grimaced. "She makes the Lyons sound like the Windsors, for heaven's sake."

If she could joke about it, she'd pulled herself together. "What did you tell her?" he asked.

She groaned. "I said I'd talk to *you!* Is that ridiculous or what? I mean, it's not like I need or even want your permission. I think that's the way she took it, though, and accepted it. Grandmère is very big on marital agreement and all that."

He nodded. "Your grandmother is a magnificent woman—a little tough from time to time, but magnificent. Your mother is, too." He cocked his head and looked at her, much calmer now than when she'd burst into the suite. Her pink lips trembled and he felt a sudden, inexplicable urge to kiss them.

He stopped himself. They were in a partnership here, not a traditional marriage. He had no special rights where she was concerned. "You don't have to do this, Les," he said.

Her head drooped. "I know, but I d-don't want to disappoint them." Her words came out muffled.

"That's what you *don't* want. Now tell me what you *do* want."

"What I want is—" she looked at him, wild-eyed "—what I've always wanted, is to make everyone proud of me."

"They are."

"But this is an ongoing issue." She chewed on her lower lip. "This anniversary celebration is important, and they want me to be a part of it. Instead, I'm just causing trouble and not helping at all."

"Trouble?"

"While I'm trying to get out of the luncheon without admitting I'm petrified, Grandpère comes in and says, 'Margie, leave the girl alone. Don't you know how much she hates that sort of thing?' Then Grandmère says, 'Paul, you can't accomplish anything without facing your fears. That's what you did and what I did and Leslie is every bit as capable. Besides, she's been over the worst of her stage fright for years. Look what a good job she did in December.' And then they start arguing and it's all my fault, because I'm *not* over it."

Michael put a gentle hand on her shoulder. "I don't think you have to worry about breaking up that marriage, hon. How long have they been together now—better than fifty years? I'm more interested in what I can do to help *you.*"

Leslie gritted her teeth, took a deep, determined breath and sat up straight in her chair. "Make me over, Michael."

He blinked in surprise. "Make you over into what?"

"The woman I want to be, confident enough to handle my public role as a member of this family without hysterics. Be my Henry Higgins. I'm tired of being a caterpillar. I want to be a butterfly, b-but even admitting that scares me. I know you can't change what's inside...well, maybe you could, but it would take a while. In the meantime, I want to change the outside. I think I can, if you'll help me."

"I'm no expert on ladies' fashions," he protested.

"I value your opinion, anyway. You can tell me which colors look good and which don't. You can help me find a new hairstyle." She rolled her eyes as if trying to see the brown hair pulled severely back into a coiled braid. "I just need a complete makeover." Nervous laughter burst from her lips. "And I need it by Friday."

He laughed, too. "Friday's a tight deadline, but we can sure get started. What's your favorite color?"

"What's your guess?"

"Navy blue?"

She laughed. "It's red!"

"I've never seen you wear red." Mostly she wore brown or black or navy blue, as she was now.

"I almost bought a red dress for the Christmas party," she said. "I wish I had."

"Then let's do it—red for the lady." He rose and reached for her hand. "Do you intend to go to that luncheon? Because if you don't want to do it, I'll be glad to tell them—"

"Don't!" she pleaded. "If this marriage was real... But why should you...? I've got to learn to stand up for myself and—"

"Les, I *want* to do this for you."

"Please don't. Just help me prepare and be there for me. Grandmère says I'll only have to say a few sentences." She gave him a bright smile. "See, I'm already feeling better."

"I'm glad someone is, because you're making this damned hard on me." He spoke through clenched teeth. Cupping her elbows, he drew her to her feet. "I want to get one thing perfectly clear about this caterpillar-into-butterfly transition, though. It's not my idea—it's yours. I think you're pretty special the way you are now."

Her expression changed into one of such vulnerability that for a moment he wondered if she'd misunderstood his meaning. Then she smiled. "Thanks for saying that. You're pretty special, too." She lifted one hand to touch his cheek tentatively. "Michael..."

He couldn't stop himself from stroking a thumb across that soft lower lip. "Leslie—"

A knock on the bedroom door startled them both.

"Yes?" Leslie's voice sounded hoarse.

"Sorry, ma'am, I thought you'd left for the day. I'll come back later to clean."

Michael was sorry, too—sorry and glad at the same time. Because there was something he had to do before they went out, something he should have done when they first moved into Lyoncrest.

MICHAEL FOUND MARGARET and Gaby in the study with a pile of folders on the worktable before them. Both women smiled when he entered, but the smiles slipped quickly.

Gaby straightened. "Michael, what is it? You look...angry."

"I am angry." He clenched his teeth and tried to be calm. He'd waited far too long to have this conversation. "Ladies, at the risk of sounding rude I have to ask you to leave my wife *alone.*"

"What in the world are you talking about?" Margaret looked mystified.

"Don't you know you're hurting her with this incessant badgering to take a bigger role in family affairs?" A world of frustration colored his tone.

Gaby's mouth dropped open, but Margaret had reclaimed her composure. "Are you referring to my little talk with Leslie at the breakfast table this morning?"

"I am."

"Michael, I in no way badgered my granddaughter. I invited her to make a simple presentation."

"Don't you get it? It's not simple to her, Margaret." He'd never called her by her first name before and he saw her surprise.

"Don't you people understand? Leslie suffers from paralyzing stage fright. If you love her—"

"How dare you suggest we don't!" Gaby came to life in an instant.

"Because," Michael said with dangerous calm, "if you loved her you'd give her a break. She's coming out of her shell, but—"

"She came out of her shell long ago," Margaret said. "You should have seen her ten years ago. She may not enjoy public exposure, but we all do many things in life we'd just as soon skip."

Annoyed by their blindness, Michael glowered at the two women. "You're wrong," he said at last. "She's learned to mask her fear a little better, that's all. Inside, she goes through hell." He inhaled deeply. "I won't have any more of it. Either you back off—that's you in the plural—or..." He hesitated, wondering if Leslie would go along with this, knowing in his heart she would. "Or we're moving out," he concluded flatly.

"Michael!" They said his name as one, staring at him as if he'd lost his mind.

"I'm sorry," he said, but there was steel in his voice. "Leslie's welfare is more important to me than good manners. Now if you'll excuse me, my wife and I are taking the day off to be together. Goodbye, ladies."

After he'd gone, Gaby turned to her mother-in-law to share her indignation. To her astonishment, Margaret was smiling.

"He really loves her," the older woman said softly. "I'll admit I wondered...but now I know they'll be all right."

"Margaret, he was incredibly rude. How can you condone—"

"Gaby, calm down. Didn't you hear what he was saying? He knows her better than we do now. Take that lesson to heart and be grateful."

LESLIE WALKED INTO DINNER on Michael's arm and everyone else in the room—with the exception of the two children—gaped. André recovered first.

"Leslie, you look wonderful. What have you done to yourself?"

"André!" Gaby, nothing if not loyal, slapped his arm lightly. "That implies she didn't look wonderful before."

Margaret took up the refrain. "Leslie's always been wonderful and tonight she looks as wonderful as she is."

Paul pounded one hand on the lace-covered table with mock disapproval. "Stop! You're embarrassing the girl."

Leslie *was* embarrassed, but gratified, too. Michael had already looked at her with warm approval, so her family's reaction was no more than she'd expected. And why not? She wore a soft, belted dress of red silk in a size she'd never thought to see again. She still wanted to lose another few pounds, but while she'd been mooning about Michael, she *hadn't* been eating.

Grandmère would probably call her lovesick.

Her hair, usually pulled back to control its curl, had been cut into a fashionable shoulder-length style that waved wildly around her face—a face she herself hardly recognized. Her makeup had been done by a professional makeup artist who'd explained every step: how to blend shadows, how to apply eyeliner and mascara—so many techniques Leslie's head was whirling. She had no idea whether she'd be able to do it herself tomorrow morning, but figured practice made competent, if not perfect.

Michael pulled out her chair. "Leslie's not embarrassed," he said staunchly. "She just decided to make a few changes."

"Michael," Gaby said, "I love you. This is your doing. I always knew that my darling Leslie was really a butterfly."

"Mama!" Gaby had always pushed and prodded, but Leslie knew her mother only wanted the best for her. Even so, it was time to call a stop to this. "I decided on a change for a lot of reasons. I'm glad you approve, but talking about how bad I was before isn't doing my self-confidence a whole lot of good."

"Leslie!" Gaby looked appalled. "That's not what I was doing at all. I just thought...I mean, the contrast is so great..." She glanced at her mother-in-law for support.

Cory jumped in. "My mommy's bee-oo-tiful. Don't you think so, Andy-Paul?"

"Yeah, sure." The boy shrugged; looks obviously weren't all that important to him.

"Don't *you* think so, Daddy?"

Michael's smile warmed Leslie more than the Louisiana sun. "I've always thought your mother was bee-oo-tiful," he replied. Leslie's hands rested in her lap and he covered one with his own. "Why don't you tell them the rest of it, honey?"

She was intensely aware of the feel of his knuckles on her thigh, heat passing easily through the thin silk of her dress. She licked her lips. "I've decided to go t-to the luncheon with Grand-mère Friday."

"And make the presentation?" Margaret asked with a quick, dubious glance at Michael. "Leslie, you really don't have to do this if you don't want to. We *do* love you. We never intended to force you."

Michael's hand squeezing hers gave Leslie courage. "I *want* to." She darted a quick glance at the man at her side and added, "But only if Michael comes, too."

"Michael?" Margaret was clearly taken aback. "I don't suppose that will be a problem, if he really wants to go to a women's luncheon." She brightened. "Actually...yes, that's a fine idea."

"Thank you." Michael shook out his linen napkin. "I don't want to let my bride out of my sight. I'm sure the ladies will understand."

Whether they did or not, *Leslie* did—and something inside her simply crumbled.

"OH, GOD!" HOURS LATER, Leslie paced around their suite's master bedroom, wringing her hands. She turned agitated, excited eyes on Michael. "If I'd passed them on the street, I don't think my own family would have recognized me."

Trying to seem relaxed, which took enormous acting ability, Michael lounged in one of the comfortable club chairs beside a small table set before the French doors. He could understand her family's reaction, because he was feeling much the same astonished confusion as he watched her tightly wound movements.

She looked like a completely different woman with red silk swirling around a body he suddenly recognized as...lush. She was behaving like a completely different woman, too. He'd never seen her so excited—or so exciting. Her brown eyes flashed and the masses of curls around her face were extremely seductive.

Belatedly he pulled himself back to the conversation. More and more of late he'd found himself thinking about her in ways inappropriate to their situation.

"Did their reaction offend you?" he asked.

"Offend me?" Her head snapped up and a deep breath made full breasts thrust up sharply beneath the brilliant silk. "I liked it. I've always said, if you're going to do something, go all the way."

That dragged a laugh out of him. "Is that why you clung to that old image of yourself? Because you were afraid to go all the way?"

She missed the wordplay entirely. "It wasn't only an image, it really *was* me." She sat in the other chair and leaned forward, her elbows on the table. The cleft between her breasts in the V-necked dress deepened. "I was never a beautiful child, not like Sharlee was."

"I'll bet your mama would disagree with you."

"That's what mothers do," she said. "But I was a fat kid, Michael. Mama and Grandmère could call it whatever they wanted, but I knew. And I got flustered easily and I stammered. I was clumsy—"

"Did you bite your nails?" She sounded as if she was getting into a serious self-critique, and he wanted to head it off.

She gave a peal of laughter. "Sometimes. Oh, I was a mess!"

"Leslie, you weren't a mess and you're *not* a mess."

"Then what am I?"

The air seemed to grow suddenly heavy and provocative between them. Only the small round table separated them, and he saw a wildness in her eyes, a glint that warned him he'd have to be careful. She was drunk with triumph, and it would be so easy to take advantage of her.

He wouldn't, although he wanted to—wanted to like hell. Living in this confined space with her, spending so much time with her, seeing how much she'd come to love his daughter, recognizing how much fortitude it had taken for her to do what she'd done today...

"Michael," she whispered, "I've led such a boring life. I've been a coward. Even when I was unhappy with myself, I was more afraid of trying to do anything about it. I've always been what Grandmère calls a homebody. I didn't have a lot of friends or much of a social life in either high school or college. I spent all my time studying and reading except..." She hesitated.

She looked delectable sitting there, head down, her pouty lower lip thrust out. He told himself he had to stop noticing such details. "Except what, Leslie?"

She looked up abruptly and her gaze locked with his. "There was a boy in college. He made a big play for me and I...I..."

He felt a stab of alarm. "You don't need to tell me anything that makes you uncomfortable."

She grimaced. "This makes me *very* uncomfortable, but I need to tell you, anyway. I slept with him. I guess you could s-say we had an affair." Her tone was almost defiant.

"Leslie—" he struggled to keep from touching her "—how do you expect me to react? Knowing you, I'm sure he must have been a great guy."

"Not so great." She shook her head. "As it turned out, he was much more interested in the Lyon name than in me." The light went out of her eyes. "Anyway, I just thought you should know."

Know that she'd been victimized by a fortune hunter? He rose, lost the fight with himself and leaned over to press a kiss into her soft hair. Why in God's name had she ever pulled those curls back and pinned them down when they were so glorious?

"Half the world's population is men and a few of them are fortune-hunting assholes," he said. "No man in his right mind would want you for anything other than yourself." He cupped his hand around her cheek. "Thank you for telling me. Now I think we'd both better get some sleep."

"All right." Her lips barely moved. "I'll see you tomorrow, then."

"Sleep tight." He turned away, hating to leave her but knowing it was the right thing to do. He also knew that if he didn't get the hell out of here fast, he wouldn't go at all.

HE THOUGHT she was telling him she'd been victimized by a fortune hunter when in fact, all she'd been trying to tell him was that she wasn't a virgin.

Damn! Men could be dense!

She fumbled awkwardly with the buttonholes on the red silk. She should undress, take a cold shower and crawl into bed—God knew, she'd done it before. But tonight, of all nights! She dreaded being transformed back into plain old Leslie Lyon after such a triumph. It was like...like discovering she had a twin, she thought, a pretty, sexy twin who could say and do all the outrageous things the dull twin would never have the audacity to attempt.

Such as seduce her own husband.

The dull twin wouldn't even know how to go about attempting such a feat. Which, now that she thought about it, was just as well. She already loved him too much. If she slept with him, heaven only knew how she'd feel afterward.

Shuddering, she crossed to the marble-topped chiffonier and yanked open the drawer containing nightwear: faded, cotton-knit sleep shirts dating back to her college days and a couple of ankle-length white cotton Mother Hubbards.

And one long, semi-sheer, very sexy nightgown sent by Charlotte as a wedding gift. Thankfully, Leslie had been alone when she'd received the package. Just the sight of it had embarrassed her, as had Charlotte's note: "They told me to get white because it matches all bedposts—which is where it's supposed to be. Best wishes for a long and happy marriage from your obnoxious little sister."

Leslie had never even tried the nightgown on. What was the use? It wouldn't be hanging on any bedposts in *this* marriage.

Staring down at the fragile silk in frustration, she crumpled the folds between her fingers. She'd be damned if she'd let this day end on such an unhappy note. Even if she was the only one who knew it, for one glorious night she was going to keep her dull, good-girl image at bay and sleep in silk.

With trembling fingers, she stripped off bra and panties and pulled the slithery garment over her head. It floated down around her to her ankles, multiple folds hiding just enough to make the body beneath look sexy and mysterious.

Running her fingers through her hair, she fluffed the curls around her face. The eyes staring back from the mirror looked almost haunted.

Turning abruptly, she walked to the lamp on the bedside table and lowered the light. The bed had been turned back to reveal eggshell-colored sheets of Egyptian cotton and lavished with multiple rows of soft cotton lace. As soon as she removed her makeup, she'd climb in—and then toss and turn until sunrise.

Suddenly she couldn't stand the sight of that bed any longer. Walking quickly to the French doors, she flung them wide. Fresh night air, redolent of flowers and dampness and unfulfilled dreams, enveloped her.

Crossing to the wrought-iron railing, she stood there motionless for a moment before letting her head fall back. Gazing up into the star-sprinkled sky, she murmured, "Star light, star bright..." She let her voice trail off but not her thoughts. If she could have the wish she wished tonight, what would it be?

"Leslie."

Michael's breath, warm and intimate, stroked across her bare shoulders like velvet. She straightened slowly but didn't turn. Her heart began to pound in a slow, intense rhythm and she felt her nipples peak beneath the bodice of her gown.

"I thought you'd gone to bed," she said.

"I...was too keyed up to sleep."

"Me, t-too."

His hands settled on her waist, hesitated briefly and then slid up to her rib cage. She didn't move. His touch was just as she'd dreamed it would be, and extraordinary sensations streaked through her to the very limits of her consciousness.

He moved closer until his body was pressing against hers, lightly but intimately. At the same time, he raised his hands to cup her breasts. She gasped and fell back against him, her head bumping softly against his shoulder.

"It's a beautiful night," he murmured, kissing the curve of her shoulder. "I needed company. But I wouldn't have...if you hadn't come outside, I think I...could have kept my distance."

She couldn't speak, could only cling to the rail while tension coiled through her. With his hands finally curved around her breasts as she had so often fantasized, she nearly groaned with relief. His fingers moved insistently, kneading the flesh, tweaking the already aroused nipples. Her head was spinning and she felt lost and drifting through that canopy of stars.

"Look," he said in her ear, "I have to tell you something."

"Oh, God, now what?" She didn't want conversation. She only wanted the rapture of his touch.

"I went to your mother and grandmother behind your back."

"My...?" She gasped; his hands on her breasts were a glory that stole her breath, made his words meaningless.

"I know this isn't the time to tell you, but I can't go on until..." He groaned, resting his chin on her shoulder. "I told them to give you some space or we'd move out. They really didn't understand, Les. I know you told me not to interfere, but I couldn't just watch them hurt you any longer. I'm sorry, but I'd do it again."

He'd stood up for her. She thought her heart would burst. She loved him for that, and for so much more.

"Leslie, say something." He spoke roughly but his hands were gentle. They left her breasts to turn her around to face him. "I've got to know what you're thinking. If you're angry—about that or about *this*—I have to know. We made a bargain and this wasn't part of it, but..." He stopped speaking and stared at her as if he'd never seen her before.

With the light spilling from the open French doors, she supposed she was fully illuminated beneath the filmy gown. Her arms jerked as if to cover her exposed body with her hands, but then she lifted her chin and gazed back at him defiantly. Let him look. She'd felt proud of herself today. She wasn't going to deny that by getting all tongue-tied and embarrassed now.

"You're beautiful," he breathed. "I already knew that, but seeing you like this—"

"Shut up, Michael." She touched his mouth with her fingers. "You've talked too much already. I don't care about any of that, just about us here and now." She trailed her other hand down his bare chest to the very edge of low-slung pajama bottoms. Slipping her fingers beneath the drawstring, she gave a light tug.

This isn't me, she thought hazily as he wrapped his arms

around her and bent her back before his kiss. *This is that other Leslie.*

I'll have to thank her.

A DOZEN KISSES LATER Michael scooped her up in his arms and carried her into the bedroom. Depositing her on the lavish bed, he stripped off his pajama bottoms, then lowered himself beside her.

She waited with open arms. His mouth closed over one tight nipple and she let out a little gasp, followed by a moan of pleasure. Her head strained back on the pillow and she twisted her fingers through his hair to pull him closer.

He'd never dreamed she was so passionate, and if it hadn't already happened, he would be instantly lost. Tomorrow he'd hate himself for his weakness, but tonight he was going to staunch the desire that had been building ever since they'd done this crazy thing and gotten married.

Still working on her breasts through the now-damp material of her gown, he skimmed impatient hands up her thighs beneath the gown. She was already prepared to accept him; he was already prepared to *be* accepted.

He poised above her, ready for the stroke that would claim her. Against the pillow, her face looked pale and rapturous, framed by those unruly curls. Long lashes swept up and she looked at him, her eyes drugged with pleasure. Lips bruised by his kisses parted and she gasped a single word: "Now!"

"Are you sure?" he gasped. "Because there's still time—"

"No, there isn't!" She lifted her hips and slid her heels around behind his knees, at the same time pulling him down into her waiting warmth.

And capturing him there until he was more satisfied...more guilty...more confused than he'd ever been before.

CHAPTER EIGHT

THE FIRST THING Leslie saw when she opened her eyes was sunlight streaming through open French doors.

The second thing she saw was her nightgown fluttering from a bedpost.

The third thing she saw *wasn't* Michael, just the dent in his pillow. Then she heard the sound of water running in the bathroom and relaxed. He was up and showering. He'd be out soon and then...

She closed her eyes and snuggled back into the nest of rumpled sheets. God, she loved that man!

After last night, he must feel something for her, too. When he walked through the door she would...

He walked through the door, golden skin glistening with moisture, hair dark with dampness. The only jarring note was the thick white towel wrapped around his midsection.

He stopped short at the sight of her. "I'm sorry I woke you," he said. "I thought I'd go for a jog before work."

His tone was guarded and his eyes wary. She felt her smile slipping. "You didn't wake me." Deliberately she yawned and stretched. Maybe he would take the hint and come back to bed. To hell with jogging. She'd keep him here all day if she could.

"You're tired," he said in that same detached manner. "Why don't you stay in bed and I'll send coffee up on my way out?"

This wasn't going the way she'd planned. "But—"

"Don't say anything, Leslie." He looked miserable. "Let me do the talking." He took a deep breath and his smooth, muscled chest lifted. "I owe you an apology," he said at last.

"Are you kidding?" She sat up abruptly, belatedly hauling the sheet over her breasts. "Michael McKay, if you think you can get away with just an apology, you've got another think coming."

"Yeah, I know, hanging's too good for me." He sounded as if he thought he was agreeing with her. "I shouldn't have gone behind your back and I sure as hell shouldn't have taken advantage of you last night. You were on such a high from dinner and you looked so great, and I really like and admire you so much—"

"You *married* me, you jerk!" She could hardly believe what she was hearing. "It's too late for that let's-just-be-friends routine."

"I know, and you can't possibly say anything to me I haven't already said to myself. On top of everything else—" his face tightened into a mask of misery "—I got so carried away I didn't even use protection. If I've made you pregnant, Les, I swear—"

"I'm not pregnant," she said flatly, her heart transforming into a shriveled knot of misery at his words. Nothing could make her happier than to bear his child—except to have his love.

"You can't be sure."

"I'm sure!" She plopped back down on the pillows. "Just leave, all right? Go jogging and forget the whole thing."

He tightened his grip on the towel. "I'm willing to do just about anything to make amends, but forgetting is asking a lot."

"Why? That's what I'm going to do."

She rolled onto her side, facing away from him, waiting for the sound of footsteps to announce his departure. Instead, he spoke.

"I'm sorry, Les, sorrier than you'll ever know. I swear to you, nothing like this will ever happen again."

"I believe you. Now get out before I kill you!"

Then she *did* hear his footsteps and dredged up the strength to wait at least thirty seconds after he'd closed the door between them before bursting into tears.

THE FRIDAY LUNCHEON was an enormous success. Even though Leslie was treating Michael like a pariah in private, their public demeanor was unchanged. Which meant that when she spoke, it could still be straight to him, because he understood.

Surprisingly enough, to her, anyway, her presentation was roundly applauded. Only with Michael did she moan, "I stammered on that first sentence and I forgot the name of the award and stumbled around a little before I got on track again and—"

"Leslie," he interrupted, his smile warmly supportive, "you were wonderful. You just proved that you can do anything you want to do. Remember that every time you look at me, and don't nitpick yourself to death, all right?"

And she hadn't.

TO LESLIE'S RELIEF neither Margaret nor Gaby ever breathed a word to her about what Michael had said to them. But they did seem to treat her with more consideration, and there were no more arm twisting sessions to get her to do things she wasn't comfortable with.

May turned to June while plans for the big anniversary celebration moved inexorably forward with minor events and promotions pointing toward the finale in July. Leslie found herself deeply involved in daily planning sessions and surprised herself by enjoying them. Of course, having Michael by her side made a big difference.

But he wasn't by her side through those long, increasingly hot nights. They'd settled into a kind of wordless truce that went into effect once they were alone in their suite of rooms. Even worse, he'd taken to working late several nights each week. Those nights were truly horrible.

There was always Cory, fortunately. The second grade wasn't much of a challenge to her, but Leslie still enjoyed overseeing homework and solving the little day-to-day emergencies. She also made sure the girl continued her weekly telephone calls to her grandmother in New York.

During one such call, Leslie was struck by inspiration. After Cory had concluded her conversation and handed over the phone, Leslie gave Cornelia a special invitation to attend the July festivities.

The woman hesitated. "I wouldn't want to intrude," she said stiffly.

"You wouldn't," Leslie said. "We have plenty of room here

at Lyoncrest, and my family will be glad to have you. Please come. You can spend time with your granddaughter and watch the Lyons go crazy.''

That drew a laugh. ''I do miss Cory terribly,'' the woman admitted. ''Let me think about it.''

She'll come, Leslie thought. That will make Cory happy, and what makes Cory happy makes Michael happy.

As if Leslie should be worrying about his happiness after what he'd done to hers. In bad moments she fully expected he'd turn to her one day and say, ''All right, Leslie, you not only survived the Lyon extravaganza, you triumphed. My ex-mother-in-law has relaxed, Kate Coleman is engaged to be married, nobody's chasing me at the moment, and it's time for us to say goodbye. Let's just shake hands—''

No! Leslie wasn't ready to think about any of that, not yet. She prayed July would never come.

BUT IT DID, and with mind-boggling speed, over a hundred triumphs and difficulties small and large. More and more, Leslie had moved into the public arena, but she'd done it on her own, without the usual trauma. As long as Michael was by her side, she did her part with good grace. With him, all things were possible. Without him, she wasn't certain she'd remember how to breathe.

Cornelia arrived in New Orleans July the first, but refused the hospitality of Lyoncrest—for all of twenty-four hours. When she gave up and moved in, Leslie breathed a sigh of relief. She hadn't been feeling very well for the past couple of weeks, since temperatures and humidity had both soared. Born and bred in these steamy lowlands, she'd never before been so drained of energy by the weather.

Fortunately most of the work was done, except for last-minute details and mountains of worry, neither of which required much of her attention. Now only two obstacles remained for her to confront: the masked ball Saturday night and the ceremonies and unveiling of the statue of the station's founders on Sunday.

She could get through that. Staring at her resplendent costume spread out on the four-poster, with Cornelia standing by to help her into it, Leslie steeled herself. She had to go forward, even knowing that next week or soon thereafter, her husband was going to come to her and say, "Thanks for everything. Goodbye."

Nausea welled up in her and she clapped her hand over her mouth and stumbled into the bathroom. When she emerged, pale and trembling, Cornelia gave her a questioning look.

"When are you due?" she asked. "And when are you going to tell Michael?"

Leslie stopped in her tracks and her eyes flew open wide. "I'm not pregnant!"

Or maybe she was. She'd missed a couple of periods, but that wasn't so unusual. The heat had gotten to her big time this summer, but *pregnant?* Indescribable joy made her wrap her arms around her middle. "Do you suppose?"

Cornelia laughed and hugged her. "I'd bet money on it," she said. "I can't believe you didn't realize."

"I've been so busy..." And he'd only made love to her once.

"Shall I tell Michael you want to speak to him?" Cornelia turned toward the door.

"No, please don't!" How *was* she going to tell him? It might be better to let him go before he knew. She wasn't sure he'd want this baby, since he obviously didn't want *her.* To Cornelia she said, "Please don't say anything to anyone until I see a doctor and know for sure."

But she did know for sure. Now that Cornelia had suggested it, Leslie knew with absolute certainty that she carried the child of the man she loved.

"I understand." Cornelia smiled as if pleased to be part of a conspiracy. "Are you going to be able to go to the ball tonight?"

"Of course." Now that she knew, Leslie felt giddy with excitement. "Just help me get into this dress and—"

But another wave of nausea hit, and then another. By the time Cornelia summoned Michael, it was clear to both women there'd be no ball for Leslie tonight.

He leaned over her prone figure, properly solicitous. "I'll bet it was that jambalaya at dinner," he said. "Your mother's feelin' a little shaky, too, but she says she's going, anyway."

"I'm sure that's it," Leslie lied. She pressed the cold washcloth against her forehead. "There's no need for you to miss the party, though. You go along with the rest of the family."

"I'll take care of her," Cornelia promised. "To tell you the truth, it's nice to be needed again."

Michael hesitated. Leslie prayed he'd insist on staying, that he'd sit by her side and hold her hand and guess what the real problem was, thus sparing her the agony of having to tell him—or not tell him.

Instead, he said, "If you're sure..."

And all her hopes were dashed.

LESLIE, FEELING MORE OR LESS herself again, walked into a hornet's nest when she came downstairs Sunday morning. Everyone was, to quote one in a succession of Lyoncrest cooks, "running around like chickens with their heads off." Margaret was trying to round everyone up for early mass, while Paul waited impatiently. André had already left for WDIX, and Gaby looked uncharacteristically nervous. Charlotte, who'd just arrived from Colorado, did not look happy to be here at all. She gave Leslie a wave and rolled her eyes the way she'd been doing since childhood.

Cornelia had the children fairly well in hand, though, and Michael surveyed the scene with good humor.

"How was the ball?" Leslie inquired. "I'm sorry I had to miss it."

"Wonderful," Margaret said, "but the details will have to wait. Out, everybody! After mass we'll get organized, I promise."

For once Margaret was dead wrong. Mass ran longer than usual; traffic was worse than usual; the children were more disruptive than usual. Once back at Lyoncrest Margaret ordered everyone to go ahead to the station while she and Paul handled a few last-minute telephone details. They'd be there in plenty of time for the one-o'clock broadcast.

Leslie had nothing to do now but go with the flow. Her part was over. She could remain calm and above the fray.

BY TWELVE-THIRTY, Margaret and Paul still hadn't appeared at WDIX. André was pacing around the executive boardroom with half a sandwich in his hand taken from the buffet set up on the conference table. He stopped and turned to the members of the family gathered there—the group from Lyoncrest, plus Alain and Charles and their branch of the family. Leslie and Charlotte were sitting together at one end of the conference table, sipping lemonade and getting caught up on each other's lives.

"I'll call home one more time and then I'm going after them," André announced, stalking to the telephone at the head of the conference table. "This isn't like Mama at all."

"But it *is* like Grandpère," Leslie said, trying to combat the sense of panic that seemed to be invading the room. She glanced at Sharlee, who shrugged. "I'm sure they're all right, Papa."

André slammed down the handset. "Busy. That line has been busy for forty-five minutes—either that or it's off the hook."

Gaby wrung her hands, her expression distraught. "Do you suppose they've already left?"

"We can't take that chance." He turned toward the door. "I'm going after them."

Michael rose from his seat along the wall. "You might miss them, André. Why don't I go, too? We can take different routes and meet at the house."

André nodded. "Thanks, Michael, that's a good idea."

"But..." Leslie's heart flipped over. She had no further responsibilities, but she didn't want to be without Michael when tempers and nerves ran this high.

Michael squeezed her hand and dropped a quick kiss on her forehead just as if they were any other happily married couple. "I won't be long," he promised, but he was obviously already thinking ahead. "André, what way are you going? I thought I'd..."

The two men hurried out. For a moment there were no sounds except the giggles of the children stacking foam cups into a tower in one corner. Then Charles said quite clearly, "Folly! Folly, folly, folly..."

AT TEN MINUTES OF ONE, Mary Boland stuck her head into the room. "They're ready for y'all in Studio A," she announced cheerfully. She did a double take. "Where *is* everybody?"

Gaby looked tongue-tied so Leslie said, "They'll be here when they're needed, Mary. The rest of us will be right down."

Mary shrugged and closed the door. Leslie looked at her mother with more sympathy than she'd ever felt before. Gaby loved Margaret like a mother, and worry twisted her face.

"Leslie, if anything's happened to Paul or Margaret..."

And to Leslie's horror, tears glistened in Gaby's eyes. "Now, Mama, everything will be all right," she said, sliding an arm around her mother's quaking shoulders. She sought out Sharlee for support, but her sister had turned away to look out the window, as if she didn't want to be part of what was happening. "Papa and Michael will bring them back," Leslie assured Gaby.

"Folly," Charles said again. "They're not coming. You women have spent all this money on a great big disaster."

Gaby pulled herself together with an effort. "What will we do if they don't arrive in time, Les?"

"We'll carry on," Leslie said staunchly. "You and Sharlee can do the honors. With cue cards and—"

"Not me." Charlotte turned sharply from the window. "I have nothing to do with this. I wasn't part of the planning and I wouldn't be here now if Grandmère hadn't...well, never mind how she did it. She got me here and that's all I promised to do—show up and smile."

Leslie's heart sank. "Then you, Mama."

"Oh, God, I couldn't possibly!" Red-eyed and trembling, Gaby shook her head vehemently. "I'm much too upset."

"Uncle Alain?" Leslie was growing desperate. "You're good at—"

"Not a chance." Alain's laugh was nasty. "Haul André's chestnuts out of the fire? I don't think so. I'm just here to show family unity."

That only left...

"No!" Leslie took a horrified step back, wanting to scream Michael's name. If he was here, then maybe. But on her own? "No! I can't and you can't ask me to!"

"I don't want to *have* to ask you, Leslie, but what choice is there?'' Gaby swallowed her tears. ''You're the only one who can do this. We have a real emergency here. We're depending on you because we must. All the Lyons are depending on you.''

''Besides,'' Charlotte put in, looking a bit more sympathetic, ''they'll probably get here in time. Why, they could be in the studio already, waiting for us. All this angst could be for nothing.''

Charlotte could be right. Leslie prayed she was.

CHARLOTTE WAS WRONG.

Standing beneath the glare of lights, listening to the countdown to air with a frozen smile on her face, Leslie wondered if she would survive this horror. Would she stammer and blush and make a fool of herself and her entire family?

Then Michael's words came back to her: ''You can do anything you want to do—remember that every time you look at me.'' But he wasn't here. Somebody *do* something, she thought wildly.

Only, there was nobody to do anything but Leslie. It occurred to her suddenly that she didn't have to actually see Michael standing in front of her. He was locked in her heart and would be until the day she died. She knew how he'd look, what he'd say with his eyes—

''We're on!''

Leslie's heart leaped into her throat and she took a shaky breath. Then the most extraordinary sense of calm settled over her. When she smiled, it was real, not the phony stretching of the lips she'd learned to do in public.

She spoke warmly to Michael as if he stood next to the camera. ''I'm Leslie Lyon McKay and on behalf of my family, I'd like to thank you all for being part of the Golden Anniversary of WDIX...''

WHEN THEY CUT to the thirty-minute documentary on the station, Leslie collapsed into a chair, hyperventilating. Her ordeal was finished. The only thing left was the unveiling of the statue in front of WDIX.

Charlotte was the first to reach her. "You were great!" she announced. "I'm so proud of you, Les."

"Th-thank you." Now that it was over, Leslie felt weak with relief—*but she hadn't tripped over a single word.*

She'd found some backbone. If she could face this, her worst fear...

Or was it her worst fear? Looking at the man she loved hurry across cables and dodge past cameras to reach her side, she realized there was one more thing she had to do before she could claim her self-respect.

He spoke first. "Les, my God, you were wonderful. I've never been prouder of you." Pulling her into his arms, he held her close.

"You know?" Confused, she clung to him.

"We watched on the TV in the limo—André and I came back with your grandparents and the doctor."

"The doctor? Is someone—"

"It's nothing. Your grandfather was feeling a little woozy and your grandmother panicked." He grinned at her, still standing in the comfort of his embrace. "He probably caught whatever was bothering you last night."

She let out an astonished gasp. "I doubt it. Michael, there's something—"

Gaby rushed up. "Leslie, you were fantastic! I knew you could do it."

"Thank you, Mama, but right now I'm busy. Could you keep everyone back for a few minutes? I have to speak to my husband." And at last Leslie knew what she had to say.

It was the right thing, the only thing.

Gaby looked surprised but impressed by Leslie's firm tone. "Of course, dear."

Michael frowned. "What is it? What's going on?"

Leslie drew a deep breath. It was now or never. "Michael," she said in a voice that trembled with sincerity, "I love you." She couldn't bear to see his reaction to her declaration—courage only stretched so far—so she stared intently at his shoulder. "I also love the family we've created with Cory—and the family we're about to create."

That silence was the longest she'd ever experienced in her lifetime. It seemed like eons before he spoke, and then it was in a croak.

"*About* to create?"

"I'm pregnant, and so happy at the thought of having your baby I can hardly t-talk about it." She dared not slow down or she'd never get it out. "I prayed you would share that joy, but if you don't and if y-you can never love me, I'll stand by our b-bargain. You can have your freedom whenever you want it, just as I promised. Whatever you decide, I'll never ever regret our time together or..." Her voice trailed away before his lack of response.

"Are you finished?" he demanded.

She blinked, frowned, dared to sneak a look at him. He was glowering at her, not an especially encouraging sign. "I'm f-finished." For good, apparently.

"Then you listen to me, Leslie McKay." He caught her just above the elbows, forcing her to look at him. "Of course I can love you—in fact, I have for longer than I even realized. Who the hell in his right mind wouldn't?"

"Are you serious?"

They stared into each other's eyes, asking questions, receiving answers, making promises. He pulled her tight against his chest and held her there, and she could feel his heart racing in time with hers.

"I've been an idiot," he muttered against her hair. "As if that stupid deal we made could ever work."

"Folly," Leslie agreed, Granduncle Charles's favorite word bubbling out along with her laughter.

"Think we should let Cory in on our good news now?" *Yes,* she thought, *tell everyone! This is the happiest—and the scariest—day of my life.*

THE DRAPERY FELL AWAY from the statue and those assembled for the grand unveiling let out a unified gasp of appreciation. Depicted in marble were the young Margaret and Paul Lyon. Making this a work of true art, Margaret was half a step ahead of Paul. Deafening applause brought a wash of youthful color to Margaret's cheeks.

The ceremonies were winding down. Standing in the front row with her husband and daughter, Leslie basked in her secret happiness. Not an audience, not even television cameras could faze her now. She had all she'd ever wanted, and she looked forward to sharing her good news at the private celebration her family had planned for later.

Paul finished his thank-you speech and turned to his wife. "Have you anything to add, Margie?"

Margaret beamed. "No, dear, but I would like to acknowledge the youngest members of the family who are with us today. Cory, Andy-Paul—children, will you come forward, please?"

The youngsters, giggling and shy, joined her at the microphone. She introduced Andy-Paul first, then said, "Tell me, young man, what have you learned here today?"

The boy scrunched up his face in an approximation of thoughtfulness. "I guess I learned the cake comes last," he announced.

After laughter and applause had died away, Margaret repeated the question to Cory. The little girl considered carefully.

Then she said, "Well, I guess the best thing I learned today is...my mama's gonna have a baby! I'm gonna be a sister!"

For once, shy Leslie wasn't the least bit embarrassed, even when everyone's attention centered on her. She was proud to help carry on the Lyon legacy, even though she had not been born a Lyon. She'd always been awed by the Lyon family loyalty, the family pride. Now she'd happily do her part to help the family prosper into the next half century, at the same time fulfilling all her own dreams.

On this golden anniversary of WDIX, she had a golden anniversary of her own to look forward to: fifty years of marriage to the man of her dreams. It really *didn't* get any better than that.

EPILOGUE

CHILDREN RAN ACROSS the graceful lawn at Lyoncrest, shrieking and giggling and heedless of generations-old beds of rosebushes.

Their grandparents, parents and aunts and uncles mingled beneath a spreading white tent, erected for the private family celebration.

And the couple who'd created the reason for the celebration fifty years ago sat on a wicker settee on the second-story gallery, watching the proceedings. They held hands and sipped sparkling cider from champagne flutes. They had retired an hour earlier and were enjoying the party from afar.

"We've done well with our lives," Paul said, giving his wife's hand a gentle squeeze.

Margaret wasn't one to mince words or hide from the truth. "It is almost over for us, isn't it?"

She looked at her husband of fifty-eight years. Even in the moonlight, his age was impossible to deny. But he still looked dashing to her. And the adoration in his eyes—that was worth everything they'd been through in their lifetime. He lifted her hand to his lips and kissed her fingertips.

"Look on the lawn, my dear Margie," he said. "Our family is thriving. Happy. Productive. There is our legacy. It's far from over for us. I'd say this is just the beginning for the Lyons."

Margaret smiled and raised her glass. "To the future."

Paul touched the rim of his flute to hers. "And to the woman who first saw it all those years ago."

Turn the page
for an excerpt from the first book
in the LYON LEGACY trilogy

FAMILY SECRETS

by

Ruth Jean Dale

Watch for it next month!

PROLOGUE

New Orleans, July 1999

SHARLEE INCHED her way through the crowd toward the door of the rehearsal hall at WDIX, trying to look inconspicuous. If she were to make a clean getaway, the time was now, while the place was still mobbed by friends, family, employees, media and Very Important People celebrating the fiftieth anniversary of the TV station established by her grandparents. No one paid Sharlee the slightest mind, which was exactly the way she liked it.

She hadn't wanted to come to this overblown extravaganza in the first place, but there'd been no way to avoid it without making relations even more strained with her family. Neatly lifting a glass of champagne off the tray of a passing waiter, she managed a mechanical smile for her father, briefly visible across the room. Fortunately, her mother was nowhere in sight.

Why couldn't her parents understand that at almost twenty-five, Sharlee was an independent woman determined to make her way in the world without benefit of the Lyon name? She felt so strongly about this that at her job as a newspaper reporter in Colorado, she went by a nickname bestowed upon her many years ago by a lost love—Sharlee, short for Charlotte—and her middle name: Hollander. She'd been essentially "gone" from the family nest since she left for boarding school almost nine years ago.

Yet here she was, pretending for the sake of public relations that she actually belonged to this illustrious clan. Her grandfather, Paul Lyon, was a television icon known and revered throughout the South as "The Voice of Dixie"; her father, André, was a devoted family man and pillar of the community who had taken

WDIX-TV to new heights. Her grandmother Margaret and mother Gabrielle had both played important roles at WDIX, while at the same time raising their children, loving their husbands, nurturing their community, and doing it all with perfect *public* grace.

At least, mama had done all that until the birth of her only son seven years ago. At that point, Gaby had "retired" to stay home with Andrew Paul, universally called Andy-Paul. Also living at the family manse in the Garden District were older sibling Leslie with her new husband and stepdaughter. Leslie's pregnancy had been revealed only minutes earlier, to the delight of all.

Sharlee hated to envy anyone anything, but this time she couldn't help herself. Just what she needed: an older sister who had everything including the approval of the entire family, and an adorable little brother to carry on the Lyon name.

A bump from behind sent her stumbling forward, a few drops of wine spraying over the rim of her glass. When she'd regained her balance, she found herself standing behind two courtly old gentlemen speaking in low tones.

Her grandfather, Paul, and his younger brother, Charles, both in their eighties, were deep in conversation. She edged closer, her curiosity roused by the almost conspiratorial expressions on their faces.

"So now the history of the Lyons is an open book," Paul was saying in a tone laced with an unusual cynicism. "The truth, the whole truth..."

To which his brother replied, "I was there, brother dear. There are more secrets in this family than there are candles on that cake—and someday they'll all come home to roost."

Sharlee frowned. *What on earth were they talking about? What "secrets"?* So far as she knew, every single Lyon was a model of decorum. Would that she could say the same! But now Granduncle Charles was suggesting something altogether different, and she waited for Grandpère to refute him.

And waited.

And began to wonder. Could it be true? Secrets—an intriguing word suggesting much but revealing little. Perhaps Charles was talking about his own branch of the family tree. He and his son, Alain, were not only active in Lyon Broadcasting but owned one of the most elegant French restaurants in New Orleans. She'd just eaten several cheese and shrimp stuffed mushrooms from Chez Charles, reminding her of one of the few things she missed about New Orleans: the food. All of Charles's descendents had moved dutifully into one or the other of the family businesses and endeavors such as this grand anniversary celebration.

Unlike Sharlee, who'd vowed early on to go her own way and had proceeded to do so, consequences be damned.

She had long since concluded that she was the only person in the family with a wild streak. In her teens, she'd been the screw-up, the kid who got suspended from school for practical jokes, who got into curfew trouble with the cops, who snuck out of the house to meet boys, who got caught drinking by the nuns. She was also the one who was arrested in campus demonstrations at college and who got into a humungous confrontation with her mother on her twenty-first birthday, resulting in her decision to take a job in Colorado instead of moving back home after graduation.

The culmination of all this rebellion was her parents' refusal to release her trust fund on schedule. Their lack of faith actually hurt more than being deprived of the money—although money was nice, too, at least from what she remembered.

This waltz down memory lane was getting her nowhere. She had a plane to catch, people to avoid. Even so, the conversation between the two old men had sent her reporter's instincts into high gear. Perhaps if she loitered for just a few minutes, she might hear a few interesting, perhaps even scandalous, tidbits about the Lyons....

But then she saw Devin Oliver heading her way, a determined expression on his handsome face. Her heart stood still. He looked wonderful with his curly almost-black hair and his deep, almost-black eyes. She'd managed to avoid him on this trip as she'd pretty much avoided her parents and anyone else wearing a serious expression, but her luck might be running out.

The last thing she needed was a run-in with a former lover

now on her father's payroll. Turning quickly away, she ducked behind a cluster of celebrants and beat a hasty retreat, resolutely ignoring Dev's voice behind her.

"Sharlee, wait! You can't go on avoiding me forever."

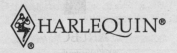

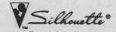